DEDICATED TO

Women everywhere who use their intellect, talent and immutable energy to reach their dreams.

This book is a work of fiction. While references may be
made to actual places or events, the names, character,
incidents, and locations within are from the author's
imagination and are not a resemblance to actual living
or dead persons, businesses, or events. Any similarity
is coincidental.

Printed in the United States of America

First Printing, 2016

Agressive Publishing, Inc.

Distributed by Bublish, Inc.

ISBN 978-0-9965195-0-2

Interior Design by ktlarosa.com

Cover Design by bergedesign.com

DEVIANT
AGENDAS

Katherine Smith Dedrick

CHAPTER

1

THE DAY WAS one of those picture-perfect Chicago days; few and far between, but unbeatable when they happened. The weather was warm and sunny, with just enough of a breeze to rustle the oak trees lining Lake Michigan's shoreline. Victoria took a deep breath as she scanned the growing crowd. Pride and contentment fought with the adrenaline racing through her veins. Moving to the side, Victoria lifted her gown and hopped on a riser so she could have a shot at finding her best friend in the sea of people.

Finally! Victoria thought. After three grueling years, she had only to get through this ceremony to become a graduate of The University of Chicago Law School. After being mentally poked and prodded by professors, spending exhausting hours up all night learning about the "eggshell plaintiff," constitutional rights, and the rule against perpetuity (some archaic rule that governed property law, which Victoria planned to never use, let alone utter, once she passed the bar), she and her peers had finally earned the right to be called "counselor," "lawyer," or "advisor."

While typically Victoria had little use for pomp and circumstance, today, she simply smiled with appreciation. For forever, the University had been hot on the heels of Harvard and Yale, always falling somewhere in the top five, yet never taking the number one or two spots. But for the first time, the predictions from those in the know were that this year's ceremony would push Chicago into the number one spot because the President of the United States, one of its most famous former professors, was to deliver the commencement address. The demand for tickets had been greater than ever, the crowd larger, security tighter and the press, everywhere. Victoria could almost taste the excitement. Good juju was in the air.

Still searching the crowd, Victoria saw the dean nod to the band, and the music began. The first few rows of Victoria's classmates had already taken their seats. As rehearsed, the rest of her peers began to meander toward their seats, knowing they had the luxury of one more song until the ceremony officially began. Victoria stretched her small frame higher one last time to find Kat.

Glancing toward the front, Victoria saw Chad move to his seat on the podium, and had to smile. He looked like he was about to puke. Unlike the other one hundred eighty students sporting maroon and gold tassels, Victoria and Chad had bright blue and yellow tassels hanging from their caps signifying their near-perfect marks. Chad had beaten Victoria by a few tenths of a point, and so would give the valedictory speech.

Victoria was actually thankful that Chad had received the honor. She wanted to enjoy the day and not worry about delivering a perfect and moving speech, especially since the President was speaking immediately after Chad.

"V! Over here." Kat waved as she moved through the crowd toward Victoria. As soon as she was in reach, she squealed and grabbed Victoria in a tight hug lifting her off the riser and twirling Victoria's petite frame around in sheer delight.

Kat smiled as she let Victoria's feet hit the ground. She was struck as always by Victoria's natural beauty. Wavy, chestnut hair, long and thick as a horse's tail but soft as butter, spilled out of the careless knot in which Victoria usually wore her hair and her beautifully proportioned face glowed with excitement.

Reaching inside her graduation gown, Kat pulled out two splits of perfectly chilled Roederer Cristal champagne. She handed both bottles to Victoria to hold while she expertly popped one, then the other, open. Victoria smiled as she felt the chill of the bottles loving the fact that Kat would never think to offer champagne, even bottles hidden away inside her commencement robe, at other than the perfect temperature.

"Congratulations, V, we did it! No more slogging through four-hour exams or staying up until all hours of the night reading boring case law! We're done! I can't wait to get off this campus and into the real world." Holding her bottle in the air, Kat toasted, "To real jobs! That pay real money!"

Victoria clinked her split with Kat's and smiled. "Cheers! To us! To the end of three years of nonstop reading, debating, writing and memorizing. To the end of totally useless pieces of information that are forever stuck in my brain! To no longer being battered and abused by professors practicing the Socratic Method simply because they can and are pissed at the world!"

After drinking from the bottle, Victoria cocked her head and offered the toast that held real meaning for her. "To the beginning of power. The kind that almost knocks you to your knees when it walks into the room. To our lives with that kind of power."

"*Salút*," answered Kat. And the two young women at the beginning of their professional lives happily chugged the remaining champagne just as the musicians concluded the "sit your asses in your place" song.

"This is it!" Flashing one of her full-kilowatt smiles, Kat pulled Victoria into a tight hug, gave her a smacking kiss on the cheek, and ran back to her spot near the front of the line.

"Don't forget to meet me after the ceremony by the basilica!" Victoria yelled to Kat's retreating back.

Victoria smiled as she watched Kat work her way back to the front. Kat had it made. She was going to work for her family's real estate business and had been groomed to do just that from an early age. She had grown up following her father around on different construction sites. All the photos of Kat and her father Victoria had seen during their time in school, had shown the two of them with matching hard hats at some construction project. In each picture, Kat wore the same expression. Determination. Whether her focus was school, men or work, it all received the same lazer-like attention. Kat, Victoria thought, with a purpose and in full pursuit, was a thing of beauty.

Victoria took her seat and tried to pay attention to the dean's opening remarks. Looking into the stands, she found Sophia watching her from her first-row seat. Smiling, her mother blew a kiss and patted her heart. Something she had done for as long as Victoria could remember. Raising her hand to wave, Victoria thought of how good it would feel to finally be able to pay her own bills and no longer be a drain on her mother's income.

The applause began as the President of the United States and other dignitaries took the stage, snapping Victoria out of her semi-daydreaming, and now a bit-buzzed state. After what seemed like forever, the speeches finally over, the first three lines of students rose from their seats and walked toward the stage, ready to receive the bit of paper that signified the beginning of their new lives. In two days' time, Victoria thought, she would begin her next life chapter at the law firm everyone said was destined to become one of the most important and powerful firms in the world. There was no doubt in Victoria's mind that it was exactly where she belonged.

CHAPTER
2

IN THE STANDS, three men stood along with the candidates' friends and family members. As the founding partners of Acker, Smith & McGowen, one of the most prestigious law firms in the country, the men were well known as they often captured the attention of the press. Either they were in the headlines to announce a new blockbuster deal or one of the three was listed as a top ten most eligible bachelor. They were well suited as partners. Each had grown up around some form of power, knew the perks and benefits it brought, and not one of them was willing to suffer a life without it. They wanted their firm to be one of a handful of respected firms with a substantial, international footprint, and they were well on their way to accomplishing their goal. Headquartered in Chicago, the firm had offices in Los Angeles, New York, Miami and Dallas, four international offices and a fifth was in consideration.

"I sometimes forget how incredibly good-looking they are at that age. Even in those God-awful robes, you can tell that they have bodies made for pleasure. I can't wait to get my hands on Victoria. I'll give her until the end of the year before she's on her knees, doing what she was made to do."

"Billy, for Christ's sake, you can't bed every new associate. We're midway into our expansion, and the last thing we need is an EEOC investigation or a sexual harassment suit to get in the way and slow us down."

Disgusted, Adam Smith shook his head, but had to admit to himself that he had had similar thoughts. He just didn't voice them aloud, nor would he ever follow through with them or pursue the young female associates they brought into the firm. He had an easier way to satisfy his urges, and it didn't involve jeopardizing the firm or his reputation.

"Really, Adam? You want to give me advice after the mess we had to bail you out of?"

"Billy, that was a one-time mistake I made while we were in law school, and the only reason it ever saw daylight was because I was young and stupidly plastered. Nothing like that has ever, or will ever, happen again."

Billy only snorted in response, remembering all too well how they had gotten a call from Adam, who had been arrested by an undercover cop because of his pre-dilection for prostitutes. Billy could never understand why Adam chose to pay for it. You could get the same or better from classy chicks for as little as a dinner, or even sometimes simply by giving them a bit of attention. As far as Billy was concerned, most women had such low self-esteem that all you needed to do was give them a few words of encouragement and they responded like hungry dogs being offered a bone.

William Acker II or "Billy," to his friends, grew up privi-leged in the fine Southern tradition of the firstborn son of a wealthy plantation family. As long as anyone could remem-ber, the Ackers had owned the rolling hills just south of At-lanta, Georgia, and had grown tobacco on their land. Some of Billy's earliest memories were of working in the fields of their plantation, The Southern Will, in the broiling summer sun and wrenching humidity alongside the hourly and often illegal immigrant workers doing the backbreaking work of picking tobacco. Billy's father, William "Big Bill" Senior, had insisted that Billy learn the business from the "dirt up," and had said so for as long as Billy could remember.

But Billy also had plenty of memories of sitting through long meetings in The Southern Will's boardroom, as it was referred to, with other growers who had traveled from different parts of Georgia and even other states to attend. Most times, when one of these meetings was in session, Big Bill would make Billy sit through it to learn the financial and legal parts of the business.

Billy not only dreaded the time he was forced to spend in the field harvesting the tobacco, he hated the meetings equally. They lasted for hours, the boardroom was always choked with smoke, and there was a lot of fist pounding and shouting, with stern-looking men in suits marching in and out, giving reports and being dismissed. Big Bill ran the meetings and commanded the room, which was only right, as The Southern Will was the largest tobacco plantation in the country. The health of its crop determined pricing each year. A bad crop would send ripples throughout the tobacco industry.

From an early age, Billy knew without a doubt that he had no intention of spending his days saddled to the plantation, like his father, worrying about crop infestations, market prices, lawsuits and kissing political ass. He didn't know what he was going to do or how he was going to do it, but he knew one thing for sure. He had much bigger plans. He was, after all, a very clever boy. Everyone said so.

As Billy matured, he learned that many of the issues discussed in the boardroom were the result of increasing litigation against the tobacco industry and the ever-growing political effort to regulate, or even outlaw, tobacco products. These issues affected not only the time and energy of those who ran the tobacco plantations, but also their bottom line. And as far as Billy was concerned, the bottom line was all that mattered.

With litigation and regulation a growing threat, it was decided Billy would become a lawyer. Much to Billy's surprise, he found that he thrived in the Socratic and bully-like atmosphere of law school. Years of being tested and emotionally abused by his never-satisfied father had made the verbal jousting dished out by his law professors seem like child's play.

When Billy took his first trust and estate class, he was intrigued and asked his family lawyers to provide him with the plantation's legal papers. Of course the first thing the lawyers did, as they were beholden to Big Bill (who paid their astronomical fees), was to let him know about Billy's request. When Big Bill asked why he wanted these papers, Billy lied smoothly and told his father it was time he understood the corporate and estate facets of the business. Big Bill could not have been prouder, and directed his lawyers to give his son full access to whatever he wanted. Billy was, after all, attending one of the finest law schools in the country, even if it was up north, and the plan was for Billy to oversee the plantation's growing legal and lobbying teams.

Billy's intentions, however, were not so pure. In fact, quite the opposite as he intended to sell The Southern Will as soon as it came into his control. So he was shocked and more than a little disappointed to learn that the estate was arranged so that it could never be sold, except for a few ironclad exceptions which were unlikely to occur.

Hearing the applause as the final graduate stepped off the stage, Billy blinked, and thanked God that he'd met his partners, even though they occasionally road each other's last nerve. The firm was the only thing he had real control over, and he had no intention of messing up their growing empire because of a predilection he had for female associates. Not that he intended to stop screwing them. He just had no intention of getting caught.

"Adam, I can assure you, I know what I'm doing. There is no way the EEOC or any law firm will ever be able to prove that I did anything." Sometimes Adam could be so dense, Billy thought. "Really, who is going to believe that a man with my passion for helping minorities and women students is going to be fishing in the same pond he's stocking? No one is going to fuck with me."

Trever chewed on his unlit cigar and cleared his throat so that his slow Texas drawl was crystal clear. "Gentlemen, focus please on the ceremony and the newest addition to our firm. We need to welcome our new associate after the ceremony and meet her family. I believe we only have Victoria in this class, correct, Adam?"

"Yes. And I have a feeling Victoria is going to be crucial to our expansion. She's not only whip smart, but speaks Spanish, Italian and is learning Chinese," Adam answered.

"I think it might be best if she starts in my group." Billy said, as he pulled his sunglasses down from the top of his head to shade his slate-blue eyes.

Adam sighed and decided to let it go. Maybe Billy was right. If there was one thing Adam had learned at an early age, it was that you couldn't change a zebra's stripes. Business was booming. And, if truth be told, the associates Billy dabbled with all seemed happy enough when he was through with them. They were, after all, big girls swimming with the big fish in a big pond, and if they chose to sleep with the boss, well then, it was their choice, after all.

CHAPTER
3

BY THEIR SECOND year of law school, Billy, Adam, and Trever knew exactly what they wanted, and it didn't involve being part of the mind-fuck of a traditional law firm. The boys had decided that the only way to make use of their law degrees, yet maintain their sanity and vision of power and wealth, was to create their own firm. But it had to be markedly different from the way other firms were organized and run. The boys had no intention of sharing either the power or profits with other lawyers that became part of their firm. So one year before their own graduation, the boys formalized their commitment to Acker, Smith & McGowen, a closely held and tightly managed, international law firm specializing in high-stakes business deals and the litigation that inevitably followed.

There were a number of reasons for their goal, one of which was that there had been few firms that crossed continents to keep up with rapidly expanding multinational businesses. Most firms did not offer seamless, international legal advice. While there were a number of explanations for this gap, the main reason, as far as the boys were concerned, was the infighting and backstabbing that formed the backbone of most law firms. With no incentive to share clients, work or contacts, it was only a matter of time before partners turned on each other, stole clients from one another, and eventually killed their firm's chance for real growth.

"Disgusting," Trever would say each day after returning from his law clerk internship to the apartment the boys shared in law school. "People pay six hundred dollars an hour or more for these idiots, when they can't even agree to host a cocktail party without an argument."

Billy had found Trever's slow loss of his legal virginity amusing. Particularly since Billy had his legal cherry popped long ago. For as long as he could remember, lawyers had sucked up to him trying to get The Southern Will's multi-million-dollar book of business. By the time he entered law school, Billy had seen inside the legal brothel during the day, and knew it wasn't pretty.

"What happened this time?" Billy would ask.

"The same shit." Shaking his head, he'd walk to their fridge, grab a beer, and swallow it in one gulp. "Not once do they consider combining their talent to work together to attract clients. They're such unbelievable fuckheads. I can't imagine becoming one of them."

"And that, my friend, is the way of the idiot, which is why we will never be in that boat," Billy would reply. Trever would finish their routine by tossing a beer to his friend and soon-to-be lifelong law partner.

During their last year of school, the boys worked relentlessly to put together the pieces for their firm. For their plan to work, they knew they had to hire the "right type" of attorneys. For Acker, Smith & McGowen, that meant attorneys hardwired to work for the better good of the firm. The kind of worker bees who would buy into the mantra that if they helped the firm grow, they would grow with the firm, when "the time was right." Of course, the time would be right for only a chosen few, and even the few who made it to partnership would have to fight over splitting a paltry ten percent of the shares.

Since "type" was critical to their plan, the boys hired Dr. Natarajan, the University's shining star and one of the country's most renowned professors of business psychology. After six months of surveys, research and test groups, Dr. Natarajan finished her work. The end result was a clear-cut list of personality types and traits. This list became the cornerstone of their firm, and was kept under lock and key. Outside of Dr. Natarajan, who remained on a steep retainer to ensure her silence, only the boys knew of the list. It was as guarded, if not more so, than the recipe for Coke.

Now, so many years later, they'd created a growing and profitable firm. The structure they'd developed in law school had withstood the test of time. They held ninety percent of the "shares," hired the right type of lawyers and the time was rarely right for any of them to become partners.

CHAPTER
4

WILLIAM ACKER SR. strode down the long marbled hallway that connected the living quarters to the business wing of The Southern Will. This was one of his favorite parts of the mansion. It was at least fifty feet long, with a sheath of glass that ran from the floor to the ceiling. Aspen trees lined the outside perimeter of the glass hallway and stood like sentries on either side of the long hall. Scattered between the trees and the glass in a haphazard array carefully placed to look as if they just happened to grow wild were dozens of different types of flowers in a rainbow of colors. William paid his landscaper hundreds of thousands of dollars each year to maintain the grounds of the plantation just so.

William was a big man. He stood six feet, four inches tall, and weighed in at a little over two hundred forty pounds. He had riveting blue eyes and a full head of light brown, wavy hair. He looked, if you could set aside his ego and temper, like what most women would describe Prince Charming might look like (if there were such a thing). Because of his looks and ready cash, he had women waiting wherever he traveled throughout the world.

"Jenny, I'll see you in a few days." William looked up as his wife came down the hand-carved, curving staircase that was the focal point of their foyer. She looked as she always did, perfectly put together, in control and calm. They had been married for twenty-five years, and Jenny had been the perfect wife and mother. Nodding at his assistant who waited by the front door, he continued, "Jeremiah will be available to help with anything you might need. Billy and I will call you when we get to the house in Bermuda."

"I'll be waiting for your call, William. Make sure you put Billy on the phone when you do. I expect to have at least a few minutes of his time, at least over the phone." She looked up for the obligatory kiss goodbye she knew William would expect so that all appearances were maintained in front of the staff. As William reached down to Jenny's demure frame, he pulled her in toward him and squeezed her ass, reminding her, as he loved to do, that he owned not only all the eye could see, but her as well.

The moment the door closed on William's retreating frame, Jenny shot upstairs to pack her bag. She had waited months for this day and had worked through every detail. She had hired a top-notch divorce lawyer in California, knowing that no lawyer in the South could be counted on to keep a secret from William. Her attorney-client privilege would have been violated in a heartbeat in exchange for William's good graces. After packing one bag with mostly cherished photos and trinkets that reminded her of when times were good, she waited patiently in her room for William's flight to leave.

After two hours and a phone call to the airline to ensure that his flight had left, she picked up her phone. "I'm on my way now. I'll let you know when I get there." She put her phone in her purse, closed her suitcase, gathered her two dogs, and walked out the front door. She was nervous. As she put her car in gear, she caught her reflection in the driver side mirror and noticed that her new yellow Chanel dress was now badly stained as her sweat had turned the fabric under her armpits an ugly mustard color. As she neared the sixteen-foot gold-leaf monogrammed gates, one of the guards leaned out of the gate house, waved, and the heavy gates began to swing open.

"Afternoon, Mrs. Acker. Doing some shopping?" The guard called out as he smiled and leaned out of the gate house.

Jenny never ceased to be amazed at how vapid the men who worked for her husband thought she was. But today she was thankful for the misperception and played it for all it was worth. "I am indeed, Jim. With William gone, I thought I would stop in the park to let the dogs play, and then head into town." Jenny leaned out of the window and smiled, doing her best to look as if she didn't have a care in the world. Her heart pounded with fear that one of William's hired goons would try to stop her.

"Right-o, Mrs. A," the guard said, and waved goodbye. Jenny sailed through the gates and watched in her rearview mirror as they lumbered shut behind her.

After driving the mile down their private drive, Jenny turned on to the two-lane country road that would take her to the highway and then on to Atlanta International Airport. Over the last six months Jenny had painstakingly put the pieces in place. She had bet correctly on William's ego. It was too big for him to ever suspect that she would walk out on him. He had no idea that Jenny knew he'd been relentlessly screwing around over the past twenty-odd years. But she did, and she was done.

Jenny was sharp and William had forgotten that fact. She was, after all, a former Georgia State's attorney, having worked in Atlanta until William had unexpectedly insisted she stop.

Jenny had never forgotten his whispered words during their first dance as husband and wife at their reception. Pulling her close and bending to whisper in her ear, she had thought he was about to utter something romantic. Instead, she heard the words that should have made her turn tail and run.

"Jenny, baby, now that you're my wife, I expect you'll be handing in your resignation as soon as we return from our honeymoon. Your job now is to take care of me and concentrate on getting pregnant."

As soon as the song ended, he patted her on her ass and walked away. She remembered thinking he was drunk and they did not discuss it further. When they returned from their honeymoon, she was shocked to receive emails from her colleagues expressing their disappointment and sadness that she would no longer be a part of their team, but wishing her well as Mrs. William Acker. She later found out that her husband had quit for her.

That was the first inkling Jenny had about the life she would lead with William. But that life was over now, and Jenny smiled as she stepped on the gas of her chocolate-brown Bentley and winged her way to freedom. Jenny was more than ready to do a little screwing of her own and Big Bill was first on her list.

CHAPTER
5

I T WAS A perfect June morning as Victoria walked out of the front door of the four-unit building she lived in on the north side of the city. A light wind was blowing in from the lake, the sun was shining, and the flowers were in full bloom. Any excuse to get outside was good on a day like this.

"Good morning, Victoria. Where are you off to?"

"Good morning, Mrs. B. I'm off to start my new life as an employed lawyer. I am officially finished living the life of a poor law student." Setting down the monogramed Louis Vuitton briefcase that her mother had given her as a graduation gift, Victoria twirled as her neighbor and friend looked down from her balcony. "How do I look?"

"Lovely. No one would ever suspect you're a lawyer."

Victoria laughed out loud and put a finger to her lips to signal it would be their secret. Mrs. B hated lawyers and had many names for them, "sharks" being one of the tamer. She couldn't understand why Victoria and her friend had chosen that profession instead of getting married or, if they felt they had to work, choosing a respectable profession like retail or the restaurant business.

"Thanks, Mrs. B. I'll take that as a compliment," Victoria said as she turned and waved goodbye.

Within ten minutes, Victoria was looking up at the gold lettering announcing the entrance to the firm where she would begin her career. Acker, Smith & McGowen owned and occupied all of the fourteen-story building where it housed its headquarters. The building sat on one of the bends of the Chicago River, so that the offices on the east side had views of both the river and Lake Michigan. The west side offered sweeping views up the river into the heart of the city.

In order to get into the building, Victoria had to press her thumbs against a recessed glass panel and once inside, present identification to an armed guard who stood behind what appeared to be a fortress rather than a reception center.

"Welcome to the firm, Ms. Rodessa. I'm Hank, part of the security team. I understand you're one of the members of our new associate class. We'll get to know each other real well. Seems the security team and the new associates always have a lot in common," Hank said.

Victoria knew he was waiting for her to ask what they had in common. Assuming it was something he did with all the newbies, she didn't want to start off on the wrong foot so she forced herself to ask, "Okay, I'll bite. What do we have in common?"

"We're the only ones here when everyone else is gone. Like weekends, holidays and in the middle of the night." Hank laughed enjoying his own humor. "Go on up to the four-teenth floor. Natalie will be waiting."

"Thanks. Nice to meet you Hank." Victoria entered the elevator and noticed the two cameras. Reaching to press the button to take her to the fourteenth floor, she saw it was already lit. Feeling a bit off balance at the tight security, Victoria shivered and noticed that the hair on her arms was actually standing on end. As the elevator whirred her to the top, she shook off the feeling and reminded herself that the firm did many confidential deals. So the tight security made sense.

As soon as the elevator doors slid open, a well-dressed woman holding a tablet engraved with the firm logo stood waiting. "Good morning, Victoria, I'm Natalie, and I run HR at the firm. You're our home-grown girl as I understand it, correct?"

"I am, yes. Am I the only one?"

"You are indeed. The rest of the twenty members of your associate class consist of nine others from the United States and the remainder are from other countries. Our international diversity is one of the core values the firm prides itself on," Natalie answered. "Come with me. I'll give you a brief tour and then show you to your office."

Natalie moved fast and there was no way Victoria would be able to remember all the departments she was whizzed through or people she was introduced to. As they came back to the place where they began, Victoria felt like she had booked at least a mile and all in heels no less. She was about to ask Natalie one of the questions she had written down as they sped about the office, but as soon as Natalie opened the door to what she announced would be her office, Victoria lost all coherent thought but one. Her office was amazing! Everything about it was breathtaking from the furniture, to the newest electronic and communication products set out on her desk, to the view.

"I see you like what you're looking at," Natalie smiled as she watched Victoria's reaction.

"I do. This is beyond what I expected," Victoria answered, as she looked out her floor-to-ceiling windows and appreciated the view that shot straight up the river to the lake. Turning, she was about to say something about the view when she stopped short as she noticed the newest mobile phone which was not yet available to the public.

"Go ahead. Try it out," Natalie encouraged. "The founding partners believe in using the most advanced technology. Since you speak three languages, you'll find that you may dictate in any of them directly into your phone and our staff will transcribe the document in the language of your choice."

Running her hand over the leather phone case engraved with her initials across the top, she then turned to an intricate phone system, laptop, printer and other electronic items she had never seen before.

"Amazing," was all Victoria could say.

"Here is your welcome packet. It has all the essentials plus your itinerary, which will be your best friend for the next six weeks. Take some time to look it over now, play with some of the equipment and I'll come back for you in an hour. We'll reconvene in the large conference room so you can meet the rest of your class and some of the senior associates. Of course a few of the partners will stop in as well." Looking down at her tablet, Natalie reviewed her checklist. "Is there anything you need or any question I can answer before I leave?"

"No, nothing. Thank you. This is amazing and I'll be ready in an hour."

Natalie took her leave, shutting the door behind her. Victoria immediately grabbed her new phone, spun in her chair like a two-year old, and dialed Kat. "You're not going to believe this, but they just gave me a private office overlooking the river and handed me a boatload of electronics, all of which are now mine. It's like Christmas!"

"If you're this excited now, you're going to be apoplectic by lunchtime. I'm glad you like it after, wait, how long have you been there? About sixty minutes?" Kat teased. "But I've got to go. We're having a meeting on our new Florida development, which I'll be taking over by the way, so let's talk tonight."

"Wow. Congrats, Kat. Okay, talk tonight, and good luck with Florida," Victoria said, spinning back around to face her desk.

According to the itinerary, the incoming associates would be spending their days at one training session after another, ending with the annual "get to know the new associates" firm cocktail party. The first two weeks would focus on firm process and protocol. The next two weeks on litigation, covering everything from learning how to write a motion "the firm way," to deposition protocol, evidence and the rules of the state and federal courthouses. The last two weeks were devoted specifically to learning about the processes and work of the department to which the associate had been assigned. For this part of Victoria's training, Armond Renoir, a partner in the international transaction group, was listed as Victoria's mentor.

Natalie knocked on the door and stuck her head in. "Ready? Let's go. We're running a few minutes behind."

Walking behind Natalie down the plush and hushed hallways, Victoria tried to mentally track their movements so she could find her way back to her office. After about five minutes of almost running to keep up with Natalie, they finally turned a corner and entered a spectacular oval conference room. All but one of the walls were windows. The free-flowing design of the large conference table in the center of the room was made of what appeared to be hand-blown glass with the firm name etched in the center. Victoria noticed that a media screen was being raised from a hidden area in the floor and there were at least twenty-five people milling about, engaged in what sounded like rather stilted "I have no idea what to say to you" conversations.

Taking Victoria by the elbow, Natalie made a beeline toward the corner of the room. "Victoria, I want to introduce you to your mentor before we get started." Natalie stopped in front of one of the best-dressed men Victoria had ever seen. "Victoria, this is Armond Renoir, one of our newest partners and your mentor for the next six weeks and longer if things work out. He'll be your guiding light at the firm. Turn to him whenever you need advice. Armond, Victoria Rodessa, our associate from Chicago and your newest protégé."

While Natalie went into the details of the importance and meaning of the mentor-protégé relationship to the firm, Armond maintained full corporate protocol. He shook Victoria's hand and nodded thoughtfully as if listening to Natalie. Victoria, on the other hand, was having a hard time focusing and instead was mesmerized by Armond's ridiculous amount of perfectly coiffed hair with not a strand out of place and his monogrammed pocket hanky.

"Armond will be initially responsible for your career," Natalie continued. "If he decides you have promise and wants to continue working with you at the end of the six weeks, and assuming you have no objections, then you'll continue to work together at the firm. He will then give you assignments, critique your work and generally, bring you along in the ways of the firm," Natalie explained. "Now, I've got to introduce others. Get to know each other a bit and we'll begin the welcome meeting within the next few minutes."

The moment Natalie left, Armond shed his corporate façade, cocked his head and began to slowly examine Victoria from head to toe. In fact, he had the *cojones* to walk all the way around her in a slow circle, quietly clucking and looking her over. When he finished his slow tour, a grin crept across his sharply chiseled face, and he nodded in approval.

"Victoria, let's be blunt, shall we? I've heard good things about you, and my own digging turned up nothing untoward. Assuming you are of the quality you've led everyone to believe, I want you to know that I will do everything in my power to ensure that you do well." Victoria took a breath and was about to thank Armond but he held up a cautionary and well-manicured finger signaling for her to remain quiet. "I suggest you let me finish, my pet, before you say something you'll regret. Now, where was I? Ah, yes. There is one reason, and one reason alone that I will make sure you do well. And that reason, my dear Victoria, is that the named partners of this firm seem to think you have talent and have issued a mandate that you be put through your paces. They have big plans for you, Victoria. I thought about it and decided that the perfect way to better my situation is to oversee the new protégé. So don't get the wrong idea and think that I care about you. It's not the case. I intend to use you, my dear Victoria. Your tireless work ethic and your skills will springboard my reputation so I'll be awarded the most shares among the partners. And if you ever bring up this conversation to anyone, I will deny it."

After finishing his speech, Armond's face lit up with a show-stopping grin as he began to circle around her once again, "Now, let's talk about your outfit and where you got it? We may actually be able to shop together when you're not busy slaving away for the good of the firm."

At first Victoria felt her anger building and thought she should perhaps report his comments to Natalie and try to get a new mentor. But she noticed that Armond had opened his man purse at the end of his little tirade and was busy digging through it looking for something. At that moment, she knew she liked Armond and suspected that the two of them would get along just fine. After all, she always appreciated honesty and prided herself on being straightforward. So she could hardly criticize him for being blunt.

"I'll tell you on one condition," Victoria said in a very serious tone.

"Oh, don't mess with me, little girl. You're not ready yet to play in my league," Armond warned, bracing for what he assumed would be some ridiculous demand from this cocky little snit fresh out of school.

"If you tell me where you got your bag, I'll tell you where I got my outfit." She smiled and held out her hand. "Deal?"

Armond smiled and shook her hand. "I think we are going to get along just fine, Ms. V. Now go play nice with the other boys and girls," he said as he sashayed out the door.

CHAPTER

6

A S SOON AS Jenny landed in Los Angeles, her assigned
driver took her and her beloved dogs straight to the apartment that would be hers for at least the next six months.
Mona Richmonds, her lawyer and one of the finest divorce
attorneys in the state of California and in fact the country, had rented it for her under one of the assumed names
her firm uses for situations just like Jenny's. One where the
spouse, typically the woman as that was who Mona usually represented, was afraid of her high-powered husband and
needed a protected place to live until the drama sparked by the
initial, and typically unexpected, service of the divorce papers
cooled down.

Jenny chose California as the stage for her next act in life
for a number of reasons. For one thing, and of utmost importance to her future financial security, it was a community
property state. Since Jenny and William owned a home in
Beverly Hills and an apartment in San Francisco, she could
claim this state as much hers as anywhere in the country. Second, it was far away from William's typical haunts and she
could move somewhat freely without running into someone
on his payroll or beholden to him every time she turned a

corner. Which would have been the case in Atlanta or almost anywhere in the South for that matter.

Jenny looked down and saw her phone light up naming the caller as "blocked." Jenny's pet peeve was people who hid their identity, yet expected that people on the receiving end of their call would pick up. Her standard retaliation against such rudeness was to not answer. But today she had a strong intuitive feeling that she should answer this one, so she took the call. But in a nod to her feelings about "blocked" callers, she refused to say "hello." The game of phone chicken was on, with the line unmistakably connected, yet no one said a word. Jenny was about to hang up when she heard, "Jenny, it's Mona. Are you there?"

"Mona, thank God it's you. Listen everything is fine. But I don't typically answer blocked calls. I've had too many people trying to get access to William through me over the years by using the 'blocked' caller identification."

"No problem, Jenny. I'll give you my private mobile line. You can call me whenever you need, and I'll use it to reach you so you'll know it's me in the future. This is the line I use ninety percent of the time with my clients because I don't want them calling me all day and all night. But the other ten percent of my clients, and you're in that group, really do need access 24/7 and I trust you to use it only for emergencies. Hold on for a minute, Jenny, my assistant is buzzing me on the other line."

Jenny sighed and pushed the speaker button on her phone and moved the device away from her ear, placing it on the seat next to her.

As Jenny waited for Mona to come back on the line, she thought about her instinct and realized how reliable it had been over the years. She thought back to the first year of her marriage and recalled the first time she had "that" feeling that something wasn't right. She remembered the time and day perfectly. It was forever seared into her mind.

They had been set to meet in Atlanta at their favorite hotel, and had planned to enjoy a romantic night swimming in the salt-water pool, followed by pampering at the spa, room service, making love, and then shopping the next day before heading home. William had been in Washington, DC for the week on business, working with his lobbyists and meeting politicians, trying to stop the building backlash against tobacco.

She spent the afternoon getting ready to meet him, still giddily in love. Excited every time she noticed that the clock had wound its way up another hour, minute, ten minutes marching toward the time when she would see him strolling purposely through the doors of the hotel lobby.

She had just finished spraying herself in all the right spots with Chanel No. 5, her favorite perfume, when he called to say he was stuck in Washington until Sunday afternoon. William was never apologetic, and Jenny had convinced herself that a man in his position had to be gruff and tough, and so she didn't take the abruptness of his call personally. But when she hung up the phone and began to peel off her skin-tight sheath dress and unclip the black garter topped with pink bows that she had slinked into just for him, she had a nagging feeling that something didn't add up. While she was still a new bride, she knew one thing for sure about her husband. William never did anything he did not want to do. She had known him to walk out of meetings he was hosting because they ran too long and he had a golf game. That was the first time she had the feeling that he might be lying. But she was in love, so she tamped down that feeling and rationalized that she had way too much time on her hands if her mind was drifting in that direction.

As the years went on, however, Jenny noted the feeling more and more. She began to fact-check his stories by doing little things like calling the hotel where he said he was staying and asking to be connected to his room to see if he was registered. But each time she checked, his stories always seemed to be true. His secretary would confirm that he was where he said he was or someone would mention that they had seen him at the convention. There had been times, over the years, when she had thought she was losing her mind. But, no. She had been right all along. He had been screwing dozens of women since the first year of their marriage.

"Jenny? Jenny?" Mona's voice came from the phone. Jenny scrambled to pick it up.

"Mona, I'm here."

"Good, I'm sorry about that. Well, you made it. Congratulations! How are you feeling? Any problem with your exit?"

"None. It was fine. Everything went just as you predicted and I'm quite sure he didn't even consider for a minute that anything might be wrong."

"I'm glad. I've dealt with men like your husband my whole career and the one thing they all have in common is that they are so involved in themselves, that they never see it coming. Listen, I only have a few minutes, as I'm due back in court. But I wanted to let you know that your apartment is set and security is tight. As of now, you're Monica Smith, one of the names I use for my high-profile clients. Can you remember to use it from now on?"

"Yes, that's not a problem, but your driver already knows me as Jenny Acker." Jenny glanced in the rearview mirror to see the driver looking back at her.

"Don't worry about Marco. He's one of my security detail. He knows all about your situation. He's there not only to ensure you get settled and everything you need, but as your driver and for your protection as well. We want the first round of this divorce to go through before William even knows what hit him. Then we'll be able to loosen up on the security and find you a place to live once we know his reaction."

"How long?" Jenny asked.

"What do you mean, how long?"

"How long do I need to assume the alias, and before I can freely walk around and be myself?"

"Right around one to two months I would guess."

"What happens next?"

"Now that you're here and out of the house, I'll file the papers this afternoon, right around four, before the court closes for the day. But as we discussed, the courts rarely allow papers to be filed using alias names, so I'm using your and William's names in the caption. The press is always at the clerk's office to get a look at the newest filings to see what stories they can break. Your divorce will undoubtedly make some of the news channels, and for sure the gossip rags will have a field day."

Jenny took a deep breath and let it out slowly before she responded. "I know, and I'm ready. Go ahead and file. The sooner we begin, the faster I can move forward."

Mona smiled at Jenny's response. After thirty years practicing family law and handling some of the most publicized divorces of the day, Mona could tell the good clients from those that would be a pain in her ass. She only gave her mobile number to the good ones, the ones who were centered and did not think of only themselves. "Good. Listen, Jenny, I'm going to have my public relations person meet you in the next half hour at the apartment. I'm sure you're exhausted, but it's critical we get our public comments in line and on point with the story line we've agreed upon for your divorce."

"That's fine," Jenny said. "I'm ready for it."

"Great. I've got to go but I'll touch base with you after I file to let you know it's done. I want you to try and relax, enjoy the rest of your afternoon and begin to acclimate to your new life in California."

Ten minutes later, Marco turned up a narrow, coast road that wound high into the hills overlooking the ocean. Jenny could smell the eucalyptus and ocean air. She closed her eyes, let her head fall back against the rich and well-polished leather of the car and breathed in deeply, wondering why she had waited so long.

The car door snapped open and Jenny shot her head up; her heart was pounding. "I'm sorry to startle you, Mrs. Acker. I called your name a few times, but you were sound asleep. We're here."

Marco held out his hand and Jenny took it, stepping out of the car. The two dogs bounded out of the car and immediately ran over to the flowers and strange stiff grass, sniffing furiously at the new smells and peeing as much as possible to mark their new territory. "Thank you, Marco. And please, call me Jenny or Ms. Williamson; that was my maiden name and I'm going to take it back. Anything but Mrs. Acker."

"Actually ma'am, I'll be calling you Monica Smith for the next little while," Marco winked, smiled and walked her in the front door of the apartment, and into the safety and privacy of her new temporary home. "Here's your home sweet home, for at least a bit. I'll get your luggage and be right back."

Too stunned at the view to respond, Jenny walked straight out onto the large tiled balcony that overlooked the sweeping coastline. Her unrestricted view traveled for miles north and south along the Pacific coast. Jenny watched the sunbathers far below on the beach basking in the glorious sunshine and the swimmers and surfers frolicking in the ocean. She smiled, feeling at home and thinking of her future as Jenny Williamson, ex-wife of William Acker and a woman of her own destiny. Jenny knew, in that moment, that she would never again allow her life to be dictated and controlled by a man. Never again.

Jenny turned and walked into the apartment to find Marco coming out of the back rooms. "I put your luggage in the master suite. Let me show you a few things. First, as you can see, it's quite large, running just over three thousand square feet. Your master, sitting room and study are up these stairs."

"Marco, this is stunning," Jenny said as she walked into the master bedroom that took up almost the entire top floor. The room was white, with lush carpets, and the furniture was a light cream color, all mixed with bright accent fabrics using the colors of the ocean. The paintings were large splashes of color on white backgrounds, each encased in periwinkle frames.

"Take a look at the study," Marco said as he walked ahead of her.

"It's absolutely perfect." Jenny set her purse and tote down on the glass cover protecting the top of the solid, white beachwood desk. She ran her fingers appreciatively over the waterworn legs of the desk, which seemed to be made from ocean wood, smooth and lovely from years of being exposed to the sea and sun.

"Of course, the house is fully equipped with wireless, even on all of the balconies, so you can sit outside and study if you like." Jenny looked quizzically at his comment.

"Study?"

"Yes, I understand you'll be sitting for the California Bar Exam. Mona told me. Congratulations."

Jenny shook her head and found some wood to knock on. "You absolutely cannot congratulate me again until I pass the exam, or you will taint me with bad luck. It's supposed to be one of the toughest bar exams in the country, and I haven't studied in years."

"You'll pass," Marco said with a smile.

"Marco, why would Mona have told you something so personal? Not that I mind, really. But it just seems out of sorts from her insistence on secrecy." Jenny asked.

"If I'm going to protect you, I need to know about you to know what is and is not your normal activity. For instance, I know you love to work out, and running, walking or hiking is all part of that, and that you do some form of exercise almost every day. If I didn't know about that part of you, I may not think it's unusual if you don't come out of the apartment to work out. Since I do know that, I would figure there is something out of the ordinary happening, and I would check on you. Make sense?"

Jenny walked back into the master suite and Marco followed. "Yes, it does. But to be quite honest, and I hope you don't take this the wrong way, I really don't think I need security. After all, I'm not famous; I just have an egocentric, self-centered husband. I certainly can't be the first and I won't be the last."

"And, not to scare you, but I need more than my two hands to count the number of attacks that some of these other egocentric, self-centered husbands have tried to wage on their wives for daring to go against their will and get a divorce. It's not even that they necessarily want their wives back. No offense meant."

"None taken," Jenny answered with a little smile.

"It's more about the fact that their wives humiliated them and they're not used to getting the short end of the stick. They don't take it well." Marco reached inside the breast pocket of his jacket and handed Jenny a black slender stick-like object. "This is your panic button. If you need me for any reason, push this button. Give it a try."

Jenny took the stick and pushed the red button on the end. She could hear and see the vibration of Marco's watch. He showed her the face of the watch, and her name was lit up along with the address of the apartment.

"Okay, I got it. Class 101 in getting a divorce. Call Marco for any problems." Jenny walked over to put the stick in her purse.

"What are you doing? You can't leave the stick there."

"Why not? What do you want me to do with it? Wear it on my clothes?" Jenny said as a joke.

"Yup. That's exactly what I want you to do. Wear it on your clothes. Here, may I?" Marco asked as he took the stick from her.

"I guess you're the boss." Jenny watched in horror as he actually clipped the stick to the inside lining of her jacket. "You must be kidding. You actually want me to wear this on my clothes?" Jenny asked.

"Not kidding, and yes. I actually want you to wear it on your clothes."

A soft chiming sound began to seep throughout the apartment. "That will be our PR consultant. Come on. Let's get you started." Marco led the way out of the master bedroom and down the stairs. Jenny followed, anxious to take the next step.

CHAPTER
7

I T WAS NOT until the next day that news of the Ackers' divorce worked its way into the public domain, and in a big way. William's Bermudan mistress, Wilhemena, was flipping through the TV channels as she usually did to get her mind off of her reality after one of William's demanding sessions. To-night he had bent her over the outside balcony off of her master suite, lifted her dress, spread her cheeks and legs, and entered her deep and hard. At least three different yachts had moved past her ocean-view balcony while he pulled hard on her hair as he rammed her from behind. He was a bit of an exhibitionist and loved having sex in possible view of others. William could stay hard and demanding for an hour or two easy, but tonight he had been quick, finishing in twenty minutes.

As she was about to flip to the next channel, she thought she heard what sounded like William's last name. Turning up the volume, her eyes widened and she quickly pushed pause. "William, you need to see this," she called from her bedroom door toward the drawing room, where she knew William was getting his nightly whiskey.

"What's up?" William asked as he walked into Wilhemena's bedroom, carrying his favorite crystal-cut highball glass. His pajama bottoms hung low around his hips, allowing his big shirtless belly to stick out over the top, prominently displayed. If Wilhemena didn't know better, she would swear he was with child. At least that's how she described his body to her girlfriends. But she was careful not to complain too much, because she was afraid someone would open her mouth and tell him some of the rather nasty things she said about him. After all, Bermuda was a very small and very close-knit island.

Overall, though, Wilhemena appreciated William, or at least, his money. He had paid for the soon-to-be-hers, lovely pink home that sat perfectly placed on a rocky outcrop right above the ocean. That purchase had come from the one and only fight they had ever had three years ago, when she told William it was the last time she would see him, because it was time she got married and started her own family. Much to her surprise, William was frantic. He told her he would not let her go, and refused to let her out of his sight for the rest of his trip. When he finally left, Wilhemena moved back into the home she shared with her mother and sister, and she thought that was the end of that. But William was relentless in his pursuit, calling her almost every other day to remind her that he expected to see her on his next trip.

Eventually, Wilhemena refused to take his calls and even threw the phone he had given her into the ocean. But about three months later, William showed up at her mother's home with flowers and begged her to at least let him take her to dinner. It was during dinner, while the sun sank slowly into the turquoise ocean, that they cut their deal. He would buy and pay for a house of her choice, after four years title would be in her name alone, and he would pay her a yearly stipend. In return, she was forbidden to have sex with anyone but him and she could not even masturbate unless he gave her permission. William made it clear those terms were nonnegotiable.

He wanted her wet and horny and ready, from the minute he landed until right before he took off. He also insisted on complete control of the sex. When, how, and where. It was all to be gentleman's choice. She would have no say unless he asked for her input. He was so much of a control freak that he even dictated during their negotiations that from that point forward, she was to accompany his driver to the airport when he was returning to the island and she was never allowed to wear panties during those airport trips.

Wilhemena had agreed on three conditions. First, there would be no sex between them until the house was bought and paid for in full, and $400,000 was deposited in cash in her bank account to cover her living expenses for the next two years. Finally, each year thereafter, another $250,000 would be wired into her account.

From that point on, the minute William arrived at the airport and entered the waiting car, he ordered Wilhemena onto his lap, spread her legs, and stuck his fingers deep inside to make sure she was wet. Then he would lift her up, and slide roughly inside her, riding her all the way home.

When she heard William enter the room, Wilhemena pushed the play button and said, "I think this will interest you." The TV sprang to action, announcing the divorce of tobacco tycoon William Acker and his one-time state's attorney wife, Jenny Williamson. The next thing she heard was William's glass shatter when it hit the cool tile of her bedroom floor.

CHAPTER
8

ARMOND HAD CREATED an intense schedule that Victoria followed over the last six weeks. He went out of his way to recruit the top senior associates to teach Victoria the basic skills she needed in order to be successful at the firm and in his corporate group. She received more training by far than the other new associates. Victoria's tutors began with simple contracts and moved on to employment agreements, from the most basic to the more complex golden parachutes created for the C-suite executives. From there they addressed complex domestic transactions until she finally graduated to international matters including the more mundane, yet extremely important pieces of information such as exchange rates, time changes, and different customs for each country in which their clients conducted business.

On the final day of training, it was time for the associates to find out whether their mentors wanted to invite them into their respective groups to continue their legal careers. While Victoria was nervous, she felt confident that Armond liked and respected her and would want to continue. But some of the other mentors had told their associates weeks ago that they had decided to continue with them and grow their relationships after the six weeks were finished. Armond, however, had never said a word. So Victoria sat and nervously waited in the assigned conference room for Armond to arrive and deliver his decision.

After a quick rap on the door, Armond entered, looking dapper in a blue pinstriped perfectly tailored suit complete with an engraved, deep navy, silk pocket hanky, and tossed a file in front of her. "Take a look," he said as he paced the room. Victoria had gotten used to Armond's theatrics and had learned that he came by them honestly. Kat had immediately recognized Armond's name and informed Victoria that his father was one of the most successful movie producers in Hollywood. Victoria learned from various sources that Armand's father had wanted him to take over the legal end of the business so he could focus on the movie producing part of Renoir Productions. Armond had declined, moved to Chicago and joined Acker, Smith & McGowen.

Victoria opened the file and began to organize and sift through the documents. "Oh for heaven's sake, it will take you past cocktail hour at that rate. I'll tell just tell you," Armond said, swinging one of the chairs around so he could look directly into her eyes, as if he was delivering a marriage proposal. "You'll be working with me from now on. You're lucky, you know. I'll expect your full attention." Armond shot out of his chair and began to pace again. "If a project needs to be finished over a weekend, late at night or over what you thought was going to be your vacation, you will simply cancel your plans and complete the project. This is not about you. It is about what you can do for me first, then the firm. *Capisce*?"

"Does this mean you like me? You really like me?" Victoria teased, mimicking a famous Sally Field's Oscar acceptance speech. She had begun using Hollywood references now and then to tease Armond whenever he began to take himself too seriously.

"Don't get carried away, my pet. You still need to prove yourself. And in my book, tomorrow is not another day," he answered with a twist on the famous closing line from *Gone with the Wind*. With one hand on the door, Armond nodded toward the file and all signs of play were replaced with aloofness. "You have twenty-four hours to digest the facts, and pinpoint the critical issues. I'll see you in my office this time tomorrow," Armond spat as he walked out of the room leaving Victoria happy as a pig in shit and alone with her first legal file.

CHAPTER
9

WHEN THEIR FLIGHT landed in Bermuda, it was for the fourth time in the last two months. William and Billy headed straight to The Western Will, Acker, Smith & McGowen's home and base of operation on the island. Big Bill had lent the boys a good chunk of the cash needed to buy the property and as part of the deal had required that they name the estate with a nod to his family's plantation. The property was magnificent and the boys would have done just about anything he asked to close the deal. It overlooked the ocean, and the house had two wings so that guests had their own private space separate from the owners. The boys each had their own suite in the West Wing, which sat on a cliff overlooking the pool, the patio, and the turquoise ocean below. Big Bill's living space was in the East Wing overlooking the golf course, as was his preference.

William and Billy grabbed a quick shower, then popped into the Maserati, the firm car Billy had chosen for his island use. They were set to present at a meeting at Highline Insurance Company beginning at two that afternoon. Highline's offices had always been a bit off-putting, at least for Billy. He preferred clean lines, open rooms and white walls. The old-world decor of the company's headquarters was anything but. Fussy, full of old-smelling knickknacks and antiques, it hearkened back to the colonial past of the island. One of the walls was lined with priceless, framed originals from the 1800s of some of the first insurance contracts ever written, complete with the slips signed by titled lords and wealthy merchants who had invested heavily in betting on the safety of ships as they crossed the oceans. It was still a fascinating business, really, Billy thought as he began his rounds to welcome each of the board members.

Big Bill was chairman of the board, and eight other men who headed syndicates that had invested significant capital to be a part of Highline's insurance pool made up the remaining members. Every major country involved in the insurance market was represented: Qatar, Japan, Australia, India, Germany, Saudi Arabia, United Kingdom, and of course, the United States.

Highline would specialize in emerging and hard-to-place risks. The more established insurance companies typically chose not to ensure such risks because the odds were not yet statistically proven to show that the insurer would win the bet of keeping the premium versus making a claim payment. Since getting involved in this new project, Billy had learned that as the world changed, so too the insurable risks, and quickly. And with each change, whether new technology or the hacking of private information or a disaster, there was an opportunity for insurers to make money. Highline had decided to target and hopefully thrive on these emerging risks. There was another twist to its business model that would separate Highline from the other insurers, but only a few people knew about that.

The room began to fill with the nine-man board, and William called the meeting to order.

"Gentlemen, good afternoon. As you know from the board packets sent to each of you, we have a full agenda and a number of resolutions to consider. I hereby open the meeting and present the agenda to the board. Randy, if you would please pass out the proposed resolutions, we can begin."

Randy Roman, the president of Highline and one of Trever McGowen's Oxford pals, passed out the documents. "First on the agenda is Highline's property product. To date, we have twenty potential investors, enough to give us a green light. The product is to be launched as soon as we can get regulatory clearance in the United States. As you know from our business plan, it will target high-risk property, from homes to large-scale condominium and commercial buildings located along the American coasts. Our product will capitalize on the rising demand from property owners and the lack of product offered by our competitors. Simple supply and demand really. Our research shows that climate change will continue with the corresponding effect of a gradual yet consistent rise in weather disasters around the world, which will hit the coasts of the US particularly hard."

Dr. Harrington, a PhD financial guru from the United Kingdom, puffed on his cigar. "What is the projected rate of return on the product, and over what period of time?"

"Billy, why don't you pull up the projected ROI and we can take a look." Randy nodded to Billy and tossed him the remote while the screen slid noiselessly from its hiding place in the ceiling.

As Billy went over the numbers, Big Bill puffed on his cigar and smiled to himself. They were set to make a killing and nothing could get in the way.

"The graph shows the projected return from your first product offering. As the product matures, your return will increase, assuming the plan is functioning as outlined," Billy continued.

"Any further questions, gentlemen?" Big Bill asked. There was no response. "Great, then is there any further discussion?" Again, no response. "Excellent, then is there a motion in line with the first resolution?"

Dr. Rodriquez nodded. "I move to approve the first resolution, approving the launch of Highline's first product."

"I second," the board member from Dubai raised his hand.

"All in favor?"

"Aye."

"All opposed?" There was no response.

"Resolution number one is approved and carried. Next on the agenda, Randy, would you take us through it?"

As Randy presented the next matter to the board, Billy thought of all the effort and time it had taken to get to today's presentation. The accumulation of enough capital to fund the company had been all consuming the last two years. But now Highline had approved the go-ahead for its first insurance policy to launch in the US. Acker, Smith & McGowen had already made over two million dollars as corporate and board counsel for Highline. But that was small potatoes compared to the money the firm stood to make from the next step of handling the regulatory work needed to bring the policy to market. He drifted off, thinking about the profits the firm would make on a going-forward basis.

When Billy brought his focus back to the meeting, the second resolution was up for a vote. It was no surprise that the resolution passed.

Four hours later, Billy finished his report to his partners back in Chicago, hung up the phone, and walked out to the veranda of The Western Will, where his father puffed on a cigar waiting to celebrate.

"Billy, you boys need to get some quality cigars for your guests. This is like smoking a turd," Big Bill said as he sloppily sucked-pulled the cigar out of his mouth and examined it as if to ensure it was not a turd. Despite his criticism, Big Bill took one more long pull on the cigar and tossed it over the cliff into the ocean. As he began to uncork the bottle of fine California Cabernet, he paused and added, "I'll do you boys one more favor. Jesus, if I haven't done enough already, but I'll tell you what I'll do. I'll set you up with my Cuban connection so you boys can get some high-quality cigars to offer to your guests. Jesus," Big Bill laughed as he walked over to hand a glass of wine to his son, "sometimes I wonder how you boys put your pants on without my help."

Billy smirked at his father's comments. God, he was a self-centered bastard, Billy thought. A condescending know-it-all. He had listened to this same kind of narcissistic dribble for as long as he could remember. There were times he wondered how much longer he could take it. But then he had to grudgingly acknowledge that it was that same cocky attitude that had enticed the caliber of men that had sat in the board room earlier that day to invest in a new company. A company that had already brought a couple million dollars to his firm. Billy could honestly say he admired his father for that. And with the thought of the millions more his firm would make if all went according to plan, he knew he would swallow his pride and deal with his father as long as the money continued to flow. Indeed he would.

CHAPTER
10

JUST TWO MONTHS after leaving Chicago to take her place in her family's real estate and development company, Kat had already developed a routine. She began her day early, as always. Walking into the plush reception area, she marched directly to the air conditioning control panel and violently jabbed at the buttons to reduce the freezing air roaring out of the vents. The subzero temperatures inside were comfortable only for people who were either overweight or women going through menopause, like her mother. Kat hated air conditioning. She pulled a sweater from her stash in the closet and threw it around her shoulders.

Kat breathed deeply and was rewarded with the rich scent of coffee, which meant that Cassie, her assistant, was already in the office.

"Morning, Cassie," Kat called as she walked through the reception area to her newly decorated office. Kat had one of the best offices on their floor. Her father and brothers, of course, had the others. Kat pressed the button on the remote, and the blinds lifted to reveal the view overlooking Houston.

Kat's corner office faced south and west. During the late afternoon, Kat often had to close the blinds as the sun, which she adored in most situations, became a demon ball from hell, gleefully shoving heat into Kat's office. But in the morning, there was nothing like her view.

"What a gorgeous day, Cassie," Kat sighed as she stared out the window. She could feel Cassie enter her office and smell the coffee that came with her.

"Really, Kat? It's too early to know yet, isn't it? God, you're a hopeless morning person. If it wasn't for the fact that I love what I do and enjoy working with you, even though you're a brutal taskmaster, I would find a job beginning at a more reasonable time of day."

Kat smiled. "Oh, Cassie, you say the same thing almost every day, and yet, when I'm in town, you always beat me to the office and have the coffee brewing by the time I walk in the door. I think you're one of those charming people who just like to bitch." Kat powered on her laptop and took the cup of black coffee from Cassie.

"What you mistake for a hardworking team player is really a covert effort to hide my overriding desire to get out of the house early so Jeff has to handle the kids and get them ready for school. I don't mind the afternoon and evening with the kids, but the morning whining just because they have to get out of bed, well, that drives me right up the wall. And since I don't score high in the patience category, as you well know, I end up screaming at them like a born-again banshee. While Jeff, on the other hand, manages to tease them out of bed." Cassie pushed her hand through her dark brown hair, sitting down to go over the day with Kat.

"Okay, what's on the agenda for today? I know I have the conference call on the La Pacifica property and then a refinancing meeting for our Southern Palm development in Miami. Have those times changed?"

"No, and they're confirmed for ten and two, respectively. However, Suzie is having problems with the insurance company for Haven Gardens. She wants some time if you can give it to her. My guess is she'll need about an hour. She's also sent some correspondence she's received from the insurer, and it's printed and in the folder titled Haven Gardens on your desk." Cassie checked her day diary. "How does three thirty sound to you? That way you'll have a bit of time to review the material she sent, and we'll still have time after that to get you ready for your trip to Chicago."

Kat frowned. Suzie was one of her most trusted property managers. She handled their property on the West Coast efficiently and independently. If she wanted to talk today, then that meant there was a real issue, and that troubled Kat. But just the thought that at the end of the day she would be with Victoria brought a smile back. "That sounds perfect, thanks Cassie. Get Suzie scheduled and let me get started."

"Done and done. I'll give you the typical fifteen-minute warning, unless you need more?" Cassie asked on her way out of Kat's office.

"No, that's perfect, Cassie, thanks." Kat's responsibilities at Fontaine Development included oversight of construction projects, as well as dealing with problems in the property management part of the business. At the beginning, Kat had felt uncomfortable taking on these responsibilities since most of the people she managed were older and had taught her the ropes when she first started working in high school. But Kat had always been good with people and her skills had only sharpened over time. She was well respected.

Kat had a good three hours before her first meeting, and got to work reviewing the documents for her ten o'clock call. After about an hour, she turned to the letter Suzie had sent from the property insurer for Haven Gardens. The insurer's claim representative had written a long ten-page letter that denied their claim and quoted gibberish policy language. Kat could feel her blood begin to boil. She had no patience for bullshit, and the letter was just that. She put her earpiece in and began to pace as she dialed one of the two lawyers they had on staff.

"Josh, have Cassie send you the letter we got from the Haven Gardens insurer and then pull the insurance policies. I want you to do some preliminary research on the issues raised by the insurer denying our claim. I want a full memo when I return next week."

Kat listened to his question about which law to apply.

"I'm not sure yet. Assume we have to file suit where the property is located. Check that state's choice of law rules and then research the law that applies. But I also want to know whether the law in that jurisdiction is followed throughout the country, or if it's the minority approach." Kat walked to the windows as she listened. "Great, email will be fine. But I want copies of the substantive cases as well as your memo."

At three thirty, Cassie put Suzie through to Kat. Kat smiled when she picked up the phone. "Hey sweetie, tell me what's going on."

"Did you have a chance to look at the letter? Those idiots at the insurance company are telling me that the roof that was uplifted during the storm and the other damage to Haven Gardens was under the deductible and not covered. Kat, our guys have done an initial assessment of the damage to the building, and it's well in excess of one and a half million dollars. There is no way we should let this slide."

"Suzie, how can the insurance company possibly say that the cost of the roof is less than the deductible? The price of roofing hasn't dropped that much, has it?" Kat asked.

"No, of course not. According to the idiot insurance adjuster who was out here, the only parts of the roof damaged by the storm were on the east and south corners. He claims that the rest of the damage is from wear and tear, which is excluded by the policy. So he figures the cost to repair the corners is well below the deductible, so according to the knucklehead, it's our responsibility to fix the roof."

"What about the other damage? Why aren't they paying for that?"

"According to knucklehead, the other damage is nonexistent, at least as damage caused by the storm and is from normal wear and tear of property on the ocean."

"How much did we pay in premiums for the policy?" Kat asked, shaking her head as she listened to the answer. "Okay, Suzie, thanks for the information. I've got Josh looking into the law, and we'll get back to you next week. For now, don't respond to this letter until we know where we stand. But I would like our guys to send me a complete scope of the damages and the cost to repair, so I know what we're dealing with."

"No problem. I doubt what I have to say to the insurance company can legally cross state lines anyway. As to the damages, my guys are halfway through their inspections. I'll let you know scope and numbers as soon as we have them, but no later than next week."

Kat sighed as she hung up the phone, made some notes about the damage numbers Suzie had given her, and put the notes in the Haven Garden file. She picked up the phone and dialed Josh's extension. When he didn't answer, she left him a voicemail. "Josh, take a look at bad faith law against insurance companies. Call me if you have any questions on where I'm going with this."

When she hung up the phone, Kat turned to the last of her tasks for the day. A few minutes later, Cassie walked in to remind Kat of the time. "You need to get going if you're going to make the flight. Ted is waiting with the limo downstairs to drop you at the airport. One of us will get your car back to your condo so it will be waiting for you on your return."

"Great. Thanks, Cassie. Call if you need me." Kat walked out of the office, looking forward to her time in Chicago.

CHAPTER
11

RMOND HAD GIVEN Victoria a lukewarm review after she reported on the first assignment he literally threw at her on her last day of training. She had no trouble digesting the information and distinguishing the wheat from the chaff. Even though Armond only gave her a mediocre response, she knew her finished product had been superb. She was already thinking of ways to move ahead of the others in her class to become the first woman partner at the firm.

"Okay, V, your first *real* project. Here you go, and don't screw it up, because my ass is on the line. And if my ass is on the line, then that means that your whole body is in front of the firing squad. Got it?" Armond handed Victoria a thumb drive marked "The Highline Group." Armond recognized how driven Victoria was, and he could not have been more ecstatic. After all, the more she did to up her value at the firm, the better he would look.

Victoria smiled. This was what she had waited for her whole life and there was no way she was going to screw this up. She was more than ready for this opportunity, and Armond's threats didn't bother her one bit. She never failed and she had no intention of changing that pattern now. "Got it, *el capitán*," Victoria said with a half salute to Armond. Over the past few months, Victoria had learned that Armond was just as power hungry as she was, and in her mind, that alone made them the perfect team.

"Smart ass," Armond smirked. "This is for the The Highline Group, a newly formed privately held insurance company. The firm has worked with the founders of Highline since day one, developing their business plan, obtaining financing and handling their legal affairs. The company's now ready to launch its first product, an insurance policy for owners of at-risk property, and we're tasked with ensuring that Highline can bring it to the United States market."

"Who's been in charge of the project so far?" Victoria asked.

"Well, Billy Acker has been running the show as general counsel for the board, as his father is chairman of the board of Highline. I've been doing all the work, while Billy gets all the glory," Armond explained. "And Trever will be involved in the company's business strategy on a going-forward basis."

"Wait, Mr. Acker's father is the chairman of the board? Isn't there a wee bit of a conflict of interest?" Victoria asked.

"Really, Ms. Hotshot? You want to begin your first assignment questioning the ethical choices of one of the founders of this firm and the chairman of the board of one of our clients, who just so happens to be his father? Do you want to rethink that question? Because if not, there are ten other people right behind you dying to get their hands on this file to show their fine legal abilities to the powers that be." Armond crossed his arms and stared down at Victoria. "But to answer your question, just this one time; what conflict? We're all in the same boat, rowing in the same direction. The firm wants what's best for Highline and Highline wants to run its business. So where is the conflict?"

"Dunno," Victoria answered. "Geez, I just asked a question."

"Well, you're not in law school anymore. No one in the real world appreciates random comments regurgitated into the atmosphere. They rarely lead to good. I suggest this is lesson number one in learning to deal in the real world with real people who have their own vested interest in whatever it is they're doing. And no one wants their vested interests screwed with, particularly not by an upstart young lawyer who doesn't know the difference between a conflict and the path to partnership."

"Okay, Armond. I heard you loud and clear the first time. Can I get going on this now?"

Armond stood up and began to leave her office. "Yes. You may. Review all the documents and details of the product offering. You'll find a memo providing a cursory overview of the different insurance regulations of all fifty states. I want a summary from you by next week setting out exactly what needs to be filed in each state and how to get it done. That means from the most important issue like necessary capital, down to the detail of the number of copies, who we send the documents to, how long it takes to get them approved, and the projected finish date for all fifty of the amazing United States to approve our client's product so they can begin to sell insurance." Armond smiled as he sashayed out her office.

"Geez," Victoria said to herself as she inserted the thumb drive in her laptop, "I gotta learn to walk like that." Laughing at her own joke, Victoria began to review the documents. There were tons of folders and hundreds of documents within each folder. "Good God," Victoria sighed. She had been handed a daunting task. It was Thursday. If she was very, very lucky, she might squeak through reviewing the documents by Sunday night. But that wouldn't even begin to address the research and contact with each state's insurance folks that had to be finished before she could even take a step toward creating the finished product Armond wanted by next week's end.

It was eight o'clock at night before Victoria looked up again from her work. She had her headphones in and had been listening to her music to drown out distractions. With only time enough to review them once, Victoria did not want to lose any level of concentration. When her phone rang, she looked at it with glassy eyes and saw that it was Kat. For a brief moment, she wondered why Kat was calling. Suddenly, Victoria shot straight up and out of her chair.

"Oh... My... God!" Victoria exclaimed as she picked up the call. "I'm so sorry, Kat. I cannot believe I did this."

"Whoa, slow down. What did you do?" Kat asked, juggling the phone between her ear and her shoulder as she pulled her luggage through O'Hare International Airport toward the pickup curb.

"I forgot you were coming. I'm still at the office in the city. I'm so sorry. Grab a cab and I'll pay for it. Okay?" Victoria said, standing, talking and packing up her work as quickly as she could. There was no response from Kat.

"Kat, talk to me. I'm so sorry, but I got my first real assignment today and it's a big one and I've been at it all day and I barely took a break to go to the bathroom. Please Kat, say something. I feel absolutely terrible."

"Well, so you should. This just leads to only one result. You're the buyer of dinner and drinks tonight. Now I'll get into a cab, but you get your skinny little ass out of that uptight office and meet me at your apartment. Make sure you open a bottle of champagne. The good stuff. Not that cheap stuff you're always trying to tell me is good enough." Kat hung up the phone, smiling, and raised her hand for a cab. Kat knew her anal best friend well enough to know that guilt would drive her to buy the priciest bottle she could find. Life was good and Kat actually laughed out loud as she got in the cab.

CHAPTER
12

VICTORIA DUMPED THE printed key parts of the file into her Louis Vuitton bag, zipped the thumb drive containing the rest of the file in the inside pocket, changed out of her four-inch heels into flats, and moved fast for the elevator. She passed security and was almost out of the building when she heard, "Hold it, young lady!"

"Hank, what's up?" Victoria turned and walked back toward the security desk in the center of the glass-surround foyer. Hank held up his thumbs, raised his right eyebrow, cocked his head to one side, and manifested a look that left no room to doubt his thoughts.

"Oh, of course. Hank, I'm sorry." Victoria placed both of her thumbs on the top of the glass security monitor and after about ten seconds, the light flashed green. She lifted her thumbs off the glass, waved at Hank, heard the telltale "click" that meant the doors had been unlocked, and revolved out into the beautiful summer evening. The minute she was a few blocks from the office, safe from the judging eyes of anyone at work, she sprinted to the liquor store and then home.

Victoria quickly stripped out of her work clothes and into her favorite jeans. She added a sexy yellow lacy top and smiled at her reflection in the mirror. She looked hot. Victoria loved that about the two of them, the brunette and the blonde. When they went out together, they could do vapid, teasing, haughty, nice, naughty or sophisticated—whatever role they wanted to play for the evening. Most guys never bothered to find out what they did or who they were, so the girls just enjoyed them for an evening and played their own game. One time, they told a group of guys they were professional football cheerleaders who had come to Chicago to learn some new moves from some of the strip-club dancers. The boys were salivating so hard that their tongues never made it off the floor for the rest of the evening. The girls fondly referred to that persona as the "slutty cheerleader." It was one of their favorites.

The door to Victoria's entry way buzzed, and she ran down to see her friend. "Hey, girl, you look so good! It's so amazingly good to see you," Kat said as she squeezed her best friend in a big bear hug.

"You too. I'm so sorry about forgetting to come get you. I really don't know what happened to me. I'm never like that."

"Forget it. Obviously you got wrapped up in your first client and by the way, yes, you're really like that. Remember in the second year of law school when you went to the library to study for your constitutional law final? You were so stressed out by that class that you completely forgot to get out of the library before it closed, and you ended up being locked in the whole night?" Kat shook her head, laughing as she followed Victoria to the spare bedroom to dump her suitcase.

"Yeah, well, I was neurotic then. Now I'm merely anal. An improvement, I think," Victoria said with a laugh. "Now, what are we doing tonight? What's your pleasure? We can go to dinner and then the bars, skip dinner and go straight to the bars, and then order a pizza after we get home and dissect the events of the night. A bunch of our classmates want to see you, and they're ready to meet us at the Lounge on Rush Street. I reserved the VIP area. I thought we should start there and go where the party leads us."

As Kat finished brushing her hair, the last of the summer day's light caught itself in her lush locks and seemed to get lost in the thickness of her mane. At times, Victoria thought, Kat looked almost ethereal, and this was one of those times. But as soon as Kat opened her mouth and began speaking, the ethereal quality was put to rest. "Let's go straight to the bars. I see no reason to eat. Send a message to our class to meet at the Lounge on Rush at ten o'clock."

"Done!" Victoria said, smiling as she sent out a mass text. "Now we have an hour before we need to meet everyone. Let's open the good champagne. Tell me about what you've been doing for the company. How do you like it? How is your new office? Everything."

As they walked toward Victoria's kitchen, Kat stopped to slip on her new heels. They were yellow leather, bedazzled in strategic places with crystals and accented with the telltale pink sole. Victoria turned with the bottle of champagne and stopped dead in her tracks. "No you didn't," she cried. "I cannot believe you went and bought your first pair without me. We had a deal. Our first time would be together. Now you're no longer a virgin, and I'm left behind," Victoria pouted as she popped the bottle of champagne.

"Victoria, I know, and I'm sorry, really I am. Okay, I was sorry for a minute, but it passed. This is not my fault. My mother bought them for me as a surprise for my graduation gift. She had no idea we had a pact. She felt bad when I told her, so..." Kat turned and ran back to her room, "wait right there!"

Victoria continued to pout as she poured their drinks. "Surprise!" Kat yelled, and held a second identical pair up high for her to see. "We bought you your pair. See, we lost our virginity together!"

Victoria stared open-mouthed at the shoes swinging by their straps and catching every bit of light in the room before they threw it right back, almost like a game. "Kat, oh my God, Kat. I don't know what to say. Well, I do, but I don't want to say it, which is…okay, here goes." Victoria took a big gulp and closed her eyes for a moment before saying, "Kat, this is an amazing gift from you and your mother, and please convey my thanks to her for me. But it's far too expensive a gift and I cannot keep them."

The silence hung in the air like the moment between when a soon-to-be new mother recognizes her first contraction for what it is and registers its meaning. Then both the girls burst out laughing at the same time. "Give me those amazing pieces of art so I can get them on my well-deserving feet before another minute passes." Kat handed the shoes to Victoria, and both girls studied them as Victoria turned them this way and that, examining every last detail before sliding them on her feet. "They are stunning, Kat. I can't thank you or your mom enough."

"Victoria, we look amazing. We'll turn heads tonight, and since we're the just-named hosts of the new reality show called Chicago Men, that searches for the most talented, single men in the city, our producers gave us matching shoes as gifts. We decided to wear them out on the town as we scout the city for men to audition for the show."

"And," Victoria added, "we have to have chosen two men by the end of the night. That will keep them coming and going."

The girls laughed and clinked their glasses to their new identities.

CHAPTER

13

K AT, TELL ME what's going on with the company? How do you like the new position, your new office, everything?" Victoria asked. They left her apartment and began walking toward the main street to catch a cab to "Viagra Triangle." Aptly named as it housed bars that attracted all types, including older men sporting the dreaded open shirt and gold chain ensemble in the age-old and never-ending attempt to attract much younger women.

"Victoria, I absolutely love what I'm doing. I'm still learning, of course, and the people who now report to me are still getting used to me as their boss. But it's not like it was a surprise to them that I would be the general counsel and VP in charge of development. I mean, I've worked at Fontaine since I was a teenager and it's a family-owned business. But best of all, I got to hire the three associates who work for me. I made that decision and I'm proud of who I chose. They're all great." Kat smiled as she began to describe them.

"They all have great credentials, but each one of them has been through something in their lives that allows their true character to shine through. I often think of Sophia, Victoria, and how she raised you on her own, and yet was always there for us through all the drama of law school. I know how hard she's had it, and so I wanted to find others that can use that boost ahead, that one little thing that might make a difference in their world. And I found Josh, Bella and Jamie. Josh was raised by his grandparents and grew up without a mother or father, and Bella and Jamie are single parents."

Victoria smiled at her friend and touched her arm as they grabbed a cab. "You're amazing and very softhearted, my friend. My mother will be so touched that you honored her in this way."

The girls hugged just as the cab pulled up in front of the Lounge on Rush. Kat paid the meter and the girls stepped out of the cab, soaking up the sight and smells of Chicago at its finest. The Lounge sat on the corner of one of the busiest multiple intersections in the city. The Viagra Triangle wasn't as crazy traffic-wise as Chicago's infamous Six Corners, but it had the added allure of being located in the posh heart of the city. The park that served as a divider between the busy streets and sidewalk swarmed with activity.

"God, I love this town," Kat said to Victoria as they steered clear of the traffic and walked into the Lounge.

The hostess recognized them at once and stepped from behind her podium where she oversaw traffic to greet them and walk them into the cordoned-off VIP area. "Girls, it's so good to see you. Kat, I didn't expect to see you again for quite some time," Celia purred to the girls.

"Celia, how could you ever think I would be able to leave this town behind? In fact, I'm actually looking for a condo on Michigan Avenue, so if you hear of anything, let me know."

Victoria grabbed Kat from behind by the arm and whipped her around. "Are you kidding me? When were you going to let me know?"

Kat smiled and yelled over the noise, "V, I wanted it to be a surprise once it was bought. But I couldn't wait any longer, so it just popped out now."

"Really, Kat?" yelled Victoria over the noise. "You couldn't think to tell me before this? Really?"

"Really," Kat answered. "I'm going to be traveling to Chicago a ton, as we're in the midst of negotiating developments for at least three new areas. Two are in the city, and the other one will be in the suburbs. It makes sense to purchase a place now and that way, I get to keep tabs on my best friend."

"Yay!" was all Victoria had time to say as the two girls were inhaled by the swarm of their former classmates.

The next morning, Victoria woke at five o'clock with a splitting headache and feeling nauseous. Despite her best intentions to not get drunk, she had. She was totally hungover and pissed at herself, as she now had to put in a full day at the office before she could get to the weekend. But even once she reached the end of the day and the coveted Friday night, her work wouldn't stop. She had a ton to do before she would be in a position to even begin to write the memorandum that Armond expected on his desk by next Friday morning.

Moaning, Victoria rolled sideways out of bed and just barely threw her feet to the floor ahead of her ass. The first thing on her very short agenda was to make coffee, take some Advil, and eat something baked and sweet and filled with grease. As she swayed down the hall toward her kitchen, she heard absolutely no sound from Kat's room. Not surprising, as Kat had always been the one to sleep until noon after one of their outings, yet still maintain straight As and rock an amazing body. While Victoria had been the one to get up at the crack of dawn to study or run or do something. Disgusting.

As the coffee brewed, Victoria berated herself for letting this happen. Why couldn't she simply have switched to water instead of drinking? If she was going to have the power she wanted to have, she was going to have to learn some self-restraint, as she would, no doubt, be confronted with many other situations like last night.

Taking the thumb drive out of her bag, Victoria picked up where she had left off. She had another two hundred pages to get through before she could even begin the necessary research to produce the fifty-state review required by Armond.

Two hours later, Victoria had waded through anther fifty pages of the file, drank two cups of steaming hot and very black coffee, downed a chocolate-chip muffin, and felt much better as the Advil had kicked in. As she was closing down her laptop to head into the shower, Kat came out of her room looking disgustingly fresh and as if she hadn't traveled across country yesterday and spent the night in the bars until 2:00 a.m.

"Mmmm, coffee, yes please," Kat said as she grabbed a seat at the kitchen bar looking expectantly at Victoria to get her a cup.

"Here," Victoria said as she handed the steaming cup across the counter. "That's all the time I have for you until tonight. I'm such an idiot for last night. I didn't tell you much about my assignment but suffice it to say that I have a ridiculous amount of work to finish before next Friday at which time, at precisely 8:00 a.m., Armond will expect me to hand him a fully completed dissertation on the regulatory requirements of all fifty states for one of our clients, a new insurance company, so it will be able to sell its insurance policy in the US. And, like a complete idiot, I go out last night and get blasted." Victoria ran her hands through her hair as tears gathered in her eyes.

"Whoa, Victoria, calm down. Nothing bad has happened. Granted, you aren't feeling as well as you would like, and you're not as perky as normal, but nothing bad has happened. You're still going into work. You'll still get through what you would have had you not drank last night. And, when you get home, bonus! Your best friend will be waiting here to pamper you and spend a quiet night in with you, catching up."

Victoria sighed as she cleaned the counter of the remaining crumbs from her chocolate muffin. "Kat, you don't understand. This is big, really big. And I feel terrible, but I don't know how I'm going to be able to spend time with you and get through the assignment on time. I feel like I need to spend my Saturday and Sunday working on this, Kat, yet we had planned this weekend to be together."

"Victoria, we've lived together for the last three years. I'm so not worried about whether we have every minute together this weekend. It's more important for you to kick some legal ass on your first assignment than it is for us to walk down Michigan Avenue shopping for the hundredth time. Anyway, I have a ton to do with the new development in the suburb. By the time I drive out there, have my meetings and get back into the city, it will probably be after eight."

Victoria ran around the counter to give Kat a hug. "Thanks. I feel better. I dreaded telling you that I had ruined our plans for the weekend."

Victoria turned and headed to the bathroom for her shower. When she was dressed, she said goodbye to Kat, who had also showered, dressed and was about to get into the town car she had hired for the day to take her to her meetings. "See you tonight," Victoria called.

"Don't worry…" Kat yelled after Victoria, but it was too late. Victoria had already run out the door to Acker, Smith & McGowen to begin her very long and tedious day. "…About anything," Kat said to herself.

CHAPTER
14

VICTORIA MADE A beeline to her office, set up her laptop, shut the door, and did not come out until hours later, when she had finally finished reviewing the last piece of information in the file. She took ten minutes to empty her bladder, get her third cup of coffee, check with her assistant Mary, and look at her emails to see if there was anything urgent. Returning her focus to the file, she began a bullet-point list of the topics that needed to be researched, the pertinent jurisdictions and the authorities that needed to be checked. When she finished the list at three o'clock on Friday afternoon, Victoria realized she would never be able to complete the assignment on time on her own.

Victoria took a few moments to think about how to handle this and began to tap her pen against her legal pad, doodling flowers and leaves while she came to her conclusion. She put down her pen, walked over and opened her office door, and called Mary into her office.

"Mary, I need your help. How many law clerks do we have on staff?"

"We just hired the last round for the year, so I think the final count is ten," Mary answered as she sat down in the chair.

"Perfect. Please head into the law clerk room and get four of them to meet in my office at four. But, before they 'volunteer,' so to speak, let them know the assignment will require that they work nonstop, so I don't want any clerks to volunteer who are not willing to sacrifice their weekend. Let them know the assignment is for Armond, so they know it's for a partner, not just for me."

"Got it," Mary said as she stood and turned toward the door.

"Oh, and Mary, make sure they know that the project is part of a showcase assignment Armond is working on for one of the firm's most prestigious clients."

Mary smiled. "Yes ma'am. Let's see what that does to the little piranhas."

Victoria smirked. Having worked as a law clerk for two summers during law school, she knew firsthand that clerks meticulously dissect the pecking order of the attorneys and they kiss ass for only those who have the power to get things done, which is code for can *get them a job*. Once they identify which attorneys have pull, they're on them like stink on shit.

As soon as she asked Mary to get her four clerks, Victoria realized that that small request was the first time she had experienced the feeling of having some sort of power over others. She liked the feeling. Victoria knew exactly what needed to be completed over the weekend and how the work needed to be divvied up among the clerks so it would be in the form she needed by Monday morning. She went back to her desk feeling a little lighter and less stressed, knowing the clerks would ease her load.

Over the remaining fifty minutes, Victoria reread her notes, highlighted important issues, and summarized the assignment she would give to the clerks. She printed the assignment, and at five minutes to four, she was ready to host her first meeting.

At four o'clock on the dot, four clerks filed into her office. Victoria handed out the memorandum that summarized the assignment and asked Mary to stay and take notes. They divvied up the fifty states. Victoria gave out her cell phone number, and told them for at least the fifth time in the short time they met how important it was for them to get it right the first time if they wanted even a sliver of a chance to ever work on another of her (code for Armond's) assignments again. Victoria made certain they understood that the most important part of this assignment was teamwork. If someone found an issue that was not on the memorandum, they were to send an immediate email notification to the team, so that the others all knew to check that issue as well in their assigned states.

Since each clerk wanted an offer from the firm, which paid the third-largest starting salary in the country, they promised they wouldn't let Victoria down. Listening to the law clerks promise an amazing product, Victoria knew she couldn't entrust any part of her career to these neophytes. They were still in school, and even though they were only one year behind her, the pressure wasn't on them. It was her career that was on the line, and anyway, it would actually behoove one of them to upstage her in front of Armond. There was no way she was going to let that happen.

"Listen, I have no doubt you will all do your best, but I think we need to meet Sunday afternoon. That means everyone will need to have finished their research and memos by noon on Sunday, sending them to me via email. That way I can review your memos, and if there are any inconsistencies, gaps, or questions, we'll clear those up Sunday afternoon, which still gives you Sunday evening into Monday morning to finalize any last-minute matters." Victoria added, "Mary, will you add the Sunday meeting to everyone's calendar?"

Mary nodded. "Got it. Do you want text reminders on your cell phones as well?"

"No, Mary, the calendars should do it. Okay thanks, everyone, and have a good, er, productive weekend."

Every one of the clerks was thinking the same thing, but none of them would say it aloud. Victoria had just upped the schedule by almost twelve hours. Still, they were excited about the chance to prove themselves and possibly get on the short list to an associate position at the firm. There were more lawyers than ever graduating from law school and, for the first time since anyone could remember, more lawyers than ever without jobs.

Before Victoria left for the night, she emailed Armond a few points of clarification she needed on the assignment and she began initial research on one of her ten states. Victoria figured it would take at least four hours of research on the first state and then a declining number of hours on the remaining states once a pattern emerged.

It was seven o'clock by the time Victoria picked up her phone and dialed Kat's number. Kat picked up on the third ring. "Hey, V, what's up? How'd the day go?"

"Hi Kat. Good, but I'm beat. I know you want to go out on the town, but I just don't think I can do it, or if I do it, I won't be any fun. I'm sorry," Victoria sighed.

"Victoria, I'm still in the horrendous traffic driving in from the shining cornfields, soon to be a large home owner association and golf course, and there's no way I'll get to your apartment for another half hour. And that's if I'm lucky. I'm beat as well. I was going to cook for you because I know you were hungover this morning, but sorry, forget it. Let's sit outside at our favorite Italian restaurant on the corner, order tons of pasta, and have a glass of wine," Kat said as she pushed to remote the other call that was trying to buzz through.

"Perfect. See you at home." Victoria put her phone down and marveled that at only eight weeks out of law school, they were already too busy and tired to enjoy one weekend together. As she headed out of her office, Armond swung by and grabbed a seat in her chair, motioning for her to come back in and sit down.

"So, my pet, the buzz is that you've commandeered four of the firm's law clerks to work all weekend in order to take some of the burden of this assignment off of your shoulders. Your other classmates couldn't wait to tell me all about it." Armond looked over his perfectly manicured nails. "They're trying to curry favor with me and at the same time throw you to the wolves, or sharks as the case may be. Rather thrilling, really, to see the backstabbing begin so soon, don't you think?"

"Armond, you knew when you gave me this assignment that there was no way I could realistically complete it in the manner it needs to be done by next Friday, even if I worked almost every minute of every day in the coming week. Anyway, we were told during training, and by you, I might add, that the law clerks are here for us to use as we see fit. So, I see fit and I'm using. Why is this a problem?" Victoria tapped her pen against her desk.

Armond put his perfectly coiffed head down and took a minute to respond to Victoria because he was trying to hide his smile. He liked this one. He really did. And he hoped that she might be the first woman to actually stay at the firm and make it to their small group of partners. He looked up from playing with the emails on his cell phone and smiled. "Victoria, it's exactly what I would have done. I love that you did it, and I love even more the buzz it's caused among your classmates."

"Really, Armond, what's the problem? Why the gossip? Don't they have assignments of their own to do?" Victoria asked, not waiting for an answer to any of her questions.

"It's simple really. Most new associates don't have the balls to give orders to four law clerks delegating their assignment within the first eight weeks at the office. And even if they did, most would have asked first. But the richest part of what you did is that you broke the trend. In other words, each one of your classmates would have assumed that they had to do it all themselves and would have killed themselves trying, but never making it to the finish line by Friday. But you, my dear Victoria, you had the balls to recognize you couldn't do it all, took charge of the situation on your own, and are making it work. And, even better, you created some juicy gossip around the office, something I always appreciate."

Victoria sighed. She hated being the center of negative attention. Seeing the look of concern on her face, Armond took pity on her. "You better get used to this type of nonsense, Victoria. The better you do at the firm, the more gossip and hate your classmates will spill about you, because you're competing with each other for only a few senior associate, then junior partner and then equity partnership spots. The last real cohesive firm function you'll be attending as a group where there might be some semblance of bonding is tomorrow night at our annual firm cocktail party. You and your classmates will be introduced as the new class, you'll be asked to tell a little something about yourself in front of the whole firm and, after that, the shit hits the fan."

"What do you mean, the shit hits the fan?" Victoria asked.

Armond tapped the tablet he always carried with him and opened the screen to a list of Victoria's classmates. Each had been assigned to a junior department chair in one of the firm's groups. Armond came around the desk to stand by Victoria. Laying the tablet on her desk, he leaned over her shoulder and pointed at the names of the junior department chairs.

"See these other guys?" Victoria nodded. "Well these, my dear V, are my counterparts, my peers, and most important of all, they're my competition. How we groom our assigned pet associates—" Victoria visibly stiffened beside Armond, "—sorry, but that's what you and your classmates are referred to here at the wonderful world of Acker, Smith & McGowen, is one of the factors considered by the troika when they make their decision on how many shares the partners will receive at the end of the year. So you, Miss V, like it or not, are critical to my success. And believe me, if you don't succeed, then I don't succeed, and if I don't succeed, the pain that a new inmate feels on his first night in prison will not hold a candle to what a pain in your ass I will be for the rest of your career here in the hallowed halls of AS&M."

As Armond was talking, Victoria began to wonder what she had gotten herself into. Where were the lofty legal ideals, the teamwork, the pulling together for the greater good of the clients and to create better and more just and seminal laws? Where was the mentoring she had been promised? This wasn't mentoring; this was more akin to slavery and active bartering of the associates' hard work for the junior partners' personal goals. But, then Victoria thought, so what? At least Armond was honest about his intent and let her know the score. She had just received a valuable education, and now she knew to avoid contact with the other junior partners, or at the very least, she knew not to trust their advice or guidance.

Armond continued, "So, to wrap up, I have no idea what the other associates are doing with their time and I don't care. What I do care about is this project and the presentation that I will make to Billy and Trever based on your work."

"Armond, don't worry about my work. It will be sterling. But if you succeed, I want to succeed. I want to be the first woman partner at this firm and I'll need your help to get that done. But I need to get going. Kat is waiting for me." Victoria pushed her hand through her hair and stood to change out of her heels and into her flats.

Armond began to walk out of her office and turned before he reached her door. "When do I get to meet this Kat? I think it's important for me to know the kind of company you keep. Tells me a good amount about your character and judgment."

Victoria smiled, thinking about the impression Kat always made on men, gay or not, and she definitely thought Armond was gay. But even more fun would be the fact that Armond had already met Kat and her family. Granted it was years ago, but it would be fun to watch Armond tilted off his even keel, even if it was for just a second, when he realized the connection. Victoria had never bothered to tell Armond her last name. In all fairness, he never asked. "You'll meet her tomorrow night at the firm party. She's my plus one."

"Excellent. Make sure you find me, and Victoria, make sure you look spectacular. This is a black-tie affair. Don't embarrass me."

With that last remark, Armond turned and walked down the now empty firm halls. Victoria heard the ding of the elevator in the distance, signaling that Armond had left the floor.

Victoria turned off her light and headed to the elevator. On the way down, Victoria texted Kat, letting her know she would be home in less than thirty minutes. This time, Victoria remembered the security clearance requirements.

Once outside and walking along the streets of the city she loved, Victoria took a deep breath and for the first time, noticed that what must have been a beautiful day had now turned into an amazing evening. The temperature had been a sweltering ninety-five degrees for the last few nights, but a cold front was moving in and the evening air felt comfortable, with a lovely light wind blowing in off the lake. Victoria walked the half mile to her apartment feeling tired but happy, knowing Kat was with her for the weekend and knowing she had just had her first meaningful conversation with her mentor. Out of all the other junior partners she might have been assigned to, Victoria felt certain that Armond was the pick of the litter, at least for where she intended to go with her career.

As soon as Victoria turned the key in her heavy wooden apartment door, she heard the sound of a champagne bottle popping open and club tunes streaming through the sound system. All the lights were on and the windows were open, sending the cooling night breeze to wander about her living room and into her kitchen. The smell that wafted throughout her apartment was like new orange blossoms in the spring in Arizona, her favorite scent in the world, and an instant reminder of travelling with her mother. Kat knew this of course, and Victoria noted the candle that Kat had obviously purchased and lit for that reason.

"Hey you," Kat said as she walked toward Victoria with a crystal flute of champagne, "tell me what you think of this vintage. I think it's perfect. Dry, not sweet, and very, very cold."

Victoria took the glass Kat handed her and took a long, slow sip. "Ah, amazing. This is the perfect end to a very long week," Victoria said as she kicked off her flats, threw her bag in the corner, and got rid of her jacket.

"When did you get home?" Victoria asked as she followed Kat to the outside balcony sitting area.

"Not more than fifteen minutes ago, but I had the driver stop first at the liquor store so I could buy the champagne, and then at the flower shop at the corner to get the candle. I knew you would love the smell and after three years of living with you, I'm now addicted to it as well. Cheers."

As they clinked glasses and sat in the chairs to enjoy the evening, Mrs. B came out on her porch below them and looked up. "I had a hunch my two favorite young women in all of Chicago would end up on the porch tonight, just like they did during all their years of law school together."

"Mrs. B, it's been a while. How are you? You look marvelous, and just as I remember. Come up and join us like old times. I'd love to catch up," Kat said. She leaned over the porch, her long blonde hair falling over her shoulders.

"I think I'll do just that," Mrs. B said. She disappeared inside her apartment, and a minute later, was knocking on Victoria's door.

"Mrs. B!" Kat said, grabbing her and pulling her into her signature bear hug. The only reason Kat didn't lift short Mrs. B off her two feet, like she always did with Victoria, was because she carried a pan filled with what could only be, judging by the amazing smell, her famous homemade lasagna with garlic bread, warm and wrapped, tucked under her arm.

"Umm, Mrs. B what is that amazing smell?" Victoria asked as she came into the living room.

"Of course I cooked for my two favorite girls. I know neither of you would think of cooking, and I don't want you eating the bastardized Italian food from the corner restaurant." Mrs. B took her food straight into Victoria's kitchen and made herself at home, turning on the oven, taking off the aluminum foil, and stacking plates and silverware. She grabbed a glass and poured some champagne. "Now, let's go out on the porch and catch up on what you're up to, shall we? The food should be ready in about thirty minutes, then I'll leave you two alone to eat."

"Mrs. B, you never stay to eat with us. We would really love it if you would stay tonight. We will bask in your Italian food and your company. We're two single girls without direction," Kat said.

"Cut the crap, Kat. I heard you two big-time lawyers come stumbling in last night at two thirty in the morning. That means that you each had about three hours of sleep last night and worked all day. Neither of you needs my direction, and you never follow it when I do give it. You both know just where you're going. And, I might add, I'm quite sure it's not to mass on Sunday morning, unless you have each turned over new leaves and would like to join me and my family this Sunday."

Victoria and Kat smiled and filled in Mrs. B on their new jobs and the people they worked with. True to her word, in half an hour, Mrs. B made sure the girls were served dinner and left them to catch up.

"What time does the cocktail party start tomorrow, V?" Kat asked after they finished eating.

"Cocktails are at six thirty and dinner at seven thirty," Victoria answered as she poured the rest of the champagne into their glasses. "It's black-tie, and Armond made a point of telling me to make sure not to embarrass him and dress appropriately."

"Okay, V, he sounds like an ass. He obviously has no idea who he's dealing with," Kat said as she sat back to enjoy the evening.

"No, Kat. He's not. He just has a dry sense of humor, and you've got to get to know him to see it. I think he is quite used to the finer things in life."

"You're not kidding. His father, Philippe, began on his own, with nothing, and turned it into one of the top-grossing production companies of all time. I still can't figure out what his son is doing in Chicago and why he's practicing law."

Victoria cocked her head. "I knew you had met Armond long ago, Kat, how do you know so much about Armond's father?"

"My parents have donated to the preservation of film museum in Los Angeles, and Philippe is chairman of the trust that is charged with the preservation. I met Armond once many years ago, when his father's tenth major film came out and his dad invited my family to the opening night in Los Angeles. I was fifteen, and I still remember that night. It was magical."

"Well, I think Armond wants to make it on his own. He really hasn't opened up to me about it yet, so I don't really know. But anyway, I want us to look so amazing when we walk into the ballroom tomorrow night that we make the partners' mouths fall open and Armond speechless."

Kat grabbed her glass and clinked one last time that evening with her best friend. "We will absolutely rock the place. Now, I'm beat; let's clean-up then go to bed."

CHAPTER
15

THE GIRLS WOKE to a beautiful day and decided to follow the routine they had when they were in law school, which meant running along the lake, followed by a quick swim, then coffee and finally, window-shopping along The Magnificent Mile.

The girls took off at a good pace and continued for about two miles until they hit North Beach. "I love this place," Kat said as the girls stopped to catch their breaths and take in the scenery. All along North Beach for as far as the eye could see, the city had set up what seemed to be endless sand volleyball courts, one after the other, readied for a tournament sponsored by one of the major beer companies and a popular Chicago radio station. Music was blasting and hundreds of volleyball players were signing in with their teams to make their entry official.

"Well, that's certainly a new look on skanky," Kat said as she grabbed a bottle of water at the counter of one of the open-air stands and nodded toward a girls' team prancing around in huggy, short-shorts with garter straps hanging down the back of their legs, topped off with little bra tops that barely covered their boobs. "I would certainly never be caught dead in that," she smirked.

Victoria laughed. "Oh, cut the crap. You know you would slither into that outfit in a nanosecond and prance around on this beach if your family wouldn't kill you for doing it."

Kat sighed, "You're right. And the bodies on those girls are insane. I almost wish we were back in law school so I could act exactly like them. Remember when we had the Halloween party and I dressed in nothing but balloons?"

"I do. I also remember when it first dawned on you that you had no way to pee except to pop some of the balloons. You ended up peeing on the side of the road on our way home from the party. I had to give you a garbage bag so you could get home without being arrested for exposure."

"Victoria, you have an awfully good memory when it comes to things I did. How about tequila Saturday? Remember when your boyfriend drove in to see you after our last final and you said you would wait for him at the hotel lobby, but wound up forgetting about that? He found you in the bar of the hotel next door, lying on the bar with your shirt off, getting a shot sucked out of your naval by some random guy."

Victoria laughed with Kat. "God, that was fun. Let's hope neither of us turns into such drudges that we don't spontaneously entertain each other anymore."

"We won't. Come on, let's run back, grab some coffee, and I need to walk down The Magnificent Mile and breathe in the fashion. We'll shop this afternoon. Then I made us appointments for facials and massages at the spa before the big event this evening."

"Yeah. Kat, I really need to work. But I do have those four lovely law clerks working for me as we speak. Oh screw it. You leave in the morning and I'll get up early and work throughout the day. Let's do it." Victoria smiled. "Feels good having someone else do the grunt work for a change. I think I could get used to this, my friend."

As the sun set on a full day of shopping and massages, the girls came out of their rooms ready for the party.

"How do I look?" Victoria sauntered down her hallway into the living area. She had on a cocktail dress designed by a friend of theirs. It shimmered an amazing shade of emerald green and fit tightly through the bodice until it fishtailed out around her knees and dropped to a slight angle in the back. She wore drop emerald earrings Kat had lent her that hinted at touching her shoulders. Her hair was swept back off her face and curled loosely, so it cascaded down her back. The sides were held in place by two antique hairpins adorned with emeralds and diamonds. They also belonged to Kat.

"V, you look like you just walked out of a fairy tale. Really. That color against your tan skin is perfect. And topping it off with our matching shoes, well, let me just say that some of these old geezer lawyers will have to pop their eyes back in their heads."

"Thanks Kat. And may I say that you are simply jaw-dropping." Kat twirled in front of Victoria. She had on a white knit dress with crystals sewn into the fabric throughout the dress. She had diamond studs of at least two carats in each ear and a diamond necklace that wrapped around her neck and came together at her cleavage, then dropped to just above her waist.

"Lord, we're spectacular. Let's go give 'em the show they want." Kat grabbed her clutch off the counter.

The girls walked into the designated high-rise and took the elevator up. As they stepped off of the elevator, the number of people and the sheer noise in the ballroom crushed them both. People were milling about in the hallway and the lounge. Kat and Victoria could feel the stares. Some of the women were obviously wives of some of the more senior attorneys at the firm, and eyed Kat and Victoria carefully.

"Don't look now, but I think we may have outdone ourselves," Kat whispered to Victoria.

"Kat, I think I made an error in judgment having us dress like this. I should have been smarter politically and recognized that the wives wouldn't want to be shown up by a couple of recent law school grads," Victoria grumbled under her breath.

"Oh screw them, V. They don't decide who goes where in the firm, and you and I both know that if a man has a choice between hiring and working with an average-looking woman and a stellar-looking woman, he'll choose the stellar-looking woman time and time again."

"You're right." Victoria squared her shoulders and held her head up high. Screw it, she thought. I worked my ass off to get here. I'm not cowering over a few wives. Besides, who's to say that I won't become friends with one of them? "There's the bar. Let's get a cocktail."

"Yes, let's. Oh, and make sure while you're standing by the bar that you turn your heels just a bit so the pink shows, so they know what you're wearing."

Victoria and Kat laughed and took in the view as they waited in line for their turn at the bar. "Stunning, isn't it, ladies?" Victoria knew that voice and turned to see Armond smiling broadly and dressed in the latest designer fashion, and what were obviously fine leather Italian shoes.

"Armond, how are you? I'm so glad you found us. Armond, I want to re-introduce you to my best friend in the world, Kat Fontaine. Kat, you remember Armond."

Victoria watched as two of the most important people in her life sized each other up. It was amazing, really, to see them take the time to look each other over with a long, pregnant pause hanging between them. Finally, Armond held out his hand and his face lit up in a welcoming smile. "Well, Kat. It's a pleasure to meet you, and I'm not disappointed. You, my dear, are exceptional. But why would you remember me?"

Kat returned his smile with a megawatt one of her own that Victoria knew she reserved for only those people she really cared about, and Victoria breathed a sigh of relief. "Armond, darling, who can turn away from such a charming compliment, and one given by a man head to toe in runway to boot? And to answer your question, I met you and your family at the opening gala for one of your father's films about ten years ago."

"Really? Why would your family have been invited to a premier?" Armond asked, stiffening his stance, suspicious about the veracity of Kat's statement.

"My, aren't we the president of 'my shit doesn't stink' club?" Kat answered, bearing her teeth just a hint, which signaled to Victoria that this introduction was quickly taking a turn in the wrong direction.

"Armond, Kat's family have been members of the philanthropic committee for the preservation of film for years. They met your father through their mutual work for the committee," Victoria jumped in before they began to tear each other's perfectly coifed hair out.

"Of course. Fontaine. I should have recognized the name." Armond reached out and took Kat's hand in both of his. "Please forgive my inexcusable conduct. People love to namedrop to get me to introduce them to my father so they can get a shot at some role they are 'meant to play.' I'm afraid I'm a bit guarded when people act familiar. Let's start over, shall we?"

"We shall. As long as you fill us in on who's who here and what V needs to know to not only survive, but stand out among the crowd of egos."

"As far as standing out, you two knocked the ball out of the park the minute the elevator doors opened. The tension and excitement level in the room shot up about twenty decibels when you made your entrance and sauntered over to the bar. As far as what V needs to know, hmmm, well as of tonight, the wives hate you. But you mustn't give a rat's ass about them. They're haters and their husbands don't listen to them anyway. More importantly, none of the troika is married and they are particularly susceptible to a pretty face. Especially Billy. Word is he likes to break in new associates in private. Enough information for complete forgiveness?"

Kat pushed her long blonde hair over her shoulder just to make sure no one missed the diamond and gold necklace dancing mischievously between her breasts. "I think that will do quite nicely. Yes."

Armond roared with laughter. "Oh, you're rich, Miss Kat, and not to worry, no one can miss your cascade of diamonds." After a pause Armond looked down and began, "I have a confession to make and I'm only letting this out so we have a clean slate. I investigated you and our little pal Victoria here months ago when I found out that she accepted the firm's offer. I then confirmed my suspicions and mentioned your last name to my father, and voila, I knew who you were months ago."

Victoria listened in amazement and gave Armond's shoulder a gentle shove. "You're a sneaky little man, aren't you? Why didn't you tell me that you knew your family knew Kat, rather than acting like you had no idea who she was and that you wanted to meet her?"

"Because, Victoria, I wanted to see for myself. You gather the information you need, but you don't tip your hand unless it's necessary. It's not like you and I have a priest-parishioner relationship and I need to confess everything I know and think to you. Not yet, anyway. Now, let me handle the liquor for us this evening, shall I? Kat, Victoria, what would you like to drink?"

Kat laid a hand on Armond's lapel to straighten his collar. "We prefer champagne, but only very good stuff. I don't suppose—"

Armond cut Kat off. "Wait right here. I'll get just what you need."

When he was out of earshot, Kat turned to Victoria. "Oh, he's charming. I like him. Funny, smart and sassy. You got lucky getting assigned as his protégée. And, since he knows my family knows his family, it should help make your bonds tighter. Because if he fucks with you, my daddy will fuck with our donations to their little films."

"Yes, well, that was quite a love-hate fest you two had." Victoria turned to look for Armond and instead saw all four of the law clerks working on her project, with their plus ones, making a beeline toward her and Kat.

"Victoria, we hope we're not interrupting," Justin said, "but we want to introduce you to our dates and we're hoping to meet your, um, friend."

Victoria and Kat glanced at each other and knew what these clerks were wondering, so without even a word between them, Victoria put her arm around Kat's waist and smiled lovingly into Kat's eyes. "Guys, I would like you to meet one of my closest friends from law school, Kat Fontaine. She now lives in Houston and is general counsel and vice president of Fontaine Development. She came back just to be with me for this event."

Victoria squeezed Kat around her waist a little harder, and Kat kissed Victoria on her forehead just as Armond was returning with their champagne. Armond raised his eyebrows from behind the clerks at the girls and shook his head, entering the group just as Kat was shaking everyone's hand.

When the clerks noticed Armond enter their group and saw that he had fetched drinks for Victoria and her "date," it was clear from the looks on their faces that Victoria's stock shot way up. All of the clerks but Jason moved on once Armond joined the group, the others feeling that they were not yet worthy to stay and engage in conversation with one of the partners.

"Armond," Jason said, holding out his hand, "I'm Jason, and this is Katie, my date. It's a real honor to meet you. I've heard so much about you at the firm, and your father is legendary."

Victoria felt Armond's demeanor shift and change. He drew himself up and used what she was fast learning was his sarcastic voice, "Jason, a pleasure. Now if you and Katie will excuse us, we have some important firm business to discuss."

Jason knew he was being dismissed and took his cue. "Of course. Victoria, I'm so looking forward to our meeting to-morrow on the project, and if there is anything else you think of that you need, please just let me know, and I'll handle it for you."

Victoria smiled and remembered when she was a clerk. "Thanks, Jason, I really do appreciate it. It's a very important project. Not only to me, but really, we're all under Armond's wing on this one."

Armond quirked his eyebrow up again. "Yes, right. Well, I look forward to a sterling job."

Kat and Victoria burst out laughing once the clerks were safely out of eye and earshot. "Oh, that was rich," Kat said. "You're now not only working for one of the hotshot and up-and-coming partners, but you have a girlfriend as well. You'll be the talk of the firm."

Armond wasn't amused. "Listen, you two, as much as I en-joy your balls-in-your-face attitude, not everyone here will, especially the troika. They're a bit conservative in their views, so I'm going to do this one favor for you this one time and then, Victoria, you're on your own. I'm going to kill the rumor that you're lesbians. Not because I give a damn, but because I don't want a dead-horse protégée. Capisce?"

The girls nodded. "Sorry, Armond," Kat said. "Since I don't need to put up with this bullshit, I forget that others do. I promise I'll do nothing other than support you and your agendas, as long as, of course, you support my V."

"Good. Now the associate introductions will be done before dinner. Make yours short, sweet and leave some mystery. Do not rattle on. Most of your peers will. Name, rank and serial number will do, and of utmost importance, my name must be said at least three times during your little speech. Got it?"

Victoria nodded. "Got it, Armond."

Armond took a sip of champagne. "If my father taught me anything, it was the importance of name recognition as a part of your personal brand."

Victoria and Kat spent the next thirty minutes speaking to the other associates in her class and discussing their speeches. They were nervous, as was Victoria. Then, the troika, as Armond called them, Adam, Billy and Trever, stepped up onto the small podium placed against the backdrop of the city. There was a clinking of glasses that grew louder, calling attention to the three men standing on the stage.

"Good evening and welcome to Acker, Smith & McGowen's Annual Firm Party. I'm Trever, and to my right are Billy and Adam. Eleven years ago, the three of us were law students at the University of Chicago complaining about professors, and perhaps most of all, the dead-end clerk jobs and boring legal positions we were being herded toward. Each of us vowed to never work in a boring, dull and stuffy law firm. So, we did what any sane, rational broke law students would do; we started our own international firm with absolutely zero clients and no prestige to our names."

There was a round of laughter as the tension eased in the crowd. Adam began, "Actually, while Trever's story is amusing, it's very true. Today, though, we're proud to say we have offices in five different countries and employ about four hundred lawyers and a staff of six hundred, and we intend to double our size within the next four years." There were applause and cheers and actual excitement in the air. The hair on Victoria's arms raised up and stood at attention, as she fully intended to be running one of those new offices.

Billy picked up the end of their show. "So, welcome to those of you who are new and to all who have been with us through the tough times as we continue our journey to provide unified and exceptional legal services to our clients worldwide. We're an exceptional group. To those who are new to the firm, you have some big shoes to fill. Lawyers are a dime a dozen. You were not chosen because you can practice law; you were chosen because we saw something exceptional in each and every one of you. Don't forget that. We expect that something special to blossom."

Trever took over again. "Now, without further ado, we begin our annual introduction of our newest class of associates. Ladies and gentleman, Billy, Adam and I proudly present the newest additions to our firm!"

As luck would have it, Victoria was the last to give her spiel. Moving to the podium and taking the microphone, she followed Armond's advice. "Good evening. My name is Victoria Rodessa. I'm the homegrown Chicagoan and I graduated law from the University of Chicago." There were a few catcalls or cheers, depending on the other alma maters in the room. Victoria smiled and took a sip of her drink waiting for the crowd to calm down. "Let's see, I love to run and compete in triathlons. However, since I am working for Armond Renoir, who is the Vice Chair of the International Transaction Department, I doubt I'll have much time to do either. Armond gave me strict instructions that I am to eat, breathe and sleep the assignment he gave me last Thursday." Raising her glass, Victoria continued, "So, I must thank the founding partners for this lovely party because according to Armond, it is the only legitimate reason I have to see anything other than that file and my desk for the next seven days. So, cheers and thanks!" Before she left the podium, someone shouted, "Who's your friend?" Victoria introduced Kat, her plus one and best friend from law school. The men in the room went nuts, and there was a short burst of stomping and whistling. It was obvious, despite the formal surroundings and attire, that the alcohol had taken command.

As Victoria stepped down from the podium, the crowd laughed and patted Armond on the back and the worst, as far as Victoria was concerned, was over. Within a few minutes, uniformed waiters walked through the throng of close to eight hundred people, ringing Ross Dinner Chimes signaling it was time to sit down for dinner. Victoria could not have been more grateful to shift the attention to something other than her and Kat.

As they sat at their assigned table, Kat leaned over to Victoria and said under her breath as she smiled and waved, "Some things never change, V. They might say they want a woman in the boardroom, but they'd still rather have her in their bedroom. Make sure you remember that here. I have a feeling you're going to need to."

Victoria was about to respond with completely inappropriate language when she felt a tap on her shoulder and turned to see the troika standing just behind their table.

Adam held out his hand first. "Victoria, we, the three of us, would like to take this opportunity to personally welcome you to the firm. Each of us travels a great deal, and as you can imagine, our schedules leave little time for us to mingle among the firm. But we wanted to be certain to give you a personal welcome."

"Victoria," Billy began as he took her hand in both of his, "I understand from Armond that the project you referred to in your introduction speech is the Highline project. That's my baby and my client. I just returned from a week in Bermuda with the board of the company. This project and the business that will roll off it have the potential to increase our revenues by twenty percent in this year alone. A hefty amount. Don't screw it up, young lady."

"Oh for God's sake, Billy, does she look like a screwup to you? Victoria, you'll have to forgive Billy. He's always on the clock and thinking about our clients and his work. But, that's also what makes him one of the best transactional lawyers in the world. Now, if you want to get a taste of some high-powered and interesting work, we'll get you on some of my international projects. We know how to have a good time traveling all over the world as we do." Trever laughed as he nudged Billy in his gut. "Plus, I heard you speak a number of languages. Seems you should have been placed under my wing instead of Billy's. How'd you feel about a change as soon as you finish up with this lil' ole insurance company project they got you on?" Trever asked, drawing out his Texas drawl as he was wont to do whenever he was making a move to center stage of a situation.

Victoria knew she was being watched for her reaction and her ability to handle a potentially politically dangerous situation. She took a deep breath and remembered what her mother had always told her. "You are a rare combination of brains, determination and survivor. So let your intuition guide you and never second-guess its path."

Drawing comfort from that advice, Victoria knew just how to respond. "You know, gentlemen, Kat and I were just discussing after our run this morning how we looked forward to actually doing real, complex work. It is, after all, what we've been training to do for the last three years at the University of Chicago. It's really what our alma mater trains us for that makes us different from other attorneys coming out of law school, don't you agree?"

Kat just sat back and watched the three men succumb to Victoria's warm charm, and total change of subject. Victoria's hit on their shared alma mater presented them with a common-denominator question that brought Victoria into their circle of power and to which they had to agree. Nicely done, Kat thought. Victoria one. Troika, zero.

CHAPTER
16

VICTORIA WOKE AT four Sunday morning and felt that familiar buzz of tense excitement coursing through her. So she got up, made coffee, worked for about an hour and a half, and then went for a run. Victoria knew from experience that her "hyperness" could overpower and overwhelm people, so her runs were not only for exercise, but for the calming effect they had on her mind. It was definitely not Victoria's goal at the three o'clock meeting with the clerks to make them feel overwhelmed. She needed them on her side, and all pulling together for a good result.

At ten, Victoria and Kat hugged and kissed goodbye, and Kat took off for the airport in a cab. By then, Victoria had finished reading all the case law and statutes pertaining to the issues in her assigned states. Ready to begin composing her memorandum of law for the meeting, Victoria opened her laptop and it sprang to life with ten new emails, most were questions from her clerks. The two most recent emails were from Armond. Victoria opened his email and was surprised to see that her four clerks were the addressees and she was only copied. The subject matter had only one word, "Critical."

I understand that Victoria chose you to work the Highline matter. I want to add my voice to Victoria's in instilling in you the importance to the Firm of this assignment and of Highline as a client. In other words, don't f*** it up. I will be at your meeting this afternoon should you have any questions.

ARMOND, VICE CHAIR, TRANSACTION GROUP.

Victoria laughed out loud. Every day she liked Armond more and more. Making sure the clerks knew that Armond stood behind her would only help ensure that they worked their asses off to provide an exceptional product.

Victoria then clicked on Armond's next email which was directed only to her.

Thought that might focus the little buggers' attention. There's no way I'm coming into the office on a Sunday, but what they don't know only helps us. See you tomorrow. Oh, btw, you got the attention of the Troika last night. Rather rare for a first year.

Victoria smiled and then frowned, as she reread Armond's email. She had no idea whether it was a good thing or not that she had the attention of the founding members of the firm, but she didn't have time to worry about it. She would see Armond tomorrow and ask him then.

By two thirty, Victoria was seated at her desk in her office with five neatly stacked piles in front of her.

"Can we come in?" one of the clerks asked as they hovered outside of her office.

"Of course, come in, and bring in some of the assistants' chairs so you can all sit down." Victoria watched as they shuffled into her office, dragging chairs and looking anxious.

"Thanks for coming in on a Sunday and working the weekend. I appreciate your time and effort. Now…"

Before Victoria could finish, Jason asked, "Shouldn't we wait for Armond to get here? He might have some direction and thoughts we should hear."

Victoria's head snapped up. She stared straight into Jason's eyes, and he stared straight back. He didn't even drop his head or glance away. Victoria smiled, but it didn't reach her eyes. "Jason, I'm in charge of this project. Not Armond. Any direction or thought you need comes from me. Now, if you would like to step outside and wait for Armond, please do so. Otherwise, consider the meeting formally in session."

Jason didn't even flinch, and that bothered Victoria. He should have been contrite and at least a tad shamed. Quite the contrary; Victoria could have sworn she saw a flicker of anger, quickly replaced by amusement, pass across his face.

"By all means, let's begin," he said.

Victoria reviewed each one of their memos while the others listened, as they had many of the same shortcomings. The meeting adjourned by four, and Victoria felt a sudden wave of absolute exhaustion and hunger. She decided to leave everything, including her laptop, at the office, order in food and watch the *Real Housewives* bonanza that was on TV.

As she walked home, she got a text from Kat, "Landed, home and safe. Great weekend. Love and see you soon." Victoria smiled and felt happy at all that had happened and been accomplished.

The week flew by in a blur. Armond had given her another two projects to work on and then a file that would be "hers" to handle. The Highline project was now fully under her wing as the clerks had finished their assignments. Victoria massaged the executive legal summary, the comprehensive state-by-state statement of law and regulations, and then the notebook of tabbed and organized case law and regulations for each state. The clerks were completing the final shepardizing of cases, checking for any legal changes that might have happened in the last week.

Midday before the project due date, Armond rapped on Victoria's closed office door as he simultaneously popped his head in. Without waiting for her acknowledgment, Armond began, "Victoria, I would invite you to lunch, but I know it would put you in an uncomfortable position because you would understandably want to say yes to spend time with me, but you would be torn because you know you should say, 'No Armond, I am just too busy.' So I thought I would spare you the uneasiness of turning me down and simply not invite you. Don't ever forget all that I do for you."

Victoria could not believe the shit that was coming out of his mouth. She had a fleeting image of a nattily dressed little dung beetle happily stuffing its face with so much poop that some of it was squirting out. She began to laugh so hard that tears gathered in her eyes. Had she not been completely exhausted from working twenty-hour days for the past week, she probably would have been able to control herself. But she was quite unable to stop laughing.

Alarmed, Armond stepped all the way into Victoria's office and shut the door. "What in the hell is wrong with you? You better not be cracking up on me already."

"No, I'm fine. Really. I'm just a bit tired," Victoria answered, wiping her eyes with a tissue. "I barely slept for the past few nights and I think it just caught up to me."

"Well, good. I don't intend to bet on a one-trick pony and I have placed my bet on you, my girl, for the long run and the big leagues," Armond said, visibly relieved.

"Anyway, the real reason I stopped by was to let you in on a change of plans. The Highline presentation was moved from next week to ten tomorrow morning. Obviously, there'll be no time to make changes to your work between the time you meet with me in the morning, and the meeting. You'll need to have your work and all the material finalized tonight so that copies can be made in time for the meeting. I've done you a favor and let Mary know and she's agreed to work all night, if you need, to see this through. While of course, I'll present the results of our Highline project to Billy, Trever and the rest of the team, you, my pet, will be there with me ready to answer any questions that for whatever reason I can't field. This means you'll need to be more than prepared with any and all support ready and at your fingertips."

Victoria was visibly shaken by his announcement. She had understood she was the grunt doing the work, but she never thought she would be part of the presentation.

"You don't look so well, Victoria. That's good. You need to take this seriously. This is your chance to impress the big boys."

"I'm fine. I just didn't expect to be invited to the presentation."

"Don't mistake this for an invite. It was my decision to include you and it's for purely selfish reasons. You're the expert on this part of the project, not me. If I am asked a question that I can't answer, I will graciously lob the ball to you. And you better not miss. Capisce?" Straightening his tie, Armond turned to leave. "I'm late for lunch. I'll see you in the morning in my office at eight." With a slight shake of his head before he closed her door, he said, "One more thing, Billy has a quick mind and when he asks a question, he'll want a direct answer. If you dance for even a minute, he'll smell blood and move in for the kill, just for the sport of it." Closing the door, Armond thought of one more thing and popped the door open again. "Sleep well, Victoria," Armond smiled slyly as he closed her door, knowing she would do anything but.

Waking early Friday morning after about two hours of sleep, Victoria went for a run, showered and then dressed in one of her favorite outfits. She had had her assistant book the conference room on her floor for their presentation and they had agreed to meet there at seven. Victoria had a set of all the material copied last night for each team member, and when she arrived at the office, Mary was going through them one last time.

"Mary, thanks for all your help this week. There is no way this would have happened without you," Victoria said as she put her bag down and opened her laptop to look over the short slideshow she had prepared at Armond's insistence. Victoria hated these types of presentations, and thought they were boring, outdated and a crutch, but Armond insisted that Billy was old-school and required them as part of every presentation.

"No problem. It's been rather fun in a weird sort of work way. Okay, you're all set. I've checked each of the copies twice. They are all in order. If there is anything you need before or during your meeting, just text me and I'll get it handled."

"I think we need an agenda. If you have something to write on, I'll tell you the five agenda points. If you can get it ready, let me take a look at it and then print enough copies for everyone at the meeting, and we'll be ready to go."

"Go ahead. I'm ready," Mary said as she sat down.

At ten minutes to ten, Billy, Trever, Armond, and six of the other team members entered the conference room. Billy's personal assistant came as well to take notes of the meeting. Mary was also there, in case Victoria needed anything. They had agreed that made more sense then Victoria trying to text something potentially long and complex in the middle of the meeting.

Victoria's heart was beating so fast and hard that she wondered whether anyone could hear it. Armond gave Victoria a quick wink and brought the meeting to order. "Each of you has a notebook in front of you which contains two parts. The first is the executive summary, and the second is the detailed memorandum, complete with summaries of each state's information. Victoria has behind her on the credenza the full array of ten notebooks that contain the relevant case law and statutes for each state. These will be housed in the firm project room and provided to each of you electronically, should you wish to review legal authority."

Billy coughed and cleared his throat. "What's the bottom line, Armond?"

Armond smiled. "It's a go. Assuming Highline has the necessary capital and is ready to execute, we will be able to legally meet its goal of becoming a registered commercial lines insurer in all fifty states."

Cheers and clapping broke out spontaneously around the room. "Congratulations, Billy. This is an amazing piece of business," one of the senior associates yelled out.

Billy smiled and then held up his hand to quiet the group. He swung his chair around and looked directly at Victoria. "Ms. Rodessa, how long will it take you to get this up and running?"

"Sir?" Victoria was caught off guard.

"I think what he's asking..." Armond jumped in to try to help her, but Billy looked at Armond and shook his head.

"How long, Ms. Rodessa? It's not a difficult question, is it?"

Victoria knew he was testing her and felt her blood begin to sing in the familiar way it did when someone was trying to challenge her. Okay, she thought, it's on.

"Well, Mr. Acker, your question is a bit vague. However, if you're referring to the amount of time it will take for the firm to get the documents in order and file them with each state, assuming I'm provided a team of five full-time lawyers and the client also assigns a dedicated team, four months. On the other hand, if you're asking the amount of time it will take before the states issue their respective certificates of authority so Highline can be fully operational selling its insurance, a total of eight to ten months. Eight months for at least two-thirds of the states, leaving a buffer of another two months for those that take a bit longer and for the possible delay or request for additional information."

Victoria sat back down, feeling fantastic. She had nailed it, and she knew it. She knew this stuff backwards and forwards. At this moment, she didn't give a rat's ass if Billy Acker thought she was cocky. The project was flawless and had taken almost every waking hour of the last week of her life, with no breaks and no coming up for air. She wanted nothing more than to head this project, under Armond, of course.

No one moved or said a word as Victoria sat down. It was deathly silent as the group waited for Billy's reaction. Staring at Victoria, Billy slowly laid down his pen on his yellow legal pad and swiveled his chair. He got up and walked around to the conference room's windows. Putting his hands behind his back, he turned and looked only at Victoria.

By God, he thought, she has some balls. She had not once taken her eyes off of his. Her breath was even, and her hands were neatly folded on the table. He actually felt himself getting excited as his mind wandered for just a minute to the challenge he imagined she would present sexually.

"Armond. I want you to run with this project. Give Ms. Rodessa the people she needs at the firm to get this done, and make certain the client gives you the team Ms. Rodessa believes is necessary. Victoria, you will move this ball down the field on the schedule you have outlined. Do you understand? No later."

"Yes sir, Mr. Acker," Victoria said, trying to tamp down her excitement.

"And I want the billing sent out on this matter at the end of every month. I want every single person who even utters the name 'Highline' to be listed on the bills and for higher than their normal hourly fee. This is a special project and the firm must be compensated accordingly for moving a substantial amount of our talent to the project so it can be completed on the fast-track schedule set out by Ms. Rodessa. The terms are payment within twenty-one days with interest accruing after the thirtieth day. I want to see an immediate and significant increase in our revenue."

"Got it," Armond said as he took a few notes.

"Nice work, Ms. Rodessa. Trever and I will meet with the client next week in Bermuda and advise them of the outcome and timetable. I'll need a meeting agenda, timeline, and executive summary for the board. Get it ready. Have it on my desk by Monday at four. No later," Billy said as he began to walk toward the conference room door. "And Victoria, call me Billy. But fuck this up, and you'll wish I never knew your name."

And with that, he walked out the door, followed quickly by his assistant, Trever and the other team members. The only three left in the room were Armond, Victoria and Mary.

Mary jumped out of her chair, walked over and gave Victoria a hug. "Congratulations. You did good. I'll leave you two to gloat."

Armond stood up, looked at Victoria, and without expression, said, "Let's take a walk. Meet me in the lobby in five."

Victoria went to her office, grabbed her bag, and on her way to the elevator, saw a number of the clerks who had worked on the project. She gave them the thumbs-up sign. They had obviously been waiting for the results, and as the elevator door closed, she saw them giving each other high-fives. Smiling, Victoria thought, things are good.

Armond had already cleared security and was waiting by the outside doors. Grabbing Victoria's arm, he propelled her through the doors and into the summer sunshine. He did not say a word.

"Armond, what's wrong? Listen, I can't keep up this pace in these heels, so either stop and tell me what the issue is or slow way down so I can keep up."

"Are you daft? I get that you're cocky and you're fearless and all that BS. But that could have gone either way. Billy might have been insulted by the fact that you essentially told the room that he had asked a rather poor question." Armond ran his hand through his hair as he now walked back and forth in front of her. They were about three blocks from the office, and apparently he felt comfortable enough to have a mini-meltdown.

"Listen. Armond. I didn't intend to be malicious or condescending or anything else negative. I simply heard a question and tried to answer it. There was more than one meaning to his question. What was I supposed to do? Act like a blithering idiot?"

"Yes. If there is a choice between you, the new rookie associate that I have chosen as my protégé, looking like a blithering idiot, or one of the Troika looking like a blithering idiot, guess which one I vote for?"

"Okay, I apologize," Victoria said. "I really didn't realize I sounded like that."

"That's what concerns me. You don't realize and even worse, I have a feeling you don't care." Armond looked seriously concerned and Victoria felt bad. After all, he had taken her under his wing, and she owed it to him to make him look good at all times.

"Armond, I'm truly sorry. I will try to be more thoughtful with my words. I promise." Victoria touched his arm.

Armond responded with a big smile and his whole mood changed. "Girl, you knocked the ball out of the park! I'm so proud of you. The fact that you had a timeline was amazing. I didn't ask for that."

"I know, but Mary told me Billy has a reputation for moving projects forward fast and suggested I might need one. I simply took her advice."

Armond grabbed Victoria's upper arm and began to walk swiftly down the sidewalk, heading directly for the corner coffee shop. Holding the door while essentially pushing her through, he said, giddy with excitement, "We're going to have to work our asses off over the next year, you know that, don't you? You did put our combined asses in a bit of a sling with that timetable, because if it isn't met, there will be hell to pay, and you can bet your life it won't be with Billy's hide."

"I know, but we can do it. I have some thoughts for the type of people we need on the team from the client's end. You'll have to come up with the best team from the firm. I simply don't know enough people yet."

Sipping his latte, Armond leaned back in his chair and a huge grin spread across his face again. Whipping out his phone, he dictated a few thoughts about possible team members and then called his assistant to arrange the first team meeting.

Geez, he was stoked about this project, Victoria thought. While Victoria was glad he was happy, she was getting worried about the demons she may have let out of Pandora's Box.

If Armond was this excited, this must be a bigger deal than she had thought.

As soon as Armond hung up his phone, he got up, threw his coffee out, and with an impish look, announced, "We're getting a cocktail after work tonight. A celebration and some planning are in order. We're going to rule this client and create a new business for the firm." And with that, he almost lifted Victoria out of her chair, and much the way he had brought her down the road, he dragged her back to the office.

When Victoria got back, she found a slew of congratulatory emails from many of the firm's attorneys around the world. Billy had, she saw, issued an announcement about the projected increase in firm revenue from the project and had noted Victoria's involvement as one of the significant parts to its success. Mary walked in while Victoria was staring at her computer in amazement. She scrolled down through the names of well-known and even some renowned lawyers, all of whom were telling her how proud they were to have her at the firm.

"A bit overwhelming, isn't it?" Mary said as she sat in the chair opposite Victoria's desk. "Trever and Adam both stopped in to see you. They asked that I extend their congratulations to you and each asked that you give them a call before the end of the day." Mary smiled as Victoria sat back in her chair with her mouth open. "Just think, this morning, a lowly associate. Just another cog in the machine. And by noon, a star is born."

"Mary, I'm stunned; not only because of all the attention, but I still don't understand why. I mean, all I did was do the work on time as asked," Victoria said, tapping her favorite pen against the yellow legal pad.

"Actually, no. That's not all you did. What you did is take charge, give deadlines, and step up and give an opinion about whether a multimillion-dollar job could get done and by when."

Victoria cocked her head. "I still don't get it. And?"

"And," Mary continued, "most people, associates and the majority of partners alike, do not step up and give resolute, unwavering opinions like you did. They're afraid to take a firm stance because of the obvious. What if it doesn't work? Then it's their butt on the line. And on this line sits not only Billy, but also the billionaire investors who are banking on Highline to turn a profit. Which depends upon, circularly, the correctness of your opinion, getting the work product done and on time."

"I get that, and I understand it's not always a popular thing to do, but…" Victoria began to doodle on her pad as this topic was making her nervous. "I was asked a direct question. A direct answer was in order. Wasn't it?"

Mary smiled again and set her coffee down on the desk. "Listen, I don't want to make you nervous, but most attorneys I have seen in similar situations would not have answered directly. Instead, they would have said something to buy time like, 'We'll take a look at it and get back to you.' Or they would have given a range of say, from six months to one year, giving themselves plenty of room and even then adding a bunch of caveats like depending on whether it snows or the lights stay on. What I'm trying to say is they would have chickened out and not answered the question. You, on the other hand, did not. Chicken out, I mean. And that, my dear Victoria, is a big deal."

Victoria began to feel like she had made a monumental error. If everyone else would have punted, why did she have to be the idiot who stepped up and stood out? What just an hour ago had felt like a victory was beginning to feel like one of the stupidest moves of her short career. If she screwed this up, she would not only be thought of as a failure, but it was unlikely that she would ever be on the road to partnership and power. But it was too late for self-pity and regrets, and anyway, Victoria had never been very good at those emotions. She had learned long ago, when her father walked out of her life, that nothing ever changed because of them.

"All right. Enough of this." Getting up out of her chair Victoria began to pace as she spoke. "Mary, I have a meeting with Armond tonight, and I want to have a fairly comprehensive outline of my plan of action done. That will mean we will need to focus on finishing it for the balance of the afternoon. How much work do you have from the other attorneys you're assigned to?"

"None. I'm all yours. That's another thing that happened. Billy issued an edict that there is to be a switch in assignments effective immediately. You're my priority. The other two lawyers have been reassigned."

For Victoria, that shift in personnel actually conveyed more to her than all the congratulations and accolades she had received. It was unheard of for a first-year associate—hell, for any associate and most of the partners—to be singly assigned to an assistant. Wow, was all Victoria could think. Wow.

Victoria spent the rest of her afternoon finalizing her plan to present to Armond that evening. She met with the clerks who had worked with her on the project and got a firm estimate from each of them on the amount of time they thought it would take for the stages for each state. Once the timeline was firm and the steps mapped out, she instructed each of the clerks to immediately pull any and all forms they would need and prepare them in reference notebooks.

By the end of that afternoon, Victoria had double- and triple-checked her timeline and wished, for the thousandth time that day, that she had done that before she opened her mouth that morning. Her initial assessment as to when the project could be finished bore out even after independent weigh-in by the clerks. While she was lucky this time, she learned a valuable lesson. She was not in Kansas anymore.

CHAPTER
17

IT HAD BEEN almost six months since Kat had seen Victoria, and she could not wait to get off the plane. Kat sat warm and cozy in her first-class window seat, wrapped in the blue cashmere throw she always took on flights so she wouldn't freeze her ass off when the crew turned the temperature down to frostbite levels. Kat looked out the window and pulled her chair back to its landing-ready position and thought she felt the plane sink lower toward the runway, fighting its way through what looked like a white-out of a blizzard. The only way anyone on the plane knew they were coming in for a landing was the pilot's say-so, and the last time anyone heard from him had been a good fifteen minutes ago.

Kat thought back to Victoria's offer that she and her mom would come to Texas for the holidays this year. But Kat knew they hated to leave Chicago during the holidays, and Kat's family loved Chicago anyway.

When they had been in law school, Kat would join in Victoria and Sophia's Christmas tradition of walking along State Street and looking at the sparkling, holiday-dressed store windows. Each year the windows revealed a different theme with moving characters telling some storybook fantasy. Mothers would read out loud from the storybook pages placed in the center of each window and inevitably, one mom would always end up reading for all the children that happened to be gathered. They were all strangers, the kids and their parents, yet in that one moment, the magic of Christmas seemed to fill the air.

The three of them would then shop away the rest of the afternoon, buying gifts for each other, friends and family and then, with a happy exhaustion and ending to a perfect day, head to one of their favorite restaurants for cocktails and dinner.

This year, Kat's dad, Anthony, had reserved a series of suites at one of the finest five star hotels right in the center of The Magnificent Mile, often called the Gold Coast. Anthony gave one of the suites to Victoria and Sophia as his family's gift to the Rodessas. After all, Mary Margaret said when Sophia protested, Sophia had watched over and cared for her baby for three years while she had been in Chicago. It was the very least they could do.

As her plane finally lowered in altitude, Kat saw a glimpse of the lights of the city. Magnificent. Most of the buildings had Christmas-colored lights or lights shaped like Christmas trees decorating their tops. Each year the mayor expanded the number of city streets dressed for the holidays, and it all kicked off during Thanksgiving week with the light parade. Victoria and Kat had seen three of those parades while they were in law school, snuggling each other and standing along Michigan Avenue in the freezing cold and sometimes howling snow with more than one hundred thousand other insane people. Fantasy floats sailed past and the streets magically exploded with light the moment the parade passed by.

As soon as her plane touched the ground, Kat texted Victoria, "landed." That was the signal. This would likely be one of the few chances Kat would have to really talk with Victoria before their families swallowed their shared time.

As soon as Kat walked out into the frigid night air, she heard the insistent honking of Victoria's car. She ran to the car to get out of the hellaciously freezing, cold night air. "Oh good God. It's amazing how easily you forget how damn cold it can get here."

Victoria leaned over to give Kat a hug before she began the drive back into the city. "I know. The temperature dropped thirty degrees yesterday. It was fifty last night when I walked home from the office."

Kat pulled a hair band off of her wrist, twirled her hair up into a high ponytail, and then put her gloves back on quickly. "Thank God for the butt warmers in your car. I can't wait to see Sophia. How is she?"

"Good. Busy as always. Happy." Kat caught a *but* at the end of the sentence.

"Well, what?"

"Well, she's dating this guy who I haven't met yet, and I don't think I like him," Victoria replied, keeping her eyes on the road.

Kat laughed out loud. "You're kidding, right? You do know how you sound, don't you? If not, I'll tell you. Insane. Yup. One word is all I need. Insane."

Victoria glanced quickly at her friend and shook her head. "You just don't get it, Kat. You've always had the complete 'family unit,' and so you have no idea how different it is not having that. Don't get me wrong, I don't miss anything, nor do I begrudge my situation or how I grew up. But my point is that I have more than a parent-child relationship with my mom. We're friends, too. She's talked to me about all sorts of things that, had there been a husband or father in our lives, I probably never would have heard about. Now suddenly, she's being mum about this guy. Telling me only the bare mini-

mum. I don't like that."

Kat tilted her head. "Well, did you consider that it just might be because she doesn't yet know how or what she feels for this guy? I mean maybe she has nothing to say, Victoria."

Victoria shook her head again. "No, that's not it. It's more like she's switching her allegiance and closeness from me to him. I don't like it. I mean, there are times when I call her and she doesn't pick up!"

"Well, Victoria, maybe she doesn't pick up because she's busy at the time," Kat replied.

"Exactly. What is that about? She has never been too busy to pick up when I call, and now suddenly she's too busy, and it's because of him."

"Hmm. Well I see what you mean," Kat responded, even though she really didn't, and thought it was about time Sophia made a life for herself. "If you want, I'll get Mary Margaret to chat with your mom. She's great at asking just the right questions to get the information we need to decide about this guy."

Victoria smiled then and glanced over at Kat. "Yes. Do it. But make sure your mom knows that this is a covert operation and should be treated as such. That means if she tells your dad, he must be sworn to secrecy, and under no circumstances can she tell those big-mouth brothers of yours."

"Done. I'll text her right now that I need a word with her before we all meet for cocktails this evening."

"Good. Thanks. I feel better. I guess it's been bothering me, and I didn't even know it was bothering me. Now, enough about me, how are you? How's business?" Victoria asked.

"Good. The rental market's been strong since the real estate market crash, and it's staying strong, since there's not enough confidence in the economy. It seems like over 90 percent of our current tenants are on track to renew for another year.

That has got to be a record."

"Whatever happened to your condominiums that were damaged by wind last year? If I recall, you were having trouble getting money from the insurance company." Her thoughts drifted back to the project and Highline as soon as Kat started talking.

"Victoria, are you listening?" Kat asked.

"I'm sorry Kat. I wasn't. My mind went to my own insurance project, the company we're bringing to the market."

"Well, let's hope it does a better job than the one we have. And to answer your question, the insurance company is simply saying that all of the damage we experienced is below our deductible. They sent one guy out to investigate and all he did was stroll around the outside of our building for half an hour, take a few photos, and leave. Based on that amazing inspection, he pronounced our damage below the deductible. Unbelievable."

"How can that be?" Victoria asked. "You sent me some of the pictures. The damage was undeniable. Did he get the photos?"

"He did. Our building will cost close to six million dollars to repair. It's one of the three we built in the last five years. It needs a new roof, the window frames were bent, and the cost to repair a high-rise is significant."

"I don't understand. How high was your deductible for that building?"

"Oh, please. It's utter bullshit. The damages are more than ten times the deductible. The insurer is sticking to its position that their adjuster found one hundred thousand dollars in damage from the storm, and all the other damage is due to wear and tear of the building and poor maintenance."

Victoria's mouth dropped open. "That's ridiculous. Did you sue them yet?"

"Well, that's the rub. We're in the process of deciding

whether to spend the money suing them or take that same money and make the repairs and yank our business. In fact, I was going to see if we could catch some time with Armond to discuss your firm possibly getting involved on our behalf. That way you would get the credit for bringing in a nice piece of business, and I would have comfort in knowing that our case was in the best of hands."

"Kat, I would love to sue those bastards for you. But we represent the insurance industry, and while we can talk to Armond and see what he thinks, it's likely there'll be a conflict. Armond, however, could recommend another firm. He's coming tonight, by the way. His parents flew in to see him, and since they know your parents, I asked if they would like to join us for drinks."

"Perfect. My parents speak highly of his family. I'm sure they'll be pleased to see them again. And on a selfish note, I can get a few moments alone with Armond and get his thoughts. That will take some of the pressure off."

Kat turned to look out of her window just in time to catch the first of the lights on Michigan Avenue. "Beautiful, isn't it? I miss all of this. Houston doesn't have the same pulse as Chicago. Hell, nothing does."

CHAPTER
18

"AT, HOW ARE you, my pet?" Armond exhaled, as he was enveloped in one of Kat's bear hugs. "Let's see the shoes," he said as Kat flashed her footwear. "Perfect. I expect nothing less from you."

Everyone was gathered in the magnificent lobby of the hotel. It was fully decked out for the holidays with Christmas trees and exotic six-foot flowers bursting from four-foot glass vases that stood on ornate tables throughout the large drawing room. At the far end of the lush room, three stairs led up to an open yet cozy cocktail area with a huge fireplace roaring at one end. On either side of the fireplace was an open entrance into the solarium that boasted floor-to-ceiling windows on three sides. The snow was falling, and while it was warm and cozy inside, the windows made it feel as if one were a part of the winter wonderland.

There was a mouthwatering collection of appetizers, all the standard treats—shrimp, fruit, cheeses, and thin slices of beef. Champagne had been opened and everyone looked beautiful.

Armond leaned over to the two girls. "Well, look what you two brought together. Everyone is happy and this beats the hell out of alone time with my father so he can grill me over when I'll enter the legal arena of the film industry."

"Oh Armond, according to my father, your dad brags about you and how far you have come in, and I quote, 'one of the most renowned and fastest growing international firms in the world,'" Kat and Victoria laughed at Armond's look of embarrassment.

"Well, then cheers to that," Armond said.

"Kat, did Victoria tell you about her little coup at the office?"

"Victoria, what's he talking about? What coup?" Kat asked, cocking her head.

"Well, I gave Victoria an assignment for one of our new clients, who is launching an insurance company. The primary market for this company is the US, and Victoria's assignment was to figure out what it needs to do in each state before it can begin selling insurance, and to be ready to work with the client to get that done." Armond paused and Victoria began to speak. Armond held up his finger.

"I know about the project of course. But I don't think she ever told me this part of the story. Tell me."

Victoria again tried to get into the conversation, only to be cut off by Armond. "We had a major presentation to Billy, Trever and a number of their cohorts, all big shots in the firm. Her finished project to the group was beyond reproach."

Kat turned to Victoria and clinked her glass to hers. "Well, of course. I would expect nothing less. I've seen her finished product before."

"Yes, well, here comes the good part," Armond continued.

"Can I say something?" Victoria asked.

"No," Kat and Armond chimed in unison and continued their private, not-so-private conversation. Victoria sighed, leaned back in the plush sofa, grabbed her glass of champagne, and decided to not fight what she couldn't change.

"At the end of my presentation," Armond continued, "Billy asked a number of questions directed not to me, but to Victoria, all of which she fielded beautifully. I mean, it was her work product after all so she should have been able to answer those questions."

"Agreed," said Kat, "now go on."

"Well, then came the fifty-million-dollar question, the one that most people would have punted or at least stalled for time. Or maybe, and here's a novel idea, maybe asked their partner in charge of the project, *moi* for instance, for his thoughts before answering. But not our Victoria. Oh no. She just stood up and answered without any hesitation or equivocation."

Kat was becoming impatient. "Well, for God's sake, Armond, what was the question?"

"The question was what all clients want to know. When can we complete the project?"

"So that's not such a big deal, is it? I mean really. Like you said, all clients want to know that," Kat said.

"Thank you, Kat," Victoria said, and the girls clinked champagne glasses one more time.

"Ah, but here's the difference. This is a client who is launching a new company, whose investors have placed millions on the line betting on when the company will launch and the success of that launch. This means that we can lose a client that will bring in seven figures in fees over the course of the next five years if everything doesn't go as planned. And Victoria here set the start date all by herself, without talking to me or anyone else about the feasibility of her projection. Just stood up and blurted it out."

"Well, that doesn't sound so bad. Can you meet the date?" Kat asked.

"I think so. We're on target so far and the tasks all seem to fit logically within the timeline. But what do I really know about meeting deadlines for the launch of an insurance company?" Victoria sighed.

"Let me continue," Armond butted in. "So then, Billy, you know as in Acker, Smith & McGowen, jumped up from the meeting and said, 'Let it be so'."

"He did not say that, Armond," Victoria jumped in.

"Not in so many words, but that's exactly what he meant," Armond sniped.

"Hey guys, this seems like an amazing opportunity for you both," Kat said. "And anyway, what's the upside for you two? It has to be significant."

"The upside is that Victoria will be on the fast-track to becoming the first woman partner, and I will have a shot at becoming the top-ranking equity shareholder, except of course for the troika. Which means, that we will both be entitled to a significant piece of the pie," Armond answered.

"Well, let's focus on that then," Kat said, noticing Victoria's stress.

"Anyway, the timeline is accurate," Victoria said. "Either we know our stuff or we don't. And I know my stuff. Now enough of boring work talk. Let's drink and eat and enjoy the holiday."

The next day, all three families celebrated Christmas together. Victoria and Kat's family went to church at the beautiful Holy Name Cathedral, one of the oldest churches in the city. Every Christmas the church is decorated in periwinkle lights, and a life-size Nativity scene is displayed under the old arches of the church's many doorways. All three families had agreed to meet for a late brunch and to exchange gifts at the top of the tallest building in the city. The spectacular views would be the perfect setting to celebrate.

After mass, Victoria and Kat finally had a chance to talk. "So, what do you really think about your job? Do you like it? Are the people assholes? Is it a sweatshop? And why, for heaven's sake, are there as of yet no female partners? Doesn't that strike you as a bit odd?" Kat asked.

"Hmmm. I think my job is just what I hoped it would be. Yes, I like it. Some of them are assholes. Yes, I work long hours, but I get paid well, so I can't say it's a sweatshop. And I don't know why there are no women partners," Victoria answered as they sat in her suite together before brunch.

"Well, the firm's been in existence now for, how long? Ten years?" Kat asked.

"Yup. About that long." Victoria sighed. She knew Kat well enough to know that she was in for her special brand of interrogation.

"And I thought I read or heard or something about the firm being renowned for its diversity, and specifically for its encouragement and hiring of women lawyers. Isn't that true?" Kat continued.

"Yup. Again."

"And if that is the case, then how can there be no female partners? What's up with that? Can I assume you've asked?" Kat finished.

"Well, if you're through with your inquisition, I will tell you that yes, I have asked. I have been told that the issue is with the women, not the firm."

"What the hell do you mean by that?" Kat fired back.

"I've heard that the women who've been eligible for partner have either gotten married, become pregnant, or chose to leave the firm for various personal reasons. You know yourself that by the time we reach partnership, about seven to ten years after law school, the clock ticking is an issue for many women, and so..."

"Oh my God!" Kat yowled. "You've drunk their Kool-Aid. You're actually buying into this bullshit." Kat got up and began pacing the room.

"Kat. What is so impossible to believe? I mean, yeah, it's not something I would do, and I don't really get the need to drop off the face of the Earth simply because you get married or have a kid, but apparently many women do." Victoria threw a pillow at Kat's head, hoping to get her off the topic.

Ducking neatly out of the way, Kat persisted, "What does Armond say about this?"

"I have no idea. I haven't asked him. And, quite frankly, I doubt he would give a rat's ass. I mean let's be real, Kat. He's intent on getting as many shares as he can. Do you really think he spends his waking moments thinking about the role of women in the firm? Anyway, remember that Billy Acker is one of the most respected and recognized lawyers in the country for his work helping women and minorities land significant legal jobs. Do you really think he's not keeping a pulse on this issue in his own firm?"

Kat had to admit that Victoria made sense. Acker, Smith & McGowen had received a ton of awards for its work in the arena. Kat shrugged as she walked over to the table to pick up her clutch so they could head out to meet their families for brunch. "Okay, I'll let it go for now. But you had better keep your eye on that golden partnership ring and how often they move it out of your reach, or you may find out you've wasted years of your life for nothing."

CHAPTER
19

THE NEW YEAR dawned crystal clear and freezing-ass cold. It was impossible to be outside for more than a few minutes. Then, with little warning, the skies opened and dumped eighteen inches of snow, delivered by hurricane-like winds. The storm began on Saturday morning, and while the first few hours were rather peaceful and pretty with puffy, sparkly, gently falling snowflakes, by the time evening rolled around, a real old-fashioned blizzard was in full swing. The streets, usually bustling, were deserted and quiet for the next forty-eight hours and an eerie, surreal peace descended on the city. By Monday morning, the chaos left by the storm was so bad that even the public schools had closed. The parochial schools were always closing, but Chicago public schools only shut down for serious things, like bomb threats or shootings, but not a snowstorm.

Walking out of her building to head to the office, the first thing Victoria saw was people standing on the tops of their cars that were parked on the sides of the streets. The drifts were so high that the snow covered the car doors, forcing their owners to dig out by standing on their roofs and digging down. All her neighbors held shovels, brooms and anything else, including the odd garden tool, that might help move the snow.

Thankful that she could walk to work, Victoria picked her way to the office by tracking in other people's snow-prints. By the time Victoria entered the lobby and put her two thumbs on the glass security monitor, she was sweaty from the exertion of simply getting to work. It was times like these that she wondered what she was doing in Chicago. Realizing she was close to being late, Victoria quickly went to her office, put her things away, and headed to the large conference room on the third floor. She heard the sound of voices getting louder as she rounded the corner and pushed through the glass doors that opened to the foyer of the main conference room.

Looking around at the crowd, Victoria grabbed a seat by one of her classmates as the room continued to fill with the close to three hundred seventy-five associates from around the world that were the primary widgets, also known as the income producers, of Acker, Smith & McGowen. Victoria couldn't help but compare herself to her peers at times like these. Her mind wandered to the school closings announced that morning, and she wondered how many of her colleagues had been bred in the parochial school environment where even the smallest, fluffiest snowflake falling from the sky became an excuse. These were the weak ones, she thought, smiling slightly to herself; the ones she needn't worry about as competition on her road to partnership.

Bored waiting for the meeting to begin, Victoria began to mentally pick out the weak ones, drawing stick figures on her legal pad. One stick figure, one weak one. After drawing twenty-five stick figures, Victoria decided she needed strong black coffee to get through the next few hours of meetings. As she pushed back her chair to begin her search for coffee, a loud screeching sound came blasting out from the front of the room. Startled, Victoria jumped as her heart slammed against her chest. The horrifying sound came again and unbelievably, a third time. The hair on Victoria's arms stood at attention and she looked to see who was responsible for such an idiotic noise.

Really? Victoria thought as she recognized the firm manager, a skinny string bean of a man who always wore a black cowboy hat and black cape that he liked to swoosh around, at center stage with the mic in his hand. No reason to have checked the mic sooner. Best to wait until there are hundreds of people in the room. After all, the meeting was only planned six months ago. I mean, who would have had time to check a mic over the last six months?

Victoria watched in disbelief and annoyance as he began to tap the head of the mic against the podium, producing some new but equally ear-splitting noises. Victoria thought, If I was the chair of the firm, I would fire every one of the idiots up there swarming around the mic staring and picking at it like some new tool that they had never seen before this moment.

"May I have your attention, ladies and gentlemen?" Shaking her out of her firing-people daydream, the firm manager finally finished fiddling with the microphone.

Three hundred–plus associates looked up for a blush of a second, then returned to doing whatever it was they had been doing. Victoria felt rather sorry for him as he unsuccessfully tried to bring about order. "Please come to order," stringbean said louder while he rapped his pen against the head of the microphone. When that didn't work, he finally picked up a gavel and banged it down on the podium, causing a vibration the likes of which had never before run through a microphone. That did the trick, as all of the associates had to stop yammering and cover their ears to try to hide from the horrific ringing sound. Even Trever McGowen, standing off to the side of the stage, covered his ears. "We have important business to address," string-bean shouted in a high-pitched, rather hysterical tone into the mic, this time bringing peals of laughter from the crowd.

Trying a different tack, he ignored the audience and simply began the meeting. "Ladies and gentlemen, welcome to Acker, Smith & McGowen's Annual Associate Meeting." The pause he made was the kind recognized all over the world: the awkward cue for undeserved applause. The ass-kissers in the room did not disappoint, and a polite smattering filled the gap. His head bobbed like a bobblehead in recognition while he continued, "We are proud to bring together over three hundred associates from seven different countries including the United States. We are proud to represent some of the most important Fortune 500 firms in the world and your excellent and unparalleled legal representation allows our clients to continue to strive toward their full potential."

"Oh boy," Victoria sighed, thinking he was a bit thick on the drama.

"The firm considers it critical that each of you have a solid understanding of the firm's financial projections for the new year. So, before the end of last year, the partners spent considerable time and effort reaching a consensus on the projections for this wonderful new year. Your department's and your personal projections will be conveyed to you by your department chairs during this first week of January, and, as you may have heard, this year is projected to bring in the largest increase in revenue the firm has ever experienced."

This time, string-bean actually held up both hands, as if he was the pope and had just finished conveying an important message from on high, while he waited for the applause that eventually rolled onto the stage.

"This meeting is to introduce you to the firm's overall financial projections so you can put your department's piece of the pie into perspective, and, of course, to answer any questions you might have. Ladies and gentlemen, possible future partners of Acker, Smith & McGowen…"

Oh good God, Victoria thought. She was close to pressing record on her phone so she could send a video to Kat, because there was no way she was going to be able to aptly convey the stupidity of this speech.

"…Consider yourselves lucky. Acker, Smith & McGowen believes in transparency, and is the only firm that allows its financial information to migrate down to the ranks of associates. You're truly blessed to be a part of this great worldwide institution."

"Wow, isn't this amazing!" one of Victoria's class members leaned over and whispered. Her eyes were all shiny and bright, and she had a dreamy look on her face that was actually kind of scary. She had definitely drunk the Kool-Aid, Victoria thought as she recalled what Kat had said to her the other night.

String-bean continued, "We're honored to have in our presence one of the foremost thought leaders on the growth and profitability of international law firms. He arrived just this morning from the United Kingdom, where he's working on another merger for Acker, Smith & McGowen continuing our plans for world domination! He agreed, as a personal favor to all of us, to come directly to the office from the airport to share the status of the firm's growth and to explain the importance of the partners' financial projections. Please join me now with warm applause in welcoming one of the esteemed founding members of the firm."

Pausing, he looked slowly around at the audience for way too long causing his hoped-for dramatic pause to turn into awkward dead space. He then wildly ripped the mic off its stand, swung his free arm in the air, and shouted, "Mr. Trever McGowen!" and once again caused the mic to squeal as if in pain.

Victoria swore she saw bits of spittle shoot out of string-bean's mouth as his introduction crescendoed. String-bean began clapping maniacally with the microphone still in his hand, which created yet another awful ear-splitting sound. Shaking Trever's hand, string-bean lead him to the podium, handed him the mic, clumsily gathered the things he had brought up to the podium and finally, to the collective gratification of everyone in the room, began to walk off the stage. But instead of walking like a normal human being, string-bean turned so he was facing Trever and began to bow and walk backward toward stage right. He continued bowing, bowing, bowing, and finally, mercifully, he was out of sight.

Trever rolled his eyes theatrically toward the heavens and smiled his sheepish and cute-as-shit grin at the audience, which elicited laughter and resounding applause and, much to Victoria's surprise, a standing ovation. Well, Victoria thought, why not? He, at least, was someone she admired. She stood and joined the fray.

Charming as ever, Trever raised his hands into the air and asked everyone to please sit and allow the meeting to begin. Eventually, everyone settled into their seats, the lights dimmed, and what looked like a six-foot dollar sign next to a large number in the millions was lit on the enormous screen that had lowered behind Trever. It was the firm revenue for the year that had just finished. One hundred million dollars. You could have heard a pin drop.

"Oh my," whispered Victoria's classmate.

"I had no idea," Victoria said in response, equally dumbfounded.

Knowing that he had their full attention, Trever used his charming Texas drawl to his advantage. "You-all know that you're the engines and brains of this firm. Billy, Adam and I depend and rely on you to keep our reputations solid and to help get us where we're going. And where we're going, as you know, is somewhere much, much bigger than the great state of Texas and any of the other little bits and pieces that make up the other forty-nine states." There were whoops and hollers, and even some floor stomping. There was no question about it, Victoria thought, Trever definitely lived up to his reputation as the most charming of the troika.

"And where we're going," Trever continued, "is to take this great law firm of ours to each of the business-centric cities around the world." More clapping and stomping as Trever paused and turned to look as pictures of London, Barcelona, Sydney and other cities flashed their way across the screen.

Trever began to pace. "Let me tell you a few stories about how we got where we are today. You know my granddaddy, the Senator from the great state of Texas, used to say, if a man can tell a few good stories, he can rule the world."

Trever held the group spellbound for the next hour, telling a few stories about his early years growing up on his family's Texas ranch run by his grandfather who was also one of the most respected right-wing Senators, (an oxymoron Victoria thought) of the last twenty years, along with a few war stories about how the firm got its first clients back in the day. He then shifted smoothly to stories about associates who "made it" into the partner ranks and what some of them had gone through to get there.

Trever told three rags-to-riches stories, each with a heavy dose of Texas humor. But the meaning was unmistakable. Enormous sacrifices were expected if one wanted entry to the hallowed partner halls. Failure to meet the working-hour requirements meant that one would be subjected to income reduction and even dismissal. Achieve more than the hour minimum, and unspecified good things awaited. These "good things" were not spelled out in detail, and no one had the balls to ask.

At the end of his storytelling, Trever unveiled the revenue projection for the current year. There was shocked silence. You could have heard a dollar drop. The partners were projecting a forty percent jump in revenue, an unheard of increase.

"That's right. You're seeing the number correctly. There's nothing wrong with your eyes. Well, my friends, let's adjourn this meeting, 'cause we got some work to do and I got a shower to take! Have a great year at the firm, and we look forward to you working like dogs." Trever exited to more applause, while string-bean ran back up to the podium to ensure the troops understood the bottom line before the meeting was adjourned.

"There is a striking difference between our firm and all others. This number," and he turned and waved his hand at the giant $140 million on the screen, "is not really a projection, because a projection is something you strive to reach. At Acker, Smith & McGowen, our projection is a number that will be reached. It's reached by ensuring that you perform, and you perform by billing the number of hours that have been allotted to you by your department chair. If you do not perform, your career will not progress. If you fall behind, we know it, and you will be brought in front of the review board to fix the problem. If the problem is you, we will work with you to fix it. If it can't be fixed, we will have to find someone else to bill the hours and you will need to find a different firm better suited to who you are."

He finally took a breath as he looked around the room. Any lightness and good feeling that had been in the room when Trever had been on stage was gone. In its place was a heavy, scary feeling.

"Now, any questions before we adjourn?" String-bean waited a beat, then barked, "No? Great! Before you leave, pick up your packet at the door. Inside you will find a personalized gift for each of you from the firm, a color-coded chart that displays your individual minimum billable hours broken down per week and month. Follow the chart and you will stay on the road to partnership. Ignore the chart, and well, I will not see you at this meeting next year." With that morale-busting statement, String-bean turned and walked toward the podium, grabbed the gavel, and banged it down hard on the mantel. "Go forth and bill! The eleventh Annual Associates Meeting is adjourned."

The room was absolutely quiet. No one moved for what Victoria swore was a good sixty seconds. As she looked around the room at her fellow associates, she saw their faces reflected her reaction. Gone was the warm and fuzzy feeling of camaraderie the firm had projected during the interviews and at the annual cocktail party. In its place stood a nasty, tense depression. Well, this will be an interesting year, she thought.

As associates opened their packets, the shit began to hit the fan. Each department had different requirements because, as Armond had explained a few weeks ago, some of the departments could get away with minimum billing, meaning the lawyers could bill more than they actually worked in a day. Litigation was one of these groups. Even if the lawyer worked only thirty minutes on tweaking the written question or interrogatory forms pulled from the firm's data bank, that lawyer could, and would, bill the client for say, "1.5 hours" with an entry like "drafting and finalizing interrogatories." The firm rationalized it was not unethical because the client was informed that some items were subject to minimum billing, and because the firm also figured it had the right to bill for this amount of time, as it was the firm's intellectual property that created these forms in the first place. This was always a point of contention, because departments like Victoria's could not minimum bill; well, at least not in the same way as litigation. So to make up for this disparity, the litigation department always had substantially higher required billable hours.

Non-billable requirements were included in the packets as well. These hours had to be spent writing articles and speeches that partners would poach and present, adding their names to any that they thought could advance their reputation as an expert in their field. Victoria had heard that it was only in the rarest of cases that a partner would credit an associate in a footnote, even though the associate was the one who had written the article.

While Victoria was less than amused with the firm's Gestapo-like requirements and the way they had been conveyed, she was not at all worried about meeting the firm's minimum hourly requirements. The Highline project, and the three other matters she had since been assigned, provided her with all the billable hours she would need. In fact, she intended to be one of the top billers in her class. No one had to tell Victoria she was hard on herself. But now more than ever, she saw no reason to change, especially since her work ethic would finally be rewarded.

CHAPTER
20

A S THE PLANE began its descent into L.F. Wade International Airport, Billy looked out his first-class window at the stunningly blue turquoise water surrounding Bermuda. He leaned over and woke Trever, asleep in the seat next to him. "We're landing."

Trever lazily came awake and smiled at his longtime friend and partner. "Thank God. I can't wait to get to our house. I need a massage and a good strong cup of coffee, and then I think I'll lay at the beach for a bit."

"I don't care what you do, my friend, as long as you're ready to present to the board at dinner tonight," Billy replied.

The plane touched down and taxied over to the tiny airport facility. As they got their overnight bags out of the carry on, Trever looked over his shoulder at Billy and said, "I want us to go over the numbers again before we meet with your father and the board. I want to be certain the big boys can afford to pay our fees for the coming year, no matter what happens to their start-up."

"I'll go over the numbers anytime you want, but my father alone can pay any legal fees we dish out. The rest of the board members are billionaires. There'll be no problem getting our fees paid."

The two men disembarked from the plane and headed toward their limousine waiting on the tarmac. "To The Western Will, please, Charles," Trever told the driver. Pressing the button to raise the privacy glass, Trever pulled out his tablet and opened the fee chart, along with the firm's retainer proposal that he intended to pass out to the board during dinner.

"Before I have Gretchen finalize this for our meeting tonight, I want to get your thoughts. Based on the amount of legal work you're projecting just to get Highline up and running and able to transact business in the US, along with the board's request to use my transaction group as lead strategists, this is my current estimate of our legal fees for this year. The next spreadsheet contains my projections for the first six months of the following year. Based on these figures, we should request our typical ten percent retainer of two million." Trever handed the tablet to Billy so he could see the numbers.

Billy smiled and handed it back to Trever.

"Agreed?"

Billy responded, "Trever, my friend, there is nothing for me to disagree with. You just showed me the highest revenue figure we have ever projected for a single client."

"If all goes as planned, your father and his merry band of billionaires will be the biggest client the firm has ever had."

Just like his father, Big Bill, Billy had a habit of pausing to light up a cigar before responding to critical points in discussions. After sucking on a few puffs of Havana's finest, Billy responded, "I'm well aware. I just want you and Adam to remember that when we divvy up the year-end distributions, equal may not work."

Billy knew that this was a sore subject with Adam, whose own family, a well-known Boston-based clothier, had essentially left their fourth child out of the family fortune. Adam's only brother had been firstborn and so inherited the position of CEO of the family company, along with most of the family's assets. His two older sisters, in the age-old tradition of the old boys' club, were married off into two scion Bostonian families and were busy with kids, charities and fashion shows. That had left Adam to make his own way. While he had significant trust funds and stock rights in the family business, he had grown up feeling left out. Everything he did was to ensure that it would never happen again.

Seeing the look of annoyance on his friend's face, Billy relented. "I'm kidding, Trever. Just kidding. Would you relax? Our agreement is solid. There may very well be a time that I won't pull in such big clients and our agreement to equal split is something that I want as well."

Trever visibly relaxed and realized that he had been actually holding his breath. Letting it out, he said, "That kind of bullshit talk is what can easily start our slide down the slippery path of traditional firms. It's really stupid."

Billy slapped him on the back as they walked up the entrance to The Western Will. "Ah, come on, Trever. Anyway, you're as much a part of this deal as I am since the board has asked that you stay involved as the business strategist for Highline."

"We need to talk about that," Trever said as the men walked into the house and out onto the magnificent back patio that overlooked the Atlantic. "I'm going to do something a bit different as far as billing for the consulting piece."

"Let's hear it," Billy said. The men pulled up two chairs to sit at the gorgeously carved patio table and ordered coffee and food from the house staff.

"I'm not going to bill hourly. I want to bill the consulting portion of this job on a reward basis. We'll get better numbers in the long run, and it removes the hassle of determining which associates to line up to create enough of a pyramid to make it worth our while on an hourly basis. It also removes the headache of the client auditing our billable hours. Since this is our first consulting gig, I think we should give it a shot."

Billy almost choked on his cigar. "Are you out of your mind? Our business plan is very specific, and our revenue forecasting depends on following that plan. We've already figured in the start-up portion of our legal fees, and you just need to add your group's hours and fees. Our way, as you well know, allows us to control our finances. Your way is a crapshoot. Absolutely not."

They had had this conversation before and Trever knew this would be a problem for Billy, the most conservative out of the three of them. "Listen, Billy, it's too late to debate. It's a done deal. Your father called me last week and told me to come up with a fee reward-type billing arrangement for the strategy piece. I did, and he agreed, subject to the board's approval tonight. It was his idea. He said if we didn't agree, they would go to another firm to get this done."

Billy's face turned bright red, and Trever knew it was not from the Bermudian heat. Slamming his fist down hard on the table, Billy made the silverware jump and the glasses rattle. "God dammit, Trever. My father is a consummate negotiator. It's what he does. I know just how he plays. He wasn't going anywhere else, but he went to you because he knew he could convince you, and he knew that I would know that he would not go anywhere else."

"Listen, Billy. Just let me walk you through it."

They spent the next hour working through the possible profit their consulting arm would make off of Highline, depending on which financial scenario worked its way to the finish line by the end of the fiscal year. Each of the paths led to significant profits for the firm and Billy visibly began to relax.

"Okay, we're agreed, then?" Trever asked Billy, noting his change in demeanor.

"We are. It's done anyway, since you already agreed with my father. One thing about Big Bill, if you back away from your word, he's relentless in dishing out the punishment. He'd pull the whole deal, including our handling the legal piece, if we tried to back out now. But don't do this again. If my father calls you, believe there's a reason he's speaking with you and not me."

Trever could not resist rolling his eyes. He had known exactly what he was doing when he negotiated the deal with Big Bill. In fact, reward-based billing was something he had pushed for at the firm for the past few years and this deal was going to bring in far more money than billing by the hour. Trever pressed the intercom button summoning the assistant who lived at The Western Will. "Gretchen, please come out to the terrace. We have some notes we need finalized into a formal proposal, and added to the board packet along with our retainer agreement, for our dinner with the board tonight."

As soon as Gretchen left with their notes and instructions, Trever pushed back his chair and stood. "Now, I'm going to get that massage. I'll see you at dinner." Trever turned and headed for his suite of rooms, looking forward to enjoying his massage on his private patio overlooking the ocean and thinking about the immense amount of money the firm was about to make.

The next day, Trever, Billy and Gretchen drove to Hamilton, the capital of Bermuda, to finalize the agreements with the board that had been made during dinner the night before. The meeting had gone well, and with a few minor changes to the retainer and risk-reward agreements that Gretchen had made, the documents were to be signed at the morning board meeting. The two-million-dollar retainer would be in the firm's account by 5:00 p.m. that day.

As the three of them walked into Highline's headquarters, Trever looked at the high ceiling and cool colors and was pleased. He had chosen the this particular building to house Highline's official corporate office for a number of reasons. Not only was the building renowned for its architectural design, as it was modeled after a traditional Bermudian home, complete with a clock tower above its entryway, but it was located in a prime spot. Rising above the other buildings at the end of the ocean walk, it was across the street from some of the wealthiest insurance companies in the world. It had been decided last night during the dinner meeting that there would be four offices set aside and support staff made available, for the Acker, Smith & McGowen team assigned to ensure Highline's launch was done on time. Trever also had an office reserved for him, as it was expected that as lead consultant he would be there often.

As they rode the elevator up to their soon-to-be Bermudian office, Gretchen showed the agreements to Trever so he could review them one last time. One of the first items on the agenda was a vote on the proposed resolutions to continue to retain the law firm for the coming year to complete both the start up and strategic work. Within ten minutes of the meeting beginning, the board approved the resolutions and the agreements were passed around the table from member to member and signed. Billy walked over to the white board and wrote three dates on the board.

"Gentlemen," Billy began, "our firm thanks you for this continued opportunity, and we look forward to a long and profitable relationship with Highline."

Jack Bowen, one of the board members, finished signing his name and asked, "Billy, every day that passes without a Highline policy in the hands of a policyholder is money out of our collective pockets. When can we expect the first rollout in the US?"

"Jack, the three dates I wrote on the board are in anticipation of that very question. The first date, is when we expect to have all of the necessary paperwork turned into the insurance regulators of each of the states. The second date, is when we expect to have the regulators' comments and final revisions completed for each state. Then, and finally, we expect all 'I's' to be dotted and 'T's' to be crossed before the third date. So we expect a full rollout, assuming certain guarantees by the board, to occur no later than eight months from now."

"Billy, I gotta tell you, I hear a bit of the tail wagging the dog in what you said. As far as I'm concerned," Big Bill said as he sunk deep into his chair at the head of the table, "we're paying you boys a shit-ton of money and I just don't like to hear caveats like you just gave us. What the hell do you mean by, 'assuming certain guarantees by the board'? I'll bet my boys here at the table all agree, our two million dollars in fine US currency soon to be in your law firm's bank account is enough of a 'guarantee' to get us past just about any problem."

God, Billy thought, he never changes. It's all about his ego and showing the world the size of his dick. Even when his own son is involved in the deal, he can't stop the grandstanding for a second. Okay, you son of a bitch, here you go.

"Obviously, Bill, in addition to money to pay for the legal work we're giving you, Highline has to respond in a timely manner to our requests for documentation and proof of capital that will be needed for each state in order to get the regulators' approval."

Big Bill would not let up. "Well, of course we understand that, Billy. You boys are dealing with nine world-class businessmen. You'll get what you need when you need it."

Trever had seen this kind of interaction between Big Bill and Billy before, and the pissing match could go on forever. He decided to put an end to it. "May I jump in?" he said as he stood up and nodded to Gretchen to pass out the next set of documents. "Gretchen is handing each of you a package containing the timeline, and the list of documents and projected capital needed from each investor and the company as a whole. Finally, it also includes the projected launch date with each piece of the puzzle that will need to come together for that date to work. If I may, I want to discuss an outline of what I will need as lead strategist in order to give you the kind of return on investment you expect."

By the end of the day, Trever and Billy had run through their projections and answered all the board's questions. After the members left to board their respective private jets, Trever and Billy remained behind to go over a few details before Billy left for Chicago that evening. Trever was staying behind to continue working on his business plan for Highline.

"Well, that went well," Trever said as he walked over to the sideboard and poured shots of whiskey into two crystal highball glasses.

"Thanks," Billy said as he took the shot from Trever. "I think it did. Jesus, Big Bill is a pain in the ass. You handled him well."

"Yeah. He is a pain. But as far as I'm concerned, for the additional ten to twenty million in revenue he's bringing to the firm, he can be as big a pain in the ass as he wants. And, by the way, I'm more than happy to deal with him on a daily basis if you prefer. You two seem to bust each other's chops, so why don't I act as the main contact?"

"Won't work," Billy replied. "He wants me to be the point person for the legal piece and you for the consulting part. By the way, if he follows his usual MO, he'll want to pit us against each other from time to time just for the sport of it. So be ready for that. Talk to me first before you take any of his bait."

Trever nodded his understanding. "No problem. When do you leave?" Trever asked.

"As soon as I can get to the tarmac. I told Gretchen I wanted to be back in Chicago this evening. The pilots are on standby and they're ready to go. As soon as we know we have word that our money is…"

"Excuse me," Gretchen poked her head in the door, "the last of the retainer just transferred into the firm account. All two million present and accounted for." Gretchen smiled before she closed the door.

The two friends were silent for a moment, appreciating the feel of being two million dollars richer. "As I was saying, I want to be back tonight as I have a meeting set first thing in the morning for the legal team. I want to ensure they don't fuck this up and that they understand any delay or movement from the timeline will be considered a fuckup."

"I assume Armond is still running the project?" Trever asked.

"He is. Although as you may recall, he's relying heavily on one of our new associates. Victoria. You'll remember her from our meeting last spring during her graduation ceremony and from our firm event. It might also refresh your recollection if I remind you that I talked about banging her. You can't deny that I have an eye for those associates who have talent, and I'm betting that this one has more than just her legal chops to offer. But for the time being, I want her to concentrate on the job at hand, rather than on giving me a hand job." Billy slapped Trever on the back as he laughed at his own joke.

Trever rolled his eyes in disgust and thought how much Billy was like his father. "Yes, well, she's far more valuable to us now as a workhorse than your whore. The last thing we want to do is distract her from putting in the hours needed for this project. Pick someone else."

Billy smiled as he thought of the juicy young associate he'd banged on his desk before boarding their plane yesterday. He had called her in to discuss a research project and within two hours she was bent over his desk letting him do as he pleased. While she had protested at first, all she needed was a bit of an education about the consequences of resisting. At the end of their little chat, she chose wisely as she did not want to spend the rest of her hard-earned legal career searching through a warehouse full of documents for a smoking gun she would never find. Maybe he'd call her when he landed for a late dinner and lesson number two. Billy got hard just thinking about it and shifted in his chair.

"Oh for God's sake." Trever recognized the look on Billy's face and knew that he already had.

CHAPTER
21

AFTER THE MEETING Big Bill made a beeline to the home he shared with his mistress. The last time he had been in Bermuda, all those months ago, he had just finished giving it to his mistress, only to hear the announcement on the news that his wife had filed for divorce. He was so pissed he couldn't sleep that night, and woke his pilots so he could get back to Georgia. He immediately contacted some of his longtime friends, who had grown up to be some of the best divorce lawyers in Georgia, only to find out that Jenny was much smarter than he ever gave her credit for. They were all forced to decline his request to represent him because Jenny had met with them, explained her intent to divorce and provided enough information to trigger the attorney-client privilege. Even though she hadn't ended up hiring any of them, she had neatly conflicted them out of the divorce match. The bitch, Bill thought. Now she was living off of him in some fancy condominium she bought on the California coast while he worked his ass off.

By now, though, he had accepted the fact that Jenny was divorcing him and other than the embarrassing things she chose to put in her publicly filed papers, he was settling into the idea of being a single man once again. While he didn't like the thought of not having a wife to take care of his homes and his personal matters, he soon realized that he could hire a young and sexy personal assistant who would do what he asked without the "discussion" he had had to put up with from Jenny.

"Hey, baby, I'm back," he called as he walked through the front door.

Wilhemena rolled her eyes. She could barely stand him anymore. His touch literally made her skin crawl. She wanted to be with men her own age; strong, solid and hard. Not some big-bellied hairy old man who still thought women looked up to him. Only a few more months, she thought, and then she would be rid of him.

"I'm in the kitchen," she called back, amazed that he never seemed to detect the sarcasm in her tone.

Big Bill came up behind her and put his arms around her so he could squeeze her breasts with his big hands. He started to knead them hard and grind into her from behind as she continued making dinner. "Just how I like to see you, barefoot in the kitchen, making food for your man," he breathed into her ear.

She could hear herself screaming inside her head, and it took all her willpower not to turn and stab him with the knife she was using to cut the tomatoes she was serving with dinner. She composed herself, knowing another quarter of a million was about to be deposited into her account next week. She could stand it for one more night, and then he would be back in Georgia and she would end it the moment he signed the house over to her.

But in the meantime, she could hear and feel his breath coming faster and harder near her ear as he reached up under her skirt to find her nakedness. He began to rub her and stuck two fingers deep inside and began to pump. "Tell me you're my whore. Tell me, now," he said as he pulled her hair back hard with one hand and began to force her legs apart.

CHAPTER
22

JENNY WOKE TO an amazing morning in Santa Monica. It was the perfect temperature at seventy-eight degrees, and the sky was a clear, azure blue with no sign of ocean fog. Breathing deeply of the ocean air, she sipped her coffee on her veranda overlooking the Pacific. Dolphins swam in the distance, and occasionally they jumped far enough out of the water that she swore she could actually see their faces. Jenny smiled to herself, thinking back over her first few months after filing for divorce. The first time she saw the dolphins, she took photos and excitedly called the few friends she still kept in contact with as the dolpins swam by. Now, it was just one more amazing day in California. She felt she had come alive again.

These past months, Jenny had learned quite a bit about herself. She was smart. She had forgotten that. She could make her own decisions, and she was good at it too. She had forgotten that as well, since she never had to make any during her marriage. But the part she had learned about herself and hated to admit was that she was a disappointment to herself, perhaps to others. She hadn't quite figured out what led her to give up everything just to be a wife to

Big Bill. A man who, if she was honest with herself, she had known had cheated on her for years. It made her sad to admit that she had allowed her life to be controlled by one man. Now, at fifty, she had to decide what to do with the rest of her life and she was intent on making sure whatever path she took was exciting and meaningful.

The divorce had been difficult. Bill was fighting her every step of the way. He had offshore accounts and was pumping cash into the tobacco business to pay off debt in an effort to prevent Jenny from getting her hands on it.

As her lawyer said, "What an asshole." In fact, Mona now no longer referred to him by his name. It was just, "the asshole," when they discussed the latest. That was fine with Jenny. He was an asshole. And as she had told her lawyer, the best way to beat an asshole was to use his weakness against him, and Bill's low opinion of women was his weakness. There would be nothing sweeter than when he realized women had been his undoing.

Jenny threw her head back, closed her eyes and breathed deeply of the sea air. A small smile flittered across her face as she drew comfort from her faith that his comeuppance was just around the corner.

CHAPTER
23

I T HAD BEEN a long year. Victoria thought of the long hours she had spent on the Highline project, and at times, she had wondered whether her efforts would pay off toward her long-term goal. But today, she knew the answer was unequivocally yes, because in about four hours she would be flying to Bermuda on the firm's private jet with Billy, Trever and Armond, to present their final briefing and kickoff package to the board. Trever would follow their legal presentation with the unveiling of the second phase of his strategic consulting plan. Victoria knew she was the envy of her associate class and without question, most of the other associates in the firm. No associate had ever been invited on the firm jet. In fact, Victoria would be the first female from the firm to ever enter the jet. Of course, speculation was high as to who Victoria had had to bed in order to receive the plum Highline assignment and now, a trip to Bermuda. Smart money had her bedding Billy.

Their flight was scheduled to leave O'Hare at ten o'clock, with their arrival scheduled for around three in the afternoon, Bermuda time. That would give them about an hour to meet with the staff at The Western Will, review the packets that had been electronically sent to Bermuda, make any last-minute changes, and discuss any remaining issues. The board meeting was set to begin at six that evening, to be immediately followed by a celebratory dinner and finally, a presentation by the public relations company in charge of the advertising campaign that would announce Highline to the States.

Billy and Armond were set to present the legal piece to the board. Victoria would be introduced, but not speak unless spoken to. Victoria could feel herself getting pissed again as she did each time she thought about those words and Billy actually saying them to her two weeks ago after their final team meeting. When Billy made that comment, Victoria was at first stunned into silence. She had been quick to recover, however, and was about to say something when she saw Armond slowly shake his head, a clear signal to keep quiet. Out of respect for Armond and trusting his judgment, Victoria said nothing.

Victoria spent the few hours before the flight at her apartment going over the presentation and highlighting important points for Armond. Once she was in the cab on her way to the airport, she texted Kat.

"On my way. Wish me luck." She got an immediate response.

"No luck needed. U R amazing!"

Once at O'Hare, Victoria headed to the section reserved for private jets and saw Armond in line for coffee. Catching up to him, she waited for him to finish buying his coffee. "Well, my little tart, ready to make history? The first time the firm has invited an associate onto its private jet. And a woman to boot! You can thank me later," Armond said as they walked alongside each other toward the boarding area.

"It's great, Armond. Really. And I do appreciate all the opportunities you've given me. I know I would never have had this opportunity if it wasn't for you."

"Damn right about that. But V, we make a great team. I can count on your work, and after having taken a few other new associates out for a test drive before you came along, well, let's just say the others are no longer at the firm." Armond winked.

While Armond meant it as a compliment, Victoria heard the double-edged sword about being fired in his statement. But knowing she needed to say what had been on her mind, she continued, "Well, thanks, I think." They walked in silence for a bit and then Victoria just blurted it out. "Armond, why is it that I'm the first woman on this plane? And what is it with Billy telling me to speak when spoken to? Is he kidding?"

Armond had been waiting for this. He knew Victoria was not going to drop Billy's comment, and she was too driven not to get answers. "Listen, Victoria, Billy's from the Deep South and hails from a long line of Southern 'gentlemen,' shall we call them? I'm sure he didn't mean it the way it came out. Remember, he chairs the American Bar Association diversity committee, and he's one of the leaders in promoting women in firms."

Victoria was less than placated. "Well then, what did he mean? And while we're on the topic, what's the deal with women in the firm? Or rather not, in the firm. There are exactly zero women partners, and only a handful who, rumor has it, are close to getting there."

Armond grabbed her arm and pulled her off to the side before they caught up with Billy and Trever, whom they could see sitting in the private lounge waiting to board the jet. "Listen V, we can talk all about this to your heart's content when we return. But now is not the time. We have a job to do. And let me be perfectly clear, this is a make-or-break-our-career job. You're playing with the big boys now. They don't give a rat's ass about how you feel or whether you like the way you were spoken to. So we're clear, I don't care either at this moment. What I do care about is kicking some ass at this meeting and getting the firm, and to be even clearer, me in particular and you by extension, retained to continue handling Highline's ongoing regulatory work and the other ancillary matters that will come up for the rest of our working days."

Armond released her arm, turned and walked over to Billy and Trever just as the captain let everyone know it was time to board. Victoria had two choices. She could either turn and leave right then and there, which would put an end to her career at the firm and likely at any firm (as there are no bigger gossips than lawyers), or she could suck it up and kick some ass in Bermuda.

That little outburst from Armond had made her more determined than ever to get to the top, and if it took being silent for a bit, well, so be it. While she was disappointed at Armond's reaction to her concerns, she grudgingly figured he was probably right. After all, he had been swimming with the sharks in the firm's political ocean far longer than she, and he had learned the fine art of negotiating from his father who was one of the top dealmakers in Hollywood. So she took a calming breath, put a smile on her face, and made one final decision as she walked up to their little group. She would stop educating Billy and Armond about the intricacies of insurance regulation. Assuming the members of this board were at least a bit curious about the security of their investments, they would want to dig into the background of some of the opinions those two would be delivering during their presentation. Whether they wanted her to speak or not, they would need her to chime in soon enough. Victoria knew she was a persuasive and captivating speaker, and she intended to use every ounce of speaking talent she possessed. And once the floor was hers, Billy, Trever and Armond would have to fight to get it back.

Victoria's satisfied smile and confident look sent a shiver down Armond's back. He raised an eyebrow at her and she just smiled back, tossed her lovely hair over her shoulder and turned to walk with Billy and Trever onto the jet.

Oh shit, he thought, this can't be good.

A few hours later, Victoria stood looking over the rocky cliffs and the turquoise ocean from her balcony at The Western Will. Her private area included an en suite bath, walk-in closet, and a full sitting area that opened by way of two hand-carved French doors onto a private massage room. The massage room opened out onto the balcony so one could have a view of the ocean while enjoying a massage from the staff masseuse. Armond had told her that the boys had a penchant for massages, and had insisted that the design of the estate included a private massage area in each living suite.

Victoria desperately wished she had time for a run on the white beach that seemed to stretch for miles just below her balcony. Running always knocked the nerves out of her and calmed her down. But they didn't have time for anything, nor would they tomorrow. Except for Trever, they were leaving tomorrow to return to Chicago. This was by far the most beautiful place she had ever been. When she was younger, her mother and she had taken vacations, but only to places like Lake Geneva, Wisconsin and Arizona. Nothing wrong with those places, but they couldn't hold a candle to the scene in front of her. Bermuda, or at least what she could see of the island, was breathtaking.

Victoria left the balcony doors open and walked back into her bathroom to try to do something with her hair. Since the ocean humidity was curling it, she decided to not fight nature and instead worked her hair into soft waves falling over her shoulders and down her back. As she finished getting ready, she thought back over the preparatory meeting held after they arrived that afternoon and was satisfied that it had gone well. Billy had been respectful and complimentary of the work she had done on the project. Maybe she had overreacted to his comment. Maybe he was under his own pressure. During their meeting, Victoria had been surprised to learn that Billy and his father didn't always get along and she had felt honored that she had been included in the discussion between Armond, Trever and Billy about how to handle Big Bill.

She had seen Kat and her dad interact on business for years now, and it was always done with respect and in a straight-up kind of manner. No bullshit. But listening to the boys discuss Big Bill and the rest of the board made Victoria realize there was an element of friction between the father and son.

It was interesting to hear the three of them assign end run-arounds for certain personalities who were going to be at the meeting. Trever said he would intervene if Billy's dad got to be too much of an ass. Victoria was very much looking forward to this meeting.

Hearing the suite door chime, Victoria went to answer it. Armond walked in, looking very dapper and dressed for an island meeting. He had the island business look perfected with a light-colored suit and an open-collared purple shirt with fine Italian leather shoes and no socks. Armond rather fancied himself a fashion icon, and Victoria had to admit, he looked good.

"Are you ready, V? This is one of the most defining moments of your career. If this goes well, we'll be set at the firm. This will be our client. Well, it's Billy's client, then mine, but you will be the one doing the laboring oar of the work and maintaining the relationships with the company management. It's a huge opportunity for you."

"I'm ready. But I don't see what there is for me to really be ready for. After all, you and Billy are presenting. I'm just watching, remember?"

"V, I saw the look on your face when you boarded the plane. Don't think I don't know you better than that. I know what you're thinking, too. Remember, I was an associate once." Armond walked over to the porch and sat in one of the outside, overstuffed chairs.

"Armond, I have no idea what you're talking about," Victoria said sweetly, sitting down to join him.

Armond knew how smart Victoria was, and he also knew that she would never be so stupid as to tell him what she was thinking. He knew, too, that she felt he had betrayed her by doing nothing when Billy had directed her to keep quiet. But Victoria needed to gain a bit more depth about the workings of their firm. Like that the male partners routinely and typically disregarded little things, like sexual discrimination rules. He couldn't even keep track of the number of times his peers had sat around and discussed what they'd like to do to one of their female lawyers without one of them showing any sign of remorse. After all, who was going to say anything to them? They were the guardians of the law. No one policed them. The sooner Victoria learned that, the better.

Armond decided he would just have to trust that Victoria's drive for the gold ring would never allow her to blow her chances by doing or saying anything inopportune. If she wanted to get ahead, and he knew she did, she would just have to learn to play the game. And if that meant standing idly by while her male colleagues made sexist remarks or ogled women, then so be it.

"Okay, then. Let's go kick some ass," Armond said as he set Victoria's arm in the crook of his elbow and walked her out of her room to their waiting car.

CHAPTER
24

NIGHTTIME IN BERMUDA was even more spectacular than the day. The sunset had been nothing short of breathtaking and the stars...well, there were so many of them that it was almost impossible to see the black of the night behind them. Victoria stood at the balcony that wrapped around the restaurant where they were gathered with the board for their celebratory dinner. As it was coming to a close, Victoria had slipped outside of the glass-enclosed restaurant to catch her breath, think back over the day and just feel.

She had imagined it would feel like this, the wave of utter relaxation and contentment that came after a job well done. She had been a hit. She always knew she would be once she got the chance. The danger had been in balancing her desire and ability to take over and run the show with the egos of her male colleagues. But much to her surprise, she had learned this afternoon that she had a natural way of walking that line by gracefully lobbing the ball back to her male colleagues. She had also learned that as long as she took the time to send that ball back, the men didn't really want it. Another surprise. Instead, they were happy to let her run with it, as long as she made it clear she was not the one in power.

"Congratulations, Miss Victoria. You did a fine job today," Billy said as he walked over to join her at the view. Victoria could never quite get used to his Southern accent, but she could appreciate the charm it brought to every sentence, whether insult or compliment.

"Thanks. I think it went well, and the board seems satisfied."

"They're more than satisfied. After you left the room, they voted to continue to move forward with the firm for the launch of Highline's and Trever's rollout plans for the year." Billy leaned his back against the railing and turned to look at Victoria. He was so close to her that she could see the flecks of gold in his blue eyes. He gave a small smile. "They asked specifically for you to remain involved in the project. Are you interested in doing so?"

Victoria's heart began to pound hard and she felt the familiar rush of adrenaline push through her body. Over the years, she had learned to fight her adrenaline's effect so she was not bouncing off the walls at inappropriate times. She fought it now, not wanting to appear too eager. "I'm glad to hear that. I've enjoyed the project and watching the company being created. I would love to be involved in the launch and the growth of the company." Victoria was bursting inside, and she couldn't wait to call Kat.

"Well, Miss Victoria, well, that's just grand. I will be the one involved in the launch and growth of Highline, and Armond will second my ship. But we'll need a solid crew to keep us on course."

Victoria heard the subtle rebuke and reminder that he was in charge, but she was less than happy to hear herself referred to as the crew. She sighed inwardly and her adrenaline spiked in a different direction. She bit her tongue and practiced turning her anger into the right thing to say to one of the most powerful lawyers in the country. "I'm excited to get this company launched. I'm on board, sir."

Billy's smile was huge. Apparently being called *sir* was all it took. Victoria had to will herself not to roll her eyes, so she turned away from him to look out over the water before her feelings were telegraphed.

"Great. Then I think we all have our marching orders for the next year, at least. Welcome on board, Ms. Victoria. Our ship sails at sunrise." He turned and walked back over to the remaining board members.

Oh my God! Victoria thought as she continued to look out over the ocean. She felt like she might puke. "I'm on board, sir?" Oh my God! She needed her ass kicked for saying that. She would have to confess to Kat in order to purge her soul for being such a suck-up and playing a game she thought she would never stoop to play.

Armond signaled to Victoria that the driver was waiting to take her back to The Western Will. Billy, Trever and Armond were staying to flesh out some of the details of the launch with the board and to watch a PR campaign presentation that might be used to launch the company's products. Apparently it was time for the big boys only, and Victoria was being dismissed. Armond knew how Victoria would react to that, so he made sure he walked her out to the car.

"Armond, I can find my own way out to the car. I'm not an idiot, whatever those Neanderthals think." Victoria walked ramrod straight and pushed the lush waves of her hair back over her shoulders. Armond knew her well enough now to know what that walk and that hair push meant. He decided to go with the "I'm so proud of you" approach.

"V, you did an amazing job today. Your timing was perfect during the meeting. You were respectful and you made sure the board understood that Billy was the mastermind and in charge of the outcome. Had you turned it any other way, the outcome for you, at least, would not have been so successful." Armond had his hand on her arm leading her through the group of men as she said her goodbyes.

"Get your hands off of me, Armond. I can say good night without you taking me through it like I'm a total idiot," Victoria hissed.

Armond sighed and released her arm. Any further restraints on her tonight and he thought she would explode. He watched the charm ooze out of her as she rounded the room to say her good nights to the board, Billy, and Trever. Then he watched as she turned to him and walked toward the door. If looks could kill, he'd be six feet under.

Walking her from the foyer of the restaurant to the car, he used their brief moment of privacy. "Victoria, it will not always be like this. Believe me."

Victoria looked him dead in the eye before sinking into the luxury of the limousine. "You bet your ass it won't." She shut the cushioned door as loudly as she could and the car drove off into the night.

CHAPTER
25

IGHLINE'S LAUNCH WAS a huge success. The public relations campaign, coupled with phase one of Trever's strategic plan, was the magic formula. The campaign used clever and funny analogies to depict other insurance companies as red-tape nightmare machines, not interested in protecting an insured's property, but in making money instead. In the time of a country just emerging from a housing crash, with an overabundance of low-paying jobs, and a weak economy, Highline offered low premiums, by providing direct access to its products without the need for the "middle man" or broker. It offered the right mix at the right time.

A few months after its splash onto the insurance market, the company began to turn a profit, exactly in line with Trever's projections. The board was ecstatic, so much so that they were considering allowing outsiders to invest in the company. Each member had been paid back almost one hundred percent of his initial investment, and management was now focusing on phase two of Trever's plan, ramping up the next product launch. The projected revenue over the next eighteen months was on target.

Armond and Victoria were involved in every phase of the business. Victoria had recently finished classes on insurance coverage. She had correctly calculated that insurance coverage, which meant analyzing the language of the policy to see if the company would accept or deny a claim, would be the next area of expertise needed by Highline. Until Victoria's push, the firm didn't have a department specializing in insurance coverage. Victoria was the mastermind of this new department.

Victoria's time was spread between Bermuda, the new Highline Chicago office, and the firm's Chicago office. Early on the Monday after the firm's thirteenth Annual Firm Party, Victoria was in the Chicago office and had just finished a meeting with her insurance team. Looking at her phone as she walked toward her office, she saw three texts from Kat. As soon as Victoria got to her office, she shut her door and called Kat.

"Hey, you. What's up?" Victoria smiled.

"Hey, yourself, Miss Victoria. How's the honorary daughter of the South doing?" Kat teased, using her best Southern drawl. Ever since that night in Bermuda, Billy had continued to address Victoria as Miss Victoria.

"I'm good. Just got out of a meeting discussing the next up-and-coming disasters about to descend upon the world."

"Must be nice." Kat leaned back in her chair and put her stilettos on the desk. "Talking 'bout the next great disaster all day long. Happy bunch."

"We do it over a nice breakfast spread too. Makes it even more fun. What's going on, Kat?"

"Say hello to the new President of Development. I'm now a woman to be reckoned with, hence the new shoes I have nicely displayed for you on my new executive desk. Check the photo I just sent you."

Victoria put down her water bottle as a smile spread across her face. "Congratulations, Kat! I knew you would run that group. How does it feel? And shit, those shoes! They're a thing of beauty," Victoria said as she scrolled through her text shot.

"Absolutely fabulous. As it should. The increase in pay and bonus potential didn't hurt either." Kat took her shoes off the desk and sat forward in her chair. "How's the creator of the newest department at Acker, Smith & McGowen and the firm's leading insurance expert doing?"

"I'm good. Really, good. I love what I'm doing, which is a far cry from how most of the other associates who came on board with me feel. I get to travel to exotic places and usually by private jet. Hard to complain." Victoria smiled, feeling really good about where she sat in her career.

"When are they naming you department chair and giving you a partnership?"

"Don't know, and I highly doubt I will ever be named department chair or get a partnership anytime soon," Victoria responded feeling a twinge of, something's not right about that, crawl into her head.

"I don't get it," Kat said, in her I'm not pleased with that answer tone. "You created a new area of expertise at the firm. You're also the one at the firm who knows the most about insurance. And, let's not forget that you're the reason Fontaine transferred all of its insurance business over to Highline. What do you mean you don't know? Haven't you asked?"

"Kat, it's not the same as a family business. The firm follows certain rules and set paths. There's no way they'll make an associate a department chair or push me ahead of schedule into partnership."

"Well, okay. I get that. I guess. But then vice chair? What's the problem with that?"

Victoria tapped her pen against her desk. "I don't know what's the problem with that. No one has said a word to me."

Kat knew that she was making Victoria anxious. She could hear the pen tapping, but she felt it was for her own good. "Well, then, more money? Money is good. Have they given you a shit-ton in bonuses or a huge raise?"

"No, nothing. You rise with your classmates in lockstep form until the firm decides one or more of you are ready for partnership. And then and only then, will the firm differentiate you from the pack." Victoria felt her head beginning to pound.

"I don't get it. Aren't you bringing in more money than your classmates?"

Victoria nodded. "Yes, by far. The nearest contender is not even close. I beat him by almost five times the revenue."

"And yet you're being paid the same?"

"And yet I'm being paid the same. Yes. And it sucks."

"Then why don't you talk to them? Bring in your numbers, summarize what you've done for the firm and ask for additional money or partnership or even better, both. Shake things up. They would be absolutely crazy not to give it to you."

"Because, Kat, that's just not the way things work. I don't want to piss them off, because if I do, I will either become persona non grata or lose what I've built so far. Coming from a family-owned business, you wouldn't understand."

That was the second time Victoria had made a point about Kat working for her family's business and it was starting to really piss off Kat. There was nothing Kat hated more, and Victoria knew it, than the implication she had gotten to where she was because she was family in a family business. Oh, she knew she got her break because of that, but her father was a tough taskmaster, and any promotion or salary increase had to be supported by quantifiable positive change for the company.

"Listen, V, you have nothing to lose. You know if things don't go well or if anything should happen, we'll hire you. We need an in-house insurance expert and risk manager, and you'd be perfect. Over the next year, I'm looking at scheduling five new developments in five of the hottest vacation spots in the world. Just think of the legitimate business trips we could take together. We would love to have you working with us."

Victoria smiled and stopped her tapping and thought for a moment.

"Really, V, don't let them define you. You're not what they're making you feel. You're not one of many and you are certainly not a cog in their wheel. You're not stuck."

Victoria began to really hear what Kat was saying. Believing that she had to wait at least six years for partnership when she was doing all the things her partners did was what her classmates would have done. Why not? Why not ask? What harm could come from that?

"You know, you're right. I'm going to not only ask for more money, but also to be bumped ahead on the partnership track for the end of this next year. One of the current equity partners did it five years ago for the same reason, because of the income he was bringing into the firm, so why shouldn't they do the same for me?"

"Exactly. Why shouldn't they? And if they won't, why won't they? May as well know now instead of spending another few years banging your head against the wall and bringing money to the boys that they aren't intending to share with you."

Victoria had already begun setting out bullet points of her accomplishments on her legal pad while she continued talking. "Kat, I gotta go. Will you and your dad look this over before I send it on to the big boys?"

"Of course, we'd love to. Send it through when you're ready."

As soon as Victoria was off the call, she finished drafting her list of accomplishments and then buzzed Mary. She asked her to take her chicken scratch and make it look beautiful and to add the projected revenue for the portions of the Highline project that were her direct responsibility.

By late that evening, Victoria had finished her summary, gathered the revenue history and projections, and pushed *send*. All she had to do now was wait to hear from Kat and her father. She was so hyper she knew she would not be able to sleep, at least not right away. Since she didn't want to run outside so late at night, she left the office and headed to her apartment to reorganize an already pristine closet.

The next morning, Victoria had just finished her Saturday run when her phone vibrated with a text from Kat, instructing her to check her personal email. As soon as she let herself into her apartment, she poured herself a cup of strong, black coffee and went over to log on to her personal account. She found a redlined version of the personal accomplishment summary she had sent to Kat and her father.

Victoria picked up her phone and dialed Kat. "Hey. I just finished looking at the changes. Can we bring your dad in for the call? I have some questions and want to hear both of your comments together."

"Yup. He should be back from golf by now. Hold on."

Victoria was so antsy waiting in the phone silence that she got up and began pacing back and forth from her kitchen to her office area. Finally, she heard the lines click back to life.

"V? Dad?" Kat said.

"I'm here, baby," Kat's dad replied in his usual lazy and comforting Texas drawl.

"Me too," said Victoria.

"Well, what do you know, Kat. We are in the presence of one of the rising titans of the mighty insurance industry. I feel like we're not worthy."

Victoria laughed, "Thanks Anthony. It means a ton to me to hear you say that. But really, guys, what do you think and most important, what do you think I should do? Should I ask to be put on the fast track and considered for partnership before next year's end? Should I ask to jump ahead of my class in salary? Here's the downside, though," Victoria said as she paced, "I've heard that any type of request to be noticed ahead of your class or out of sequence of associate-to-partner track is considered bad form. Like you only care about yourself and not others. I'm told it's viewed as selfish. What do you think?"

"I think it's bullshit, V. That's what I think. Daddy, you're more level-headed and even tempered than I am. What do you think?" Kat said sounding exasperated.

"Well, here's what I can tell you from years and years of being in business, first with partners, and then on my own. First, some people can be trusted and some can't. Simple, right, but finding those in business who have your back is key. So find those who have your back at the firm and talk to them about this. Don't let their opinion stop you from doing what you think you need to do, but try to line them up to support you once you do it. Second, when you do good work, and particularly when it's better than others, then you should be rewarded for that work. Otherwise, unless you own the business, if you don't get rewarded, what's the point? And finally, when someone threatens you for asking for what you're entitled to, it's definitely time to move on. There are people out there who will appreciate what you bring to the table, so don't be afraid of the unknown."

Victoria listened and she began to feel another adrenaline rush, even though she had just finished her run. She knew what he was saying made sense, but she also knew that if she went forward with this plan, she might be out of a job or put on the penalty track. "What if they get pissed or think that I'm taking too much credit? After all, I didn't bring the client or the business to the firm. I just worked on what was brought to the firm."

"Okay, that's a fair point," Anthony responded. "Let's look at that for a moment. Didn't you work on the first part of the project? In other words, weren't you the one who was assigned the task of determining whether and how Highline could operate in each of these United States?"

"Yes. That took months of my time."

"Then didn't you make a presentation to the board about your findings?"

"Well, eventually yes. But that was after I presented to one of our managing partners and the team."

"Go on. What happened next?"

"Then we orchestrated the rollout of Highline's first insurance policy, which was a success, and then I began a new department, so to speak, at the firm."

Anthony interrupted, "Let me ask, did your firm have the ability to do this type of work before you began all of this?"

"No. Not really. It had done transaction work for insurance companies before. You know, working on mergers and acquisitions and other similar things, but nothing like what we're currently doing for this company."

"As far as I can see, you're not saying anywhere in the summary of your work that you're responsible for bringing the client in the door. Correct?"

Victoria finally felt calm enough to sit on her sofa. "Of course not. No."

"Well, have you accomplished more than your classmates?"

"The numbers say I have."

"Victoria, that's my point. All of these things you're talking about in your summary are a direct result of your good and hard work. If they don't recognize you as the star you are or if they try to make you feel that you're bad or out of place for asking for recognition, why are you there? What's the point?"

There was a long pause on the phone.

"Yeah, Victoria," Kat piped in, "why are you there? I mean it's not like you're working for your family so that you have ties to these people other than work, and it certainly isn't to get an attagirl at the end of the day. Remember your ultimate goal."

Victoria sat up straighter on the sofa and said quietly, almost to herself, "To get to the top. To have the power to control my destiny."

"Well, you ain't gonna get it by not taking risks. Right, Daddy?" Kat asked.

"Listen, Victoria. I know it seems easy for Kat to say things like that because she works for her family. And in one sense it does make things easier, but in another sense, it makes things tougher. But even so, her point is well placed. If what you want is to rise to the top, then you must be working somewhere where they want that to happen too. If they won't let that happen, then why are you there? The place is not aligned with your goals."

Victoria was writing thoughts that were coming into her head as she listened: *what reaction, partners, first female and power.*

"So I say go for it, Victoria. Unless, of course, you're happy to wait in line, while you continue to work above the line. Which makes no sense to me, but some people don't mind. They want the security of the job. Nothing wrong with that."

"Thanks, guys. I know what I'm doing. I'm going for it."

"V, I'll call you later, and Daddy, thanks."

"Okay, Kat, and thanks, Anthony. I feel better. I know the path I'm taking, and I got this," Victoria said as she stood and began to pace again.

"Honey, any time. You know that. You and Kat are my two up-and-coming business moguls. Not much I enjoy more than watching you two walk into a room and having the boys think there's nothing much going on in those pretty little heads of yours other than shopping. Throws 'em off guard. Love it."

As soon as Victoria was off the phone, she reviewed the redlined version Kat and her father had sent one more time, accepted most of their suggested changes, and then placed a call to Armond. He was the one she could trust. No question. Anyway, she felt she needed to give him a warning before she pushed the button sending a potentially volatile email to the troika and the partnership committee. All hell could break loose, and she didn't want Armond blindsided.

Victoria dialed Armond's cell phone and cringed as she listened while the phone continued to ring. Armond absolutely loathed to be bothered on Saturday mornings. He considered it his one respite and had declared it the only time he was off-limits. Typically, during what he referred to as his sacred time, he turned off his phone, or so he had told Victoria. Breathing faster with each ring, she jumped up and began to pace again.

"This better be good," Armond growled.

God, he sounded sleepy and pissed. Victoria closed her eyes, took a breath, and rushed out, "Hi, Armond. I'm so sorry to bother you. I know this is your personal time. I would not have called you if it wasn't important."

"So far, nothing good. You have ten seconds tops to capture my attention before I hang up. I only answered because it was you."

"I want to give you a heads-up about something I'm about to do. I'm about to send an email to the troika and the partnership committee setting out my accomplishments and the revenue I've been responsible for bringing into the firm. I'm asking for an accelerated path to partnership and an immediate increase in salary."

There was a loud crashing noise from the other end of the phone, followed by "son of a bitch," and then silence. The phone was dead. Victoria stopped pacing and stared at the face of her phone. Just as she was about to hit redial, her phone rang.

"What the hell did you say?" Armond asked in his very low I'm so unbelievably coiled right now, if I was a snake I would strike and bite the shit out of you voice.

"Ummm, are you all right? What was that crash?"

"That crash was me pouring hot coffee on my hand instead of the cup, because one of my associates, the one who I have taken under my wing and mentored and raised from attorney birth, is about to commit professional suicide and take me along with her."

"Armond. Listen. Just give me a minute. I'm not taking you along with me anywhere. You can say you had no idea or that you told me not to do it or that you disagree and don't think I'm that great. Say whatever works for you. I understand completely. But I need to do what I need to do. I'm making a ton of money for the firm, working insane hours, taking no vacations, always on call for Highline. I'm still getting paid the same as my classmates, who are not bringing in even fifty percent of the revenue I am, nor are they in charge of projects the way I am, nor have they developed a whole new line of business for the firm."

Armond pushed his uninjured hand through his heavy wave of hair. "Listen, V, I know what you've done and so do they. Your time will come. But you need to let it come. There is a process. You can't change it."

"Listen, Armond. I know. And I realize I might be put on the slow track to nowhere if this pisses them off. But I need to know where I stand. I want to be an equity partner, sooner rather than later. There are no women there yet. Which is another topic I won't go into right now. So let's see what they do with this. Worst case, they say no."

"Let's meet for coffee in an hour to discuss. You need to calm down and think. Meet me at the bistro on Rush and State at eleven. We'll discuss all the ups and downs of your plan."

"No. Armond, I respect your opinion immensely. You're my mentor and I'm lucky enough to consider you one of my closest friends. But, no. I've already decided and I know you'll only try to talk me out of it. And I just might listen. Just say you had no idea. That's why I didn't email it to you. I know that one of the first things they'll do is see if you're behind it or support it and they'll check our email traffic.

Victoria heard a long, deep sigh. "Damn it, V. This is unheard of. They'll think you're ungrateful for the opportunity they gave you. They can crucify you, V. You have no idea."

"Armond, they gave me the opportunity, that's true. But I took it and ran with it and made it work. That's all I'm saying. Give me what I'm worth. Nothing more, nothing less. It's not like I joined a sorority where some weird, kind of never-ending loyalty is expected in exchange for teaching me a secret handshake. It's business, after all."

Armond recognized Victoria's tone and knew there was nothing more he could say. But she was wrong, he thought. It was indeed like joining a sorority, or really more like a cult, and unwavering loyalty and a no-questions-asked type of respect was exactly what was expected. Sighing, he asked, "When are you going to do it?"

"Now. As soon as we hang up. Shall I copy you or leave you out of it completely?"

"Copy me. What the hell. It's happening, and they may as well see that I at least know what's going on, even if I can't control my associate."

"Will do. Call me anytime if you want to talk over the weekend or we'll talk next week. Wish me luck."

"You'll need it, my pet. And that is the understatement of the year."

The minute Victoria was off the phone, she walked over to her laptop, read the final version one last time, composed a suitable short, introductory email and in the subject category wrote, *Victoria Rodessa—request for partnership candidacy*. She added Armond's name to the copy line and pressed send. It was done. She sat for a minute and tried to drink her coffee. She got back up yet again, put her running shoes on, and decided this was a day for firsts. The first time she asked for a promotion and the first time she went for two runs in one day. She'd see how they both turned out soon enough.

CHAPTER
26

MONDAY AFTERNOON, KAT heard a sharp knock and looked up from the motion she was editing for court to see Cassie peek her head around her office door. "It's gaining speed and they're now predicting landfall tomorrow at about five in the evening, right about rush hour. You might want to take a look."

"Shit," Kat replied. She picked up the remote and clicked on the television built into her office wall.

Cassie made herself comfortable on the white leather sofa Kat had bought for herself to celebrate her promotion. After listening to the weather bunny do her best to use the big words necessary to convey the path and speed of the approaching hurricane, Kat got up and went back to her desk. "Contact all our managers on the East Coast. Set a conference call for one hour from now. I don't care where they are or what they're doing. Attendance on the call is not an option. Trigger our disaster-response protocol and let them know the call is phase one. They need to be prepared to discuss their respective protocols for each of their buildings."

"Got it. I'll let you know when they're all on line."

Cassie turned to leave, but Kat stopped her. "Also, print the protocols and bring them to me, so I have them for the call. Call our vendors and make sure they're tracking this. Get confirmation from each of them by the time of our call, that we have their guarantee that they will get to our buildings first if anything happens. If we're not first on their list, we better be second, and I'll want to know why we're not first."

"Got it. Anything else?"

"Yes." Kat sat at her desk and held up the brief she had been working on. "This needs to be filed today. Give me another fifteen minutes with it. No more. Then get it out of my hands and on file with the court."

"Got it." Cassie was almost out the door when Kat stopped her again.

"One more thing." Kat dug in her purse and pulled out some cash. "A large cappuccino and something chocolate, please. Get whatever you want as well. I have a feeling we'll be here a while."

As soon as Cassie shut the door, Kat opened her live webcams of Fontaine Development's buildings. Kat then pulled up the satellite maps on her second screen and zeroed in on the first four Fontaine properties in Hurricane Ileana's path.

Fontaine Development owned twelve high-rise buildings located along the East Coast, beginning in Southern Florida and stretching to Atlantic City and the boardwalk in New Jersey. Five were hotels in various stages of development, which Fontaine would keep and have managed by an outside group. The other buildings were finished and consisted of three hotels and four mixed commercial and residential buildings.

Hurricane Ileana was over the Caribbean and gaining speed. The computer-generated path projected her making landfall in Miami first and then turning and traveling right up the coast. Kat emailed Cassie to pull the insurance information for all buildings in the projected path and to set an immediate call with her brothers and father.

Ten minutes later Cassie buzzed Kat, "Your brothers and father are on the line."

"Great, thanks, Cassie. Make sure we're off in time for the next call."

"You got it," Cassie answered as she walked in and took her seat.

"Hey all, how are my big brothers doing today and how is my favorite father?"

Her eldest brother, Troy, who oversees the development of their properties on the East Coast got right to the point. "I'm doing like shit out here. We are in a full-blown state of emergency to lock down all the cranes and equipment and building components before this bitch comes roaring through. I'm losing my crew, the majority of whom left already, as they're all worried about their families and property. I could use another ten hands here to get all that has to be done finished in time."

"Have you tried raising people on the Internet to help? You might find a good ten who are willing to jump in to help for some quick cash. If it will help, Cassie can run the search and send the best ten to wherever you need," Kat said, speaking loudly as the wind in the background on Troy's end had picked up.

"That's a great idea, Kat." Anthony jumped in. "Cassie, why don't you run with that plan. Track with Troy and send whomever you chose to wherever he needs next. If Kat doesn't mind, why don't you go start that right now."

"Will do," Cassie responded as she left Kat's office to begin the search.

"Kat, give me a report on our other buildings," Anthony said.

"We have a conference call with the building managers in thirty minutes. We'll run through our disaster protocols for each building and work toward whatever help they may need. I also have a meeting with my clerks on the insurance to put all the proper parties on notice. I'll of course do that for all our facilities including the ones in development."

"Okay, then call any of us if you need help. Buzz," Anthony said to his youngest son, "your job is to stay tight with Troy. Make sure he is not taking any unnecessary chances. Keep in close contact with him. I want to know where he is every step of the way."

"Got it, Dad. Troy, turn on your tracker device on your phone, will you and I'll alert our security team as well."

"Okay, guys, I suggest we touch base later this evening to get a rundown. Troy, I know it will be hard, but do everything you can to be on that call or at least let us know you are okay if you can't get on that call so we know about you and the status of our buildings." Just as Kat was hanging up, Cassie buzzed, letting her know Victoria was on the line.

"Hey V. I'm about to get on a conference call. Can I get back to you later?" Kat asked just as Cassie poked her head in and held up five fingers.

"I'm calling to see if you need anything. I've been watching the storm and thought there might be something I can do. Calls I can make? Anything you need?" Victoria said. "So just give me a call when you're through or text me. I'm here for you."

The door opened again, and this time Cassie came into Kat's office with her pad and sat in one of the two chairs in front of the desk, nodding to indicate that conference attendees were on line and waiting. "Yeah, since we switched our business over to that insurance company of yours, make sure it pays our claims if anything happens. V, I gotta go. I'll call you when I can." Kat pressed the button for the other line and let Cassie do her thing. "Hello everyone. Let's begin with a roll call, please."

Once the role call was complete, Cassie nodded at Kat. "Good evening, everyone," Kat began. "I know it's late on the East Coast, but Hurricane Ileana has picked up speed and, as I'm sure you're all aware, landfall is predicted for early tomorrow evening. We'll begin by reviewing our new disaster protocols, followed by a report from Cassie on her communications with our disaster vendors for each region, and then we'll close with any problems or questions. I want to remind you all that there are absolutely no stupid questions. I mean that. If you're not sure, ask. If you think we discussed it in the past, but aren't sure, ask. The only thing that will piss me off when this is all over is if you didn't think to ask something or consider doing something that could have saved a life or preserved our buildings." Kat paused. "Okay, let's begin. Donna, your two buildings look like they'll be the first in line. Why don't you start us off by running through your disaster protocols, where you are in the process, and whether you're running into any problems or issues?"

Hours later, Kat sat in her high-rise condominium eating take-out and allowing herself to indulge in a glass of her favorite red wine, after having tried to relax in a very steamy hot shower. Cozy in her favorite sweats, she walked over to her windows and looked out at the calm and starry sky over Houston, while the weather channel's breaking bulletins about Hurricane Ileana played over and over in the background. Kat sighed heavily and took a big gulp of her wine as she heard the meteorologist (apparently now that the storm was serious, weather bunny had been relegated to a different skin-tight-red-dress-required job), announce that Ileana had picked up speed yet again. She was now a Cat 4, with predictions having her at a Cat 5 by the time she reached the Florida coast. According to the weather report, the water temperature was just right to encourage the wind speeds to continue to increase.

Kat called Donna. "Hey, boss," Donna answered almost immediately. "I thought you might call after she moved up to a Cat 4."

"How're you doing?"

"Not too bad. We have seventy percent of the buildings boarded and we're scheduled to finish the rest by about three in the morning. We've issued warnings both by way of email and recorded telephone messages to all of the residence owners and to the commercial lessees. We posted the signs we all agreed on during our call. I'll send you a picture of how they turned out. Our emergency line is activated and staffed. We've already been responding to questions from our residents. I'm not gonna lie, it's getting creepy. Hold on a minute."

While she waited for Donna to come back on the line, Kat walked into her kitchen and refilled her glass, figuring she was going to need a bit more to calm her down. Wandering back to her living room, she picked up the remote and turned the channels. Just then Donna came back on the line. "Shit, Kat, turn on CNN."

"I'm looking right at it. Shit," Kat repeated. Both women were quiet as they listened to the mayor of Miami.

"We are issuing an evacuation order for the city effective immediately. Within the last fifteen minutes we have been advised that Hurricane Ileana is now a Category 5 hurricane. This means it has sustained wind speeds of 157 miles per hour or higher. We are ordering that everyone evacuate from Miami city limits and Miami Dade County by ten tomorrow morning. After that time, public services including police, fire and emergency personnel, will no longer respond to individual

calls until the storm has passed and some semblance of order is restored. Again, let me repeat…"

Turning down the volume Kat went back to Donna. "That's the first time I've ever heard a public official tell the people that elected him that they may be on their own. I wonder how that will go over reelection time."

"I'm not surprised," Donna said. "In fact, after the past storms down here and Hurricane Sandy, I thought this directive would come earlier. I've been waiting for it, so as soon as we hang up, I'll initiate our final protocol and evacuation order."

"Promise whatever you need to promise to get our guys to move faster so they finish the boarding as soon as humanly possible. I want our staff to knock on each of the resident's doors immediately to let them know about the evacuation order and that they must be out by tomorrow morning. You need to revise our announcements to let the residents know that there will be no one from property management available after nine in the morning and that we insist everyone follow the mayor's order. In the morning, then, Donna, I want you and your team to begin knocking on the doors by no later than eight to ensure that everyone is out or if they refuse to leave, that they know no one will be there to help. Keep a roster documenting that you went to all of the units in each of the buildings."

"Wait, Kat. Do you mean you want us to break protocol and not even leave a skeletal staff at the building? I don't think we should do that."

"That's exactly what I'm telling you. There is an executive order issued by the mayor to get out. There is no way I'm putting you or anyone else at risk. If anyone decides not to follow my instructions on this, tell them I'll fire them immediately when this is over. And Donna, just so you're very clear, that goes for you too."

Kat was feeling guilty. Damn it, she should have flown out earlier that afternoon so she could be there, she thought. But there was nothing she could do about it now. Anyway, Troy was there and he would be the family boots on the ground. "Copy me on all emails so I can track the progress."

"Will do. I'll text you as soon as the boarding is complete."

"Okay. Oh, and Donna, call me anytime, day or night. Whatever you need. Even if it's just to say you're scared shitless or you just need to hear someone's voice. I don't care. I'll pick up no matter the time."

"Thanks. My phone is not leaving my side. It's my new best friend." Kat heard banging noises in the background. "Kat, I've gotta go. The emergency crew is heading to the lobby and then to finish the windows in the common areas. I need to be with them and then get into the office and send out the evacuation notices."

"Go. Call if you need. We'll talk first thing in the morning."

Hanging up, Kat poured herself a smidgen more wine. As soon as she took her first sip, she remembered she hadn't called Victoria back. She pushed speed dial.

Victoria picked up on the first ring. "Hey, how're you doing? I've been thinking about you. I bet you're insane."

"Exactly on the nose. I am insane. But at least I'm safe. The damn storm is tracking directly toward seven of our projects. Five of which are our most valuable properties in the east, ringing in at over eight hundred million in combined value. That's not even including the income from rental, parking, assessments, and all those additional items. Not to mention the lives at stake. There's always idiots who ignore the evacuation warnings and then are stunned that they can't get out of their building or leave their neighborhood."

"Our Miami office shut down as of 5:00 pm. Only a skeletal security staff remains, and we've ordered all the employees to work from home or if that's not safe, to leave the area until the all clear is given," Victoria replied.

"Well, your security staff is going to have to leave as well. I don't know if you saw, but the Miami mayor was just on the news issuing an evacuation order." Kat's phone began beeping. "Listen, V, my father's on the other line. It's going to be a long forty-eight hours. Wish us luck. I'll talk to you later."

CHAPTER
27

OPENING HER EMAILS, the next morning, Victoria found two marked as "important." One from the troika to the "firm," containing information about the approaching storm, the evacuation of Miami and the closure of the Miami office. The email outlined how business was to be conducted with the now closed Miami office. The second "important" email was from Billy to Victoria copied to Adam, Trever and Armond.

> I received your missive. We have a pending disaster on the East Coast to contend with at this time. We will respond at the appropriate time. We expect you will continue with your duties and responsibilities as a member of the Highline team.

Mary walked in with Victoria's cappuccino, as she did almost every morning. Mary loved working for Victoria and couldn't be happier. Over a year ago, Victoria had insisted that Mary accompany her on trips to Bermuda, arguing to the powers that be that Mary knew almost as much about Highline as she did, and working with Mary by her side allowed Victoria to accomplish three times as much as she could without her. So, Mary had been to Bermuda and The Western Will five different times so far, and by way of the firm jet, no less. Mary had worked at the firm for twenty-five years and had worked with all shapes and sizes of attorneys. Victoria was different. She had grit and guts. She did what had to be done, and said what needed to be said. Most of the lawyers Mary had worked with said whatever the client wanted to hear, not really caring about the good of the client, but rather knowing that if they continued to say what the client wanted to hear, chances were good that they could continue billing and the client would continue paying. Mary worried about Victoria. She knew the troika tolerated her outspoken nature for only one reason. They needed her, for now. She had done a flawless job of bringing Highline to the market, which in turn had generated significant revenue.

"Morning, Mary."

"Good morning, Ms. V," Mary said, setting the cappuccino on Victoria's desk. "Armond called. He wants you to call him the minute you walk in. He sounds stressed."

"When is he not stressed?" Victoria said, picking up her coffee and taking a sip as she dialed Armond.

Before she could say a word, she heard Armond say, "I'll be right there. Don't move," and the line went dead.

Not more than five minutes later, her door opened and closed firmly. Victoria looked up from her emails and waited. She knew Armond expected her to react to the email or to ask what had happened or if he had heard anything. She refused to bite. Instead, she folded her hands together and sat still. Not an easy feat, she thought, feeling proud of herself for this unusual show of patience.

"Give me a pen and that legal pad," Armond demanded.

Victoria slid it across her desk and watched as Armond took his time writing something he was shielding from her view.

When he looked up, Victoria could no longer take it. "Well?" she asked.

"Well, this about sums up your situation." Armond turned the pad around so it was facing Victoria and shoved it back toward her across the desk. Victoria felt her stomach drop. He had drawn a game of Hang Man, only he had filled in the spaces with her name and finished the stick figure so it was clear it was her hanging in the noose. Great.

Victoria knew she had to compose herself. "Armond, what are you, five? What does this mean? Am I fired? Should I pack up and leave?" Victoria didn't realize how mad she was until she felt herself stand up and begin to open her desk drawers to pack her personal items. She had no intention of playing some stupid cat-and-mouse game, and particularly not if the cat was Armond.

"V, sit down and calm down," Armond ordered.

"Not unless you intend to tell me what's going on and where I stand. I refuse to be treated like some sort of an idiot and with disrespect simply because I dared to ask for more."

Armond stood up and walked over to her office door and made sure it was shut all the way.

"What are you doing?" Victoria asked.

"Please, V. Sit down and listen. Have I steered you wrong yet?"

Victoria thought about all the political traps Armond had so far cleared out of her way, and sat. And waited, again, while Armond was silent. Okay, that's long enough, Victoria thought.

"Listen, Armond. I don't know what's going on, but either you tell me now or I'll assume your drawing is an accurate representation of my career at this firm and I'll pack my things and go."

Armond ran his hand through his mass of hair, trying unsuccessfully to move the one unruly wavy lock off of his forehead and back into slicked down perfection. "Okay. What

I'm telling you is absolutely confidential. My career will be over if you say a word. Do you understand?"

"Yes. I get it. I won't say anything. When have I ever? Now, what happened?"

"Okay. Not more than two hours after you sent that stupid email of yours that I told you not to send, the troika had me on a conference call. All three of them were on the line."

"You've got to be kidding me. Why would they take that kind of time to deal with one little request from one of their hundreds of associates? It just doesn't make any sense."

"Are you insane? It makes perfect sense. Law firms are about partner control of associates, and this relationship is built on hundreds of years of tradition. Firm revenue depends on associates working like slaves for seven or eight years. And then, only then, a small percentage of those worker bees get to share in the bowl of honey. Your email is dangerous. It's a threat to that control. At least that's how they feel."

Armond stood and leaned forward, bending his long frame over Victoria's desk, and whispered, "They're pissed, Victoria. Really, really pissed. Adam thought you should be booted out of the firm immediately. You're lucky the other two didn't agree. Billy was the most vocal defending not firing you today. But don't get it twisted. He doesn't give a rat's ass about you. He's worried only about how that would affect his reputation and who would take your place with Highline. In fact, Billy called me privately after the conference call to let me know that you made him look like a horse's ass in front of Adam and Trever and that they criticized him for letting you get too much power and that he's holding me personally responsible to get you under control."

Victoria saw red. She knew she should calm down and not overreact until she had a chance to think, but she knew one thing for sure. She would not stay at a place that did not want her. She stood up and began opening her desk drawers.

"What are you doing?" Armond jumped up and went around to shut the desk drawers, putting things back in while Victoria continued to take them out.

"I'm packing. Get out of my way," Victoria answered calmly.

"No, you're not. If you do that, they'll know I told you and you'll have single-handedly ruined not only your career, but mine as well. You owe me more than this temper tantrum."

Victoria saw the panic in Armond's face. She paused long enough to hear him say, "Just let me finish." Sitting back down, she waited.

"They told me to scare the shit out of you. Obviously they have no idea you're ready to walk if you don't get the response you're after. The whole hanging man thing was Adam's idea. Not mine."

Victoria finally recovered enough to respond. "That's sick, Armond, really. I mean, telling you to draw a figure of me hanging because I asked to be put on the fast track to partnership is really out of whack. And worse still is the fact that you did it. I thought you had at least some balls, Armond."

"Not really, Victoria. It's really not out of whack, whatever that means. This is their firm after all, and they intend to continue to run it in a certain way. All firms have an order and designated path to partnership. Your little email challenges that. They reminded me that they expect any associate who is a serious contender for partnership to do good work and work his or her ass off for six to seven years. So why should you be treated differently?"

Victoria gripped her coffee and walked around to the seat across from her desk and next to Armond. She didn't want anyone to overhear their conversation so she leaned in close to Armond. "Because I am different, Armond. I'm the number one revenue-producing associate at the firm. And not just by a crevice. But by a canyon. I also started a new department specializing in insurance coverage. Something the firm never had before. No other associate has ever done that, as far as I know. So why not reward me?"

Mary knocked on the door. "Victoria, Armond, sorry to interrupt, but Victoria, you've been summoned to Billy's office. He told me to interrupt whatever it is you're doing and tell you to go to his office immediately."

"Okay, thanks, Mary."

As soon as the door closed, Victoria jumped up out of her chair and walked around her desk to grab a pen and a legal pad, as well as her phone.

"Crap, V. I know that look. What are you planning to do?" Armond asked.

Victoria felt the familiar "look the fuck out," sensation building inside. It was the same sensation that pushed her to do things, which in retrospect, she sometimes wished she hadn't. In her first year of law school, it pushed her to be the first idiot in her criminal law class to volunteer to answer the questions thrown, one after the other, by their crazy yet TV-famous criminal law professor, who liked nothing more than to scare the shit out of his students. It was that day, when without even knowing each other, Kat tried to push Victoria's hand down before she was called on. It was too late and the professor proceeded to summarily crucify her.

Victoria decided she didn't want to talk about it any further with Armond. What more was there to say anyway? What's done is done. Best to simply deal with it, whatever "it" might be. As she walked toward the door to head up to Billy's office, she turned back to look at Armond's worried face. She felt almost sorry for him. "Don't worry. I'm not suicidal. Everything will be fine."

CHAPTER
28

THE NEXT TELEPHONE call Donna would make, as soon as she left the last of the two properties she managed for Fontaine, would be to Kat. But before she could leave, she had two more units to check, and then she would help her husband, who was downstairs, load the office electronics into their van to protect them from destruction. Taking the elevator up to the thirtieth floor, she stepped out into a burst of wind and held on to the railings and walked the curve of the building until she reached the west end. She knocked on the penthouse door and got no response, so she moved over to knock on the expansive windows that formed a good portion of the wall. No one answered and there was no sound. She cupped her hands around her face as she leaned forward onto the glass to see inside. There was no movement. Good. One down and one to go, Donna thought.

As she traveled to the other side of the building, she felt the wind grow even stronger, and its hot, humid breath licked her body, leaving it wet enough to stick her shirt to her back. As soon as she knocked on the east penthouse door, she thought she heard a faint noise. She knocked again but this time couldn't hear anything. She moved over to try to see through the sheer curtains covering the window and was sure she saw movement. She went back to the door and turned the knob. Much to her surprise, the door flew open and she felt as if she had been sucked inside, while the wind pushed her from behind.

As soon as her eyes adjusted to the darkened room, Donna was stunned to see the Hendersons, both in their late seventies, huddled together in the dark on their living room sofa, with blankets all around and over them and their two pug dogs tucked in the middle.

"Mr. and Mrs. Henderson, what are you still doing here?"

"Donna. Why are you still here? Now you take yourself right out of here just like the mayor said," Mrs. Henderson said, visibly shivering.

"I'm not going anywhere without the two of you. Now get up and let's go. My husband's downstairs and we'll help you. You can come with us."

"But this is our home and we have nowhere else to go. We're not leaving, and we can't leave Juno and Blue," Mrs. Henderson said as she hugged her boys tight.

"I tried to get her to go." Mr. Henderson looked helpless. "She just refused."

"Listen. I'm not asking you, I'm telling you. I cannot leave you here." Donna reached for her two-way and let her husband know what was going on. While she waited for Dave, Donna spent the next ten minutes walking through the penthouse to ensure everything was as secure as it could be. When she came back into the main room, her husband was walking in the front door and she felt a huge wave of relief.

"Dave, this is Mr. and Mrs. Henderson. This is my husband, Dave."

Dave walked over to the couple and politely shook their hands as if they had all the time in the world and the winds just outside the front door weren't gusting upwards of sixty miles an hour. "Nice to meet you. And who are these two handsome guys?" he said, petting the dogs.

"Juno and Blue," Mrs. Henderson answered. "But listen here, I know just what you're doing and we're not leaving. I don't care how nice you are."

At that, Mr. Henderson stood up and put both the dogs on their leashes. Turning to look at his wife, he held out his hand and said, "We're leaving, Lila. We're going with these nice folks. We're not gonna risk all of our lives because you're a stubborn old woman. Now get up off your behind and git."

The septuagenarians did a nice job of staring each other down, Donna thought. In fact, it was one of the finest stare-downs Donna had ever seen. But they didn't have all day. The clock was ticking, and if they weren't out of there by ten, the mayor would close some of the exit routes and they might end up stranded. The ocean water was rising fast and beginning to flood some of the major roads.

Just when Donna thought Dave was going to have to hoist the old lady over his shoulders, Mrs. Henderson said, "Well, if that don't beat all, you old coot, talking to me like that. Well, then, I guess I got no choice in the matter. Let's go."

It took a few minutes for the group to figure out the safest configuration they could walk in to give them the best chance to block the wind and flying debris. As soon as Dave opened the front door though, it seemed to have a mind of its own as it tried to fly off its hinges to join the other debris already cluttering the sky in a mad frolic. Dave had to fight to get it closed at the same time he pushed the Hendersons against the outside wall of the building to try to shield them with his body. They had to hug the wall. The winds were so strong they could feel a kind of suction trying to pull them toward and over the balcony rail. The dogs were too light and small to move against the force of the winds, so Dave put both of them in his jacket and zipped until only their wet and twitching little black noses peeked out. Once his hands were free of the dogs, Dave put Mrs. Henderson under his arm and led the way in an effort to block some of the wind for Donna as she held on to Mr. Henderson. They could not chance the elevators, so they had to take the stairs. It took at least thirty minutes to get down to the ground floor.

As they began their drive out of the neighborhood, they heard a loud crash and looked back just in time to see the windows, out of what looked like the top ten floors of their building, plucked out of their sockets and tossed into the dark sky. Many of the concrete railings that had been built for safety and surrounded the outside walkways were now hanging by rebar threads.

"My God, Dave, the buildings," Donna said.

"Never mind the buildings. Look," Dave said, pointing to a number of already blocked inlet roads. After traveling a few blocks farther, they came across police who opened a road so they could fall in line with the traffic heading out of the city. As inky darkness began to fall, silence fell within the car. It was only ten fifteen in the morning, but it looked like ten at night. All hell was about to break loose.

CHAPTER
29

A S SHE WALKED into her office, Kat continued to reach out to Donna, but with no luck. Apparently, the cell towers were already down. The last she heard from Donna was a text at six that morning that they were beginning the unit walk-through. Kat dialed Troy. Nothing. She called Frank next, Fontaine's property manager in Ft. Lauderdale. Blessedly, she heard ringing and then Frank's voice on the other end. "Frank, thank God! I can't reach anyone in Miami. What have you heard?"

"Kat, all indications are that we're next after Miami. It's like she's pissed as hell at the Eastern Seaboard and has every intention of showing us all just how much of a bitch she can be," Frank said in a rather excited tone. He wasn't much of a talker and this was more than Kat had ever heard him say at one time.

"Donna. What about her? Have you heard anything?" Kat repeated. She really wasn't ready to focus on the next group of buildings when she didn't know what had happened in Miami.

"We've been in contact throughout the night. Last we spoke, it was about eight this morning and they were working their way through the last of the unit checks. She said

Dave was helping her finish and then they planned to evacuate right from the complex. I haven't heard anything since. But a number of the cell towers are blown according to the news reports. I think it'll be awhile before we hear from her."

"Where are you in your process?" Kat asked.

"We don't yet have an evacuation order, so we aren't as far along."

"What do you mean you aren't as far along?" Kat asked.

"Well, I figured we shouldn't start the final protocol of full boarding and evacuation emails yet. Since the focus has been on Miami, I didn't want to trigger the Ft. Lauderdale disaster budget unless it was absolutely necessary."

Kat wanted to reach through the phone and rip his throat out. She had little patience for stupid. But he was the Fontaine man in charge of Ft. Lauderdale right now, and so he was all they had. She took a deep breath and let it out to try to calm herself before she spoke. "Frank, I want you to listen very carefully. Begin full final protocol immediately. I've made the decision so it won't be on you as far as affecting your expenses at year's end."

"Are you sure, Kat? I mean, it hasn't even hit Miami yet."

"I'm sure. Now in one hour, I want you to call me back with a full status. Got it?" Kat demanded.

"Yup. Got it."

"One more thing," Kat said before he disconnected the line. "If you hear anything, and I mean even one peep or one text out of Donna, I want to know about it immediately."

"Of course. As soon as I hear anything, I'll let you know." Kat heard Frank's name being called in the background.

"Kat, I gotta go. The winds just started kicking up and one of the maintenance men said there's a problem. I'll let you know what's what as soon as I can." Before Kat could respond, the line went dead.

Kat turned back to the news. The storm had picked up speed overnight and was now expected to hit Miami by noon, five hours ahead of the previously predicted landfall. According to the bulletins flashing across the screen, Ileana was currently toggling between a Category 4 and 5, with wind gusts up to one hundred sixty miles per hour and sustained wind speeds of ninety miles per hour. If it kept up at this rate, it would beat the force of any other storm to have hit the Florida coast.

Picking up her office intercom, Kat buzzed Cassie. "Yes, boss?"

"Cassie, bring me our insurance binder. I want our insurer on notice of potential claims for our properties up and down the coast. I'll draft the notice, but I want you to ensure that it goes out tonight."

"Will do. Have you heard from anyone?"

"Only Frank. Donna, not since six in the morning, and it was only a text. Frank heard from her a few hours ago and that was the last time."

"She'll be fine. Shall I send an alert out to all the managers to let us know if they hear from her?"

"Do that. And then get my father on the line for me, please."

The storm hit hours earlier than predicted. The city of Miami, normally bustling and filled with life, was vacant, dark, and dead. The wind ripped around and up and over the high-rise jungle that was Miami. Ileana seemed to delight in the towering buildings, using the narrow paths between them to her advantage to gain even more speed. As she played in the concrete jungle, she learned the taller the building, the faster her speed as she raced to reach the top. Sparks flew high in the air as she gleefully ripped the conduits of electricity from the ground and watched their wires snap like dry twigs.

As Ileana showed off wind speeds never before experienced, she unleashed her other tool of destruction, suction, on the inside of every building. She caused internal walls to crumble like dried crackers, and the building skeletons to shake and moan and twist in ways even the best architects and engineers had never imagined and so had not planned for. Windows popped loudly as they were sucked out. Glass crashed and shards flew about like deadly bullets looking to impale anything in their path. Pipes burst, elevators flooded, and roofs were uplifted only to take flight and land miles away on unsuspecting buildings and cars. As the eye of the storm closed in on Miami, it looked like the end of the world.

Donna had never seen anything like it and she had lived through many Florida hurricanes. For the last three hours, Donna, Dave and the Hendersons had been in a race, trying to outrun the fierce grip of the storm. Their group, along with hundreds of thousands of others fleeing the storm, had been stopped by the sudden green and murky surge of ocean that had come careening over the beaches, through the neighborhoods, and onto the bordering streets and highways. Palm trees over a hundred years old and no less than fifty feet high had been yanked out of the ground and thrown, like giant spears chucked by some angry Greek god, more than two football fields in length inland. They lay across roads and were rammed through windows and even the concrete sides of buildings.

Donna and Dave had kept the Hendersons with them as long as they could. But the water continued to rise and combined with the wind, their heavy SUV began to slide along with the water rushing onto the streets, as if it were a boat being lifted off the shore by the incoming tide. Fearing for the safety of their elderly passengers, Dave waved down some first responders who had commandeered private boats to use in an effort to get people to safety. The elderly and the children were being loaded out of cars first, with those strong enough being asked to swim or slosh their way to safety or to stay in their cars. No advice was being given as to which was the better bet; stay in your car, or make a break for somewhere safer. No choice offered any guarantee of survival, as no one knew whether or when another surge of water would hit, wiping out those who tried to walk or whisking those who chose to stay in their cars out to sea.

As soon as Mr. and Mrs. Henderson and their two dogs were safely on a boat, Donna and Dave decided to abandon their car and all their possessions and make a break for dry land and, hopefully, some form of shelter. After about a half an hour of exhausting and slow work through the murky water, worrying about everything from alligators to live electric wires, Donna said, "Listen." Everything was suddenly still and quiet.

"It's the eye," Dave said. Taking Donna's hand, he pulled and then pushed her exhausted body as fast as he could through the muck and mess. "Donna, this is our best chance to reach safety. I don't know how long we have, but you've got to use every bit of energy you have left to move. We won't get another chance until this is all over."

As exhausted as Donna was, she was more scared. She put her head down and didn't talk as she held on to Dave. She had no idea how long they walked, but after what seemed like hours she heard Dave say, "There it is. There's our safe haven." Looking up, Donna saw a large church on the top of a hill. It had to be at least another mile away, but it was not yet engulfed by water, ripped apart by the wind, or torpedoed with a tree. Smiling to herself, she put her head back down and marched relentlessly forward toward their piece of heaven.

CHAPTER
30

VICTORIA WALKED TOWARD Billy's executive assistant, perched as always behind her ornate desk in her own antechamber outside his cavernous office. Jody guarded the entrance to Billy's office like a marine protecting the President of the United States. She was always dressed impeccably, and with long blonde hair, huge boobs, and nails perfectly coiffed, she was the quintessential executive secretary every red-blooded male dreamed of one day having at his beck and call. Jody lauded her position over the associates and most of the partners. If ever there was an example of power by association, Victoria thought, it was Jody.

Victoria stopped and stood directly in front of Jody's desk and waited for her to finish her call. Of course Jody took her time just to make sure Victoria knew that she, and not Victoria, held all the power. Victoria was used to Jody's bullshit and had let Jody have her day in the past, waiting patiently for the queen of Billy's time and attention to acknowledge her. But today was a new day, and it was the wrong day for Jody to fuck with Victoria. After holding on to her rising temper for about another minute without yet being acknowledged, Victoria turned and walked the length of the hall toward the carved wooden double doors of Billy's office. A smile spread over her face as she heard Jody almost have a coronary as she tried to hang up and sprint around her desk in an effort to beat Victoria to the entrance. Which she did, just a moment before Victoria's outstretched hand hit the levered door handle. That'll teach her to fuck with me, Victoria thought, and watched with unrestrained wonder as Jody literally suctioned her body to his doors like a leach on skin.

"What are you doing?" Jody screeched. "I didn't tell you to go in!"

"Oh, Jody. Yes, I know. I did stand there for a few minutes, right in front of you, in fact. When you didn't even see me, I knew it must have been because you were on an important business call, so I didn't want to interrupt. But, since Billy asked that I see him immediately, I didn't want to be late and have to tell him that I'd been standing outside his office for a while, waiting for you to finish a call. But, if you'd rather I wait out here and then explain that to him," Victoria shrugged her shoulders, "I'm okay either way." Victoria spoke as if each of her words was coated in maple syrup.

When Jody stood there, dumbfounded and not moving, Victoria's tone changed to more of a growl. "Jody, either get out of my way, or announce me now. You have two seconds to make up your mind."

The look that Jody gave Victoria was one of pure panic. "I'll announce you now. Please wait here." As Jody opened the door to slip through, Victoria walked in with her.

"Sir, I'm so sorry," Jody began. "I asked her to wait and she just pushed her way through."

"Jody, it's fine. Will you please excuse us now and close the door on your way out? Oh, wait one minute. Victoria, what would you like? Coffee? Water?"

"I'll have a cappuccino, thanks, Billy."

"Jody, we'll both have skim cappuccinos, please. You take yours fat light, don't you?" Billy looked at Victoria.

"I do, yes." Victoria took a seat in the chair opposite Billy and called over her shoulder, "Thanks, Jody. Oh, and please make mine extra hot and a grande." Victoria smiled as she heard the door slam shut. Turning toward Billy, she was not in the mood to mince words or waste time. If they were going to fire her, she wanted it over and done. "So, what's up? What's so urgent?"

"Victoria, you know you're a valuable part of the Highline operation," Billy said, folding his perfectly manicured hands in front of him.

"I do," Victoria nodded, crossing her legs.

"And while that may be true, no one is irreplaceable. You understand that as well, do you not?" Billy asked as he pushed back his ginormous carved chair, stood and began to walk around his office, requiring Victoria to turn in her chair to follow his movements.

"That's what I hear. Although I do believe that while you may find someone to step into a spot, it doesn't mean that person will do the same quality of work as the other. Don't you agree?"

Billy came back to his desk and sat down. "I do indeed. That is why I want to have this discussion. Obviously, we read your submission and request to be placed on a fast track to partnership and to receive more money immediately. Never, in the now thirteen-year history of the firm, has anyone made this type of request."

Victoria stayed silent, waiting for his point. "I will tell you it did not go over well with my other two partners. Both of them wanted to fire you immediately." Again, there was a long silence. Victoria waited, having no intention of responding until she knew what his point was. "But I intervened on your behalf." Billy stopped doodling on his legal pad and looked directly at her, waiting, for some show of gratitude.

"I do appreciate your show of support, Billy," Victoria said. Still waiting.

"Yes, well, don't get it wrong. I didn't do it just for you. I did it for the firm and for the benefit of our client Highline as well. You're undoubtedly, as you know, the one at the firm with the most knowledge of all facets of their business."

"I do work very hard, Billy," Victoria answered.

"You do. So here is what I have proposed to my partners," he said getting up and walking around to lean back against the front of his desk, which placed his groin awkwardly and directly in front of her face. "Let's get through the storm that is hitting the East Coast and then let's see where we are with the aftermath. Undoubtedly, there will be a barrage of claims filed and they will need to be dealt with before we can focus on too much else. Once we know where we stand, we'll review your request at the appropriate time."

Victoria remained silent. She wasn't sure how she felt. But she knew that she wanted to see the first disaster through with Highline, who she thought of as her client.

"May I give you some advice? Don't be too aggressive, Victoria, particularly as a woman, or the partners will think you're greedy and not grateful for the opportunities the firm has given you. Be patient; in due time the firm will repay you. You have my word."

A quick, hard rap sounded and the outer doors burst open as Jody entered with the two cappuccinos. As Jody served the coffee, Victoria glanced at her phone and saw that she had received an unusual number of text messages in the short time she had been with Billy. Three were from Armond, at least five were from Kat, and a number were weather alerts. She looked up at Billy as he sipped his coffee, obviously waiting for her to respond. Apparently, he was done.

Victoria took her time, tasted her coffee and cleared her throat. She thought about the firm and had to admit that she had been fortunate to have had the Highline opportunity thrown in her lap. Plus, she really didn't want to start over somewhere else with people she neither knew nor trusted. At least at Acker, she knew the poison was in the well and could try to avoid it. Making a quick decision, Victoria stood so she was at eye level with Billy. "Billy, I love working here and I want to be a part of this firm. I'm fine with waiting to discuss this further until after Highline safely weathers this storm. Let's focus on that, and I'll trust the firm and you to stand by your word that if I'm patient, I'll be rewarded." Pausing to glance at her texts, she said, "In fact, Billy, it seems as if the storm has ratcheted up a notch, based on these weather alerts. We need to call an emergency meeting to get the team on board here, and then we need to connect with Bermuda to ensure the proper procedures are up and running for the claims that are sure to come in the door."

"Great minds, Victoria. That was going to be my next suggestion. Why don't you gather our team for a meeting this afternoon? Follow that with a conference call with Bermuda. In the interim, I'll set an emergency call with the board. They'll want to know what's going on and how much of their money is at risk. I'll coordinate with Trever and make sure he's at the meeting and on the call." Billy reached out and clasped Victoria's shoulder. Turning toward the door, he slipped his arm around her shoulder and pulled her close. "I'm glad we had this chat. You're a valuable member of this firm. I hope you feel you can come to me anytime. Day or night. I'm here for you, Victoria, whatever your needs. I hope you feel you can turn to me."

"Thank you, Billy. I appreciate your vote of confidence," Victoria said. "I'll see you at the meeting."

As Victoria left Billy's office, she felt satisfied, as if something had been accomplished to move her forward on her career path. But the farther she walked away from Billy's office, the more she wondered exactly what she felt satisfied about. Nothing had been accomplished. Well, except for pushing her requests to the back burner and an agreement from her that she'd continue to work hard for the firm without a raise. On the other hand, Billy promised, hadn't he, and why would he say those things if he didn't mean them? After all, Victoria thought, his word must be his bond. If it wasn't, how could he have made it this far in business if he wasn't trustworthy? After a few minutes of wrestling with her uneasy feelings, she managed to push them into the forest of her mind, there to lurk until they found their way out to the clearing of reality.

As she got back to her office, Mary looked up from her cubicle and quirked her eyebrow and tilted her head as if to say, "Is everything okay?" Victoria just nodded and went into her office. Surprisingly, Armond was still sitting in her office.

"Well, that didn't take too long. Since you're not accompanied by the firm security, I take it he didn't fire you. What happened? What did he want?" Armond asked. He jumped up to shut the door so fast behind Victoria that it almost sliced off a piece of her ass.

"He wanted me to know that they're taking my requests seriously, that his two other partners wanted to fire me, that he saved my ass with a subtext of how grateful I should be to him, and the pièce de résistance is that we table any discussion about me until our client gets through the storm and the legion of claims which will no doubt be a critical part of the storm's aftermath."

"Well, that's good news. All of it, don't you think?" Armond was visibly relieved.

"Well, let's recap, shall we? In a matter of a few minutes, I was masterfully played and agreed to continue working for the same amount of money. In fact, let's correct that. Due to the hurricane, I'll likely work harder than I've ever worked, while all my requests have been pushed off into an indefinite holding pattern. So, how do you think I feel? The only good thing, I suppose, is the fact that I wasn't fired on the spot. Which only makes me circle back to the reason I was pissed off in the first place which is, why should I work for people who don't value my unique abilities and who act like a request to be adequately rewarded is akin to a suggestion that the US and the UK reunite?" Sensing that Armond was about to dive further into the topic, Victoria held up her hand before he could speak. "Armond, we're calling a team meeting for two o'clock this afternoon," Victoria paused while she began typing an email to Mary directing her to set the meeting while she continued speaking to Armond, "with all hands on deck. I need to get organized, so let's talk about this another time."

"That's fine. I'll see you at the meeting. Call if you need me before then." Relieved to get back to the relatively safe topic of work, Armond turned and left.

CHAPTER
31

KAT HAD HAD no contact from any of her Miami employees, or Troy, for the past six hours. From the pictures just beginning to come through on the Internet and TV, it looked as if hell had decided to move up from the netherworld and set up shop on the Earth's surface. Everything was broken from the trees to the cars thrown on top of one another to the buildings that had balconies hanging off their sides, roofs ripped off, and objects speared through their walls. There was no sign of life. No movement from anything. No birds. No animals. No humans. Just quiet. The broadcaster announced that the photos depicted the eye of the storm and the second half promised to be even worse. Kat got up from her desk and started pacing as she tried her brother and Donna again. "Answer, damn it," she muttered out loud. This time, there wasn't even a ringing sound on the other end.

Kat hung up and dialed again. "Dad, anything?"

"Not a thing, baby. Nothing. We have our emergency crews within the vicinity but just out of range. I'm not sending anyone in until the second half passes through. I'm sorry, baby, but I won't risk any lives."

"I know. I know." Kat sighed, and they were both silent but stayed connected on the line to each other. After a few minutes of silence, Kat said, "Dad, I'm going to call V and see what she knows. She told me that Highline has crews ready to go up and down Florida to try to help with the cleanup. Maybe they have more sophisticated communication channels for disasters like this."

"Okay, Kat. Call me immediately if you hear any news."

"I will, and you do the same. I love you."

"I love you too, Kat. Don't worry, yet. We'll get through this."

As soon as she was off the line, Kat called in her assistant and one of her associates she had put in charge of the insurance review. While the lives of people were of course most important, the livelihood of their company was at stake as well.

"Well, guys, tell me what we have. Outline it by building."

For the next three hours, Kat, her associate, and her assistant ran through all the twists and turns of the insurance agreement they had with Highline and they came up with an overall plan to report the damage.

"Cassie, set up a meeting with our engineers and general contractors. I want them ready to inspect the damage, tell me if it's repairable and if it is, I want a full scope of works and an estimate of the cost on my desk no later than two weeks after inspection. Let them know the purpose of the meeting so they're not coming in here cold. Give them until tomorrow morning to come up with a feasible and comprehensive plan of action that they can present at the meeting. If there are any questions, have them accumulate them and I'll answer them as best I can before I leave this evening."

"Got it. Do you need anything else?"

"Yes. A call from our people," Kat said. She turned her chair around and stared out her window at the peaceful view, and wondered about the hell that was happening in Florida. She picked up her phone and dialed Victoria.

CHAPTER
32

L ISTEN, WE NEED this to run like a well-oiled machine. Highline will need to have answers to any questions immediately. This is their, and our, first run-through with a disaster and unfortunately it happens to be one of record-setting magnitude. We need everyone ready to do his or her part. Please give your reports. Review where you stand as to readiness first, and then focus on any problems. We have three major departments that need to report: underwriting, claims, and reinsurance. Let's start with underwriting." Victoria sat down and gave the floor over to Bart, who ran the legal piece of Highline's underwriting department.

"All of the underwriting files involving any property in the area of the storm have been electronically flagged. We're checking to ensure that the complete policy, as well as the pre-Ileana property condition report, is available for each property. We've also coordinated with Ben's department so that each claim handler will have access to this information."

"Any problems, Bart?" Victoria asked.

"None yet. But we'll see how it flows as soon as the claims begin to come in."

Victoria nodded and looked down at the flow chart their team had created about a year ago for just such a situation. So far, so good, she thought.

"Ben, go ahead," Victoria said, nodding at Ben.

"Right," Ben said as he stood and walked over to the white board in the room and began to draw as he spoke. "The claim reps are ready to go. They'll receive a claim number, connect with the policyholder, and gather as much information as possible about the damage. They'll also assign an adjuster to inspect the damage. So within one week of reporting a claim, the policyholder will have had at least two solid interactions with Highline."

"Thanks, Ben," Victoria said.

"What about payment?" Ben asked.

"No amounts in excess of thirty thousand dollars will be paid without management approval," Victoria answered.

"Who is on the management team?" Ben asked.

"They're all Highline employees. In fact, Trever personally picked each Highline manager. So if one of them turns out to be an idiot, the firm's to blame, so let's hope we find everyone levelheaded and highly intelligent, shall we?" Victoria said, smiling, and everyone around the conference room table laughed.

"Okay, great." Victoria made a note to have Armond check with Trever to ensure everything management needed to make payment decisions was in place. "Alex. Reinsurance, please."

"Yes. Well, we pulled the trigger and notified the reinsurers of the likelihood of significant property losses on their policies insuring Southern properties."

Victoria snorted as she looked up and smirked, "I bet that went over well."

"As you'd expect. We received immediate responses that the reinsurers don't consider their money in play yet. In short, call us when you have a real claim."

"That's fine. How's their solvency?" Victoria asked.

"All grade A. Nicely financed and cash heavy."

Victoria smiled. "At least there's a bit of good news." She looked down for the first time at her cell phone and saw that Kat had called her two times.

Armond and Billy walked into the meeting just then. Victoria gave a summary recap of the teams' reports. Billy asked a few questions and then asked everyone but Armond and Victoria to leave the room.

"I don't have to remind you that Highline and its shareholders are in the insurance business to make money. So, while it's great that we get them ready for the worst, it's not our job to get involved in management's payment decisions. Any questions about our role?"

Both Armond and Victoria shook their heads no.

"Good. I'll expect you to hold daily meetings with the team. By the end of each day, I'll expect an executive summary to be on my desk." Billy got up and left the room.

Armond looked at Victoria and said, "You're well aware, aren't you, that our careers depend on this?"

"Yes, I'm aware."

"So, with that as the backdrop, do you see any gaps in our processes or in legal that I'm missing?"

"No. Everything is tight. I expect things to go wrong though. Don't you? This is Highline's first time through a disaster, and there'll be some flaws in our process or with people. But whatever it is, we'll fix it," Victoria said as she closed her legal pad and scooted her chair back to stand.

CHAPTER
33

LEANING ON HER balcony railing and cradling a cup of coffee, Jenny looked out over the Pacific. She couldn't believe she was still not divorced. Bill was playing hardball. Mona's words, not hers. He was arguing that California's community property laws did not apply to their situation, which is what they had expected him to do, but they hadn't expected him to accuse Jenny of stealing money from his paternal grandfather's trust and moving it to offshore accounts. It was ludicrous, of course. Jenny had never thought of doing any such thing, and even if she had, she would never have done it. She was honest to a fault. But the court had delayed the proceedings to allow his ridiculous accusation to be fully investigated. Sighing, Jenny pushed back from the rail and turned to go inside for more coffee.

Feeling the buzz of her cell phone, she pulled it out of the back pocket of her jeans. "Mona, hi. What's up?"

"Jenny, I just got a call from Bill's lawyer. They're ready to drop the investigation into the alleged stolen funds and will not press charges, if you'll agree to return all items of value within the next twenty-four hours, including documents you have in your possession which they say belong to Bill and which they claim you stole from his private safe." Barely stopping to take a breath, Mona continued, "Jenny, what the hell is he talking about? I can't represent you if I don't know what you have and if you've done something illegal, you need to tell me now or I'll file a motion to withdraw as your lawyer by the end of the day," Mona said, sounding both stern and really pissed for the first time since Jenny had met her.

"Mona, I have no idea what he's talking about. Did you ask what items he wants returned?" Jenny said, feeling rather annoyed that Mona had insinuated she was hiding something.

"Of course I asked. All he said was he didn't know, and when he asked Bill, all he said was that you would know."

"For Chrissake! This is stupid. No one knows what the hell that idiot is talking about, and yet we're all talking about it. Anyway, I didn't take any money, and he knows it. The forensic accountants are almost done with their review, aren't they? They'll be able to prove that, right?"

"Yes. But that's not the point. Think about it for a minute. He's known all along you didn't take any money, and he doesn't really care about the divorce because he has a mistress, so why is he stalling? What is it you have that he wants? I feel like there's something important here, and whatever it is, I don't think he's even shared it with his lawyer." Mona took a breath and continued in a rush, "Listen, I've been doing this for thirty years and I have a feeling that something's not quite right, and when I get this feeling, whatever it is always ends up playing a significant role in the divorce. There can be only a few reasons he doesn't want his lawyer to know about it. Either it concerns something that is illegal or borders on the criminal, or it's something that can ruin his reputation or that of one of his businesses. Otherwise, he'd be screaming to the court for an order requiring you to return whatever it is. If we can figure out what he thinks you have, I'll bet you one dry martini that we'll be able to nail his big ass to the wall. He'll cave on the divorce and settlement, as it will be the least of his concerns."

"I'll think about it, Mona. I'll let you know if I come up with anything." After hanging up, Jenny sat and watched the ocean far below her rise and fall, and listened to the faraway squeals and shouts of excitement drifting up from the tanned and sunburnt bodies playing in the frigid Pacific and on the sandy beach. After about fifteen minutes, Jenny pushed herself out of her chair, walked into her bedroom, and opened the safe. There was nowhere else she could think of to look for hints of what Bill was talking about.

Inside she found the papers she had shoved in her suitcase as an afterthought, really, when she ran from her home and left Atlanta. They were bunched together, somewhat crinkled and in a cylindrical shape and stuffed in the back, behind her jewelry. Pulling them out, she placed them on her desk and began to go through them. She had no idea why she was even looking at them, as they had little to do with Bill and more to do with information about her and her side of the family like birth certificates, wills, death certificates, passports and Social Security information. Nothing else.

As she rolled them open, a thumb drive fell from the crinkled fold of the middle document and landed on her thick carpet with a soft and muted thud. Jenny picked it up and stared at it. She went over to her laptop and put it in. As it powered up, Jenny went into the kitchen to grab a glass of wine. Glancing at the clock, she saw that it was only four in the afternoon. For God's sake, it was seven on the East Coast. Late enough, Jenny thought.

When Jenny returned with her wine, she sat at her desk, expecting to see old family photos of vacations gone by or something equally mundane. But when she glanced down, she stopped with her mouth open and her wine glass halfway there. "Oh my God," she breathed out aloud. After clicking through the documents for a few minutes, she grabbed a pen and her notebook and took notes of a few critical points. She was paranoid she would push the wrong button on her laptop, accidentally erasing the information. Leaving the computer on, Jenny grabbed her phone off the balcony table and dialed as fast as she could and got voicemail. "Shit," Jenny said as she paced back and forth while waiting for the beep so she could leave a message. "Mona, you're never going to believe what I just found. You need to call me back as soon as you get this."

Jenny pored over the documents for the next two hours until Mona finally called her back. "Sorry about that, I've been in court in a custody hearing for the last two hours. God, the bastard husband—"

"Mona, did you listen to my voicemail?" Jenny interrupted.

"No. Like I said, I just walked out of court, saw you called a while ago, and I wanted to get back to you right away. What's going on?"

"I think I found the answer to why Bill won't get on with the divorce. You might want to come over."

"I'm on my way."

While she waited for Mona, Jenny printed two copies of all of the documents on the thumb drive. One for Mona and the other for her own use. She knew Mona would need a clean copy for court, if that was where they ended up taking this. Finding a yellow highlighter, Jenny walked back out onto her balcony and began to read, this time highlighting. Jenny's heart began to beat faster. She was elated. However, she also knew she may have the key to the demise of the family fortune, which was not in her best interest. This would take delicate timing and handling to achieve a positive outcome, at least for Jenny.

The doorbell rang just as Jenny finished going through the documents for a second time. Opening the door, she stood back and allowed Mona to walk in. Hugging her, Mona said, "What is it? You're not usually prone to drama."

"You'll want to take a look at it for yourself. I've made a copy for you, one for me, and the original is in the safe. I put it back in the same order it was in when it was stored at The Southern Will and then here."

"Jenny, can I get a glass of wine? And, I'm starving," Mona said, descending from a towering five foot eight to a more petite five foot four as she stepped out of her heels.

"Of course. I'll get you a glass of cab, and how does cheese, fruit, and crackers sound? Will that hold you for a bit while you read?"

"Perfect."

"Great. Sit wherever you like. Here's the document."

Mona found a spot on Jenny's sofa and sat back, gathering her breath. She glanced at the title of the papers Jenny had handed to her. "Highline: Turning Claims Into Cash." Mona knew, of course, that Big Bill was a major investor in the new insurance company and that he sat on the board of directors. Other than that, the title did little for her, one way or the other.

"Here you go. Enjoy and relax," Jenny said, handing the wine to Mona and setting a tray down on the table in front of her.

Jenny watched as Mona smelled her wine, closed her eyes, and took an appreciative sip. Mona sighed out loud as the first sip ran past her tongue and, as she popped a few grapes into her mouth, she settled back to read. Jenny went into the kitchen and found something to do. She was so hyper, she knew if she stayed in the same room she would interrupt Mona's reading, nagging her for her opinion after each page. After about five minutes in the kitchen doing nothing, Jenny walked back into her great room and a smile spread across her face.

Mona was sitting upright, on the edge of the sofa, her reading glasses on the bridge of her nose, as her pen and high-lighter danced across the pages. Mona was writing comments in the margins, and almost the whole page she had read was doused in yellow highlighting. "Son of a bitch," Jenny heard Mona say to herself at one point. Looking over Mona's shoulder, Jenny noted the page number, went back into the kitchen, leashed her two dogs, and called over her shoulder that she would be back in about half an hour.

Taking the elevator down to the beach, Jenny felt a jumble of relief and excitement, along with a deep sense of foreboding that something monumental was about to happen. She had experienced this unique combination of feelings in only one other situation in her life, and that had been each time she had stepped in front of a jury as a prosecutor. It had been almost twenty years since she last practiced law, and she had forgotten about this unique combination of emotions. They came slamming back now. She remembered feeling excited and nervous, as well as relieved because she was prepared and ready to romp and stomp (as her colleagues used to call it) her opponents, yet at the same time being scared as shit that she might lose and wanting to go home, close the curtains, lock the doors and shut out the world. Jenny remembered loving and hating this jumble of emotions.

But now, Jenny noticed as she walked her dogs down the boardwalk on this perfect summer evening, smelling the ocean air and feeling the warm breeze, she relished the feelings.

Whatever Mona said about the documents, whatever it meant, Jenny realized she wasn't scared. It would take her down one path or the other, and she was ready for either one. As she walked, Jenny glanced at the shoreline, taking in the grace of the early evening surfers and the beauty of the sun as it inched toward the horizon. Breathing in the ocean air, feeling the beauty all around her, Jenny knew she was at the end of one journey and the beginning of another. A feeling of utter contentment flowed through her body.

Turning around to head back, Jenny thought about her future. She was set to take the California Bar. She had been studying for the last few months and was almost ready. The timing was perfect. Everything was falling into place. Once she passed the bar, she intended to do something to help women. She wasn't certain what that meant yet, but each day, her thoughts were getting clearer.

Opening the door to her condo, she heard Mona in the kitchen. As she let the dogs off their leashes, Mona called out, "In here, replenishing my wine." As Jenny entered the kitchen, she saw Mona sitting on her counter with her second glass of wine almost half-gone. Before Jenny could even speak, Mona said excitedly, "Jenny, let me ask you. What do you think is the significance of those documents?"

Jenny had to smile. Ever since she had begun studying for the bar, Mona took every opportunity to quiz her to make her think like a lawyer.

"No, really, Jenny. I'm not quizzing you this time. Let's round table this a bit," Mona said, tilting the glass upward and finishing off the rest of her wine.

"I think the significance is extraordinary," Jenny said, and then paused to collect her thoughts. "But I'm not sure how. Certainly, the information in that document would be harmful to the company if it were to get out. But I don't know how that helps me. I'm also wondering whether we have information that requires that it be given to some sort of authority, although I don't know who that would be."

Mona jumped off the counter. "Jenny, I need to think about this and research a few areas before I give you my recommendation. But I have a feeling it will all be okay. Come on, I'm taking you to dinner, and you can tell me all about where you found this, what you knew, and answer questions about anything else I can think of to interrogate you about."

As Mona began to move past Jenny toward the living room, Jenny grabbed her arm to stop her. "Mona, I want this kept confidential until I hear your suggestions and agree to them. Do you understand?"

"Agreed. Now, let's go. I'm famished. Getting ball-busting evidence always makes me hungry. Shit, this turned out to be a good day after all."

CHAPTER
34

THE TRAINING HAD completed a mere three weeks before Ileana threw her temper tantrum in Florida. Victoria, Armond and their team had spent the previous six months leading different training classes for Highline's claim representatives and adjusters. One of Victoria and Armond's goals had been to create such well-prepared and savvy claim handlers that Highline would avoid the spike of lawsuits that were typically filed against insurance companies after a disaster.

Since the storm, Victoria, Armond and Billy had gathered together in Bermuda for three days straight, with little stop for sleep, developing a final reporting channel for the claims that would soon be pouring into Highline.

"Okay, we're done. My team will handle the claims and you two will focus on the regulatory and reinsurance reporting," Billy said as he stood and stretched. "I'm grabbing coffee and then heading to The Western Will for a shower. If you need me, give me a call. Victoria, great work coordinating all of this over the past few days." As he walked past her, he stopped and moved a piece of her hair back behind her shoulder.

Victoria visibly jumped at Billy's unexpected touch.

"What the hell was that?" Armond asked as soon as Billy was out of earshot.

"How the hell do I know." Victoria spat. "He got so close to me the other day in his office, his crotch ended up almost in my face. I thought it was an odd place to stand at the time. But now, I'm not so sure he didn't do it on purpose."

"You can't be serious, Victoria. A grown man putting his crotch in your face is like the Titanic sending up a flare after it crashed into that giant iceberg. There was a reason for it and it wasn't accidental."

Victoria sighed and put her fingers to her temple. "I'm getting a headache."

"Listen, Victoria," Armond said as he got up to shut the door, "Billy has a reputation among the men at the firm for… hmm…how shall I say this? Ah, providing extracurricular educational sessions to the female associates."

"What are you talking about? He's the diversity chair of the firm. He's received awards for what he has done for women in the law," Victoria argued.

"Right. I'm aware. All I can do is tell you what is understood among the partners of the firm."

"And you're just choosing to tell me now? Seems a bit late in the game to come clean about that, doesn't it? Why now?" Victoria spat back.

"There was no reason to say anything to you before. He's our department chair and he is well known for his work with women." Armond could not help but smile at his rather clever unintended play on words.

"Jesus, Armond. Really? You find it funny?"

"No. I'm sorry, I really don't. You've never had an issue with him as far as I knew, so there was no reason to put any bad juju into your working relationship. I'm sorry I said anything.

I just thought you should know based on what I just saw. I care a great deal about you and I would not want anything to happen to you," Armond said as he squeezed her arm.

"Let's just focus on what we can deal with at the moment, shall we?" Victoria said. "Billy is going to run the claims, the success of which depends on the oversight of the management team chosen by Trever."

"Right."

"Well, how will we know what is and is not working? Who is keeping us in the loop?"

"We have enough on our plates, Victoria. Trever is good at what he does as is Billy. If they need our help, they'll ask for it. Let's just focus and get through our final team meetings tonight without stepping in anyone else's shit."

"Fine with me. I'm tired and I can't believe I'm saying this but I can't wait to get off of this island," Victoria answered.

"Hey, why don't we meet for a late dinner tonight at our favorite restaurant overlooking the ocean. Meet me in the bar as soon as you've finished with your team."

"Done. That sounds perfect."

Six hours later, Victoria walked into the bar and saw Armond as he waved to her from across the room, already seated at one of the high top tables. Victoria smiled and walked to him, greeting him with a hug and a kiss on his cheek.

"Well, so far so good, my little protégée," Armond said as he popped open the bottle of champagne he had waiting for her arrival. "Our deliverables are about to be tested. If this works, and Highline keeps its claim management and legal fees below industry average, we'll have a whole new area the firm can tout. You and I will be sought after by not only other insurance companies, but also by other law firms as well."

"Armond, I think we'll need to let the training settle in, and then we need to do a second round in another two weeks. What do you think?"

Armond sighed in response. He knew Victoria so well, and recognized that if her mind was not done with something, there was little hope of getting her to focus on the bigger picture, so he gave in and went with her flow. "I agree. If we're going to do another round, we had better agree on the agenda and schedule the tentative dates and send it up the chain for Billy and Trever to okay before we leave. Otherwise, it will be too late to get it going when we both come back after our vacations."

Victoria took out a pad. "Let's get it done now. By tomorrow, I won't want to deal with this. We'll figure it out in draft today and finalize it on the plane home tomorrow. When we get to the office in the afternoon, your assistant can get it out to them, so if there are any changes to the schedule, hopefully they'll weigh in before we leave on our trips."

Over the next half hour, they knocked out a rough draft that they were each happy with. Closing her notebook, Victoria poured another glass of champagne for each of them. "Armond, you know I love my work, but our book of business will bring in close to eighteen million this year, and I'll be taking home not even a pittance of that amount. I know I told Billy I would wait until this is all over, but I've changed my mind. It will be years and years before these claims are resolved. I'm not going to wait that long before I get more money and become fast tracked. In fact, I'm no longer interested in waiting on a fast track. I want and deserve partnership now. As you said, if this goes as planned, there will be a slew of insurance companies and law firms vying for us."

Armond smiled, "Ah, so you were listening."

"Of course I heard you, and don't think I hadn't already been thinking about that. Listen, I know you think I should wait. But…"

"No. I've changed my mind. I agree with you. If you wait until it's up and running and all the bugs are out and fully functioning, you're in danger of making yourself obsolete."

Victoria stopped with her glass midway to her mouth and stared at Armond. It was the first time he had ever admitted something like that to her. She cocked her head and just stared at him. "Armond, I'm stunned to hear you say that. You've always been so rah-rah firm in the past. You know, be patient. Wait until it's your time. It will all come out like a Disney movie in the end."

"Well, I want my fair share as well. I was promised great things last year, and I haven't seen anything that rocks my boat yet. I'm having my own meeting with Billy the day after I get back from my vacation. I want to be compensated now, not later. And my thoughts are the same as what I've told you. I'm very relevant now. If I don't use that to get what I want, who knows when I will be again?"

Victoria reached across the table and squeezed his hand. "Armond, you deserve it more than anyone I know. Except me." She smiled and Armond leaned back and laughed.

"To us," Armond raised his glass. "To our successful futures at Acker, Smith & McGowen."

"To us. To our continued friendship," Victoria happily responded.

CHAPTER
35

A FEW WEEKS after returning from Bermuda, Victoria finally took a vacation. She and Sophia traveled to Houston to visit Kat and her family. On the last night of the trip, Kat took Victoria aside for a private meeting.

"Victoria, you know we insured our property with Highline. While we're big boys and girls, we chose them in part because of your involvement in creating the company and high recommendation. So I thought you would want to know that I'm getting word from our risk manager that while he put our claims in about three weeks ago, we haven't yet heard a word from anyone at the company. You know that eighty percent of our Florida property was hit, and hit hard. We need to begin repairs as soaon as possible to get everything back up and running and rented or occupied. To do that, we need payment by our insurance company. I hate to ask for favors, but is there anything you can do to find out about our claims? We're bleeding cash."

"Kat, you should have let me know right away. You should have received contact almost immediately after your claims were reported. Of course I'll look into it for you. This is the exact type of information we need to make sure the processes we launched are working. Clearly, something is wrong. Have one of your people send me the list of properties they made claims on and I'll look into it and get back to you. Don't worry, we'll keep on this and get it done."

"Thanks, the last thing I want is to have an issue with the company you helped create."

When Victoria returned to work the following Monday, she had received the email from Kat's assistant listing their damaged properties. She forwarded the email to Armond, Billy and Trever. Victoria also instructed Mary to keep a running list of all of the complaints they received so she could ensure that each one was handled and the cause identified and rectified.

Armond emailed Victoria. "That's a pisser. Are you sure Kat's information is accurate, or is she just trying to get special attention?"

Victoria was so pissed when she saw that response, her head almost exploded. She knew that what she wanted to say should not be put in an email. Victoria calmly walked out of her office, up the inner set of stairs and into Armond's office without knocking. "Are you kidding? What the hell is that supposed to mean?"

Getting up from his desk, Armond walked past her and shut his door, returned to his desk, and sat. "Well, hey there, Miss V. My vacation was great and yes, my family is doing just fine. Thanks for asking. How was yours?"

"Don't give me that bullshit. What kind of an email is that? You know Kat. Why would you assume that she's trying to get favors rather than simply letting me know exactly what they're experiencing? Which, quite frankly, in my mind and I would think in your mind, is a significant problem. Let me summarize it for you, as you obviously missed the point. After one month, her company, which by the way is a significant policyholder, aka client, for Highline, has received absolutely no response about their claims. Not even a, 'Hey, how you doing? We're here and alive. Don't worry. We've got it.'"

"Well Victoria, let me break it out for you. Did you consider for even one minute that every time something negative comes across the wires like that, it's a mark against what we set up? Against you and I, Victoria. Not the firm. Not Billy or Trever. You and I. So each time you document it or make a big stink about it, you're fucking with our careers. Did that little bit of reality fail to cross your logical mind?"

"It's you and me, Armond. Not I," Victoria said, annoyed at the tone Armond was using with her.

"Whatever." Armond stood up and began to pace. "You and me. It's our asses on the line. You don't think for one minute that either Billy or Trever will stand with us as a team or take any type of blame for any problem, do you? And in the long run, hell, even the short run, each of these problems is a cut against our careers. Can't you tell your friend to tell you that information over the phone and just look into it for her without making it the first recorded item? Are you that daft?"

"Daft? Really? What the hell happened to you on vacation? And she's your friend too. Or so I and she thought."

"Yes, she's my friend, but she's your best friend. Like sisters, or so you've both told me time and time again. And as sisters, don't you think it would float through that pretty little head of yours that you should pick up the phone and call her and explain the situation to her?"

"You've gone daft. Did you get too much of the California sun? Or maybe you watched one too many movies on your trip home to La-La land."

"Listen, Victoria, I'm not kidding. Our setup is being watched by the insurance industry. We hold the key. This is more than just Highline. Don't you get it? If we do this right, we will be able to sell our formula to the rest of the industry. And who do you think will be the keepers of the key? It's us, V. You and I."

"God, you idiot. It's you and me."

Walking to his corner sofa, she sat down and poured herself a glass of water from the pitcher he always kept on the table. As she gathered her thoughts, she began to feel all of the pressure Armond had apparently been holding in begin to settle on her. She took a deep breath and looked at Armond, who had moved to sit on the coffee table in front of the sofa.

"Do you see, now, V? This thing is bigger than both of us, and without either one of us intending it to, it controls us. We're no longer in control." Armond looked sad and exhausted as he looked down at his shoes.

Victoria refused to take on his pressure. She was on her way up the ladder, and she had no intention of being thrown to the wolves if something didn't go as planned. And anyway, what was wrong with Armond? He was suddenly such a Debbie Downer over one simple little notice from Kat. It didn't make sense. Maybe he was being pressured by his family to go back into the movie business.

"Armond, I'm not sure what brought this on, or really why you're acting like this. Nothing has gone wrong. We received one alert from one policyholder, not tens of thousands. And, actually, it's a good thing really. This way we can fix it before it gets out of control. And it fits in perfectly with the plan we developed in Bermuda to have follow-up meetings with the teams to correct any problems that crop up."

Armond ran his hands through his hair and looked up and smiled a weird, quirky little smile that did not reach his eyes.

"You're right. I'm sorry. I invested the last few years of my life in this project and I'm edgy, I guess, waiting to see how it will go."

"Let me handle this little glitch, Armond. You'll see. It'll be a good thing. But I want you to promise me one thing."

Armond looked up and waited.

"You will never again keep anything from me. If you're worried about something, let me know, in real time. I don't want any further blowups between us. We have enough to deal with from outside competitors and competition within the firm. We don't need it from each other. Agreed?" Victoria stood up and looked directly into his eyes.

"Agreed."

"Great. I'll call you later and let you know what I find out about why this happened. In the meantime, why don't you begin organizing the agenda for our team meeting next week." Victoria turned and walked out the door without waiting for a response from Armond.

Victoria called her assistant from her cell phone and told her to forward the message from Kat's team to the project leader at Highline to find out what had happened. Victoria told Mary to stress in the email that she expected a call by the end of the day with both the reason why it happened and confirmation that the cause and the problem had been handled. Victoria was beyond pissed that after all the best practices and training her team had given the claims group at Highline, one of the easiest things to do, communicate, had already been royally screwed up.

CHAPTER
36

THE HEAVY, CARVED wooden doors remained closed as the executive session of the board meeting continued while Trever and Billy sat outside in the antechamber after having made their presentations. Much to their surprise, and with a hit to their egos, they had been excused from the meeting so the members could have the final session in private. So far, they had been cooling their heels for fifty minutes, like truant school boys waiting outside the principal's office.

"Jesus. What's going on in there? I thought we handled the questions during the meeting," Billy quietly asked Trever.

"I'm not surprised. These guys have been swimming in clean water and now that the water's become a bit murky after the hurricane, they're probably feeling a bit of buyer's remorse. They'll come around for a number of reasons, not the least of which is your father won't let them leave this island until they do." Trever turned to look at Billy and gave him a smirk. "I envy your dad's skills sometimes. He's a true negotiator. I've never seen anyone say no to him. Bet you can't wait to hone that same talent one day."

Billy got the implied insult but chose to ignore it. He was used to these types of shitty comments as he had heard them for as long as he could remember. He couldn't stand the way everyone danced to Big Bill's tune and thought he was so high and mighty. Billy knew what a bully he could be, and how manipulative. His father had no sense of honor and did whatever it took to win whatever game he was playing at the moment. Whether it was fucking around on his mother or negotiating a deal. But Billy had to agree with Trever; he had never seen his father lose the momentum in a room.

Loud laughter came from the other side of the door, and Trever and Billy turned to see Big Bill ushering the men out, taking their memos and telling them he would be in touch. As soon as the last of the members were on the elevators on their way out of the building, he turned toward them with a big smile on his face and a cigar clenched between his teeth and jerked his head inward.

Billy and Trever followed Big Bill into the room and as the doors closed behind them, Big Bill growled, "God, those pansies are a pain in my ass. Had I known they would be constantly whining, I wouldn't have brought them into this deal."

"What's the issue?" Trever asked.

"Nothing concrete. They want reassurance that our plan is sound, that it's ethical, that there will be no wrongdoing. They reminded me about their 'sterling reputations,'" Big Bill said as he made quote marks in the air, "that they don't want damaged. Blah, blah, blah."

"And, what did you say?" Trever asked, as he pushed the intercom signaling for their assistant to come in to collect, and then shred, the memos.

"What do you think I said? I pointed to you two. I told them that we had two of the finest lawyers in the world standing right outside our doors advising us, and that your licenses and livelihood were on the line if you had advised us to do anything improper or unethical. All we can do is rely on our lawyers, and if they say it's good to go, then who are we to say otherwise?" Big Bill slapped Trever on the back and laughed out loud, but the serious glint in his eyes revealed his point.

As their assistant opened the door, Big Bill turned to walk out. Pausing to let her enter first, he waited a beat to appreciate her rear end as she walked into the room. As soon as she was past, he turned, smiled and said, "I'll see you boys next month at the board meeting. I expect everything to go smoothly."

As soon as their assistant had left the room, Trever put his arm around Billy and maneuvered him out to the balcony off the board room, and shut the French doors so they could talk privately. "Are you fucking kidding me? Did he just warn us that our asses are on the line? Would he seriously throw his own flesh and blood under the bus?"

Billy pulled his gaze from the ocean and turned to look at Trever with sympathy, but no pity. "It's what I've tried to tell you all along. But you weren't listening. As usual, Trever, you thought you knew better."

Victoria hung up her cell phone and stood in the middle of the boardwalk. She was unbelievably pissed and completely confused. The call she'd been waiting for had come through during her evening run, and she had slowed to a walk to take the call. As she listened to the information, she suddenly stopped walking and stood dumbfounded in the middle of the path, not noticing the bikers, skateboarders and runners as they tried to avoid clipping her. As she turned to head home, she stepped directly into the path of a biker who had to screech on his brakes so hard it threw his rear wheels over the front. Victoria watched in horror as he flew off of his bike as if in slow motion and came crashing down with an audible "thud" on the concrete paved surface.

"Son of a bitch, lady. What the hell are you trying to do?" the man moaned as he raised himself up on his elbows.

"Oh my God. I'm so sorry," Victoria said as she saw his gashed knee and reached out to help him off of the ground. "Let me help you."

"No. Don't touch me. I'm fine. Just get the hell out of the way before you do further damage to someone else." He winced as he wiped the blood with the front of his shirt, clipped into his pedals and took off.

Shaking her head to herself, she knew she had to focus and decide what to do. What she wanted to do was pick up the phone and call Billy and point-blank ask him what the hell was going on, but something warned her that was the wrong choice. Instead, she decided, she needed to talk to Armond. She tucked her phone back into her sports bra, and ran back to her apartment.

Armond took a quick scan through his emails as he got ready to head out for the evening. He stopped just as he was leaving his apartment when he read the last one in the chain. He was stunned to see that Billy had canceled Armond and Victoria's Highline team meeting. Armond felt heat shoot through his body. Not only had Billy not discussed canceling their meeting, but Billy had totally usurped Armond's authority, and made him look like an idiot in front of his team. Aside from the personal affront to his ego, Armond couldn't understand why Billy would cancel such a critical meeting without discussing it first. As he stood and stared at his phone, deciding whether he should let this unexpected bit of news ruin his evening, Victoria's name popped up on his phone.

"Victoria, you're not going to believe this," Armond began, answering her call without waiting for her to say anything.

But before he could even finish his sentence, Victoria interrupted, "Armond, hold on, we have a major problem, and we need to talk. Can you come over right away?"

"Yup, I'll be right there. Hopping in a cab now." Armond hung up, sent his friends a quick text letting them know that he would not make dinner, grabbed his laptop and headed out the door.

Victoria took a quick shower, and then dressed in casual, torn jeans. Just as she finished combing out her hair, she heard the knock on her door. Looking through her peephole, she saw Armond. "Hey, come in," she said, opening her door.

After hugging her, Armond said, "I need to discuss something with you, but you go first. Yours sounds urgent."

"Armond, I have no idea what's going on, but Michelle rang from Bermuda about an hour ago to report on why Kat's company has received no information or contact from Highline. She told me that the claim group received explicit direction that under no circumstance was any contact to be made with policyholders. Instead, any information that was received was to be sent to the management team and once they had a chance to review the information, they would advise when and what contact was to be made with the policyholders. So far, according to Michelle, claims has not heard a peep from management and no one has had the balls to ask questions."

Armond walked directly to the wine rack and grabbed the first bottle he touched without scrutinizing the origin and year. "Geez, what happened to you?" Victoria asked as she cocked her head to watch his uncharacteristic behavior. Typically, Armond would not go near a wine bottle without channeling its lineage.

"Our meeting was cancelled. Just today. If you haven't looked at your emails, Billy sent out a notice cancelling our team meeting," Armond answered as he poured two glasses and handed one to Victoria, watching her reaction to his news.

"You've got to be kidding. Why would he do that? Especially now with the information I just received from Bermuda. A meeting to correct this needs to happen right away. We should move the meeting date up, not cancel it," Victoria almost screeched. "Armond, you do understand that whatever the hell is going on now is nothing remotely like what the claim team was taught, don't you? If this is the way Highline is beginning their claim process, the response time will be way off, information will be lost and screw client satisfaction. The amount of litigation that will be filed will be through the roof. All of our projections will be off. We need to get ahold of Billy and Trever right away and let them know what's going on."

Victoria had thought Armond would react as she had, but she watched in amazement as he calmly walked to her tiny kitchen, and poured himself another glass of wine. "Armond, did you even hear me? What the hell is the matter with you? This is serious. As you pointed out, our asses are on the line, and if someone is changing our landscape, don't you think we should know who that is and what's going on?"

Armond sat on Victoria's couch and took a sip of the wine. Then he said, "Victoria, did you know that Billy had cancelled our meeting? I assumed he spoke to you about it and that you two had made the decision. Did you?"

"Of course not. It was my idea to have the meeting in the first place, remember? Why would I cancel it, especially in light of Kat's experience? That's what I wanted to correct." Victoria walked over to the kitchen and poured herself another glass of wine. "Why did he cancel the meeting? Did he move it to another day?"

"I have no idea. And, no, he didn't move it. He didn't bother to discuss it with either of us, apparently. He just cancelled it."

"Armond, we need to call him and let him know about the changes to our process and find out what he knows. I think this is important enough that you need to call him tonight." Victoria sat across from Armond on her sofa.

"Why should I call him? You're the one in charge of the best practices, and that's what's been violated."

Victoria cocked her head and just smiled at her friend. "Because you, my friend, are the partner between the two of us, the vice chair of the department to be exact, while I'm just a lowly associate who has recently and continuously been reminded of that fact. This is why you make the big bucks." She picked his phone up off of her table and handed it to him. "Now, make the call."

Armond flipped her off, took another sip of wine, got up, began pacing and dialed Billy's number. After four rings, Billy's phone clicked to voicemail. "Billy, this is Armond. I'm sorry to bother you, but we have a development with Highline that we believe needs to be immediately addressed. Please give either me or Victoria a call."

As he turned around to head back into the kitchen for more wine, he tried not to look at Victoria but couldn't avoid it. "What now?" he said.

"What do you mean, 'Give me or Victoria a call'? How about just give you a call back."

"Victoria, you want to play with the big boys, you'll need to get used to being pushed on the playground. Welcome to the sandbox."

Victoria flipped him off and joined him in the kitchen to open another bottle. It was definitely a two-bottle night.

CHAPTER
37

AS SHE WALKED into the firm the following morning, Victoria headed directly to Armond's office as planned. As she got close to his office at the end of the plush hall, she saw him pace back and forth across his doorway. As soon as she walked through his door, Armond walked behind her, shut his door, and handed her a revised handwritten draft of a memo that they had worked on the night before.

"Your opinion, please," Armond snapped. "I want to get this out in the next thirty minutes."

Trying to read through the multiple revisions and chicken scratch on the paper, Victoria read aloud, "We received information this weekend that our best practices have been aborted. We were not advised of a change in our process. For this reason, we are rescheduling the team meeting that was recently cancelled. It will take place tomorrow at noon. Attendance is mandatory." The memo was addressed to all team members and copied to Billy and Trever. Sighing heavily, Victoria smacked her hand against the paper.

"I don't understand, Armond. We agreed we were going to speak with Billy this morning. We decided against sending an email. Why are you giving this to me now? What changed?" Victoria asked.

"Because I've already tried to set an appointment with him and was told that he was out of the office for the next two weeks. He still has not returned my call. We need to communicate this any way we can," Armond responded. "The last thing we want is to have Billy or Trever claim that we never advised them about what was going on, and we have nothing tangible to show other than my phone calls to Billy."

"What about Trever? Have you tried him?"

"No. Since he wasn't directly involved in best practices, I thought we should first put it in writing to Billy, wait twenty-four hours, and then call Trever," Armond said.

"I disagree," Victoria said, as she walked over to Armond's window and looked out at the bustling intersection. She paused to think through whether she really wanted to do what she was about to suggest. "I'll call Trever," Victoria said as she dug her phone out of her bag. "I'm not waiting twenty-four hours to find out what's going on and whether we should take action."

Taking out her cell phone, Victoria dialed Trever's office and asked to speak with Trever. Jamming the phone between her head and shoulder, Victoria grabbed paper and pen from Armond's desk and wrote, *out of the country; unavailable*, showing it to Armond as she continued to speak with his assistant to try to get information about his accessibility or return date. "I see," Victoria responded. "Well, please let him know when you speak with him that Armond and Victoria tried to reach him about an urgent matter having to do with Highline."

Victoria disconnected the call and looked at Armond. "Houston, we have a problem," she said. She began to pace.

"Armond, let's see how much information we can get before we receive calls from Billy or Trever. Maybe there's a logical explanation for this and we can sort this all out. If there isn't, then we'll need our own information anyway. Why don't we give it until the end of the day and then if we don't have a satisfactory explanation for this, we'll send out the email. Agreed?"

Armond signaled his agreement by pressing the intercom to his assistant, and when she picked up, asked her to get Michelle from Highline on the line. Victoria sat quietly waiting for Michelle to be put through. She had already quizzed her, and all she really got from Michelle was more questions. But she knew Armond needed to hear it for himself, as she would have wanted to. Anyway, Victoria thought, Armond was a consummate interrogator; perhaps he would find a stone she had left unturned.

The next few hours proved interesting. Michelle relayed to Armond the same information she had given Victoria. She also forwarded to Armond and Victoria the email her team received, directing that they were to do nothing with the claims until further instructions. The email came from "Peer Review." Bizarrely, the email was sent from the group and not from any one particular member, and even more bizarre, no one recognized the email address. Victoria and Armond figured that if they could find out who sent it, they could at least speak to that person to begin to unravel what was going on. Victoria asked Mary to find out who had sent the email and to use the firm's top IT guy for the investigation.

Later that afternoon, Mary poked her head into Victoria's office and said, "Victoria, I have Kat's risk manager Malcom Dwyer on the line. Do you want to take it?"

Victoria sighed and thought, shit no, but said, "Yes, of course." A moment later, her line flashed, indicating the call was waiting.

Pushing the flashing button, Victoria picked up her phone. "Malcom, how are you?" She listened as Malcom explained that he was anything but fine, and that while he knew she was like a sister to Kat, could she please forgive him if he was blunt, and, "What the hell is going on with that shithole of an insurance company?" His office could get no one to respond to their questions. In fact, no one was even answering the phones anymore.

Victoria stood up quickly, and almost knocked her chair over. "What do you mean, no one is answering the phones?"

"Exactly what I said. No one is picking up a damn phone. We've been calling continually for three days. Nothing. Not a recording. Not a peep. Not a person on the other end. We started again this morning and still nothing. Victoria, I don't have to tell you how much of our company's assets are tied up in the property that was hit by Ileana. Operations has already contracted out the repair work, but the amount of capital outlay to get the buildings into shape, without insurance contribution, will come close to...well, it's not for me to say. But just understand it feels like we're sitting here with no insurance. Just, please do what you can."

"Malcom, let me call you back. I promise I'll reach you by the end of the day. Give me your mobile so I can reach you after hours if necessary." Victoria hung up the phone and immediately pressed her speed dial. While waiting for an answer, she sent an email to Billy and Trever copied to Armond, documenting the complete breakdown in High-line's communication channels and requesting an emergency meeting within the hour.

"Damn it," Victoria said out loud as Armond's office line rang.

"Armond Renoir's office," Charlotte answered.

"Charlotte, it's Victoria. Will you please let him know I'm on the line?" Victoria said.

"Oh, Victoria, hi. How are you? I'll let him know as soon as he comes out of the department meeting. But they usually last two hours, so I doubt he'll be available for another hour at least," Charlotte told her.

"Charlotte, I've never asked you to interrupt him in all the time I've known you, so I want you to understand how serious this is when I tell you to get him out of that meeting, however you have to do it, and have him call me immediately. When I tell you this is an emergency, I'm understating it. Got it?"

"Yup. Got it. Hang tight and I'll get him to call you."

"Have him call my mobile. Thanks, Charlotte." Victoria hung up and paced back and forth. Going online, she pulled up Highline's website and then searched online for any bulletins or new information, and saw nothing out of the ordinary. Everything looked the same. Maybe Malcom was exaggerating.

Gathering her laptop and cell phone, Victoria headed out of the office to work from the coffee shop down the street. She needed to get some space without interruption so she could think clearly. What the hell was going on? They had just run through all the training exercises. Everyone had understood the process, and the management team was on board with the best practices. Who sent the email canceling communication to claimants? Who made that decision? And, oddest of all, perhaps, where the hell were Billy and Trever?

Once at the coffee shop, Victoria settled herself with a cappuccino at an outside table. As she opened her laptop and prepared to make some calls, her body relaxed for the first time in what seemed like a long time, as she felt the warmth of the sun. It was an amazing fall day. The breeze was slight and still warm, and the trees were just beginning to change color. Where the hell was Armond? Victoria wondered as she checked her cell phone. It had been thirty minutes since her conversation with Charlotte.

Scrolling through her emails, Victoria checked to see whether she had received a response from either Billy or Trever. Nothing yet. Odd. Especially for Billy, as he was addicted to emails and never took more than a few minutes to respond. She picked up her cell phone and scrolled through her contacts until she found Michelle's number.

"Good afternoon. This is Michelle Baumer, Highline claims."

"Michelle. Hi, it's Victoria. I'm hoping for an update. Have you or anyone on the team received any further communications or directives from anyone? Have you begun the next phase of processing the claims?"

"Victoria, none of us have heard a thing. We're receiving hundreds, if not thousands of claims from people whose property was damaged by Ileana, and the only thing we're doing is logging them into the system with whatever information they're providing to us. We're working nonstop, but we have no outgoing communication. What is going on?" Michelle asked.

"I'm working on the answer to that question, Michelle. Believe me. As soon as I find something out, I'll let you know. It will help if you keep in contact, and if there are any new developments, let me know right away, will you? I'd prefer if you gave me a call so we can discuss it, rather than communicate by email."

"That's fine. No problem. But, what should I tell the team? They're confused, and I feel a bit of hysteria growing within the rank and file," Michelle said, pulling her voice down to a whisper.

"Tell them to continue to gather the information, that everything is fine, and that we're simply gearing up for the next phase. Will that hold you for now?"

"I don't know if it will hold them, but if it's all we have, then it will have to do," she responded. "Listen, Victoria, why don't we touch base two times a day, once in the morning and again in the afternoon? I'll feel better about having direct contact with you."

"That's a great idea. Let's do that. I'll leave it up to you to contact me. Call whenever it works for you, and if you need me more often, call. I'll talk to you later then, if not sooner." As Victoria hung up, Armond was beeping through.

"Armond, God that took you a long time to call," Victoria said pissily.

"Victoria, Jesus Christ. You're not the only human being on the planet. I left the meeting as soon as I could during wrap-up. It was the best I could do, and even leaving then violated our department meeting rules. No interruptions of any kind are allowed, even for the equity partners in the group. What the hell is the problem now?"

"Armond, I thought you would want to know that Kat's risk manager called me. He was extremely upset and actually seemed to be a bit hysterical. According to him, not only have they still received no communication from Highline, but now no one is picking up the phones when they call the service number. I thought you might want to know. But never mind. I'll let you know information as I gather it through email, and then you deal with it as you see fit."

Victoria hung up on Armond and wished she had been on a landline so she could have slammed down the receiver. It would have been much more satisfying than silently disconnecting on a cell phone. She had never hung up on Armond before and it wasn't her usual style, but she had no intention of letting Armond bully her.

Her phone began to buzz as Armond tried to call her back. She didn't answer. She had more important things to do. Picking up her phone, she called Kat.

"Victoria, hi, what's up?"

"Kat, I spoke with Malcom this morning, and I wanted to speak with you directly. We've been looking into the situation at Highline. I was told this morning that they're logging in all the information they receive from claimants before they begin responding. I'll call and tell Malcom what I'm telling you, but I suggest you provide all the information you have on the repair or rebuild you intend to do, including contracts with outside vendors, and your own company costs if you're using your own crews for the work. You should also maintain the time and cost expenditures of your staff spent on gathering information for the claim."

"I appreciate the head's up, V. But we're already doing those things. I'm glad you called because I was just about to call you. You must know that we don't have enough capital set aside to do all of the work that needs to get done from the hurricane. The insurance company needs to kick in, and quickly. We can't afford to wait much longer for some type of assurance from the company that they have our back, and most importantly, when we can expect to begin receiving payments. I hate to tell you this, but if we don't get a response and some payment from the company soon, we're filing suit. We have no choice. Some of these properties are still mort-gaged and the banks are breathing down our necks to do the repairs or to pay them off. We can do neither without the in-surance money. Our lawyers sent a letter advising of just that to Highline about an hour ago, and it's copied to your firm as the attorneys of record for the company. We can't wait any longer, V. I'm sorry."

Victoria was dumbstruck. She hadn't expected Kat, or any policyholder, for that matter, to move so quickly to litigation. She thought they had at least six months before even the inkling of a lawsuit became a gleam in some lawyer's eye. Not only was the lawsuit a problem, but now Victoria would be thrust into an adversarial position with Kat's company. She had ethical obligations to her client to protect it and, shit, what a mess.

"Kat. I understand. You need to do what you need to do. I want you to know that I'm doing everything in my power to find out what is going on."

"I know you are. But you know this will place us on different sides of the playing field. Our lawyers have advised that I should have no further communication with you about the claims. From this point forward, everything will be channeled through them. I'm sorry, Victoria, but I need to take their advice."

"Kat, I understand. If I were your lawyer, I would tell you the same thing."

"Thanks, V. I knew you'd understand. I hate to cut you off, but I have a full plate today. We'll talk later. And Victoria, take good care." The line went dead and Victoria sat and stared at her phone. Everything felt like it was running downhill and fast. Perhaps worst of all, was the growing feeling that there was little she could do to stop it.

Victoria's phone began to buzz again. "Mary, what's up?"

"Victoria, I hate to bother you, but I thought I'd give you a heads-up. There's a special executive committee meeting that's been convened on an emergency basis, and Charlotte called to tell me off the record that there is only one topic on the agenda, and it's you."

"Mary, what are you talking about? What do you mean it's about me? When is this happening?" Victoria felt a rush of heat run through her body, and she suddenly felt nauseous.

Trying to keep her voice low, Mary responded, "It's happening now. According to Charlotte, Armond is in the meeting, and the only reason Charlotte found out about it is that she was asked to bring your timesheets and fee receipts into the boardroom."

"Armond is in the meeting? I can't believe this. I just spoke to him. He told me he was finishing a department meeting, and said nothing about going into an executive committee meeting and he sure as shit didn't say anything about it being about me. Who else is there?"

"All the executive members who are in the city, and the others have called in. When Charlotte walked in to give Armond your financials, she saw the light on the conference phone, and she heard Billy comment through the speaker. She thought you would want to know. And Victoria, you can never tell anyone how you learned of this or Charlotte and I will be let go immediately," Mary said.

"Mary, of course not. I won't say a thing, and thanks for the heads-up," Victoria said as she hung up the phone.

Victoria sat and thought for a moment then redialed Mary. "Does Charlotte have any idea why I'm on the agenda? What it's about?"

"No," Mary answered. "And that's what's so odd. The agenda she saw had only your name on it and no topic. She has no idea other than she was asked to bring your time and income receipts into the meeting."

"Okay, thanks. I'll see you soon."

Victoria felt sick to her stomach and was afraid to return to the office. She didn't know what they were meeting about but she had a feeling it wasn't good. On the other hand, perhaps they were considering her request for early partnership. But she doubted it. She felt like she was in an altered universe and her equilibrium was off. She really needed some support, and the two people she was closest to, Kat and Armond, were off-limits at the moment. She decided there was only one thing to do, and that was to head back to the office and deal with whatever it was. Running away would do no good. Whatever "it" was would find her sooner or later, and she would rather look "it" in the eye than have "it" stab her in the back.

Closing her laptop, she walked the few blocks back to the office. As she got off the elevator and headed down the corridor to her office, she thought she felt the staff watching her. Good God, Victoria thought. Either she was now fully paranoid and delusional, or the meeting was no longer secret and everyone but her knew what it was about.

"Hey Mary," Victoria said as she passed by her desk, "can you come in?"

"Be right there," Mary said as she ended her call and came in, shutting the door behind her.

"Well?" Victoria said, knowing Mary well enough to see that she had more to tell.

"That was Charlotte. The meeting just broke up, and Armond and Jack are on their way down to see you. Listen, Victoria, if you need anything, anything at all, just let me know and you know I'm here for you," Mary said.

"Jack? That's bizarre. Why would he be coming to see me? I don't think we've said more than ten words to each other since I've been here."

"I have no idea and neither did Charlotte," Mary answered. "Just remember what I said. Anything at all you just let me know."

"Mary, there are a few things I need if you can swing it without putting your job in jeopardy." Victoria just finished giving the list to Mary when there was a knock on her door. It swung open before she had a chance to respond, and Jack sauntered in with Armond trailing behind him.

"Mary, we need a minute with Victoria," Jack said as he walked over and sat down without even asking whether Victoria was busy or had "a minute." Jack O'Leary was one of only ten other equity partners in the firm, besides the troika. It was rumored he held the largest number of firm shares out of the other partners. He billed himself as a ruthless litigator, and the "ruthless" part had become legend. His clients were some of the largest companies in the United States and he litigated only the sexiest of cases and those he knew he could win.

"Thanks, Mary. I'll let you know if I need anything further. Hello, Armond. Jack. What can I do for you?"

"Victoria, I'm afraid we have some unpleasant business to discuss," Jack said as he leaned forward and handed Victoria a letter on Welder & Jackson letterhead. Victoria immediately recognized the firm as the lawyers Kat's company used. Welder & Jackson was one of Acker, Smith & McGowen's competitors, and they had one of the best litigation departments in the world. Victoria knew what the letter would say, but took her time reading it anyway. When she finished, she looked up at Jack and then over at Armond, put the paper on her desk in front of her, folded her hands and waited. She refused to start babbling.

After a rather pregnant pause, Jack picked a few pieces of lint off his perfectly creased pants, crossed his legs and said, "Needless to say, Victoria, the executive committee was quite surprised to receive this letter, as was the board of Highline. Litigation like this coming so soon after the claims began and by one of your close friends is a disgrace to the firm.

Moreover, as you have been the lead with this client in ensuring the best practices are in effect, the committee considers this unfortunate development your responsibility." Jack stopped, obviously waiting for some reaction from Victoria. She did nothing other than set her pen down, lean back in her chair and wait.

"The executive committee convened an emergency meeting a short time ago and came to a consensus. This is your mess, but you have laid it on our doorstep. We need to clean it up, and step one, insisted on by the Highline board, and agreed to by the executive committee, is that you be relieved from your position in the insurance group here at the firm and that you be immediately removed as firm liaison with Highline."

Victoria was stunned. She had not known what to expect but it certainly had not been this. Particularly when she had kept alive the hope that they might have called the meeting to consider her request for advancement into the partnership. Without taking time to think through her response, she shot off, "How is this my fault, Jack? We've been trying to reach Billy and Trever to discuss the odd directive someone gave to the claim handlers that they were not to respond to any claims. I'm sure Armond explained that to the executive committee." Looking over at Armond for agreement or some indication that her assumption was correct, she got nothing as he stared at the floor. "Who gave that directive? That's the person you should be looking for and talking to. Why is this being laid at my doorstep? In fact, Billy is the one who took over the claim handling. What does he say about all of this?" Victoria felt the nausea return.

Before she could continue, Jack held up his hand as if he was a king commanding his subject. "Victoria, I'm sure you have many opinions about how we should handle this and

I'm also sure you would no doubt like to voice them, as you have done throughout your tenure at this firm. And, might I add, often without being asked. You have, in my opinion and that of many of the other partners, routinely overstepped your boundaries at the firm and unfortunately you were allowed to do so without any consequences. There was only one reason you got away with that and it was because you were handling an immensely profitable client. Now, however, that Highline no longer needs or wants you, neither does the firm. Effective immediately, you are no longer part of our firm. You have one hour to gather your personal items, which will be checked by the security team before you leave. They will remain with you and escort you out of the building."

Victoria could not believe what she was hearing. These were people she worked her ass off for, and with over the last few years, and now they were simply telling her to get out? She had done a great job and brought in millions of dollars for the firm. This made no sense. And Armond, of all people, was just sitting there. She couldn't help herself as tears sprang to her eyes. "Armond, are you a part of this?" she asked in a quiet voice.

"I am, Victoria. I think it's for the best," he said, looking directly at her with zero signs of remorse. It was as if they didn't even know each other.

Looking Victoria direct in the eyes, Jack allowed a smirk as he handed Victoria two pieces of paper. One was a resolution that announced "her decision" to leave the firm, and the other was a settlement agreement which provided that the firm would give her six months' severance at her current salary in return for agreeing to not sue the firm, and holding all information about the firm and her decision to leave in confidence. "You have the next thirty minutes to make up your mind about this. I suggest you take this offer. It's very generous.

If you don't, your pay ends today and it will be necessary for us to advise any and all potential employers of your blunder and the effect it had on our firm. I doubt you'll work as a lawyer anywhere in the country, or world, for that matter, ever again. If you agree to our offer, we'll highly recommend you, continue your health insurance for a time and pay for a headhunter to help you find another job. Very generous."

"I'd take it if I were you," Armond spoke up as he pushed the settlement agreement closer to Victoria.

Victoria couldn't even stomach looking at Armond. But right now she needed to focus on the decision these assholes were forcing her to make. She certainly had not expected to make a decision like this when she woke up that morning. Having no idea what was "typical" in these situations, Victoria had no idea whether this was, in fact, "very generous." It really didn't matter though, as Victoria knew she had made up her mind almost within the minute Jack had presented her with the firm's offer. And while she knew what she should do to make her life easier, she knew that wasn't what she would do.

Sighing, Victoria pushed the papers back across the desk and stood, placing her fingers lightly on the polished wood top. She noticed the light in her office had shifted slightly, and there was now a full beam shining in on the scene. Looking down at Jack as he was still seated in the chair across from her desk, Victoria said calmly, "Fuck you, Jack, and fuck the firm's deal. I'm not signing anything. I'm being pushed out for something I did not do. I'm being made to be a scapegoat and you and Armond know it. Now both of you, get the fuck out of my office while I'm still here."

Jack stood, leaning forward over Victoria's desk until he was inches from her face, and snarled, "Don't fuck with me, little girl. You have no idea what you're up against. If you try to come after this firm or do anything other than sashay your sweet little ass out of this office, I will unleash an arsenal the likes of which you can't even imagine." Taking a step back Jack walked around the back of the chair he had been sitting on and held on to it. In an instant his tone changed from menacing to soothing. "Let me give you some advice. Sign the agreement. Take some well-deserved time off. Find yourself a man, get laid and have a few babies. Then when the dust has settled, oh let's say maybe three to five years from now, dip your toe back into the legal field on a part-time basis. I think you'll find that will be your best option and by then all of this will have been forgotten."

Jack's little speech and attempt at manipulation had had only one effect and that was to make Victoria more resolute in her decision. "My answer remains. Now get the hell out of my office. Both of you."

Jack pushed back from the chair and walked over and opened her office door, signaling the two firm security brutes into her office. "Don't let her out of your sight. She's got thirty minutes to gather her personal items. Watch her the whole time and check everything she takes. Then kick her ass out on the street like the bitch dog she is." Turning to Armond, he said, "Let's go, now."

Armond walked toward the door to follow Jack and turned to look at Victoria. "I'm sorry, V. I really am."

"Fuck you, Armond," Victoria said with tears in her eyes as the door closed behind them.

CHAPTER
38

EXACTLY THIRTY-ONE minutes after Jack's directive, Victoria stood outside what she once considered her firm and her future. She could not believe what had just happened. For a brief moment, she had the sensation that she had been dreaming and was waiting to wake up. But as she stood squinting from the glare of the late afternoon sun, she realized it was real.

She had no idea what to do. Unlike all the other times she had needed help or support, this time she couldn't call Kat or Armond.

"Hey Victoria." Some of the other associates were heading in or out of the firm, depending on their schedules. That snapped her out of it. Victoria smiled weakly in return. The realization that she was no longer part of them came slamming home. Rather than sitting at the top of the heap, she would now be the fodder of gossip, and, what a prime piece of gossip. The queen of coverage, as she had been called, was officially dethroned. This would be rich. There was nothing people loved more than fallen royalty. She had to get out of there. Move, she told herself. Now.

Without really thinking, Victoria began walking. She had no idea where she was going or what she should do next. She had no phone or laptop. Both had been firm issued, and the security goons had them now. She hadn't even had a chance to download her personal contact information stored on the phone. What an idiot to trust so completely. She had zero backup of her contacts, and no copies of the articles she had written, or presentations she had given. She would need those as proof of her credentials in order to get another job. Oh my God! A job! Who would hire her now? Jack made it clear that he intended to ruin her. As she walked, she lifted her hand to brush stray hairs off her face and realized her face was wet. She was crying. When was the last time she had done that?

Action. That was all Victoria's brain was saying to her, over and over. Action had always been what she had relied on in difficult times and it had always gotten her through. She hailed a cab and went to buy a laptop and a phone. That took about an hour. Once her phone was up and running, Victoria immediately entered as many contacts as she could recall by heart. Next, she found the closest coffee shop with Internet access and immediately tried to access her emails and contacts. Much to her stunned surprise, her password was not rejected and she was in. Either no one had shut it down yet or Mary was helping. Whatever the reason, Victoria was grateful and moved as quickly as she could, downloading documents, emails and contacts before she was shut out of the system. Just as her phone reported 95% complete transfer, everything stopped. She had been locked out.

Victoria smiled. Either way, the firm hadn't been fast enough to prevent her from downloading all she might need to guard against the firm slandering her reputation. After saving all the information on to a backup, she called Sonia.

"Hello, can I help you?" Sonia answered, sounding formal.

"Mom, it's me, Victoria."

"Well, this is a nice surprise. To what do I owe this, and why are you calling me on someone else's phone?"

"It's my new number, Mom. Listen. Please let me get through this. I'm going to explain, but I'm going to go quickly because I have a lot to do," Victoria responded without pausing for breath. When Victoria was stressed, she spoke quickly and had little patience for anyone who interrupted her flow. Sonia knew this about her daughter and vowed to be patient.

"I was fired this afternoon. Kicked out of the firm and escorted out by two security goons. They took my phone and laptop, and—"

The firing part was all it took for Sonia to forget her vow of patience. "What are you talking about, Victoria? I thought you were on track for early partnership? Where are you? I'm coming to you." Sonia knew she was babbling but couldn't help it. Juggling the phone between her shoulder and ear, she headed toward the door, grabbing her coat and keys on her way out.

"I'm headed home, Mom. Meet me there. I have no idea what's happening. All I know is that I tried to right some wrongs going on with the insurance company, and the next thing I know, I'm out of a job."

"Well, call Armond and tell him to meet us at your apartment. He'll know what this is about," Sonia said as she walked out her door and headed to her car.

"He was part of it. He sat right there and looked directly at me. He said it was for the best and didn't even flinch. He's been a part of whatever this is all along."

Sonia stopped dead in her tracks. "Victoria, there must be some mistake. He would never abandon you. You two are as close as if you were brother and sister."

"I thought so too. I don't understand what's happened. But it's true. He sat there and supported that dickhead Jack while he told me I could either sign an agreement to not sue the firm and get six months' severance and a good recommendation from the firm for another job, or I could leave with nothing."

"Something's just not right with this picture, Victoria. None of this makes any sense. At least you have six months' severance. That will give you plenty of time to find another position and not worry for a bit about money."

"Mom, I didn't take the deal. I told them to fuck off and walked out the door."

Sonia sighed. While she was not surprised, she wished Victoria would have, for once, been selfish and thought about herself.

"Sit tight. I'll meet you at your place. We'll figure this out. Just as we always have."

"Love you Mom. Come quick." Victoria tried one more time to access her email. This time she received a warning advising her that she was illegally trying to access private IP property, and she must cease and desist or be subjected to penalties. Victoria smiled at the new warning, as it sounded like something Jack would have dictated to the techies at the firm. She imagined that Jack's head must have almost exploded when he learned that she had access after she had been escorted out of the firm. As she thought about Jack's head exploding Victoria's heart beat a bit faster, and she felt a little lighter, at the rightness of it.

As soon as Victoria entered her apartment, she went online and researched first Highline for the latest news, and then the firm. There was no indication that any lawsuits had as of yet been filed against Highline and there was no negative publicity. She also noted that her name had not yet been removed from the firm's roster of over five hundred attorneys, and she was still listed as a member of the insurance coverage department.

Victoria next dialed Michelle in Bermuda.

"Michelle Baumer, Highline claims."

"Michelle, it's Victoria."

"Victoria. Oh my God! What the hell is going on? I mean, first we can't do our job, and no one knows what is going on. The number of claims is rising at an astronomical rate and the reported damage is off the charts. Then I received an email from your firm that you've been relieved of all responsibilities and are no longer with the firm. What the hell is going on?"

"About two hours ago, Michelle, Jack and Armond walked into my office and told me that due to the fiasco with Highline's claim handling, the board and the firm were relieving me of all my responsibilities. I could either sign an agreement to keep my mouth shut and receive severance and a recommendation or I could be escorted out the door with nothing but a tarnished reputation."

"Let me guess, Victoria. You chose the tarnished reputation."

"Yup. Probably not the best choice, but I was pissed. Listen, I have a feeling that I was let go because I was looking into Highline's process failure. Do you have anything new to tell me that will help me figure this out? I need to get to the bottom of this."

"Hold on a minute." Michelle was silent as she got up and walked toward the courtyard outside her office. It was eighty-five degrees outside and humid. No one was outside in the middle of the day if they could help it and so she would be guaranteed privacy. "I hate to tell you this, but a minute before you called, Armond called me. He told me you had been fired, that there had been some inappropriate conduct that was firm related, nothing to do with Highline, and that I would be coordinating with him from now on as the firm liaison. When I asked him what had happened, he refused to tell me, being very polite but in no uncertain terms letting me know that it was private firm business and he could not discuss it further."

"This is unbelievable," Victoria whispered into the phone.

"I know. Listen, Victoria, he also told me that if you called, I was not to talk to you anymore."

Victoria was silent. All of the connections she had built over the years were in danger of being blocked by the firm, and it had enough power to do it.

"Victoria, listen. I'm not going to do that. Here's my personal cell. Call me on that number from now on. Is this number a firm phone or your own?" Michelle asked.

"Michelle, are you sure about this? I don't want you getting into trouble or losing your job," Victoria said weakly.

"Hell yes, I'm sure about this. You're the one who trained me and put me into this position. I would have still been selling shells to tourists on Hamilton Street had you not taken a chance and hired me. Anyway, something's not right. First we're told not to interact with the claimants, and then you're fired for no apparent reason. Something smells bad, and the stench is getting worse by the minute. Listen, don't get it twisted. I'm doing this not only because I like you and consider you my friend, but also to protect my own ass. If you were fired, obviously anyone can be let go, and I have no intention of going down with this ship."

Victoria smiled. She was sure that none of the firm boys imagined for a minute that one of their subordinate women wouldn't do what she had been told to do.

"Michelle, thanks. I need all the help I can get. For now, sit tight, watch the communications you receive from your management and the firm. Print those that seem at odds with the protocol or discuss my removal and any others you have a gut feel about. Let me make some calls and do some homework, and I'll get back to you. Call me if you need anything."

"Got it. Victoria, I'm sorry about this. You don't deserve it, and I know how hard you worked to make it at the firm," Michelle said before hanging up the phone.

That was true, Victoria thought. She didn't deserve it. And she was tired of getting the short end of the stick, from her shit of a father walking out on her, to her shit of a friend Armond turning his back on her...actually, stabbing her in the back, when she needed him. Well, there was at least one good thing about the shit storm of a situation she was in, and that was she had no choice but to fight. At least all of her brain power and energy could focus on doing just that, rather than second-guessing whether she had made the right decision.

Victoria heard a knock, saw her door knob jiggle and turn, and in walked her mother. "Honey, come here," Sonia said as she opened her arms and enveloped Victoria in a comforting hug. "I'm here for you, and we'll get through this together. No one fucks with my daughter and gets away with it."

Victoria had felt herself begin to break down and weaken when she was in her mother's arms, but when Sonia said "fuck," she pulled back with tears in her eyes and stared at her mother, who had a saucy grin on her face. "That's right, I said the F word. And I'll say it again if I need to."

Victoria began laughing, and then they both were cracking up. It felt so good. Then Sonia opened her purse, pulled out a notebook and said, "Okay, Victoria, let's get serious. I have a few things to tell you. First, I spoke with my principal at the school. In confidence of course," Sonia said as Victoria opened her mouth to speak. "He knows everything about everyone and everyone who is anyone. He's highly connected in the city. He gave me the name of two lawyers who specialize in employment law, one of whom does the labor negotiations for the school unions and is a pit bull. Both are top-notch, well known, and tough as nails. Both of them were already advised that you may be calling them."

"Mom, I don't see the need for this. I'm fired. It's done and over. It's a bit late now."

"Sometimes, Victoria, when it comes to you, you can be so daft. You need expert advice. These idiots just walked into your office this morning and fired you without any notice or basis, and after you've received nothing but sterling reviews and accolades. On top of that, something's not right with the insurance situation. You said so yourself."

"I did. Something's wrong, and I'm going to find out what it is. But here's the thing; I'm not sure I want to spend my time going after the firm. They're powerful and have unlimited funds. I'm not and don't. I need to focus on saving my reputation and getting a job. I can't believe I'm sitting here in the middle of the day without a job and with no one to turn to. I'm such a loser. Maybe I deserve this," Victoria said as she pulled a blanket around her and laid down on the couch.

All her life, Sonia thought, Victoria had functioned at two speeds, full throttle and off. But this was new, this despair. "Well, maybe you do deserve it. I mean you told me yourself that you were asking for promotions and partnerships ahead of the typical time frame that everyone else had to wait for. If you think about it, that's pretty self-centered. Maybe this is just a way for the universe to tell you this is not your chosen path and you're meant to do something else. Teach, perhaps? Maybe a law professor or some other sort of academic post is your calling? Teaching does run in the family after all."

Victoria sat up and looked at her mother. "I know what you're doing. Can you say reverse psychology? Really, Mom. It's a little obvious."

"Well, fine. Then think about it logically, Victoria; if you give up and don't fight, where will you be? Nowhere. You'll be damned by your silence, and people will think you did something wrong and must have deserved it. The gossip will grow and you'll become a legend for the wrong reasons. Now get off your ass. I'm making appointments with these two lawyers. We'll go together and see what we think. We're hiring one of them today."

Victoria knew what her mother said was right. She had already decided that she had to fight. But she had wanted her fight focused on moving forward, guarding her reputation and finding a new job. She had not intended to fight the firm as well. But the more she thought about it the more she realized the fights were inextricably intertwined. Pushing herself into a seated position, Victoria responded, "Fine. You set up the appointments. Give me about two hours if you can before we see the first one. I need to go through the information I downloaded and pick out the documents I think the lawyers will want to see. I'm going to work in my room and you work out here. Oh, and please look up all you can find out about these lawyers. I want to know more about them than their fancy degrees and bulldoggedness. I want to understand where they came from."

"Got it. Now go do your stuff. I'll let you know when it's time to go."

CHAPTER
39

MONA HAD BEEN practicing law for thirty years, and had never yet put her license on the line for a client, and didn't intend to start now. She had been concerned that if she used the information Jenny had found without notifying the authorities, she might violate one of the bazillion ethical codes, most of which were clear as mud. Jenny readily agreed to bring the authorities into the picture, as she had no interest in being even remotely involved in anything that might jeopardize the license she was hopefully about to receive from the State of California which would allow her to finally practice law again.

After having spent the last few days being interviewed by both the California State's Attorney's office and the feds, the feds advised Mona that they had asked all the questions they had at the moment, and gave Jenny and Mona the green light to proceed with their divorce strategy. They had been told that their main contact would be the federal agents, as they would be in charge of the investigation.

That afternoon, sitting in her condo with Mona by her side, Jenny picked up her phone and nervously dialed Big Bill's private line. The call was being taped. He picked up on the third ring. As was his way with his private line, he never said hello. The silence was unbearable and Jenny nervously shouted, "Bill, it's Jenny." They had not spoken in over two years. She could hear him breathing. There was no response and his silence was difficult to withstand.

"What do you want?" he finally responded tonelessly.

"I think we should talk," Jenny said. She thought she sounded like a mouse and didn't like it, so she cleared her throat and tried again. "I thought that since the lawyers have been unable to untangle our marriage, perhaps we could try to hammer out the resolution without them." Jenny paused and waited. Again, it seemed to her as if an eternity was passing by slowly.

"What's really going on, Jenny? You finding out that life without me and all the money you're used to isn't so easy? You hoping to come on back and settle into the lil' ole mansion you left behind in such a hurry?"

Good God, his ego was unbelievable. Jenny felt herself getting pissed, and she was amazed at how easily he could make her angry and want to pop off. She looked up at Mona, who was sitting on the other side of the table listening to their conversation. Mona shook her head from side to side and mouthed the word "no," warning Jenny not to follow her instinct. Jenny knew she had to be careful. She didn't want to bruise his ego or he would get off the phone, and if she heard too much more of this she would say something that would make him hang up anyway.

"Listen, Bill. You're right. Life without you is not easy, and perhaps I was a bit hasty in my decision to leave you and our life behind. But—"

"Damn right you were," he interrupted. "Do you realize the scandal you left in your wake? Shameful what you did to my family name."

"I know, Bill. I could have handled it better." Jenny was about to continue, but Bill interrupted again.

"You never were very good about thinking things through. Your mind was always jumping from one point to the next without any rhyme or reason."

Jenny put the wireless headpiece on so she could pace while she talked. She needed to move or she would blow this whole deal, federal task force or not. "Well, you were always the more logical one. There's no doubt about that," Jenny said as she walked into the kitchen and poured herself a cup of coffee.

"Now, let's talk about how we're going to do this. Before I even consider taking you back, there'll be some new rules. The first of which is, I don't want that damn man-eating bitch of a lawyer involved. You'll need to fire her ass and use one of the firms that I tell you to use, and it certainly won't be one of those liberal-assed California firms. I'll arrange for one of our firms here in Georgia to handle this for you."

Jenny stopped mid-pace. To say she was dumbstruck by his assumption that she wanted to come back would be an understatement. "What did you say?" she said, to give herself time to think. She looked over at Mona who gave her a rolling signal with her hand. Jenny nodded her head to let her know she understood and played along. "What else, Bill?" Jenny asked softly.

"Well, we're not going to have the marriage we used to have, Jenny. I want an open marriage."

Jenny was dumbstruck. While she knew Bill had been sneaking around on her and screwing half the world, she never thought he would agree to let her do the same. "What do you mean, Bill?"

"I mean that I'm not giving up my mistress. I have one and I'm keeping her. I'm also not sneaking around anymore, wasting my time trying to think up reasons why I won't be home for the weekend or creating some phantom business trip. When I want to see my mistress, I'm going to see her, and that's it."

"And by open, do you mean that I can have relationships as well?" Jenny asked. She had no idea why she was following this path, but she couldn't seem to help herself.

Bill chortled, and her stomach turned. She'd always hated his laugh. "Holy shit, Jenny. You haven't changed a bit. Smart on the inside but naive on the outside. Of course the fuck not. I'm not letting my wife be the whore of Atlanta. No, honey. You'll be the typical ol' Southern cuckolded wife, and you will do so with grace and suffer in silence as the good women of the South have done for centuries. Hell, you never even really liked sex anyway."

Mona was now up and walking around as well. She went over to Jenny and put her hand on her hand to give her support as she listened to her ass of a husband spew garbage out of his mouth.

"Bill, I'll have to think about all these new rules. Is there anything else?" Jenny asked.

"There might be, and if there is, I'll let you know. You've got one week to think about my offer. After that, all bets are off." The next thing Jenny heard was a click and the phone went dead. Big Bill had done what he had been doing to her for the last twenty years. He had manipulated her and controlled their conversation so much so that she had never even broached the reason she had made the call.

Jenny was embarrassed. She looked at Mona and expected to see disappointment on her face because she hadn't done what Mona and the task force had wanted her to do on the call. Instead, and much to Jenny's surprise, Mona was laughing.

"Oh my God. What an asshole," Mona said, trying to catch her breath as tears started running down the side of her face.

"Mona, it's anything but funny. I'm so embarrassed. I couldn't even get a word in. I look like such a fool," Jenny said, suddenly breaking down and crying.

Mona stopped laughing immediately, surprised to see the extent of Jenny's distress. She went over and hugged her as Jenny let out racking sobs. "Jenny, you did a great job. There's not one thing I would have changed about that conversation."

"What do you mean?" Jenny gasped. "I didn't get any information out of him, and he doesn't know I found the information he wants back. I'll never be divorced. I'll never amount to anything but Big Bill's cuckolded wife."

"No, no. You're wrong. It was a perfect job. Don't you see? His ego is so huge that he got off track by working so hard to belittle you and he has no idea whether you found what he knows you have or if you did find it whether you understand the significance. That's the best striking position we could possibly have. He's so comfortable and cozy in his belief that you want to go back that soon he'll be rolling over and exposing his soft underbelly. Once that happens, we'll take such a big bite out of that belly that he'll never recover."

"Are you just saying that, Mona? I can take the truth," Jenny said as she got hold of herself.

"No, I'm not just saying that. Why do you think I was laughing? It's too perfect, really. Now, come on. Go get those dogs of yours, take them for a long walk on the beach, and then focus on studying for the bar exam and let me do my thing. Okay?"

"Are you sure? Maybe I should just call him back now and tell him what I have and that we know what it is and we have him by the balls."

"Absolutely not. Now I want you to follow my instructions. You're going to put all thoughts of this out of your head. Meanwhile, I'll be plotting and scheming for you."

Mona pulled Jenny to her feet and got the leashes out of the drawer. Once the leashes were visible, Jenny's two dogs went nuts and ran around in circles, demanding their walk. Jenny had no choice but to smile and take her dogs for a walk.

"Okay. I'll agree to put this aside for now. But at the end of the week, I'm making a beeline for your office so you can fill me in on what's hatched in that cunning mind of yours. Agreed?"

"Agreed."

"Great. Come on, I'll head down with you, walk the beach a bit, and then come back up to focus on the always riveting Federal Rules of Civil Procedure."

CHAPTER
40

VICTORIA FINISHED PRINTING the last of the emails she thought her soon-to-be lawyer, whoever that might turn out to be, would need. With the emails in a folder, she walked into her living room and plopped down beside her mother on the sofa. Sonia was just about done finding out all she could about the two lawyers they were going to see.

"Victoria, take a look at the information I found on these lawyers while I freshen up before we go. They're both incredibly experienced and qualified. Let me know which one you like." Sonia handed her tablet over to Victoria and showed her the bookmarked pages. After about five minutes, Victoria knew which of the two she preferred, with the only caveat that she wanted to meet them first to ensure that the one she thought she wanted didn't turn out to be different in person than he appeared on paper.

Two hours later, Victoria had finished her meetings with the lawyers and had hired Robert Towner, the one she thought she would like. Robert had a comforting and positive demeanor, and most important to Victoria, he had represented quite a few women in disputes against their former employers. But the kicker was that at least three of them were female attorneys who had at one time worked at Acker, Smith & McGowen. Because Robert had already been involved in disputes with the firm, he had a good reserve of knowledge and documents about the firm. Victoria was also able to speak to each of these women as they had agreed to act as references for Robert. While they were happy to speak with Victoria and gave Robert glowing reviews, none could discuss their particular situation involving the firm, why they left, or share information that might help Victoria because they had agreed to sign confidentiality agreements when they settled their claims.

After hiring Robert, Victoria gave him the documents she thought would be important and promised to send the rest by email. He agreed that none of what had happened at the firm made sense, and that while it sounded like she had a case, until he did a deep dive into the facts, he couldn't tell for certain. He also had made certain Victoria understood that while being suddenly fired is not a pleasant or fair experience, since she was not employed under a contract, she was an "at will" employee, meaning, that she could be fired at any time with or without cause. However, the one thing the firm could not do was discriminate against her. If they could show that her firing was tied to some form of discrimination, she would be sitting pretty.

"And with the Acker firm, I'll bet we'll find some nasty dirt hidden just under the surface," Robert said. He gave Victoria a reassuring wink as he walked her out of his office and back to Sonia, who had been impatiently waiting in his lobby.

While Sonia had an opportunity to meet Robert when they first arrived, he had asked that she wait in reception so he could speak privately with Victoria to preserve her attorney-client privilege.

"What do you think that means?" Sonia asked Victoria as they headed down in the elevator.

"I have no idea. But he's obviously had some revealing and profitable dealings with the firm in the past."

"You should go back in there and ask him what that means," Sonia said, grabbing Victoria's arm.

"Mom, it must mean that he's seen this type of behavior or something like it before with my firm. I mean, former firm. And that he knows of information he can't yet share. But I think it's a good sign," Victoria responded.

Sonia put her arm around her daughter as they walked out onto the sidewalk into the still warm evening air. "Me too. I think, Victoria, this will all turn out for the best."

"Thanks for forcing me to hire a lawyer. I would never have done it without you," Victoria said as she laid her head on her mother's shoulder, suddenly feeling exhausted.

"Oh, you would have figured it out sooner or later. But you're welcome. Now, let's go have some Italian food and drink some wine while we plan our next steps. I was doing some additional investigation that you should take a look at, too," Sonia said.

Hailing a cab, Sonia gave the name of their favorite Italian restaurant on the south side on Taylor Street. Victoria had never been so thankful for her mother's guidance and comfort as she was at that moment, sitting in the cab with her, and heading to dinner. Just as they had done numerous times since she was a little girl. Victoria glanced at her mother's silhouette and thought how very lucky she was.

Once they were seated in the restaurant, Sonia opened her tablet.

"Here, take a look at this," Sonia said proudly. She turned her tablet toward Victoria so she could see what she had been looking at.

There were links to articles regarding Billy's parents' on-going divorce. They all had the same information about the high-profile divorce between William Acker Senior, one of the wealthiest men in the country, and Jenny, a former Atlanta prosecutor and his soon-to-be ex-wife. The articles went on to describe the juicy details of his Bahamian mistress ensconced in an ocean-view home in Bermuda. There was a brief mention of Billy as their only child, head of one of the largest firms in the world and thought to be the sole benefi-ciary of The Southern Will Plantation. Finally, the articles mentioned Jenny was living in California and thought to be trying to restart her legal career.

"I don't get it. So Billy's parents are getting a divorce. Nothing unusual about that, happens every day," Victoria said, putting the tablet down and signaling for the waiter to take their order. She felt herself nearing total exhaustion, and knew if she didn't eat and get home so she could fall into her bed, preferably within the next hour, she might not make it through dinner.

"Yes, I know. It's not the divorce. It's the fact that there is a chink in the armor, meaning you're on the outs and this Jenny is on the outs. She's also trying to get started in the legal field. What if you gave her a call and asked if you could speak with her? Perhaps she knows something. After all, she was married, well, is still married into that family, and has been for years," Sonia said.

"I'll think about it, Mom. Calling someone out of the blue to see if she might happen to know something about any-thing that might help me is not my top priority right now, and it's a real long shot. I need to focus on getting a job. Surviving, when no one will hire me. What do I say during my interviews? 'Yes, I was fired from one of the best firms in the world and no, they will not give me a recommendation.

You'll just have to take me at my word when I tell you it wasn't my fault and I have no idea why I was fired, except that something is fishy and I was poking around into it and the firm didn't like it. So if you hire me, maybe I'll poke around in your stuff too and you won't like it.'" Victoria teared up. "This is hopeless."

The waiter came to the table and Sonia ordered two glasses of red wine, despite Victoria's protest that it would knock her out after one sip, and the specialty of the house for dinner. Once the waiter left, Sonia said, "Victoria, you are being a bit melodramatic. You graduated second in your class at Chicago, you helped create and were legal counsel for an insurance company and you really developed the insurance coverage group at one of the largest firms in the world. Someone will see the benefit in that."

"Not if the firm calls them and tells them not to hire me. And Jack was adamant that he would make sure he would kill any opportunity I have to work in law anywhere. Worldwide. Period," Victoria said.

"Well, Victoria, that's a very sorry picture you're painting and even if I wanted to mope around in it with you, which I do not, you have no choice but to move forward. We cannot allow your future to be controlled by fear of what Jack the asshole may or may not do. So stop wallowing. Now, let's go over what you've done so far today. You purchased a new phone and laptop and best of all they are private and yours. You downloaded documents and contacts into your new phone and laptop. You've hired a lawyer who is working for you and is on your side. All in all, you've accomplished quite a bit, I think. Don't you agree?"

"Yeah. Well, while that's all fine and good, I still have no idea about my career. Practicing law is what I've dreamed about for as long as I can remember and I've managed to end it in a few short years. Now what do I do? I'm screwed. Maybe I can get my old job back in the bakery I worked at during high school," Victoria responded in a defeated tone.

"Now, we continue to plan. Here are my suggestions. Get out some paper and take notes," Sonia said, ignoring her daughter's efforts at self pity.

For the next hour and a half Victoria and Sonia ate, drank and exchanged ideas, and by the end of dinner, they each had a list of tasks they were going to accomplish over the next day or two. They had also sketched out a possible career path for Victoria, at least for now. She would open her own firm. She had no idea who her clients would be, but she would figure something out. She had a fledging thought in the back of her mind that if the insurance industry wouldn't hire her, because if Jack was true to his threat, he would make sure of it, then maybe the policyholders would. Maybe she could now work for the other side and represent those wronged by insurance companies. Victoria felt a small tingle of hope run up her spine. Maybe it was just the wine, but whatever it was, she felt better when they left the restaurant.

Victoria woke the next morning to the glorious sound of birds singing and the smell of fresh coffee. She smiled and snuggled in bed and felt cozy and so good until, "Shit!" She sat straight up as the memory of getting fired came rushing back. Sighing, her good mood broken, she put her running clothes on and wandered into the living area to find her mother sitting at the small table on the balcony with a blanket wrapped around her, sipping coffee and intent, again, on her tablet. Even though Victoria insisted it wasn't necessary, Sonia had spent the night.

"Morning," Victoria said, going over to give Sonia a kiss.

"Morning, baby. How'd you sleep? Get some coffee. I put cinnamon in it, just like you like," Sonia responded.

Victoria grabbed a cup of coffee, and as the first sips ran through her, she could feel her body return to the living. She walked out to the balcony and sat with Sonia while she put her running shoes on.

"Good," Sonia said. "I was going to suggest you go for a long run this morning. It always seems to clear your head."

"I'm running by the lake. Why don't you come with me? You can walk and I'll run and then catch up with you on my way back, and we can walk the rest of the way together."

"Done. Let me get my shoes and I'll come right back." Victoria pulled Sonia's tablet over to see what she was up to. She could not believe what she saw. Her name was all over with links to what seemed like hundreds of articles. Clicking on the one, she quickly read what was being said in the "About Town" section.

> Victoria Rodessa was removed from her position in the Insurance Coverage and Transaction Group at Acker, Smith & McGowen yesterday. While many in the industry thought her to be on track as one of the elite up-and-comers in the rarified silk stocking, legal world, she's apparently off that track and without a job. When asked for a comment, the firm said that for legal reasons, it could not answer any questions.

Victoria ran inside and found her mother brushing her teeth. "Mom! Did you see this? When were you going to tell me? What am I going to do now?"

Sonia spit out the last of the toothpaste and wiped her mouth. She grabbed Victoria in a hug. "Darling, we're going to do what we have always done. We're going to show them. Now, let's go for that run, and then we're going to call your lawyer and see what he says about this. We may need a spin of our own." Sonia turned Victoria around by the shoulders and marched her out of the bathroom and out of her apartment into the warm sunlight. "Now go. Run."

Victoria took off toward the lake. It felt good, she realized, to use her body and not her brain. As she settled into her pace, she let the feel of the run take over, changed her music to one of her favorite songs, and let her body take her into the zone and away from her ever-racing mind.

CHAPTER
41

ARMOND WANDERED AROUND his office, feeling like a caged animal. Everything was wrong. Frustrated, he kept thinking of that cartoon. The one where the brakeless train is chugging toward the cliff where the track inevitably runs out, pouring the train into a deep cavern and certain destruction in the rushing waters far, far below. When he was a kid, he always came up with a hundred different ways he would save the train, and he would scream each one at the TV while he pealed with laughter. *Inflate the hot air balloon hidden in the last car, pull the switch to inflate the cushions in the secret compartment at the bottom of the train, lasso the tree so the train will ricochet up and land on the other side.*

Now here it was, twenty-five years later and he was still trying to figure out ways to stop a brakeless train heading toward a cliff. Only this time, it was not a cartoon and there was nothing funny.

CHAPTER
42

WILHEMENA WANTED OUT of this relationship.
Now. Big Bill had promised that he would sign the
house over to her and be out of her life. Well, that was
years ago, and she was still waiting for him to do what he
promised. He had not signed over the house and he was
stalling. Last night he changed tactics, and suggested that
they stay together as he was about to have more time to spend
with her as he would soon get carte blanche from his wife to
do what and when he chose. When Wilhemena responded
that she still wanted out and had not changed her mind, he
got nasty and implied that if she continued to nag, he might
feel like she was blackmailing him and that would present a
problem he would have to resolve. His threat was clear. He
had a lot of high-powered connections in Bermuda, certainly
more than she would ever have.

Little did Big Bill know that his suggestion that he might
not follow through on his promise, coupled with his threat
of blackmail had pushed her last button. Now she was done,
and she intended to play hardball.

As soon as he left the house to play his round of morning
golf, Wilhemena got her cell phone, flattened a crumpled

piece of paper out on the counter, and dialed the number. She was nervous, so she walked over to her back porch to have the call. The sound and smell of the ocean always calmed her.

The phone was on its fifth ring and she was feeling relieved because she could hang up and avoid the call, justifying to herself that she had tried. But just as she took the phone away from her ear to press disconnect, she heard a rather cheery, "Hello."

Wilhemena didn't respond immediately. Much to her surprise, she felt her throat tighten and a rush of heat ran through her body and sweat formed under her arms. This could backfire, she thought. "Hello?" The woman on the other end had a little less cheer in her tone that time, snapping Wilhemena out of her thoughts and into the present.

"Hi," she began a bit timidly. "May I please speak with Jenny Acker?"

"This is she."

She sounds pleasant enough, Wilhemena thought. Well, let's see how she sounds after she hears what I have to say.

"You don't know me and this is awkward to say," Wilhemena said in her clipped and precise British accent, "but I'm your husband's mistress and have been for a number of years. I understand you're going through a rather tricky and difficult divorce. I have some information I thought you might be interested in," Wilhemena finished in a rush before she could chicken out.

Jenny was stunned into silence. Her mouth dropped open while she stood dumbstruck, holding the phone to her ear. After a good long minute of silence, Jenny got over her surprise and felt anger. How dare this woman call her. How did she get her phone number? That part of her life was over and she had moved on, and she had no intention of allowing this bimbo to drag her back into the drama of her old life. Instead of saying all the things she was thinking, Jenny responded in a controlled and monotone voice, "I'm quite sure we don't have anything to say to one another. If you want money, you'll have to ask your keeper."

Jenny was about to hang up when she heard, "Wait, I have information for you. It's what I can do for you," Wilhemena said, knowing she was about to lose her only chance.

"What kind of information could you possibly have that I would want? What is it that you really want?" Jenny said coldly.

"Nothing. I want nothing from you. What I do want is out of this relationship with your husband. He made promises to me he's not keeping. My one goal is to get him out of my life. Your goal is to get him out of your life. I think if you hear the information I have, both of us will be able to get what we want. I'll get him out of my life, and you'll have enough to bring him to his knees and get your divorce."

"At the risk of sounding cliché, why in the world should I trust you?" Jenny asked as she went into her kitchen to grab paper and pen to write on.

"Of course I can't give you any reason or basis to trust me. In fact, there is none. On the other hand, you've got nothing to lose. What harm is there in listening and taking a look at the information I have?" Wilhemena asked. "If you aren't interested or don't like what you see, then fine. You get on the plane and go back home. We each resume our lives."

"Get on the plane? You want me to come to you? I don't even know who you are or where you live."

"I know that and I understand your concern. I live in Bermuda. I'll give you my contact information and full name. Investigate me. Do whatever you have to do to get comfortable. But come. You and I share a common goal. I have what you need to reach yours, while you have the power to make mine a reality."

"Why don't you come to me or we can meet halfway? Better yet, email me whatever you have," Jenny said.

"No. It has to be a face-to-face meeting. I have never left the island and I don't intend my first trip to be for you. If you want this, you come. I'll give you five days to get here. If not, I'll use the information to benefit me in a different way and it'll be lost to you," Wilhemena said, deciding it was best to respond to Jenny's rather highbrow attitude with attitude of her own.

"Give me your contact information and I'll get back to you," Jenny said, placing the phone on speaker while she wrote.

After getting Wilhemena's contact information, Jenny hung up and walked out onto her balcony and stared at the ocean. This is incredible, she thought. What other skeletons are going to come crawling out of Bill's closet?

The more time passed, the more Jenny realized how very little she had known her husband. Hadn't it been exhausting for him to constantly have to sneak and hide who he really was? Thank God his mental state and well-being were no longer her concern.

She called Mona at her office and was told she was in a client conference and could not be disturbed. Jenny left a message for her to return her call.

Next, Jenny called the airline and booked a flight for the next day. She would just have to lug her material with her and study on the plane. There was no avoiding either the bar exam or Wilhemena's deadline. She would have to do both. She booked a hotel, deciding she would stay two nights in case there were other pieces to the puzzle that was the real Bill that might reveal themselves while she was in Bermuda. Enough sitting on the outside, waiting for life to happen. She was flying straight into the headwind, literally and figuratively, and was ready to face whatever was waiting for her.

CHAPTER
43

A T THE SAME time Wilhemena and Jenny ended their call, Billy and Trever sat on their porch at The Western Will overlooking the ocean. Each had just rid themselves of their women from the night before and met, as agreed, to have breakfast and discuss the board meeting scheduled for that afternoon.

"How was your night?" Billy asked.

"Just as it should be. Yours?"

"Perfect. I'll tell you one thing about the women on this island, they understand how to please a man. If I could harness the energy mine showed my cock last night...." Billy sighed in utter contentment.

Billy disgusted Trever when he rambled on about his sexual larks. Changing the subject, Trever asked, "How are we situated for the board meeting today?"

"We're going to be put through our paces. My father was all over my ass last week, wanting to know how we're going to explain Victoria's removal as Highline's counsel and termination from the firm."

"Listen, the board won't give a rat's ass about Victoria after I give them our report on the return on investment numbers.

They're making money hand over fist right now, and once they see how much, that's all they'll care about," Trever responded. "Let's be real, not one of these men care about anything other than lining their pockets and that's how it should be. In fact, I suggest we don't bring her up unless one of them asks."

Billy wasn't satisfied with Trever's typical "everything's rosy at the moment" answer. So he pushed back, "Yes, and while the numbers are good news, the point is that up until now, it's been easy to put those kind of numbers on the board, Trever. But that changed when Ileana destroyed everything in her path. Highline hadn't yet experienced a major disaster, and this is the first time it's been in a position where it's faced with paying out millions upon millions of dollars. The claims have been pouring in, and we're beginning to get some negative comments from policyholders about the company's lack of response. Armond is doing his best to keep a lid on it, but even he's starting to sound like Victoria, and hinting that perhaps someone should take a look at why the best practices are not being followed."

"Listen, we're fine. The beauty of this business is that all insurance companies get complaints. They're a part and parcel of the business. In fact, complaints by policyholders are expected." Trever pulled out a fresh cigar, signaled their housekeeper for more coffee, and leaned back in his chair.

Billy wasn't so sure. But he had seen Trever turn even the angriest crowd around so that when he was through dispensing his charm, each person felt like he or she had won the golden ticket to Willy Wonka's chocolate factory.

"However," Trever paused to puff on his cigar before finishing his thought, "we're going to have to explain the lawsuit threatened by that stuck-up spoiled bitch Kat and her company and what we intend to do about it."

"I've got that in hand," Billy said. "While we pulled the trigger and fired Victoria later than we had intended, it's actually fitting in to place quite nicely. Of course, I'll explain to the board that as soon as we learned of her total ineptness with Highline's claim process, we took control, gave Armand the reigns and fired her ass. That will explain the threatened litigation and put Armond next in line should there be any more bumps in the road."

"Fine, I'm leaving that part of it to you. But," Trever continued, "in order for our strategy to work, the claim team must document that they are providing the highest caliber of claim handling to Highline's policyholders. That part is also under your watch. If you fuck that up, the whole thing will go down the toilet," Trever warned.

"Everything is under control. Everyone on the claim team has a script to follow. All staff has been instructed not to have any communication, other than emails requesting damage and policy information, with the claimants. No telephone communication of any kind is currently allowed. Any incoming calls are sent to an automated system and responded to with a computerized email. We've taken almost all human interaction out of the process which means that we're in control," Billy responded in an annoyed and clipped tone. "Speaking of responsibilities, you need to get the PR running nationwide about the importance of fraud prevention to buttress what we're doing on the claims end."

Trever enjoyed a long inhale of his cigar and slowly exhaled it as the wind grabbed the smoke and ran with it toward the ocean. "You needn't worry about anything on my plate. It's still too early, as only a few people are complaining right now. We need to wait until just before the complaints reach a fevered pitch. Then, our public relations team will explain that a full investigation is critical to shareholders and policyholders alike to ensure that only true and rightful claims are paid. They'll make sure the public understands that fraud is in the air and that fraud leads to increased premiums. Soon, the public and those policyholders not affected by Ileana will be insisting that Highline take all the time it needs before it pays out any money. Self-interest is a powerful tool and we're going to spin it so that it becomes the wind beneath our client's wings, so to speak. Simple, really."

"Then what, Trever? Surely at some point claims will need to be paid."

"Indeed," Trever answered and leaned forward to flick the ash off his cigar and into the shrubbery, "but by then those hurt by Ileana will be desperate for money and inclined to take whatever Highline offers. At that point, Highline will end up paying out only pennies on the dollar, leaving Highline with a substantial profit."

"But then litigation will increase, which will simultaneously run up expenses and tarnish the company's reputation. It will lead to never-ending problems and that is not the kind of legacy any of the board members, or our firm for that matter, wants. They'll fire our asses if that happens"

Trever shook his head and smiled at Billy, "In fact, I predict the opposite. Statistics show that the longer people wait for their money, the less they want to engage in litigation for two reasons. One, they have had it by that time. They want to move on with their lives. And two, only a very small percent of people have the discretionary funds to pay for lawyers, particularly after surviving a disaster."

Trever watched Billy as he finally understood how it was going to work. Billy's face lit up with a broad smile and he jumped up and walked over to Trever and slapped him hard on the back. "My God, that's brilliant. It can't really fail, can it? We wrap it in the cloak of fraud prevention to keep premiums low and soon the public will be pushing our agenda for us." Billy paused though and sat back down and leaned forward. "I assume you don't intend to communicate this in writing?"

"Of course not, no," Trever answered. "At least not in the way I explained it to you. The explanation the board and internal teams will receive will be couched in terms of fraud prevention."

"But what about our firm?" Trever continued. "Getting rid of Victoria was a necessary first step in keeping our plan in place. But now, who will indoctrinate our lawyers so that they can correctly explain to Highline's staff the 'need' for the lengthy investigations and 'reasons' for delayed payment? The last thing we need is some young, idealistic lawyer digging around and trying to make a name for himself," Trever pontificated between puffs on his cigar. "Independent thinkers are not what we want in this group."

Annoyed at Trever's holier-than-thou attitude, Billy's first thought was to tell him to fuck off, focus on handling his side of the equation, and stop opining about things he knew nothing about. Instead, pulling on the restraint he had learned from years of dealing with the same type of condescending bullshit from his father, he managed to answer calmly. "I'm handling our people. I've cleared out those loyal to Victoria or too attached to the damn process she put in place and I've instead replaced them with some of our mommy lawyers."

"Why in God's name would you do that?" Trever asked, leaning his head back against the cushioned chair and watching the clouds float across the sky.

"Think about it, Trever. These women need the paycheck but they also need to get home at the end of the day to take care of their kids. They don't have time for anything else. No questioning. No digging. It also gives me a nice little group to brag about at the annual Diversity Convention. Kills two birds with one stone," Billy answered with a smirk.

Sick of Trever, Billy stood up. "I'm heading into town. I'll see you at the meeting," Billy said as he turned and walked toward the house.

Trever sighed and turned his gaze to admire the intense colors of the ocean. He watched the water ebb and flow as it caressed the island in a way, he thought, could only be described as lovingly. Trever had unexpectedly fallen in love with Bermuda and now thought of it as his second home. If this went off as planned, and Trever had no doubt that it would, Highline would come out of the hurricane claims as one of the country's highest-valued insurance companies. The firm would receive enormous income and he would be even wealthier. As he stood to get ready for the board meeting, Trever smiled, and envisioned the not-too-distant future when he would add to his growing reputation by being not only a successful lawyer, but also a sought-after business strategist. He'd then be in the perfect position to throw his hat in the race for Senate to represent the great state of Texas, just as his grandfather had done.

CHAPTER
44

AFTER SONIA AND Victoria finished their walk/run, they agreed that, because Victoria was so emotional, it would be best if Sonia met with Robert to discuss the story in the paper and find out if there was anything that could be done about it. Victoria, in the meantime, would begin looking for office space, choose a name for her firm, form her company, and begin putting all the parts in place so she could open her doors as soon as possible. They agreed to meet for coffee at about two in the afternoon to see where they were and figure out what more needed to get done.

As soon as Sonia left for her appointment with Robert, Victoria got online and began searching for office space. She was surprised at the number of choices. She quickly made a few calls, and set up two appointments with those all-inclusive business center-type places. They sounded perfect. They supplied the receptionist, staff, telephone service, and office furniture. All she had to do was pay the monthly fee and show up. Easy. As soon as she showered and dressed, she headed out the door and walked to her first appointment, a high-rise only six blocks from her apartment. As she reached the second block, the good mood Victoria had earned from running began to disappear to be replaced by a feeling that at any minute someone would recognize her, point her out as the loser who was fired from her job and the subject of the lead story in the paper. Just as she was beginning to sink into depression, her phone rang. She looked down and saw Kat's name and face light up her screen.

Victoria was smiling as she answered. "Hey you. It's been awhile. How are you?"

"Victoria, what the hell is going on? I'm so pissed off. I don't mean to pull rank, but damn it, I have no choice. My people tell me they still have not spoken with a human being at the company, and that even though they've sent in all the information we currently have on the damage to our buildings, they continue to receive emails asking for more and more information over and over again. And my lawyers tell me there has been no response to their letter."

"Kat, I thought your lawyers told you not to talk to me about this. Why are you calling me?" Victoria said in a flat voice.

Kat paused then said, "Listen, V, I hate to do this to you, but I don't have any other option. I've instructed my lawyers to up the ante in the lawsuit we intend to file to include the board of directors of Highline. I don't know how much that will affect you, and I wanted to give you a heads-up."

Victoria waited until Kat finished. On the one hand, Victoria felt irrationally angry, thinking that if she had still been at the firm and overseeing Highline, Kat filing a suit going after the board would likely drag Victoria smack into the middle of it. On the other hand, Victoria was happy that Kat was going after the board, as that would likely affect the firm negatively and right now anything that hurt the firm made Victoria feel good.

"Victoria, you're not saying anything. Listen, I'm sure you're upset and probably pissed off at me for taking this route. You know you're like my sister. In fact, you are my sister. But I have my whole family's business to consider," Kat continued. "I have no choice, and frankly, I'm disappointed. From what I can tell, your team's done nothing to help." Kat finally stopped to take a breath, realizing that Victoria had said absolutely nothing, which was not like her. It was rare that Victoria would stand still for a tongue-lashing without coming out of her corner swinging.

Maybe she hung up on me, Kat thought, working herself up even more. "V, are you there? And why did I have to call Sonia to find out you changed your phone number?"

"I'm here, Kat," Victoria said.

"Well, why aren't you saying anything? What's going on? My family's whole business is at stake and you're just sitting there, mute, as if you could give a shit. What's wrong with you?"

Listening to Kat made Victoria feel like she had one less friend in the world and that Kat was just one more person who had decided to dump on her. How dare she call and lambast her without even finding out what was going on? Kat knew Victoria better than that, and even if she had doubts about what Victoria may or may not have done regarding Highline, shouldn't she have given Victoria the benefit of the doubt?

Victoria let the silence sit heavy for a beat before answering Kat's question. "I was fired yesterday. I was given thirty minutes to pack my personal items and get out. Two security goons stood guard and then escorted me out of the office."

Now the silence hung heavy from Kat's side. "Are you still there?" Victoria asked.

"Victoria, yes, of course I'm here. What are you talking about? How can that be? What happened?"

"Listen, Kat, I don't understand it myself. They said it was because of the suit you intend to file which, according to them, was a result of the mess I created. I think it has something to do with my inquiries into what was going on at Highline. That's about as much as I can figure out right now. On the other hand, maybe I did create this mess. Maybe they were right and I was too pushy, too greedy and this is all a consequence of that."

"Okay, now you sound like a Stepford wife. Stop talking like that. How did it happen?"

"Yesterday, the head litigation partner, Jack, with Armond in tow, walked into my office, showed me the letter your lawyers had sent, and told me that I had totally fucked up Highline and that the board had requested I be removed as its counsel. Jack told me that in order to protect the firm, and because I had a bad attitude, the firm wanted me gone. Immediately."

"That's insane. What did Armond say?"

"Well, that's rather interesting. Armond said absolutely nothing. Just sat behind Jack and let him do his thing. Until, that is, I asked him what he thought. He didn't even hesitate, looked me right in the eyes and said he agreed with the firm's decision. I haven't spoken with him since," Victoria explained, feeling sad reliving Armond's betrayal over again.

"This makes no sense. Why would Armond act like that?"

Victoria felt tears gather again and she began to lose the little control she had as she thought about Kat's question. "I have no idea. He stood by and said nothing while Jack ordered the security goons to watch me and make sure I was escorted out of the firm." She started to sob quietly but heavily into the phone. "I thought we were friends," she said, wiping the tears as fast as they fell to prevent her mascara from totally screwing up her face.

"Oh, V, I'm so sorry. I had no idea. Why didn't you call me?"

Through her sobs Victoria responded, "Because I couldn't. I didn't want to involve you in case it somehow affected your situation or our client's business. I felt like I had nowhere to turn." She started crying again and her sadness was palpable through the phone.

"I'm getting on the first plane I can find space on this afternoon. I'll be there for dinner. What are you doing now?"

"No," Victoria managed to spit out, as she tried to regain control. "No. Don't come. Not yet. I need to figure some things out."

"I'll help you do that, Victoria. I want to be there with you and I want to see Armond, that lousy son of a bitch. I intend to break his balls, assuming I can find them, small as they apparently are."

"Not yet. Sonia's been with me every step of the way. She's been great. We've got a plan and it's under control right now. To be honest, I don't want to be seen with you right now and have them accuse me of helping you with your lawsuit. I wouldn't put it past them to make those kind of accusations and I can't take any more pressure."

"Okay, I'll accept that for now. Will you consider coming to work for us?" Kat asked.

"No. Not yet. But thanks for the offer. Let me get through the next few days and see where I am, okay?"

"Of course. But, what are you doing for money? I'm assuming they are paying you a hefty severance?" Kat asked.

"The firm wanted me to sign a release agreeing not to sue them. In return, they would have paid me six months' severance and agreed not to sully my good name."

"What did you do?"

"I told them to go fuck themselves."

Kat started laughing so hard she almost fell off her chair. "Oh My God. Good girl. I would have paid good money to see that. What did they say?"

"Jack didn't take that too well. I'm quite sure no one has ever spoken to him like that. He's used to everyone hanging on his every word and accepting his ultimatums. He didn't like it. I'm sure I'm in his crosshairs now."

"Listen, Victoria, I want to help. What can I do?"

"You can send me business. I'm opening my own practice. I'm heading over now to look at office space, and I've hired a lawyer to look into suing the firm. Sonia's with him now, discussing what we can do about an article that appeared in the paper this morning about my firing. I'm incredibly embarrassed, Kat. I thought I was a star and on track to be the youngest-ever partner at the firm. Now look at me. I'm embarrassed, without a job and totally disgraced," Victoria finished, feeling the heaviness of dejection settle into her chest.

"Victoria, stop that. Don't let those assholes define you. You're one of the most brilliant people I know. To be honest, I always thought that firm was stuffy and parochial and full of partners who clearly don't value women as their equals. I know this is trite, but in this case, I think this will turn out to be one of those times where something horrible turns into one of the best turning points of your life."

"Ah, thanks Kat. You have no idea how much that means to me. I just don't feel very positive right now. I mean, the only thing I have ever done is insurance work. Seems like a pretty narrow specialty right now," Victoria sighed.

"Listen V, if I was there with you, I would give you a big hug then a swift kick in the ass. Now listen, I'll send you business. Don't worry about that. Insurance is all contract work, so what you are is an expert in negotiation, contracts and regulations. We'll have you up and running in no time. I'm so sorry I was all over your ass, as if you were responsible for Highline. I know you better than to think you would have allowed one of your clients to act inappropriately."

"I understand, Kat. Actually, though, something isn't right. The last time I tried to call a meeting, it was cancelled by the top dogs at the firm. Neither Armond nor I could get it reset. Now that I have seen how Armond reacted to my being let go, perhaps he was involved in preventing that meeting and didn't want me to know."

"Let me think about this for a bit, V. Something seems off about the coincidence of your firing and Highline's lack of response, especially now that you tell me you were trying to set meetings to discuss the issue. Do you mind if I do a bit of digging?" Kat asked.

"I don't mind as long as you don't poke the bear until I'm ready and you don't publicize anything about my situation."

"No, I'll ensure that won't happen. I think I might have a way to help both of us. But I want to check with my lawyers first."

"No problem," Victoria responded. "Oh, but I do need a publicist. Do you have a good one you can recommend?"

"Yes, and she's fantastic. I'll email her contact information to you. I'll let her know that you may contact her, and I'll be sure to let her know you're family. That should move anything you need done to the top of her list," Kat said.

"Thanks, my tart. You're always there for me. I've gotta go, I'm late."

As soon as Kat was off the line with Victoria, she called the partner who was handling their case against Highline and relayed her conversation. Clearly something was going on between the Acker firm and Highline. It made no sense that someone would thwart an effort to improve one of its client's services by firing the person who was trying to fix the problem. Kat didn't know what was off, but she sure as shit was not going to sit around and let someone screw with her company or her best friend. When she was finished, she sat back and sighed. Now she would wait to see what trash her digging would unearth.

CHAPTER
45

JENNY FIDGETED AS she was uncomfortably stuck in a window seat. She preferred an aisle, but the flights to Bermuda had been booked solid as it was nearing the end of the high season and tourists from all over the world had come to bask in the sun and swim in the warm water. But as the plane banked and turned sharply on its descent toward the island airport, she changed her mind about her seat as she was rewarded with a breathtaking and panoramic view. Why have I never been here before? She wondered. The scene that unfolded below her window was absolutely stunning. The colors of the water that surrounded the small, quaint-looking island ranged from bright turquoise to deep teal and it was so clear she swore she could see bottom. Jenny was smitten.

But anxiety soon washed away her feeling of enchantment. Meeting the woman who had been her husband's mistress for, as far as the private investigator Mona had hired could figure out, the last ten years, had not been on Jenny's bucket list. Jenny felt a strong and familiar wave of hot anger mixed with shame bubble to the surface. It was a feeling she had come to know well as it revisited each time Mona told her, "regrettably," about another one of the women their investigator had turned up. The anger wasn't so much over the fact that Bill had relentlessly screwed around, although she was pissed over the possible health risks. Rather, it was over what Jenny considered a waste of a large part of her life spent tirelessly trying to please a man who clearly could not be pleased and never, apparently, gave a rat's ass about her.

The hard smack of the plane's wheels hitting the runway jolted Jenny out of her negative thoughts. She reminded herself that she was far beyond those old feelings and had successfully and happily moved forward with her life. She loved living in Southern California, would soon be practicing law there, fingers crossed, and was set to begin a job as an intern at a firm in Los Angeles, thanks to Mona. Gathering her carry-on bag, Jenny determinedly changed her perspective. As she walked out of the plane, she reminded herself that whatever was going to happen now would be part of her path forward. And as far as Jenny was concerned, any forward movement was good movement.

Wilhemena sat waiting in the hotel lounge. She was surprised to realize she was sweating. She was never hot, as she had little body fat. Today was different. Today she was playing a dangerous game that would determine the outcome of her long-awaited future.

Wilhemena straightened her pencil skirt and fiddled with her diamond stud earrings. She had dressed conservatively and formally, chic yet sophisticated, like the woman she imagined herself to be. She never thought that sleeping with Big Bill in return for money and other benefits was in the same category as the prostitutes on the island who turned a quick trick for cash. After all, it wasn't like she rented her body out to different men for money. She had been in the same relationship for the past decade, since she was seventeen. She had done what she had to do so she wouldn't end up like her mother, cleaning toilets in one of the fancy hotels for the rest of her life and forever worrying about paying the bills.

A text brought her phone to life. *On the way,* texted the limo driver she had hired to get Jenny from the airport. Wilhemena flagged the waiter and ordered champagne. She was nervous and needed a few sips to calm her down. Her life was in the hands of this privileged woman from the mainland whom she had never met. An intolerable situation, and one that Wilhemena swore she would never allow happen again. Once this was over, she would be the only person in control of her life.

Checking her watch, Wilhemena glanced anxiously at the entrance to the darkened bar. She took a deep breath and waited for her future.

CHAPTER
46

SONIA'S MEETING WITH the lawyer had been productive. During the meeting, Victoria had texted Sonia the contact information for the public relations expert Kat had recommended. Robert smiled when Sonia told him her name, explaining that he had used her before and agreed she was one of the best. Sonia and Robert drafted a statement they were both happy with, received approval from Victoria, and had a conference call with the expert. She agreed to take Victoria on as a client and Robert had his assistant send her both the article that had appeared in the paper and their draft response. She promised to have a plan of action within the next hour and would contact Victoria and Robert for a conference call.

That done, Robert turned next to the matter of the Acker firm. While Sonia was still in his office, he drafted and, after reading the letter to Victoria over the phone and receiving her approval, sent via email and hand delivery, a letter to Acker's chairman. It warned first that further communication of any information about Victoria would be met with swift and immediate action, including holding the firm accountable for any character damage, defamation or privacy violations. Finally, the letter advised that a claim was going to be filed seeking damages for the improper firing of Victoria and demanding that, pursuant to the Federal Rules of Civil Procedure, the firm refrain from destroying any evidence about Victoria and Highline.

After Robert sent the letter to the firm, he looked up, and said with the gleam of someone who loves a good fight, "Hang on, this is where the fun begins." Sonia actually laughed out loud. For the first time in forty-eight hours, she felt good. Really good. There was nothing like taking positive action when people were trying to shit on you. And no one was going to shit on her little girl and get away with it.

Armond read the email from Trever to all partners and then he opened the attached letter from Victoria's lawyer advising of the claim he would be filing on behalf of Victoria. Trever's email called for an emergency meeting that afternoon at four o'clock, and instructed all partners not to discuss Victoria in any way or with anyone. Any inquiries, even from staff or associates, were to be directed to Jack.

Armond couldn't help but smile. Good girl, he thought. "I was hoping you'd have the balls to do just that," he said under his breath as he continued to load documents onto a USB stick. He checked the time. Almost two thirty. He had only a precious few moments to finish before the meeting. As soon as the meeting was finished, he planned to return to his office, pack his "man purse," as Victoria had dubbed it, and leave. Armond smiled as he thought about all the shit Victoria used to give him about his many clothes and accessories. He missed her, but the die was cast and he had chosen his path. He pushed thoughts of her out of his mind.

He was bone tired. He had been at the office until one that morning, returning five hours later at six. He figured he had gotten maybe two hours of sleep. His physical state, however, took a distant second to his mind, which was racing. Everything was nearing the boiling point. He had to be extremely careful. Execution and timing were critical, and he had no intention of screwing it up.

Victoria loved the first space she saw. It had amazing views of the lake and the city skyline. She signed the contract leasing the space for six months and completed all the final arrangements before she left. She even met with her assigned staff and gave them a list of items she needed them to handle over the next few days. When she left, she felt rather good about things, and freer than she had since she began working at the firm.

On her way home she called her mother and texted Kat, telling them the good news. She also tried out the name she had come up with for her new firm, saying it out loud for the first time. While she had been waiting for the final paperwork at her new space, she had toyed with a description of her firm. *Rodessa Law. Specializing in contract and insurance matters.* A bit disjointed and it definitely needs work, but it's a start, she thought.

At the same moment Victoria was heading home after leaving her new office, Armond was walking into the firm's large conference room for the four o'clock meeting. He had weathered other emergency meetings over the years, but never one where the tension in the room had been this thick before the meeting had even begun. While the partners in the room found their seats, the wall cabinet moved slowly back into specially designed recessed pockets, revealing a big screen that would allow Trever and Billy to chair the meeting via satellite as they were still in Bermuda.

At precisely four o'clock, the screen flickered to life and the firm's IT security chief was the first to speak. "We have a secure line, sirs," he said to Trever and Billy.

"Thank you. You may leave," Trever ordered. They waited in silence while the security chief walked the long stretch of the formal conference room and closed the door behind him. The room remained silent. Every lawyer in the room knew how to play the pregnant-pause game. Idiots, Armond thought. You're like a bunch of sheep.

"Gentlemen, thank you for rearranging your busy schedules on such short notice. We have, as you've all heard by now, a situation that began yesterday when the firm made the decision to relieve Victoria Rodessa of her position. Jack and Armond handled the dismissal for the firm and they will answer any questions you have before we adjourn this meeting. However, as you see from the letter her lawyer sent earlier today, she's quite full of herself and is threatening a federal employment and gender discrimination action. This is a problem for the firm on two fronts. First, we're well regarded as a firm that supports and funds the growth of women in the law. Litigation of this nature will obviously call our record into question. Second, it may shed unwanted light on Highline Insurance, one of our largest clients. Obviously, we can't let either happen." Trever paused long enough to take a pull from the cigar he had smoldering on the table in front of him and allowed his words to hang heavy in the air. As he knew would be true, no one dared say a word. They were all waiting for the opportunity to kiss his ass. Trever allowed himself a quick smile at the thought and then came back to the moment. "Jack will be the lead for the firm on this little bitch's litigation. But we need each and every one of you to refrain from speaking about this young woman and to gather any documents, witness names, and personal accounts that will support our decision to remove her from our firm. We intend to drive Ms. Rodessa so far underground where the sun don't shine that she'll never rear her pretty little head in the legal arena ever again. When we're through with her, she won't even be able to get a job as firm coffee lady."

Laughter broke out among the men as they murmured their approval of the plan. Assholes, Armond thought as he doodled on the pad in front of him. When he looked up, he saw that everyone had turned to look at him, silently questioning whether he was on board. Trever almost laughed out loud as he watched the expressions flit across Armond's face. He could have predicted his responses down to the exact second. But he needed Armond on his team so he would protect him, for now. "Armond has been one of the driving forces behind our decision, and while he worked closely with Victoria while she was here, he was the first to admit that she had set up what has turned out to be a dysfunctional system at Highline. He was instrumental in bringing matters to a head so we could jump in, begin to correct the missteps taken with our client, and rid ourselves of the problem. Armond, have I left anything out?" Trever asked.

"No sir. Except the fact that Miss High-and-Mighty told Jack and me to 'fuck off' before she was escorted out of our offices." There was a smattering of laughter and hooting, as Armond could have predicted. "She was quite pissed at the time, so I'm not sure her retaining a lawyer is a big surprise. But no sir, you left nothing out," Armond finished, playing his part in this horrific game.

"All true. Thank you, Armond." Taking another pull on his cigar, he turned to Billy, whose hair was being gently and perfectly blown by the Bermudan breeze. "Billy, anything to add?"

"No. The less time spent on this bitch, the better. Looking around the room and with our collective hourly rates, we've just tossed about $20,000 out the window. Let's wrap this up."

Trever smiled. "Right you are. Okay, our public relations person will be handling all communications on this topic, both internal and external. So please, gather from anyone in the firm all of the negative information about Victoria you can get. Do not, however, say anything negative or discuss the situation. After the close of business this evening, I will send the letter we received from her lawyer, along with a short explanatory email to all the employees of the firm. That will allow us to demonstrate how seriously we take such matters to any judge assigned to this case and keep us on the right side of this thing. Now, unless there are further questions or comments, this meeting is adjourned and let's get back to what we do best, making shit piles of money!" The screen faded to black to loud applause, with the image of Trever's fisted hand slamming down on the table like he was some politician making a particularly important point.

Armond smirked. Nicely done, he thought. But he had little time to think about anything, as he was immediately surrounded by partners who wanted to relive the incredible moment that must have been Victoria's firing. Most of them were jealous of Victoria and hadn't liked her, as she had been knocking on their partner door in what they considered an overly aggressive fashion, trying to be the youngest and the first woman partner at their firm. Now, to a man, they all thought she had got what she deserved. Armond was not in the mood to discuss what he felt had to date been one of his worst moments, so he steered them all to Jack for answers.

"Jack was the one who really ran the show. He's the best one to give you the play-by-play."

Just as Armond knew he would, Jack loved the attention and picked up the conversation as if on cue. "Gentleman, I'll be more than happy to answer your questions at another time. Right now, though, my top priority, really our top priority, is to gather evidence against Ms. Rodessa. Did people consider her difficult to work with? In other words, was she a raging bitch? Was she hell-bent on getting ahead? Did she abuse people to do so? Was bettering her career her goal so much so that she acted to the detriment to our clients? Was she screwing anyone at the firm or one of our clients' employees? Who was she friends with both here and at Highline? We will need to neutralize those people. All of this information will help me craft our defense and, even more important, our offense."

Armond watched as his idiot partners actually took notes so they could be certain to try to dig up the best and dirtiest secrets about Victoria in order to curry favor from the troika. Armond got up to leave, having no further stomach for this display, and was stopped by Jack. "Armond, hold up a minute. Gentlemen, one more thing before we break," Jack said, looking directly at Armond. "I expect each of you to give me at least one piece of damning information I can use against Victoria, and I want it by the end of the week. No excuses will be tolerated. So if you never worked with her, find someone who did, befriend them, and get the information we need to put her down. I repeat, no exceptions will be tolerated. None." Jack stared at Armond with a slight smirk on his face, daring Armond to protest his newest edict.

Armond looked Jack directly in the eyes, nodding as if in agreement, all the while thinking about what a prick he was. Turning to leave, he headed directly to his office. Once there, he gathered as much as he could carry of his belongings without drawing attention to his intent, headed down the elevator, through security and out into the evening air, leaving behind forever the building he once thought would be his home for the whole of his career. It wasn't until he had walked six blocks, turned the corner onto Wacker Drive, and caught a glimpse of the boats heading up the Chicago River on their way toward Lake Michigan, that he let out his first full breath.

CHAPTER
47

BEFORE THE CALL began, Kat reviewed the complaint her lawyers had drafted and were about to file, which would signal the start of Fontaine's lawsuit against Highline. Kat was not happy and she let her lawyers know it. "It sucks," she told them in no uncertain terms. "I want headline grabbing and sexy. I want the board members added as defendants. I want their balls against the wall. I want passion. I thought I had made that perfectly clear. This complaint contains nothing passionate, sexy or ball busting, for that matter."

"Kat. Let me—"

"Let me finish," Kat interrupted one of the lawyers working on her case, "because it seems that you did not understand me the first time. I want a show-and-tell for whichever federal judge ends up being assigned to our case. Of equal importance, I want the reporter assigned to the courthouse to salivate once he or she reads our complaint so much so that the story they write in the paper screams the verdict in our favor before the first deposition is even scheduled. Most of all, I want to scare the living shit out of Highline and the board so they do what should have been done from the beginning— pay for my company's property damage."

"Kat, we need solid fact to sue the board and make those kind of allegations in federal court or we'll be sanctioned, and we don't have them yet," Joseph, the partner in charge of her case said.

"I'm connecting some dots on my end and we'll see where it leads. It's a long shot but it just may pay off. In the meantime, I don't give a rat's ass if you have to hire ten investigators to get the backup you need. You've got precious little time to revise the complaint to create the masterpiece I just described or you're fired. I want the board to understand that it is not only their company's ass that's on the line, but theirs as well. I expect creativity in the next draft and I better get it."

Just as Kat hung up on the call with the law firm, her cell phone began to vibrate and make that irritating buzzing noise. As she was about to push the ignore button, she was stunned to see the caller ID announce, Armond. She almost dropped the phone trying to answer it before he hung up. "Hello?" Kat asked, skeptical that Armond would really be calling her after what he had done to Victoria.

"Kat, listen, it's Armond. Don't hang up, please."

"How could you have done that to Victoria?" Kat demanded. "What's wrong with you? What the hell is going on?"

"Kat, please. There is a lot at stake, and neither you nor V really understand. I don't have long to talk. Just let V know that I'm with her, but I have to handle things my way. She'll understand soon enough."

"Armond, I don't understand. What are you talking about? Why did you let them fire Victoria and throw her out of the firm? None of this makes any sense."

"It will, Kat. I promise. Please just convey that message to V for me. Please." Armond's pleading sounded so pitiful Kat couldn't help but relent just a bit.

"Fine. I'll convey it. But just for the record, if you hurt her, you'll be next on my hit list."

"I get it. You'll have to wait in line, though. There'll be a few ahead of you. One more thing. Might I suggest a meeting?"

"About what?" Kat asked.

"I can't discuss it over the phone and I suggest you have your legal team present. Someone will be in touch with you to arrange it." Armond disconnected the line.

Kat sighed. Trying to relax, she turned, looked out her windows, and watched the sun sinking in the west. She took a few calming breaths while trying to think of the best way to deliver Armond's cryptic message to Victoria. Fuck the calming breaths, she thought. Walking over to her office bar, Kat opened a bottle of particularly good red she just had shipped from Australia. Pouring a glass, she picked up her phone to deliver the message to Victoria.

Victoria's days had been filled with doing all the thousands of little odds and ends that are necessary to open a legal practice. She hired a marketing person she found on the Internet, and with her help, decided on a logo, branding, and a marketing campaign—most of which, due to her shrinking savings, would be directed to her contacts and a specific market they had decided to target. She worked with a web designer recommended by the marketing guru, and together they finalized the design of her web page. Victoria then spent time creating the content. She wanted to have a blog so she could discuss new case law as it came down, as well as some of the developing trends around the country and in the world of insurance law.

Actually, Victoria thought, when she had a moment to think about it, this whole endeavor felt right. Really good, actually. Like she should have been doing this all along. While the opportunity to work for Highline and learn insurance law and regulations had come from being a part of the Acker firm, she alone had been the one primarily responsible for creating the insurance coverage and transaction group. The more she thought about all she had learned and accomplished, the better she felt about being on her own. She had been the laboring oar at the firm. She had suggested they create the insurance group. She had no reason to be nervous about being on her own. She had always, now that she thought it through, essentially been on her own at the firm. Well, having Armond in her corner and for brainstorming sessions had been a godsend. But she'd just have to make due.

The thought of Armond's odd message to Kat made Victoria feel sad. She had no idea what he was talking about. What she did know, however, was that he had marched into her office and fired her. Victoria knew she would never forget the look in his eyes that day or the tone of dismissal in his voice. It was as if they had never been friends. She thought they were so close that she had actually thought of him as the brother she never had. Well, whatever was up, Victoria knew she couldn't sit around and wait for him to let her in on it. Anyway, her lawyer had told her not to take any calls from Armond due to the lawsuit he was about to file.

CHAPTER
48

FOR THE PAST week, Armond had been busy poring over the history of emails and documents that went into the formation and running of Highline. He had called in sick the first three days after the "Victoria conference," as he thought of it. On the third day, he emailed his assistant letting her know he had decided to use the rest of his vacation days and he would not be back in the office until the third week in October. He needed time to organize his strategy and to allow his father to use his considerable contacts to find and retain the best lawyer to represent him. Someone to keep him clear from violating criminal laws or ethical codes of conduct. Armond had no intention of getting himself embroiled in a mess that was not of his making. He thought of himself more as a whistleblower. Unfortunately, and ironically, there was no such protection for lawyers who chose to reveal improper conduct. He intended to ensure that what he did, and how he did it, did not violate any attorney-client or work-product privileges or any other confidential or protected rights.

As he swept through the documents and communications, he simultaneously added the critical information to a timeline. He had learned during his legal career that this simple tool was the best way to reveal hidden agendas. Whatever story was hidden by the moving parts or as of yet unrecognized allegiances, would always emerge. He sat up straight, pushing his hands against his lower back, stretching the muscles that were tight from being hunched over his desk. He got up and walked to his kitchen to make a fresh pot of coffee. He wanted to finish the first draft before he slept. Time was now of the essence. Not only for him, but Victoria and countless others as well.

While he waited for the coffee, he bent over the kitchen counter with his head in his hands. Suddenly, it came to him. His timeline was one dimensional! That was the problem. He needed to add some of the other non-Acker players like Billy's father, since he was the chairman of the board of Highline and had been the one to suggest retaining their firm in the first place. He searched the Internet for Bill Acker, and four hours later, at three in the morning after adding information, he finally went to bed. He knew he had most of the story, and while he didn't have it all yet, he had enough. Exhausted, he went to his room and fell asleep with his clothes on.

The constant buzzing of his phone worked its way into his dream. He couldn't understand why his assistant kept buzzing him when he had given her specific instructions that he did not want to be bothered. He would have to let her go. Reaching to answer her call, he was surprised to hear his father's voice coming from outside his office. He rarely came to Chicago. "Why are you here?" Armond mumbled.

"What the hell are you talking about? Are you drunk or high? Jesus Christ, you sound just like some of these idiot actors I have to deal with day in and day out."

Armond sat up and looked around. Holy crap. It had been a dream, and his father was on the phone, which he had apparently answered in his sleep. "Dad. Sorry. Sleeping. You were in my dream," Armond managed to get out, yawning as he looked at the clock. Eight in the morning. He had gotten about five hours of sleep. That will do, he thought.

"I take it you saw my email yesterday?" his dad asked.

"Jesus. No, sorry. I worked until the early morning hours on the theory. I don't have it yet. I'm close. I can feel it," Armond said excitedly.

"Well, that's jim-dandy. Bring it with you but get your ass to the airport. You're booked on a flight to Houston leaving at noon. I'll see you there."

"Did you find a lawyer?"

"I did. One of the best in the country. But judge for yourself. He's flying into Houston for the meeting. I have to go. I'll see you in a few hours."

Armond grabbed leftover coffee and heated it in the microwave while packing his laptop and timeline. He had one person he wanted to connect with before he got on his flight. Placing the call, he waited for her to pick up. The answering machine took his call. Rather than leave a message, he left his name and number and asked that she give him a call.

By the time Armond landed and got to his hotel, it was three thirty. While checking in, the front desk clerk handed him a note from his father with his room number and telling Armond to call as soon as he was settled.

By four o'clock, Armond was in his father's suite meeting the lawyer retained by his father. His father let the two men talk in private. Armond explained what he had from the firm and pulled out his timeline. He explained the situation leading up to Victoria's firing.

Armond listened to his lawyer's advice, which was to go to the meeting with Kat's team and listen to what they had found out thus far. That way, Armond would not be revealing anything, and if some of these facts were already known, he would never have to. If they weren't known, then they would determine the next steps.

CHAPTER
49

EVER SINCE JENNY'S enlightening and productive meeting with Wilhemena, Mona and she had been busy connecting the dots, making phone calls and perfecting their strategy. It was eight at night, and they weren't quite yet ready to stop. They had at least two more hours before they would be ready to put it, and themselves, to bed. As Jenny waited for Mona to come back to her conference room with much-needed coffee, her mind wandered over the strange turn of events that had brought her to this unexpected place. Much to Jenny's surprise, she liked Wilhemena, not that she intended to keep in touch. But once she understood Wilhemena's limited opportunities to make something of herself on the tiny island, Jenny had a hard time blaming her. After all, Wilhemena had been a young girl of only seventeen when her stupid husband had directed the full force of his charm, power, and money in her direction. Heady stuff for any young girl. Jenny herself had fallen for it, and she had been older, highly educated and had a career.

Now, however, Jenny found their surprising joint goal of getting Bill out of their respective lives to be refreshing and almost comical, in a sick sort of way. Both of them had been used and manipulated, and now it was their turn at bat. And with what they each had on him, they'd need only step into the batter's box once to hit a home run. Mona now represented Wilhemena as well and as soon as she could arrange it, she would deliver to Big Bill a copy of the complaint, alleging various inappropriate and lewd acts performed on a seventeen-year-old girl. Statutory rape for sure, with prison time possible, and the sullying of his reputation a reachable outcome. No one wanted to do business with a pervert and criminal nowadays; the Internet was too powerful a tool and everyone knew everything about everyone.

"Here you go," Mona said, handing Jenny a cup of dark, black coffee. "If this doesn't keep us awake, nothing will."

"Thanks. Okay, now what?" Jenny asked.

"Well, oops, hold on," Mona said. Looking at her phone, she read the text and smiled.

"Well?" Jenny asked. "Did they get him?"

"Not yet. Apparently he's still in Bermuda. But they've got The Southern Will staked out. As soon as he walks in that door, he'll get a little welcome-home present he won't soon forget." The package Mona had created for Bill gave him forty-eight hours to accept Wilhemena's demands before she made his life a living hell by filing the lawsuit which would make his life a public nightmare. Mona put her coffee down untouched and walked over to push a button in the conference room wall. "Screw the coffee." There was the slightest whirring noise, followed by a portion of the panel sliding back into the wall, pocket-style, to reveal a beautiful room stocked full of bottle after bottle of fine wine. "A celebration is in order."

Grabbing a bottle of champagne, Mona popped the top and filled two glasses. Handing one to Jenny, Mona lifted her glass in a salute to their handiwork. "To us and the fish we're about to skewer."

"I'm worried he'll try to contact me," Jenny said.

"He might." Mona shrugged her shoulders. "Just don't respond. Anyway, I'm sure I'll get an irate call from his lawyer as soon as he receives my newest missive. And, I bet the first words out of his mouth will be, 'What the fuck do you think you're doing?'" Mona smiled and sat back as she sipped the champagne. "And then," Mona sighed, "I'll tug on the line a bit more to set the hook so we get our meeting, where we'll lay it all out. And you, my dear, will get to kill two birds with one stone. You'll get to right a wrong, and have the pleasure of seeing your soon-to-be ex-husband squirm like a helpless fish."

Jenny smiled at the thought and took another sip of champagne. "Let's get back to work. I want every piece in place before we get on the plane tomorrow."

Seven people milled around Kat's conference room. Three from her outside legal team, Armond, his father, his lawyer, and Kat rounded out the group. They were just settling in around the long conference table when Kat's assistant knocked on the door, peeked in and announced, "They're here. Shall I bring them in?"

"Give me a minute, Cassie. I'll come out and get them in a moment." Everyone, including Kat's lawyers, looked at Kat for an explanation. Armond almost laughed out loud. Looking at the expressions on the faces of Kat's legal team, it was obvious she had not filled them in on whatever was about to happen. Had Armond not been so concerned about his own situation and the safety of his own ass, he would have undoubtedly sympathized with them. There was nothing lawyers hated more than being surprised by their own client.

Kat pushed her chair back from her position at the head of the table, leaned back, crossed her legs and explained. "I wasn't sure they were coming so I didn't want to say anything. But when I open the door, we'll be meeting two women who claim to have important information that they thought might be of interest to our insurance matter with Highline. Apparently, our company's little problem with our insurer seems to have crossed paths with a divorce case. Anyway, they refused to discuss it over the phone, which seems to be a trend at the moment," Kat said, smiling at Armond. "So let's be gracious and give them the floor, shall we?"

Stunned, the group sat still and said nothing while Kat walked over to greet their visitors. Before she opened the door, she turned and said, "I assume everyone will keep any information they have to themselves and not speak or discuss anything with these ladies until we have had a moment to digest whatever information they choose to share and we figure out what privileges apply to whom." Turning, Kat walked out the door.

Armond almost fell out of his chair as Kat came back into the conference room followed by the well-known Mona Rivera and then, he couldn't believe his eyes, but Jenny Acker, whom he had tried to call yesterday. As Kat made the introductions, Jenny smiled at Armond. "I received your voicemail, but I thought rather than return your call, we could speak in person. I hope you don't mind?"

"Not at all," Armond mumbled, trying to force his face into a composed expression.

"Do you two know each other?" Kat asked after hearing their exchange.

"Not personally. No. But I know of Armond, of course, as he's one of the partners at my son's law firm. Billy and I used to talk quite often. From time to time, he'd mention some of the up-and-comers. Armond is one of them." Jenny smiled at Armond.

"Well, this is a tangled web," Mona said, smiling while she made the rounds to introduce herself to the others in the room. God, she thought, you can't make this stuff up. Loving it, Mona thought she'd stir the pot a bit more. "Armond, why did you call my client?"

Armond's lawyer jumped in before Armond could answer, suggesting that they allow Mona and Jenny to share whatever it was they came all the way from California to share before his client answered any questions.

Mona smiled. She would have said the same. "Certainly. If you will all take your seats. A bit of background is in order, I think. Kat do you want to do the honors or shall I?"

"The floor is all yours," Kat responded.

Mona looked around the room and relished the tension etched on each person's face. Nodding to Kat she began. "I received an unexpected call—from Kat. After explaining a bit about her situation, she asked if my client's divorce had reached a point where we might want to work together to turn up the heat on a certain Highline board member. She also wondered whether we might have obtained information during the divorce proceedings that might be of interest to Fontaine. My, or rather our," Mona said nodding at Jenny, "response was to book two seats on the next flight to Houston. And, well, let's play show and tell shall we?" Turning to look over her shoulder Mona asked, "Kat, do you have a screen I can use?"

Kat pushed a button and a screen slid down from the ceiling. Mona opened her laptop and the screen came to life revealing handwritten notes with the word "Highline" scrawled along the top, a date four years ago, and a series of bullet points. There was also a list of names. "As I'm sure you know, the people listed are the current board members of Highline. Big Bill, sorry, Bill Acker Senior is the chair of that board." Mona paused to enjoy the tension in the room.

"As you can see, the remaining notes list a series of numbers which we believe were projected returns on investment to Highline over different periods of time after the company's launch. There are two different sets of numbers. The first set gives you an average ROI based on insurance companies that are publicly traded and have been in the business for at least fifteen years. The second set has the title Highline ROI and lists numbers at least twice the ROI of the first group. As you continue to read, you'll see why we're here. I'm sure you'll all agree that the last line sums it up nicely." Mona sat back and waited.

Kat read the line out loud for the group, "Delay claim payments—creates new profit center—increases ROI; the Highline way."

One of Kat's lawyers actually laughed out loud. "Son of a bitch," he said, "in all my years of practicing law, this is the first time I have been in a case where there is an actual, proverbial, 'smoking gun.'"

"Whose handwriting is this?" Kat asked. Turning to Mona, she said, "Of course the document is essentially useless unless we can get someone to authenticate it."

Jenny leaned forward. "That's where I come in." She paused and looked around the room. "The handwriting is my husband's, Bill Acker Senior."

The room erupted as the lawyers all tried to ask different questions in tandem. "How did you get these? Where were they kept? Does your husband know you have this?" Armond's lawyer stood up and walked over to the table to get more coffee and asked, "What's in it for you? Why share this with people you don't even know?"

Mona held up her hand, signaling to Jenny that she'd answer. "My client has been trying to finalize her divorce from her husband for almost three years now. He has dragged his feet and stalled at every stage. The more pressure there is on him from other avenues, the more he'll want to dump one of his problems. And with the things that are bubbling to the surface, I expect he'll be chomping at the bit to finalize the divorce so his remaining cash can go to protect his other assets."

"Plus, I don't like seeing innocent people harmed by big business," Jenny piped in.

"I assume since you're here that Mrs. Acker will agree to testify in court and swear that these notes are Mr. Acker's handwriting?" Kat asked.

"Of course. Correct. There are other documents we have as well. But we thought this would be enough to see if you have an interest in working in with us," Mona answered.

"What is it you have in mind?" Kat asked.

"We'd like to suggest that whatever lawsuit you intend to file against Highline include the chairman of the board. Of course, we would expect that you would do so only after you've had a chance to review the other documents and satisfy yourselves that there are sufficient facts to include Bill Acker Senior," Mona answered. "It seems to me though, and I admit I know nothing about insurance law, that with the information we have, you should be able to create a meaty little tell-all that will keep Highline and its board busy for months, maybe years, to come. We'll help you with the authentication of the documents we have, as well as provide access to a key—but for now secret—witness, to whom Bill bragged that he was the genius responsible for, as he apparently put it, 'launching this ingenious slice of his American dream into the market.'"

"Mona, I respect your abilities as a lawyer. You're well known and you have made quite a name for yourself. So as you know, perhaps better than any lawyer sitting at this table, I cannot and will not authorize the filing of a lawsuit based on a secret witness whom we have not vetted and know nothing about," Kat said, getting up to pour herself a cup of coffee.

"I realize that. Our witness is in California now for the next four days. She's agreed to allow you and your lawyers to vet her story," Mona said.

"Why would she want to get involved in all of this?" Kat asked. "What's in it for her?"

"Jenny, it's up to you," Mona said, turning to look at Jenny. "This part of the story is not something they need to know."

"Bill essentially made her his sex slave for the past ten years. It began when she was just seventeen," Jenny answered without the slightest hesitation. She was tired of all the bad juju Bill had created and she wanted to clean house and move out and on. "She recently tracked me down and I flew to Bermuda to meet her. Ironically, she thought that perhaps we could be of some assistance to each other. Turns out she was right."

"In short, she has her own considerable bone to pick with him," Mona continued.

"I assume she has a birth certificate and other corroborating documents we can see?" Kat asked.

"Indeed," Mona answered with a slight smile, loving the way her plan was clicking along like a well-oiled machine.

That's all Kat needed to hear. Turning to her legal team, she ordered, "Make arrangements to go to California immediately. Review their documents and interview the witness. Get whatever you need and get this complaint on file. No excuses. I want to read all about it in the paper by this weekend."

Turning to Armond, Jenny asked, "May I ask what it was you wanted to speak with me about?"

Armond looked at his lawyer, who nodded his okay.

"I was going to ask some questions about your knowledge of some of your husband's activities with regard to Highline. I knew you were in the process of getting a divorce, and I thought you might have information you would be willing to share. It was a long shot. But apparently, from what we've just heard, not so long."

"May I ask why you're here and involved in a discussion that may ultimately implicate the firm?" Mona asked.

"I've left the firm. I tendered my resignation via email this morning."

"Why?" Mona pressed.

"A number of reasons, one of which is that one of my very dear friends, a former colleague at the firm, was fired. It all involves Highline, and she's being made a scapegoat. Instead, she's the one who raised the alert and began to put the pieces together that something was wrong. When she tried to get to the bottom of what it was and fix it, the shit hit the fan."

"Your friend is female?" Jenny asked.

"Yes. One of the best attorneys you'll ever find."

"I may have some information for you. Why don't you come out to California?" Jenny said.

CHAPTER
50

THREE DAYS LATER, a few minutes before the close of business, a gentleman dressed in Bermuda business attire consisting of shorts with a button-up shirt and tie walked into the well-appointed lobby of Highline and handed a sealed envelope to the receptionist. "Will you please deliver this to the CEO, and sign here to accept delivery?"

"Certainly. May I tell his assistant who this is from?"

"Tell him Highline has just been served."

Billy walked through the house in Bermuda to find Trever sitting in his favorite chair on the back porch. "My father's just called. He's on his way out to the house. Some sort of emergency developing," Billy told Trever.

"What about?" Trever asked.

"No idea. He hung up before I could find out. He'll be here in about fifteen minutes."

Trever sighed. Leaning forward, he pushed the intercom. "Bring a bottle of pinot noir and a cigar around to the south porch, please. Oh, and we're expecting Acker Senior momentarily. When he arrives, bring him straight back."

Within a few minutes of uncorking the wine, Big Bill came barreling through the French doors. He looked, Trever thought, like a giant Clydesdale snorting and pawing at the ground, frustrated at being held back. With a few long strides, Big Bill crossed the wide expanse of the stone patio, and threw a rolled-up document at his son.

"Goddamn it. You two idiots told me you had everything under control," Big Bill thundered. As he paced back and forth, Billy opened the document and began to read. Before he finished even the first page, Big Bill snatched it back and waved it in the air. "We've been sued for breach of contract and a bunch of other legal bullshit. Who knows what the fuck this thing says. Fuck lawyers. Goddamn bane of the world. I'd like to round every last one of 'em up, boat them out to an island, and blow it up."

"Bill, calm down," Trever said, pouring a glass of wine. "Here, try this. It's some of the best pinot noir I've ever tasted. I think you'll appreciate the subtleties."

Big Bill grabbed the glass and smashed it on the stone pavers. He then rounded the table and handed the document back to his son. "Well? What does it say? And why in God's name am I and the other board members named in this shithole of a document?" Without waiting for Billy to answer, Big Bill continued, "You need to get this taken care of, and fast. The board will flip, and some of them might even want to sell their stake and step down. That would be disastrous."

"Dad, calm down. Let me finish," Billy said.

Big Bill finally walked over to the empty chair, sank heavily into it, and took the second glass of wine offered by Trever. Silence descended on the three men as Billy began to scribble some notes in the margins of the document. After a few minutes, he looked up.

Oh my God, Trever thought, as he watched Billy's face, he's actually enjoying being center stage for his father.

"Okay," Billy began, "they've sued Highline for breach of contract and bad faith. In other words, for failing to pay what they allege is owed under the policies."

"What does any of this gibberish mean, and why are the board members named?" Big Bill interjected.

"The board members are named because Fontaine Development is alleging that the members approved and instigated a pattern and practice of delaying the investigation and payment of claims for their own personal benefit," Billy answered, stunned at the detail in the document.

"Well, how would they know about anything like that? Where are they getting their information? We need to stop this immediately and remove it from the public domain. Our reputations will be ruined unless you get us out of this mess in the next twenty-four hours," Big Bill said.

"I'm afraid there's nothing we can do about this, and certainly not within twenty-four hours. That's not how the system works, Dad. We have thirty days to respond to the complaint, meaning we can either answer it or we can move to dismiss some or all of the counts. If we move to dismiss, briefs will have to be filed setting out the reasons for dismissal and finally, a hearing will need to be held before the court. Then, when the judge gets around to it, he or she will issue a ruling so, oh, I'd say in about six months your names will be out and things will return to normal."

The sudden stillness, after Billy finished his little speech, was unnerving. Big Bill slowly pushed back his chair and stood to his full height. Downing the last of his wine, he set the crystal glass back on the table so hard the stem cracked and the glass toppled over. Sounding more animal than human, he growled, "Get this matter sealed and out of the public eye. I don't care what bullshit you need to make up to get that done. Then have this matter resolved. Forty-eight hours, Billy. No more or you and your firm are fired."

"Dad, we can't possibly..." he said to Big Bill's retreating form.

"Shut up. Will you please? He's already out the door. Stop groveling," Trever demanded, disgusted.

"Trever, what you fail to understand, since you've never set foot in a courtroom, is that we're no longer in control. The court is. No matter what we do, we cannot force anything to be withdrawn or removed from the public eye unless we have court approval to do so," Billy said, annoyed at his father's typical condescending attitude and Trever's even more typical superior one.

"Billy, let me translate what your father just said into simple English. He doesn't give a rat's ass about the courts or anything or anyone else. He cares about one thing. And that is that we clear this up now. He doesn't care how or what we have to do. Legal or illegal. Do you understand? And if we don't do what he's asked, we'll lose Highline as our client. This will not only reduce our revenue, but it has the very real possibility of ruining our reputations and affecting our other clients. Now come with me. We need to get Jack on the line and we need to speak with the plaintiff."

"You mean the plaintiff's attorneys. I know the firm and this lawyer in particular. He'll take my call immediately," Billy said, walking alongside Trever toward the conference room to hook up another secure line to the States.

"No. You're not listening. We need to cut a deal now with the plaintiff directly. Not through their lawyers."

"Trever, we can't do that. It's unethical. They're represented by lawyers, and as such, we need to go through their lawyers to communicate with them. Even you remember enough about the law to know that," Billy responded.

"Here's the thing, Billy. I don't care about the law and neither does the board. They care about themselves. I care about us. If we don't fix this, and do it fast, the possibility exists that if this matter goes far enough, we will be the targets of litigation. You do understand the danger in that, don't you?"

Trever saw the light finally go on in Billy's head.

Walking swiftly to The Western Will's boardroom, Trever asked their assistant to obtain a secure line and visual with Jack. Within five minutes, the screen flickered to life and Jack appeared. "What's going on? You pulled me out of a client meeting."

"Highline was served today. Complaint filed on behalf of Fontaine Development in Miami Dade Federal Court. It's being scanned now. You should have it momentarily."

"So what? Insurance companies are sued all the time. We knew this was coming," Jack said.

"While that may be true," Trever answered, "they typically don't name the members of the board, and our firm is not usually the architect of the strategy that is at the heart of the matter. I, for one, don't intend to be placed under oath so that a bunch of idiot lawyers can ask what we meant when we told Highline that the path to increasing revenue is to maintain their invested capital longer by 'investigating' claims thoroughly and paying nothing until they were fully satisfied, meaning sued."

"Holy shit," Jack responded.

"Yes, that's my thought exactly," Trever answered. "In addition, Big Bill gave us forty-eight hours to clean up this mess or we're fired. And by clean up, he means he wants this gone from the public eye without a trace."

"We'll have to contact Fontaine directly and work through a settlement, a confidentiality agreement, and a request to seal and remove from the public record. Who are their lawyers?"

"A firm out of California. I have a good relationship with their managing partner," Billy answered and gave the firm's name.

"Yup. I know them as well. They handle primarily class-action plaintiff work. Which is bad for us, as it's likely they're floating this lawsuit to see what kind of a response they get from other policyholders who are pissed at Highline. If they get enough interest, this thing will be in the courts for years," Jack answered.

"Gentlemen, let me make this perfectly clear. If this thing gets any bigger before we launch our full-fledged attack on Victoria and ride in on white horses to correct the poor claims-handling process she put in place at Highline, we'll all be fucked," Trever said.

"Well, what the hell, Trever?" Billy interjected. "You're the one who launched this whole scheme. You're the one who said that Highline should delay payment of their insureds' claims and keep that money as long as possible to invest for its own benefit. A 'win-win' is how you described it. Now you're sitting back and acting as if you had nothing to do with it. Tell me, Trever, while we're running around trying to clean up your mess, what are you going to be doing?"

"Billy, my part of the plan has gone as it should have. It's your end that's fucked up. You should have fired Victoria as soon as she finished the claim process and had it up and running. Had you maintained the agreed upon schedule, there would have been no one asking questions and calling staff in Bermuda to find out why her perfect protocol wasn't being followed," Trever said, as he pointed at Billy. "She gave us the perfect opportunity too, when she asked to be placed on the fast track. No one would have been surprised or suspected anything, had we fired her then. All the partners would have understood that she needed to be controlled. Hell, Billy, you knew years ago at that first meeting, when she answered your question about the launch date, that she was showing signs of not fitting our trait requirements."

"Have you forgotten that Armond was fully involved in the setup of the claims? So, even if we had gotten rid of Victoria, we would have had a bigger problem with him," Billy pushed back.

"Oh please. Let's get real, shall we?" Trever exploded as he stood to pace. "Armond's interested in one thing, and that's getting more shares and power in the firm. It would have taken only a few mentoring words and promises from you, and he would have fallen in line and conveniently forgotten any questions he might have had."

"We still would have had the issue with Fontaine. Without Victoria at the firm, her friend Kat would have pushed even harder. So keeping her on longer actually helped," Billy argued.

"Are you totally delusional?" Trever spat as he slammed his fist on the table. "How much worse could it be? Fontaine's not only sued Highline, but the board as well, and that bitch somehow knows details about our strategy that only three people were aware of—you, me and your father," Trever bit back. "Had we gotten rid of Victoria at the proper time, it would have given us the space to maneuver all the pieces so the blame could sit squarely on her shoulders. The only reason you didn't stick to the plan and fire her ass is because you hadn't screwed her yet. She was a challenge, and one that you wanted to win. Your uncontrollable predilections have led this firm into the sewer." Trever turned to leave, signaling he was done with the meeting. "I'll leave you legal geniuses to clean this up. Get rid of this so Victoria can once again become the headline."

CHAPTER
51

SONIA AND VICTORIA sat outside, sipping their coffee on Victoria's balcony, watching the streets come to life and feeling the sun as it began to warm the day. "I like this one best," Sonia said, sliding a sketch across the table.

"I do too. It's different. I love it, actually. Okay, it's decided. This is it." It was an intricate and flowing combination of her initials, V and R.

"I have my first client," Victoria revealed, feeling excited. "Kat's company hired me with a large retainer to work with her risk team to ensure Fontaine Development has the right insurance in place, and to handle any property claims that develop in the future."

Sonia smiled and squeezed her daughter's hand. "Victoria, I'm so proud of you. The moment you told me what your firm had done to you, I knew it was going to be one of those door-closing, window-opening things."

Victoria cocked her head at her mother and couldn't help but smile. "You mean one of those times where when one door closes and another opens?" Her mother never got those sayings right. She typically combined two or three of them together, creating some weird combination of a "feel better" slogan.

"That's it," Sonia responded with a smile.

CHAPTER
52

IMMEDIATELY AFTER LAMBASTING his son, Big Bill called each board member and advised them of the lawsuit. The last thing he wanted was for them to find out about it through the media. After assuring each of the men that the matter would be handled and put to bed within forty-eight hours, reminding them of the profit they stood to gain, and promising an update the next morning, he could finally put an end to what had turned out to be a horrible day.

Now, he thought, he could head home to Wilhemena, who would be waiting for him with one purpose on her mind. To make him happy. Thinking back over his past while driving the winding road alongside the ocean that lead to his home, he could not for the life of him recall why he had gotten married. But one thing he knew for certain, once Jenny was back in Georgia and he could keep his money and estate intact, he would spend most of his time in Bermuda. He would continue to pay Wilhemena so she would remain under his control. He certainly had no intention of turning his Bermudian home over to her as he had promised. Smiling at the naiveté that allowed her to believe such a thing was even possible, he gunned his car. The more he thought about the control he had over her, the hornier he got.

Twenty-four hours later, Big Bill walked through his front door at The Southern Will, thoroughly and utterly exhausted and a bit off-center. The last day had been a cluster fuck. Not only had Wilhemena not been at home waiting, but she had answered none of his calls and had not returned home before he had to leave the island. Moreover, contrary to the instructions he had given to the board members, each of them had told their personal lawyers about the Fontaine lawsuit and every one of their cock-sucking lawyers wanted to make the mess bigger so they could bill the hell out of it, instead of making it go away. He had called his son and told him to get these walking, talking paid pricks under control before they blew all of them out of the water.

Since then, he heard that Jack had a meeting with all the lawyers and convinced them to lay low and let Jack coordinate their plan of attack. As long as the lawyers got to continue billing the shit out of their respective clients, they agreed to sit tight, but only for the next forty-eight hours.

Walking into the library to fix a drink, Bill heard the doorbell ring. As he was pouring himself a vodka neat with a twist, his housekeeper knocked on the door and announced a man was waiting for him in the foyer.

That's odd, Bill thought. Irritated, Bill walked into the foyer and felt the hairs on the back of his arm raise.

Before he could decipher his body's warning, the man handed him a sealed envelope. "An urgent message for you, Mr. Acker. Have a nice day." Bill opened the envelope and stood, dumbfounded, in his perfectly maintained foyer in his perfectly kept mansion. He could not believe Wilhemena would turn on him. After all he had done for her.

Mona's phone lit up indicating a text had arrived. Jenny watched as a smile spread across her face. "What happened?" Jenny asked.

"My little package was delivered. About an hour ago. In the foyer of his home. 'Said nothing,' according to the messenger and I quote, 'Just stood there with his mouth open.'"

CHAPTER
53

KAT AND HER legal team had perfected the timing of their strike scenario. So far, so good, things were proceeding as planned. Subpoenas had been issued to a slew of Acker lawyers, including Victoria and Armond. Everyone who had anything to do with Highline had been the lucky recipient, commanding their appearance at their very own deposition.

Trever and Billy each received one within five minutes of their private plane landing at O'Hare International Airport. Hearing their names called as they walked from the tarmac into the main terminal, they turned to see a leggy blonde dressed in a captain's uniform filled with dancing double-D boobs that looked like they were fighting to get out of their shirt cage.

Their egos made her job easy. Neither could resist watching and waiting for her to catch up to them. They were sitting ducks. Her smile got bigger, and her teeth, outlined by her red lip gloss, seemingly became whiter as she got closer. Reaching into her briefcase as it swung from her shoulder, she pulled out two sets of documents.

"What can we do for you, captain?" Trever asked, almost drooling as he said it.

"Gentlemen, I have something for you." They each willingly took the packet she offered. "Consider yourselves served. Mr. McGowen, Mr. Acker, have a good evening." She tipped her captain's hat and turned and walked away.

Victoria sat in Robert's conference room with a cup of coffee, trying to focus on the content of the complaint to check for accuracy before it was filed. After fifteen minutes, she still had not gotten past the caption on the first page naming her as the plaintiff against the mighty international Acker, Smith & McGowen law firm. While Victoria had been around litigation during her years at the firm, she wasn't at ease with the process and truth be told, she was concerned about the ramifications of airing dirty laundry. After all, Chicago was rampant with whispered rumors that female lawyers who complained of sexual harassment or discrimination were quietly excluded from future legal business and thus, their career in law tanked.

Victoria brought herself back to reality and sighed as she forced her way through to the end of the complaint. She called from the conference room phone, letting Robert know she was through. She felt edgy. She hadn't run that morning, and that had been a mistake. Standing, she began pacing the length of the conference room.

The door swung open, and Robert came in with his assistant. "Okay, I know you're worried. Let's talk it through," Robert said.

"My reputation. My career. It's what I've worked for my whole life. If I do this, I'll be seen as a problem. I'll be known as a troublemaker. Who will want to deal with me? To you, this is just another case. But to me, it's the public airing of my life and rehashing an embarrassing situation. I'll have to live with how this turns out forever."

Robert took a chair at the head of his conference table and sipped his coffee. "Do you mind if I sit? You keep pacing. But I'm going to sit. Let's run through the history of events. The firm fired you, blaming you for the problems of Highline. They did this even though you know, from a company insider whom you trust, that the process you put in place has not been followed, and in fact, has been countermanded. Correct?" Without waiting for an answer, Robert continued, "Next, the firm makes your firing public by slipping it to a well-read Chicago newspaper. Correct?"

"Yes, but no one cares about that. All they'll remember is that I claimed discrimination against a firm."

"Hold on," Robert said, holding up his hand. "Keep pacing and listen. Next, Kat's Florida property has been essentially abandoned by Highline and her business is stretched to its financial limits from trying to repair the damage from Ileana without the insurance company's money. True?" Holding up his hand to signal that his question was rhetorical, Robert continued. "Moreover, Kat's family has filed suit against Highline and the shit's about to hit the fan. The firm's already put the pieces in place to say it was your fault, and once they found out about the inept process you put into place, they fired you. Add to that the random, yet I believe related, fact that there are no female partners or any even on the horizon at Acker, and yet the firm is touted as one of the premier places to work for women."

"Now, putting all of this together, how can you afford not to state your case?" Robert asked. "Even if you don't do it, no firm will hire you now anyway. Why? Because Acker has already sullied your reputation and intends to make you a target. The only way back, and frankly, Acker made the choice easy when you think about it, is to sue them and fire back strong, loud and proud."

That was all Victoria needed to hear. She knew he was right. They really had left her with no choice. She nodded.

"Okay. Let's go. You're filing today, right? What do I need to do?"

"Not a thing. Just sit back and watch the fireworks. Public relations will give you a few comments this afternoon that you should use to respond to any press inquiries. All press will flow through PR and they'll tell you who you can, and can't, speak with and what to say," Robert added. "Now go take your run. Things are about to get interesting."

Thirty minutes later, Victoria was on the lake, loving the feel of the breeze and watching the boats bob on the water. She felt good. She was committed. She would win this battle.

The following morning, the receptionist at the Chicago head-quarters of Acker, Smith & McGowen had just returned to her desk after grabbing her second cup of what would be at least four cups of black coffee for the day. She adjusted her headphones and returned to fielding calls when the elevators opened to showcase a tall, well-dressed man heading straight toward her desk. "Hello, are you the receptionist?" he asked.

"Yes, sir. Who are you here to see?"

"You. You're perfect." Handing over an envelope, she took it and signed the form he stuck in her hands. "These are papers notifying the firm of a lawsuit filed against it. You've been served. Have a nice day."

A few weeks later, Kat sat in a packed courtroom at the Miami Federal Courthouse on a sweltering hot and humid day. Working out of their hotel's conference room, her legal team had finished incorporating the final changes to their Motion to Preserve Evidence just last night. A hand-delivered copy of the motion had been provided to both the judge and the opposing counsel this morning.

"Fontaine Development versus Highline Insurance Company and other defendants," the clerk called through the microphone. At least twelve men in dark suits walked up to the podium.

"Joseph Williams for Plaintiff, your Honor," Kat's lawyer introduced himself as he stepped up to the podium. After seeing all the other lawyers that stood on the defendants' side, he couldn't help but turn and wink at Kat. They had hoped this would happen.

"Jack O'Leary for Highline and the board, your Honor."

"Good morning, gentlemen. We're here on a status this morning. However, my clerk has handed me a number of motions seeking to allow new lawyers to file their respective appearances on behalf of individual board members. It seems these motions were filed this morning. Gentlemen, please introduce yourselves for the record." The judge nodded toward the other men.

One by one the lawyers introduced themselves and each stated that they represented a different member of the board.

"Mr. O'Leary, it seems you may only be left with two clients in fairly short order, the insurance company and Mr. Acker. What say you?" the judge asked.

"Your Honor, I did not receive these motions until I walked into court this morning. I would like time to confer with my clients and these gentlemen before you allow these motions."

"Request denied. Motions to Appear are granted. Gentlemen, you have some other motions?"

"We do, your Honor. We are seeking leave to file cross claims against Highline and the chairman of the board *instanter* and we have provided our claims to you and to counsel this morning."

"What say you, Mr. O'Leary? I see no reason why I shouldn't grant their motions. Do you have any objections?" the court pushed.

"We would respectfully request time to review the motions and consult with our clients, your Honor. From my brief review this morning, they contain some serious allegations," Jack answered, trying to stall for time.

"All matters filed in my court are serious, Mr. O'Leary. I'll give you fifteen minutes to review the motions and consult with your clients. Then come back here and I'll listen to any valid, and I'm stressing the word 'valid,' objections. I'll rule right after our discussion. I'll then address Fontaine's motion. Miss Clerk, call the next case."

Fifteen minutes later, it was done. The new lawyers were in the case, their cross claims were filed and the other board members were lining up to point their respective fingers at William Acker Senior. It was a plaintiff's dream and more than Kat could have hoped for. The motion was granted and Highline and the board members had thirty days to produce all requested documents, including any handwritten notes. The pressure was building, balls were being squeezed and Kat was smiling as she left the courtroom.

CHAPTER
54

ARMOND WAS STUNNED at the information Jenny had told him about the firm and its hiring of women. While he had always known it was a misogynistic playground, he had never imagined it was as deep-seated as Jenny implied. If what she said were true, it would be enough to ruin the firm. But perhaps best of all, Jenny had given Armond a valid reason to contact Victoria. He had wanted to call her for days, but he didn't know if she would ever forgive him for not including her in his plans and for putting her through hell. He had known, though, that the best way for him to find out what was going on was to let the firm continue with its plan to use her as the scapegoat for Highline's slow pay, while he dug for information.

Victoria felt good. She had two new clients and she was busy. Not as busy as she liked to be, but busy enough for now. Her lawsuit against the firm had been filed and had been the first item in the legal gossip columns. Since then, three former female lawyers of the firm had contacted her and they all wanted to join her suit. Hearing her cell phone buzz in her purse, Victoria pulled it out and was surprised to see Armond's name.

"Hello? Armond, I'm quite sure you shouldn't be calling me. Contact my lawyer if you have anything to say." Victoria hung up. Whatever he had to say, Victoria had no intention of listening. She had to admit that she still missed Armond terribly, even though he had betrayed her. And that almost made it worse. How could she still miss and want to see someone who had caused her so much pain? She really did need a good shrink.

Ten minutes later she got a call from her lawyer. "Victoria, I just spoke with Armond. He told me you refused to speak with him and hung up on him. He called me right after you slammed the phone in his ear."

"Yes, well, I have nothing to say to him and I don't want to hear whatever it is he wants to say to me. Anyway, you told me not to speak to anyone at the firm. Why would I take a call from him of all people? What's going on?"

"You're not going to believe this, but Armond has information from a source he won't yet reveal that he says will begin to explain why there are no women partners," Robert responded excitedly.

"Yes, we know why. We've heard it before. It's the women's fault; they have babies, quit to stay at home, and when they finally come back, they only want to work part-time. It's the same line over and over."

"No, no, no. This is different. He said the firm has a personality index the boys use to help them hire those women most likely to quit or bow under pressure. That way, they get at least seven to eight years of hard labor out of them before they increase their non-billable duties to such an extreme that they quit. In other words, their whole plan is to use women and then, when it's time for partnership, push their buttons so they quit. For those women who don't quit, it seems the firm finds a trumped-up reason to force them to leave with the choice of either getting six months' severance and signing a release or firing them on the spot and ruining their reputation. Sound familiar?"

Victoria listened, stunned, thinking back to things that were said to her when she had asked about the lack of women partners. "I can't believe this. What about all the awards for the firm's promotion of women?"

"That's just it. They're clever. They operate on the doctrine that perception is reality. While there is no real promotion of women, the firm hires so many women and runs so many programs for them, knowing that the perception that they give a shit will turn into the public's reality. It's beautiful, really," Robert said, getting excited as only a lawyer can over new evidence.

"Robert. You're starting to get on my last nerve," Victoria said.

"No, no no. You know what I mean. It's a good thing for our case. Not for women, but we'll be able to change things. Armond told me he's left the firm and that he only went along with your firing as a ruse to be able to learn what was really going on regarding Highline and the firm's seemingly simultaneous firing of you." Robert stopped talking to let that sink in.

"He misses you, Victoria. He told me to tell you to contact Kat and you'll understand."

"You told me not to speak with him. Are you telling me I can?" Victoria asked.

"Why don't you call Kat and let me know what happens?"

Victoria called Kat. Within the hour, she and Armond had agreed to meet at their favorite corner bar later that night.

CHAPTER
55

THREE MONTHS AFTER her meeting with Armond, Victoria walked into her new office. She had had to move from her temporary space as business was booming. She had hired one associate and two paralegals, as well as staff. Mary was her office manager and loved her new position.

As she walked by reception, she noticed the headlines in the paper, "Highline CEO and Board Removed. New CEO Announces Hurricane Claims to Be Resolved in One Year." Victoria smiled. She knew the pressure Kat's suit had brought to bear. The shit had hit the fan. It had also finally made sense. The firm had to get rid of Victoria in order for Highline to carry out its scheme to delay payment of claims. All those cancelled meetings to try to correct the situation—no wonder they didn't happen. They hadn't wanted her to correct the situation. The delay was the end game. Neither she nor Armond had known because they were going to be served as the scapegoats.

What bothered Victoria, though, was that as of yet no charges had been brought against the boys at the firm for any part they may have played in the scheme, and nothing solid had resulted from her allegations of the firm's discrimination against women. Robert assured her both would happen. That she had to be patient.

Victoria smiled as she thought about how far she had come. Time was on her side now. But even better, she finally had the power she had always craved. She had every intention of putting them both to good use in the coming days. While she promised Robert she would give him time to get it done, she had a few ideas she wanted to run up the flagpole that she thought just might speed the process along.

Walking into her office, she saw Kat sitting in her chair talking on the phone. Victoria smiled. Kat waved and Victoria heard her say, "Jenny, congratulations. I'm glad it worked out. We'll be in touch. I'll tell her."

"That, my dear friend," Kat said as she put her phone down, "was the infamous and newly divorced Jenny. I promised to introduce you two one day. She thinks perhaps you could be an amazing team, righting some wrongs together. I happen to agree."

Victoria smiled at the thought and bent down to hug Kat. "I look forward to it. But first I have a few loose ends to tie up. Are you in?"

CPSIA information can be obtained
at www.ICGtesting.com
Printed in the USA
FSHW010453180319
56453FS